W9-BUQ-595

THE IVY TREE

THE IVY TREE

MARY STEWART

Cover design: Sarah Olson
Cover image: The Marsden Archive

This unabridged edition is reprinted by arrangement with William Morrow, an imprint of HarperCollins Publishers.
Copyright © 1961 by Mary Stewart
All rights reserved
This edition published in 2007 by
Chicago Review Press, Incorporated
814 North Franklin Street
Chicago, Illinois 60610
ISBN-13: 978-1-55652-726-5
ISBN-10: 1-55652-726-8
Printed in the United States of America
5 4 3 2 1

For Fredith and Thomas Kemp

A north country maid up to London had stray'd,
Although with her nature it did not agree;
She wept, and she sighed, and she bitterly cried:
"I wish once again in the North I could be!
Oh! the oak and the ash, and the bonny ivy tree,
They flourish at home in the North Country."

"No doubt, did I please, I could marry with ease;
Where maidens are fair many lovers will come:
But he whom I wed must be North Country bred,
And carry me back to my North Country home.
Oh! the oak and the ash, and the bonny ivy tree,
They flourished at home in my own country."

Seventeenth Century Traditional.

CHAPTER ONE

"Come you not from Newcastle?
Come you not there away?
Oh, met you not my true love?"

Traditional.

I MIGHT HAVE BEEN ALONE in a painted landscape. The sky was still and blue, and the high cauliflower clouds over towards the south seemed to hang without movement. Against their curded bases the fells curved and folded, blue foothills of the Pennines giving way to the misty green of pasture, where, small in the distance as hedge-parsley, trees showed in the folded valleys, symbols, perhaps, of houses and farms. But in all that windless, wide landscape, I could see no sign of man's hand, except the lines—as old as the ridge and furrow of the pasture below me—of the dry stone walls, and the arrogant stride of the great Wall which Hadrian had driven across Northumberland, nearly two thousand years ago.

The blocks of the Roman-cut stone were warm against my back. Where I sat, the Wall ran high along a ridge. To the right, the cliff fell sheer away to water, the long reach of Crag Lough, now quiet as glass in the sun. To the left, the sweeping, magnificent view to the Pennines. Ahead of me, ridge after ridge running west, with the Wall cresting each curve like a stallion's mane.

There was a sycamore in the gully just below me. Some stray current of air rustled its leaves, momentarily, with a sound like rain. Two lambs, their mother astray somewhere not far away, were sleeping, closely cuddled together, in the warm May sunshine. They had watched me for a time, but I sat there without moving, except for the hand that lifted the cigarette to my mouth, and after a while the two heads went down again to the warm grass, and they slept.

I sat in the sun, and thought. Nothing definite, but if I had been asked to define my thoughts they would all have come to one word. England. This turf, this sky, the heartsease in the grass; the old lines of ridge and furrow, and the still older ghosts of Roman road and Wall; the ordered, spare beauty of the northern fells; this, in front of me now, was England. *This other Eden, demi-paradise. This dear, dear land.*

It was lonely enough, certainly. We had it to ourselves, I and the lambs, and the curlew away up above, and the fritillaries that flickered like amber sparks over the spring grasses. I might have been the first and only woman in it; Eve, sitting there in the sunlight and dreaming of Adam. . . .

"Annabel!"

He spoke from behind me. I hadn't heard him approach. He must have come quietly along the turf to the south of the Wall, with his dog trotting gently at heel. He was less than four yards from me when I whirled round, my cigarette flying from startled fingers down among the wild thyme and yellow cinquefoil that furred the lower courses of the Roman stones.

Dimly I was aware that the lambs had bolted, crying.

The man who had shattered the dream had stopped two yards from me. Not Adam; just a young man in shabby, serviceable country tweeds. He was tall, and slenderly built, with that whippy look to him that told you he would be an ugly customer in a fight—and with something else about him that made it sufficiently obvious that he would not need much excuse to join any fight that was going. Possibly it is a look that is inbred with the Irish, for there could be no doubt about this young man's ancestry. He had the almost excessive good looks of a certain type of Irishman, black hair, eyes of startling blue, and charm in the long, mobile mouth. His skin was fair, but had acquired that hard tan which is the result of weathering rather than of sunburn, and which would, in another twenty years, carve his face into a handsome mask of oak. He had a stick in one hand, and a collie hung watchfully at his heels, a beautiful creature with the same kind of springy, rapier grace as the master, and the same air of self-confident good breeding.

Not Adam, no, this intruder into my demi-Eden. But quite possibly the serpent. He was looking just about as friendly and as safe as a black mamba.

He took in his breath in a long sound that might even have been described as a hiss.

"So it is you! I thought I couldn't be mistaken! *It is you*. . . . The old man always insisted you couldn't be dead, and that you'd come back one day . . . and by God, who'd have thought he was right?"

He was speaking quite softly, but just what was underlying that very pleasant voice I can't quite describe. The dog heard it, too. It would be too much to say that its hackles lifted, but I saw its ears flatten momentarily, as it rolled him an upward, white-eyed look, and the thick collie-ruff stirred on its neck.

I hadn't moved. I must have sat there, dumb and stiff as the stones themselves, gaping up at the man. I did open my mouth to say something, but the quiet, angry voice swept on, edged now with what sounded (fantastic though it should have seemed on that lovely afternoon) like danger.

"And what have you come back for? Tell me that! Just what do you propose to do? Walk straight home and hang up your hat? Because if that's the idea, my girl, you can think again, and fast! It's not your grandfather you'll be dealing with now, you know, it's me . . . I'm in charge, sweetheart, and I'm staying that way. So be warned."

I did manage to speak then. In face of whatever strong emotion was burning the air between us, anything that I could think of to say could hardly fail to sound absurd. What I achieved at last, in a feeble sort of croak that sounded half paralyzed with fright, was merely, "I—I beg your pardon?"

"I saw you get off the bus at Chollerford." He was breathing hard, and the fine nostrils were white and pinched-looking. "I don't know where you'd been—I suppose you'd been down at Whitescar, blast you. You got on the Housesteads bus, and I followed you. I didn't want you to recognize me coming up through the field, so I waited to let you get right up here, because I wanted to talk to you. Alone."

At the final word, with its deliberately lingering emphasis, something must have shown in my face. I saw a flash of satisfaction pass over his. I was scared, and the fact pleased him.

Something, some prick of humiliation perhaps, passing for courage, helped me to pull myself together.

I said, abruptly, and a good deal too loudly, "Look, you're making a mistake! I don't—"

"*Mistake?* Don't try and give me that!" He made a slight movement that managed to convey—his body was as eloquent as his face—a menace as genuine and as startling as his next words. "You've got a nerve, you bitch, haven't you? After all these years . . . walking back as calm as you please, and in broad daylight! Well, here am I, too. . . ." His teeth showed. "It doesn't necessarily have to be midnight, does it, when you and I go walking at the edge of a cliff with water at the bottom? Remember? You'd never have come mooning up here alone, would you, darling, if you'd known I was coming too?"

This brought me to my feet, really frightened now. It was no longer imagination to think that he looked thoroughly dangerous. His astounding good looks, oddly enough, helped the impression. They gave him a touch of the theatrical which made violence and even tragedy part of the acceptable pattern of action.

I remember how steep, suddenly, the cliff looked, dropping sharply away within feet of me. At its foot Crag Lough stirred and gleamed under some stray breeze, like a sheet of blown nylon. It looked a long way down.

He took a step towards me. I saw his knuckles whiten round the heavy stick. For a mad moment I thought I would turn and run; but there was the steep broken slope behind me, and the Wall at my right, and, on the left, the sheer cliff to the water. And there was the dog.

He was saying sharply, and I knew the question mattered, "Had you been down to the farm already? To Whitescar? *Had* you?"

This was absurd. It had to be stopped. Somehow I managed to grab at the fraying edges of panic. I found my senses, and my voice. I said flatly, and still too loudly, "I don't know what you're talking about! *I don't know you!* I told you you'd made a mistake, and as far as I'm concerned you're also behaving like a dangerous lunatic! I've no idea who you think you're talking to, but I never saw you before in my life!"

He hadn't been moving, but the effect was as if I'd stopped him with a charge of shot. Where I had been sitting I had been half turned away from him. As I rose I had turned to face him, and was standing now only two paces from him. I saw his eyes widen in startled disbelief, then, at the sound of my voice, a sort of flicker of uncertainty went across his face, taking the anger out of it, and with the anger, the menace.

I followed up my advantage. I said, rudely, because I had been frightened, and so felt foolish, "And now will you please go away and leave me alone?"

He didn't move. He stood there staring, then said, still in that edged, angry tone that was somehow smudged by doubt, "Are you trying to pretend that you don't recognize me? I'm your cousin Con."

"I told you I didn't. I never saw you in my life. And I never had a cousin Con." I took a deep, steadying breath. "It seems I'm lucky in that. You must be a very happy and united family. But you'll excuse me if I don't stay to get to know you better. Good-bye."

"Look, just a minute—no, please don't go! I'm most terribly sorry if I've made a mistake! But, really—" He was still standing squarely in the path which would take me back to the farm track, and the main road. The cliff was still sheer to one side, and the water, far below us, smooth once more, glassed the unruffled sky. But what had seemed to be a dramatic symbol of menace towering between me and freedom had dwindled now simply into a nice-looking young man standing in the sunshine, with doubt melting on his face into horrified apology.

"I really am most desperately sorry! I must have frightened you. Good God, what on earth can you think of me? You must have thought I was crazy or something. I can't tell you how sorry I am. I, well, I thought you were someone I used to know."

I said, very drily, "I rather gathered that."

"Look, please don't be angry. I admit you've every right, but really—I mean, it's pretty remarkable. You could be her, you really could. Even now that I see you closely . . . oh, perhaps there are differences, when one comes to look for them, but—well, I could still swear—"

He stopped abruptly. He was still breathing rather fast. It was plain that he had indeed suffered a considerable shock. And, for all his apology, he was still staring at me as though he found it difficult to believe me against the evidence of his eyes.

I said, "And I'll swear too, if you like. I don't know you. I never did. My name isn't Arabella, it's Mary. Mary Grey. And I've never even been to this part of the world before."

"You're an American, aren't you? Your voice. It's very slight, but—"

"Canadian."

He said slowly, "*She* went to the States. . . ."

I said violently and angrily, "Now, look here—"

"No, please, I'm sorry. I didn't mean it!" He smiled then, for the first time. The charm was beginning to surface, now, through what I realized had been still a faint filming of disbelief. "I believe you, truly I do, though it gets more fantastic every minute I look at you, even with the foreign accent! You might be her twin. . . ." With an effort, it seemed, he dragged his uncomfortably intent stare from my face, and bent to caress the dog's ears. "Please forgive me!" The swift upward glance held nothing now but a charming apology. "I must have scared you, charging up like that and looming over you like a threat from the past."

"My past," I retorted, "never produced anything quite like this! That was some welcome your poor Prodigal was going to get, wasn't it? I—er, I did gather you weren't exactly going to kill the fatted calf for Arabella? You did say Arabella?"

"Annabel. Well, no, perhaps I wasn't." He looked away from me, down at the stretch of gleaming water. He seemed to be intent on a pair of swans sailing along near the reeds of the further shore. "You'd gather I was trying to frighten her, with all that talk."

It was a statement, not a question, but it had a curiously tentative effect. I said, "I did, rather."

"You didn't imagine I meant any of that nonsense, I hope?"

I said calmly, "Not knowing the circumstances, I have no idea. But I definitely formed the impression that this cliff was a great deal too high, and the road was a great deal too far away."

"Did you now?" There, at last, was the faintest undercurrent of an Irish lilt. He turned his head, and our eyes met.

I was angry to find that I was slightly breathless again, though it was obvious that, if this excessively dramatic young man really had intended murder five minutes ago, he had abandoned the intention. He was smiling at me now, Irish charm turned full on, looking, I thought irritably, so like the traditional answer to the maiden's prayer that it couldn't possibly be true. He was offering me his cigarette case, and saying, with a beautifully calculated lift of one eyebrow, "You've forgiven me? You're not going to bolt straight away?"

I ought, of course, to have turned and gone then and there. But the situation was no longer—if, indeed, it had ever been—dangerous. I had already looked, and felt, fool enough for one day: it would look infinitely more foolish now to turn and hurry off, quite apart from its being difficult to do with dignity. Besides, as my fright had subsided, my curiosity had taken over. There were things I wanted to know. It isn't every day that one is recognized—and attacked—for a "double" apparently some years dead.

So I stayed where I was, returned his smile of amused apology, and accepted the cigarette.

I sat down again where I had been before, and he sat on the Wall a yard away, with the collie at his feet. He was half turned to face me, one knee up, and his hands clasping it. His cigarette hung in the corner of his mouth, the smoke wisping up past his narrowed eyes.

"Are you staying near by? No, I suppose you can't be, or everyone would be talking. . . . You've a face well known in these parts. You're just up here for the day, then? Over here on holiday?"

"In a way. Actually I work in Newcastle, in a café. This is my day off."

"In *Newcastle?*" He repeated it in a tone of the blankest surprise. "You?"

"Yes. Why on earth not? It's a nice town."

"Of course. It's only that . . . well, all things considered, it seems odd that you should have come to this part of the world. What brought you up here?"

A little pause. I said abruptly, "You know, you still don't quite believe me. Do you?"

For a moment he didn't reply, that narrow gaze still intent through the smoke of the cigarette. I met it squarely. Then he unclasped his hands slowly, and took the cigarette out of his mouth. He tapped ash off it, watching the small gout of grey feathering away in the air to nothing.

"Yes. I believe you. But you mustn't blame me too much for being rude, and staring. It's a queer experience, running into the double of someone you knew."

"Believe me, it's even queerer learning that one *has* a double," I said. "Funnily enough, it's a thing one's inclined to resent."

"Do you know, I hadn't thought of that, but I believe you're right! I should hate like hell to think there were two of me."

I thought: and I believe *you;* though I didn't say it aloud. I smiled. "It's a violation of one's individuality, I suppose. A survival of a primitive feeling of—what can one call it—identity? Self-hood? You want to be *you,* and nobody else. And it's uncomfortably like magic. You feel like a savage with a looking glass, or Shelley seeing his *Doppelgänger* one morning before breakfast."

"Did he?"

"He said so. It was supposed to be a presage of evil, probably death."

He grinned. "I'll risk it."

"Oh lord, not your death. The one that meets the image is the one who dies."

"Well, that is me. You're the image, aren't you?"

"There you are," I said, "that's just the core of the matter. That's just what one resents. We none of us want to be 'the image.' We're the thing itself."

"Fair enough. You're the thing itself, and Annabel's the ghost. After all, she's dead."

It wasn't so much the casual phrasing that was shocking, as the lack of something in his voice that ought to have been there. The effect was as startling and as definite as if he had used an obscene word.

I said, uncomfortably, "You know, I didn't mean to . . . I should have realized that talking like this can't be pleasant for you, even if you, well, didn't get on with Annabel. After all, she was a relative; your cousin, didn't you say?"

"I was going to marry her."

I was just drawing on my cigarette as he spoke. I almost choked over the smoke. I must have stared with my mouth open for quite five seconds. Then I said feebly, "Really?"

His mouth curved. It was odd that the lineaments of beauty could lend themselves to something quite different. "You're thinking, maybe, that there'd have been very little love lost? Well, you might be right. Or you might not. She ran away, sooner than marry me. Disappeared into the blue eight years ago with nothing but a note from the States to her grandfather to say she was safe, and we none of us need expect to hear from her again. Oh, I admit there'd been a quarrel, and I might have been—" a pause, and a little shrug—"well, anyway, she went, and never a word to me since that day. How easily do you expect a man to forgive that?"

You? Never, I thought. There it was once more, the touch of something dark and clouded that altered his whole face; something lost and uncertain moving like a stranger behind the smooth façade of assurance that physical beauty gives. No, a rebuff was the one thing he would never forgive.

I said, "Eight years is a long time, though, to nurse a grudge. After all, you've probably been happily married to someone else for most of that time."

"I'm not married."

"No?" I must have sounded surprised. He would be all of thirty, and with that exterior, he must, to say the least of it, have had opportunities.

He grinned at my tone, the assurance back in his face, as smoothly armoured as if there had never been a flaw. "My sister keeps house at Whitescar; my half-sister, I should say. She's a wonderful cook, and she thinks a lot of me. With Lisa around, I don't need a wife."

"Whitescar, that's your farm, you said?" There was a tuft of seapink growing in a crevice beside me. I ran a finger over its springy cushion of green, watching how the tiny rosettes sprang back into place as the finger was withdrawn. "You're the owner? You and your sister?"

"I am." The words sounded curt, almost snapped off. He must have felt this himself, for he went on to explain in some detail.

"It's more than a farm; it's 'the Winslow place.' We've been there for donkey's ages . . . longer than the local gentry who've built their park round us, and tried to shift us, time out of mind. Whitescar's a kind of enclave, older than the oldest tree in the park—about a quarter the age of that wall you're sitting on. It gets its name, they say, from an old quarry up near the road, and nobody knows how old those workings are. Anyway, you can't shift Whitescar. The Hall tried hard enough in the old days, and now the Hall's gone, but we're still there— You're not listening."

"I am. Go on. What happened to the Hall?"

But he was off at a tangent, still obviously dwelling on my likeness to his cousin. "Have *you* ever lived on a farm?"

"Yes. In Canada. But it's not my thing, I'm afraid."

"What is?"

"Lord, I don't know; that's my trouble. Country life, certainly, but not farming. A house, gardening, cooking—I've spent the last few years living with a friend who had a house near Montreal, and looking after her. She'd had polio, and was crippled. I was very happy there, but she died six months ago. That was when I decided to come over here. But I've no training for anything, if that's what you mean." I smiled. "I stayed at home too long. I know that's not fashionable any more, but that's the way it happened."

"You ought to have married."

"Perhaps."

"Horses, now. Do you ride?"

The question was so sudden and seemingly irrelevant that I must have looked and sounded almost startled. "Horses? Good heavens, no! Why?"

"Oh, just a hangover from your looking so like Annabel. That was her thing. She was a wizard, a witch I should say, with horses. She could whisper them."

"She could *what?*"

"You know, whisper to them like a gipsy, and then they'd do any blessed thing for her. If she'd been dark like me, instead of blonde, she'd have been taken for a horse-thieving gipsy's changeling."

"Well," I said, "I do know one end of a horse from the other, and on principle I keep clear of both. . . . You know, I wish you'd stop staring."

"I'm sorry. But I—well, I can't leave it alone, this likeness of yours to Annabel. It's uncanny. I *know* you're not her; it was absurd anyway ever to think she might have come back . . . if she'd been alive she'd have been here long since, she had too much to lose by staying away. But what was I to think, seeing you sitting here, in the same place, with not a stone of it changed, and you only changed a little? It was like seeing the pages of a book turned back, or a film flashing back to where it was eight years ago."

"Eight years is a long time."

"Yes. She was nineteen when she ran away."

A pause. He looked at me, so obviously expectant that I laughed. "All right. You didn't ask . . . quite. I'm twenty-seven. Nearly twenty-eight."

I heard him take in his breath. "I told you it was uncanny. Even sitting as close to you as this, and talking to you; even with that accent of yours . . . it's not really an accent, just a sort of slur . . . rather nice. And she'd have changed, too, in eight years."

"She might even have acquired the accent," I said cheerfully.

"Yes. She might." Some quality in his voice made me look quickly at him. He said, "Am I still staring? I'm sorry. I was thinking. I—it's something one feels one ought not to let pass. As if it was . . . meant."

"What *do* you mean?"

"Nothing. Skip it. Tell me about yourself. You were just going to. Forget Annabel; I want to hear about you. You've told me you're Mary Grey, from Canada, with a job in Newcastle. I still want to know what brought you there, and then up here to the Wall, and why you were on that bus from Bellingham to Chollerford today, going within a stone's throw of the Winslow land." He threw the butt of his cigarette over the cliff, and clasped both hands round the uplifted knee. All his movements had a grace that seemed a perfectly normal part of his physical beauty. "I'm not pretending I've any right to ask you. But you must see that it's an odd thing to accept, to say the least. I refuse to believe that such a likeness is pure chance.

Or the fact that you came here. I think, under the circumstances, I'm entitled to be curious—" that swift and charming smile again—"if nothing else."

"Yes, of course I see that." I paused for a moment. "You know, you may be right; about this likeness not being chance, I mean. I don't know. My people did come from hereabouts, so my grandmother told me."

"Did they now? From Whitescar?"

I shook my head. "I never heard the name, that I remember. I was very little when Granny died, and she only knew what my great-grandmother told her, anyway. My own mother was never much interested in the past. I know my family did originally come from somewhere in Northumberland, though I've never heard Granny mention the name Winslow. Hers was Armstrong."

"It's a common name along the borders."

"So she said, and not with a very savoury history, some of them! Wasn't there an Armstrong once who actually lived just here, in the Roman Fort at Housesteads? Wasn't he a horse thief? If I could only 'whisper' horses like your cousin Annabel, you might suppose—"

"Do you know when your people left England?" he asked, not so much ignoring my red herring as oblivious of it. He seemed to be pursuing some very definite line of his own.

"I suppose in my great-grandfather's time. Would that be somewhere about the middle of the last century? About then, anyway. The family settled first at a place called Antigonish, in Nova Scotia, but after my father married, he—"

"What brought you back to England?" The singleness of purpose that seemed to be prompting his questions robbed the interruption of rudeness. Like an examiner, I thought, bringing the candidate back to the point. . . . Certainly his questions seemed to be directed towards some definite end. They had never been quite idle, and now they were sharp with purpose.

I said, perhaps a little warily, "What brings anyone over? My people are dead, and there was nothing to keep me at home, and I'd always wanted to see England. When I was little, Granny used to talk and talk about England. She'd never seen it, but she'd been brought up on her own mother's stories of 'home.' Oh yes, I heard all about 'bonny Northumberland,' and what an exciting city Newcastle was—I almost expected to see the sailing ships lying along the wharves, and the horse trams in the streets, she'd made it all so vivid for me. And Hexham, and Sundays in the Abbey, and the market there on Tuesdays, and the road along the Tyne to Corbridge, and the Roman Wall with all those lovely names—Castle Nick and Borcovicium and Aesica and the Nine Nicks of Thirlwall . . . I read about it all, too. I've always liked history. I'd always promised myself that some day I'd come over, maybe to visit, maybe—if I liked it—to stay."

"To stay?"

I laughed. "That's what I'd told myself. But I hadn't seen myself coming back quite like this, I'm afraid. I—well, I was left pretty badly off. I got my fare together, and enough to tide me over till I got a job, and that's my situation now. It sounds like the opposite of the usual story, doesn't it? Usually the lone wolf sets out to the New World to make his way, but I—well, I wanted to come over here. The New World can be a bit wearing when you're on your own, and—don't laugh—but I thought I might fit in better here."

"Because your roots are here?" He smiled at my look. "They are, you know. I'm sure I'm right. There must have been someone, some Winslow, way back in the last century, who went to Canada from here. Probably more than one, you know how it was then; in the days when everybody had thirteen children, and *they* all had thirteen children, I'm pretty sure that one or two Winslows went abroad to stay. Whitescar wouldn't have been big enough, anyway, and nobody would have got a look-in except the eldest son. . . . Yes, that's it, that explains it. Some Winslow went to Canada, and one of his daughters—your great-grandmother, would it be?—married an Armstrong there. Or something like that. There'll be records at Whitescar, surely? I don't know, I wasn't brought up there. But that must be it."

"Perhaps."

"Well," he said, with that charmingly quizzical lift of the eyebrow that was perhaps just a little too well practiced, "that does make us cousins, doesn't it?"

"Does it?"

"Of course it does. It's as plain as a pikestaff that you must be a Winslow. Nothing else would account for the likeness; I refuse to believe in pure chance. You're a type, the Winslow type, it's unmistakable—that fair hair, and your eyes that queer colour between green and grey, and those lovely dark eyelashes. . . ."

"Carefully darkened," I said calmly. "After all, why go through life with light lashes if you don't have to?"

"Then Annabel's must have been darkened, too. By heaven, yes, they were! I remember now, when I first came to Whitescar she'd be only fifteen, and I suppose she hadn't started using that sort of thing. Yes, they were light. I don't even remember when the change took place! I was only nineteen when I came, you know, and straight from the back of beyond. I just took her for granted as the most beautiful girl I'd ever seen."

He spoke, for once, quite simply. I felt myself going scarlet, as if the tribute had been aimed at me. As, in a way, it was.

I said, to cover my embarrassment, "You talk of me as being a 'Winslow type.' Where do you come in? You don't seem to conform."

"Oh, I'm a sport." The white teeth showed. "Pure Irish, like my mother."

"Then you are Irish? I thought you looked it. Is Con short for Connor?"

"Sure. She was from Galway. I've her colouring. But the good looks come from the Winslows. We're all beauties."

"Well, well," I said drily, "it's a pity I haven't a better claim, isn't it?" I stubbed out my cigarette on the stone beside me, then flicked the butt out over the cliff's edge. I watched the place where it had vanished for a moment. "There is . . . one thing. Something I do remember, I think. It came back as we were talking. I don't know if it means anything. . . ."

"Yes?"

"It was just—I'm sure I remember Granny talking about a forest, some forest near Bellingham. Is there something near your 'Winslow place,' perhaps, that—?"

"*Forrest!*" He looked excited. "Indeed there is! You remember I told you that Whitescar was a kind of enclave in the park belonging to the local bigwigs? That's Forrest Park; the Park's really a big tract of land enclosed in a loop of the river, almost an island. The whole place is usually just spoken of as 'Forrest'—and the Forrests, the family, were there for generations. It was all theirs, except the one piece by the river, in the centre of the loop; that's Whitescar. I told you how they tried to winkle us out of it. The big house was Forrest Hall."

"Was? Oh, yes, you said the Hall had 'gone.' What happened? Who were they? This does sound as if my great-grandmother, at any rate, may have come from hereabouts, doesn't it?"

"It certainly does. I knew it couldn't be sheer chance, that likeness. Why, this means—"

"Who were the Forrests? Could she have known the family? What happened to them?"

"She'd certainly have known them if she lived at Whitescar. The family wasn't an especially old one, merchant adventurers who made a fortune trading with the East India Company in the seventeenth century, then built the Hall and settled down as landed gentry. By the middle of the nineteenth, they'd made another fortune out of railway shares. They extended their gardens, and did a spot of landscaping in the park, and built some rather extravagant stables, the last owner ran it as a stud at one time, and did their damnedest to buy the Winslows out of Whitescar. They couldn't, of course. Another cigarette?"

"No, thank you."

He talked on for a few minutes more about Whitescar and Forrest; there had been in no sense, he said, a feud between the families, it was only that the Winslows had held their small parcel of excellent land for generations, and were fiercely proud of it, and of their position as yeomen farmers independent of the family at the Hall, which, in its palmy days, had managed to acquire all the countryside from Darkwater Bank to Greenside, with the single exception of Whitescar, entrenched on its very doorstep.

"Then, of course, with the mid-twentieth century, came the end, the tragic Fall of the House of Forrest." He grinned. It was very evident that, whatever tragedy had touched the Hall, it didn't matter a damn if it hadn't also touched Whitescar. "Even if the Hall hadn't been burned down, they'd have had to give it up. Old Mr. Forrest had lost a packet during the slump, and then after his death, what with taxes and death duties—"

"It was burned down? What happened? When you said 'tragic,' you didn't mean that anyone was *killed?*"

"Oh, lord, no. Everyone got out all right. There were only the Forrests themselves in the house, and the couple who ran the garden and house between them, Johnny Rudd and his wife, and old Miss Wragg who looked after Mrs. Forrest. But it was quite a night, believe me. You could see the flames from Bellingham."

"I suppose you were there? It must have been awful."

"There wasn't much anyone could do. By the time the fire brigade could get there the place was well away." He talked about the scene for a little longer, describing it quite graphically, then went on: "It had started in Mrs. Forrest's bedroom, apparently, in the small hours. Her poodle raised the place, and Forrest went along. The bed was alight by that time. He managed to drag the bedclothes off her—she was unconscious—and carry her downstairs." A sideways look. "They were damned lucky to get the insurance paid up, if you ask me. There was talk of an empty brandy bottle in her room, and sleeping pills, and of how there'd been a small fire once before in her bedroom, and Forrest had forbidden Miss Wragg to let her have cigarettes in her room at night. But there's always talk when these things happen—and heaven knows there'd been enough gossip about the Forrests . . . of every sort. There always is, when a couple doesn't get on. I always liked him, so did everybody else for that matter, but the old woman, Miss Wragg, used to blackguard him right and left to anyone who'd listen. She'd been Crystal Forrest's nurse, and had come to look after her when she decided to be a chronic invalid, and she had a tongue like poison."

"Decided to be—that's an odd way of putting it."

"Believe me, Crystal Forrest was a damned odd sort of woman. How any man ever—oh, well, they say he married her for her money anyway. Must have, if you ask me. If it was true, he certainly paid for every penny of it that he'd put into that stud of his, poor devil. There can't have been much money, actually, because I know for a fact that when they left England after the fire they lived pretty much on the insurance, and on what he'd got for the horses. They went to live in Florence—bought a small villa there, but then she got worse, went right round the bend, one gathers, and he took her off to some man in Vienna. Till she died, two years ago, she'd been in one psychiatric clinic after another—or whatever is the fashionable name for the more expensive loony bins—in Vienna, and that had taken everything. When Forrest got back from Austria eventually, to finish selling up here, there was nothing left."

"He's back, then?"

"No, he's not here now. He only came over to sell the place. The Forestry Commission have the park land, and they've planted the lot, blast them. That's the whole point. If I'd been able to lay my hands on a bit—" He broke off.

"The whole point?"

"Skip it. Where was I? Oh, yes. The Hall's gone completely, of course, and the gardens are running wild. But the Rudds—they were the couple who used to work at the Hall—the Rudds have moved across to the other side of the Park, where the West Lodge and the stables are. Johnny Rudd runs the place now as a sort of small holding, and when Forrest was over here last year, he and Johnny got the old gardens going again, as a market garden, and I believe it's doing quite well. Johnny's running it now, with a couple of local boys."

He was gazing away from me as he talked, almost dreamily, as if his attention was not fully on what he was saying. His profile was as handsome as the rest of him, and something about the way he lifted his chin and blew out a long jet of smoke told me that he knew it, and knew I was watching him, too.

"And Mr. Forrest?" I asked, idly. "Does he live permanently in Italy now?"

"Mm? Italy? Yes, I told you, he has this place near Florence. He's there now, and the place is abandoned to Johnny Rudd, and the Forestry Commission . . . and Whitescar." He turned his head. The long mouth curved with satisfaction. "Well? How's that for a dramatic story of your homeland, Mary Grey? The Fall of the House of Forrest!" Then, accusingly, as I was silent, "You weren't even listening!"

"Oh, I was. I was, really. You made a good story of it."

I didn't add what I had been thinking while I watched him; that he had told the dreary, sad little tale—about a man he liked—with rather less feeling and sympathy than there would have been in a newspaper report; had told it, in fact, as if he were rounding off a thoroughly satisfactory episode. Except, that is, for that one curious remark about the Forestry Commission's planting programme.

He had also told it as if he had had no doubt of my own absorbed interest in every detail. I wondered why.

If I had some suspicion of the answer, I wasn't prepared to wait and see if I was right. I looked round me for my handbag.

He said quickly, "What is it?"

The bag was on the ground at the foot of the Wall. I picked it up. "I'll have to go now. I'd forgotten the time. My bus—"

"But you can't go yet! This was just getting exciting! If your great-grandmother knew about Forrest, it might mean—"

"Yes, I suppose it might. But I'll still have to go. We work Sunday evenings at my café." I got to my feet. "I'm sorry, but there it is. Well, Mr. Winslow, it's been interesting meeting you, and I—"

"Look, you can't just go like this!" He had risen too. He made a sudden little movement almost as if he would have detained me, but he didn't touch me. The rather conscious charm had gone from his face. He spoke quickly, with a kind of urgency. "I'm serious. Don't go yet. My car's here. I can run you back."

"I wouldn't think of letting you. No, really, it's been—"

"Don't tell me again that it's been 'interesting.' It's been a hell of a lot more than that. It's been important."

I stared at him. "What *do* you mean?"

"I told you. This sort of thing isn't pure chance. I tell you, it was meant."

"Meant?"

"Ordained. Destined. Kismet."

"Don't be absurd."

"It's not absurd. This thing that's happened, it's more than just queer. We can't simply walk away in opposite directions now and forget it."

"Why not?"

"*Why not?*" He said it almost explosively. "Because—oh, hell, I can't explain, because I haven't had time to think, but at any rate tell me the address of this place where you work." He was searching his pockets while he spoke, and eventually produced a used envelope and a pencil. When I didn't answer, he looked up sharply. "Well?"

I said slowly, "Forgive me, I can't explain either. But . . . I'd rather not."

"What d'you mean?"

"Just that I would rather—what did you say?—that we walked away in opposite directions now, and forgot all about it. I'm sorry. Please try to understand."

"I don't even begin to understand! It's perfectly obvious to me that this likeness of yours to Annabel Winslow *isn't* pure chance. Your people came from hereabouts. I wasn't only joking when I said we were long-lost cousins."

"Possibly we are. But can't you grasp this? Let me be blunt. Whitescar and Winslows and all the rest may mean a lot to you, but why should they mean anything to me? I've been on my own a good long time now, and I like it that way."

"A job in a café? Doing what? Waiting on tables? Cash desk? Washing up? *You?* Don't be a fool!"

"You take this imaginary cousinship a bit too much for granted, don't you?"

"All right. I'm sorry I was rude. But I meant it. You can't just walk away and—after all, you told me you were nearly broke."

I said, after a pause, "You—you take your family responsibilities very seriously, don't you, Mr. Winslow? Am I to take it you were thinking of offering me a job?"

He said slowly, "Do you know, I might, at that. I . . . might." He laughed suddenly, and added, very lightly, "Blood being thicker than water, Mary Grey."

I must have sounded as much at a loss as I felt. "Well it's very nice of you, but really . . . you can hardly expect me to take you up on it, can you, even if our families *might* just possibly have been connected a hundred years or so ago? No, thanks very much, Mr. Winslow, but I meant what I said." I smiled. "You know, you can't have thought. Just what sort of a sensation would there be if I did turn up at Whitescar with you? Had you thought of *that?*"

He said, in a very strange voice, "Oddly enough, I had."

For a moment our eyes met, and held. I had the oddest feeling that for just those few seconds each knew what the other was thinking.

I said abruptly, "I must go. Really. Please, let's leave it at that. I won't annoy you by telling you again that it's been interesting. It's been—quite an experience. But forgive me if I say it's one I don't want to take any further. I mean that. Thank you for your offer of help. It was kind of you. And now this really is good-bye."

I held out my hand. The formal gesture seemed, in these surroundings, and after what had passed, faintly absurd, but it would, I hoped, give the touch of finality to the interview, and provide the cue on which I could turn my back and leave him standing there.

To my relief, after a moment's hesitation, he made no further protest. He took the hand quite simply, in a sort of courteous recognition of defeat.

"Good-bye, then, Mary Grey. I'm sorry. All the best."

As I left him I was very conscious of him standing there and staring after me.

CHAPTER TWO

"Or take me by the body so meek,
Follow, my love, come over the strand—
And throw me in the water so deep,
For I darena go back to Northumberland."

Ballad: *The Fair Flower of Northumberland.*

WHEN THE KNOCK CAME at my bedroom door, I knew who it was, even before I looked up from my packing.

My landlady, Mrs. Smithson, was out; but even without this knowledge I could never have mistaken the tentative, even nervous quality of this knock, for Mrs. Smithson's forthright rapping. As clearly as if the thick, shiningly varnished door were made of glass, I could see who stood there; the stodgy, brown-clad woman who, for the past three evenings, had haunted the Kasbah Coffee House, staring at me as if her life depended on memorizing everything about me—"as if," one of the girls at the Espresso counter had said, "she was a talent scout looking for a new film star." Or as if (I said to myself) she thought that perhaps she recognized me, and was trying to nerve herself to speak. . . .

With the recent encounter on the Roman Wall still fresh in my mind, I had, in my turn, watched her a little wearily. Though I had never, to my knowledge, seen her before, there was about her something that was faintly familiar, and also (though I had no idea why) disturbing.

Outwardly, there was nothing in her appearance to alarm anyone. She could have been anything between thirty-five and forty. She wore goodish, but badly chosen country clothes and a minimum of make-up—powder, I guessed, and a touch of lipstick which did little to lighten the dull, rather heavy features. The general effect of dullness was not helped by the browns and fawns of the colour scheme she affected. Her hair under the slightly out-of-date felt hat was dark, and worn plainly in a bun. Her eyebrows were thick and well-marked, but untidy looking over badly set eyes. The outer corners of brows, eyes and mouth were pulled down slightly, giving the face its heavy, almost discontented expression. One got the curious impression that the woman only just missed being good-looking; that the features were somehow blurred and ill-defined, as if they had been drawn conventionally enough, and then the artist had smoothed a light, dry hand carelessly down over the drawing, dragging it just that fraction out of focus. She could have been a bad copy of a portrait I already knew; a print blotted off some dramatically sharp sketch that was vaguely familiar.

But even as I tried to place the impression, it slid away from me. I had never, to my recollection, seen her before. If I had, I would scarcely have noticed her, I thought. She was the kind of woman whom, normally, one wouldn't have looked at twice, being at first sight devoid of any of the positive qualities that go to make up that curious thing called charm. Charm presupposes some sort of vivacity and spark, at least what one might call some gesture of advance towards life. This woman merely sat there, heavily, apparently content to wait while life went on around her.

Except for the tireless stare of those toffee-brown eyes . . .

She had left the café at last, without speaking, and I had dismissed her with a mental shrug. But the next day, Tuesday, she was there again. And the next, still watching me steadily and disconcertingly from under the brim of the brown hat, until finally, in a moment of exasperation, I had gone over towards her table, intending to speak to her.

She had watched me coming, without moving, but in her heavy face a sudden spark of animation showed, momentarily lighting the plain features. . . .

I saw it then, the likeness that had troubled me; the poorish copy of that dramatically handsome face, the sepia print of Connor Winslow's Glorious Technicolour. *"My half-sister keeps house at Whitescar,"* he had said. *"With Lisa around, I don't need a wife"*. . . She would be some half-dozen years older than he, with the different colouring she had probably got from her Irish father, and none of the good looks that his Winslow blood had given Connor; but the likeness, ill-defined, shadowy, a characterless travesty of his vivid charm, was there.

I had walked straight by her table without pausing, out through the swing doors into the café kitchen, and had handed in my notice then and there.

And now, the same evening, here she was, at my door. It could be no one else. How she had found me out, why she had followed me, I could only guess. I hadn't heard her come upstairs, though the bare and echoing linoleum of the two flights to my room was a more than sufficient herald of approach. She must have come up very softly.

I hesitated. She must know I was here. I had seen no reason for silence, and the light would be showing under my door.

As the soft, insistent rapping came again, I threw a swift look round the room.

The ash tray by the bed, almost full . . . the bed itself, disordered, evidence of the time spent smoking and staring at the fly-spotted ceiling and wondering at myself and the impulse of panic which had driven me from the café, and even to consider leaving my lodgings. My cases stood, half-filled, in the middle of the floor.

Well, it was too late to do anything about them now. But there, on the table near the window, was a still more cogent witness to the impact that my meeting with Connor Winslow had had on me. The telephone directory, borrowed from downstairs, lay open at the page headed: "Wilson–Winthorpe. . . ."

I went silently across the room, and shut it. Then I turned back to the dresser and pulled open a drawer.

I said, on a note of inquiry, "Yes? Come in."

When the door opened, I had my back to it, lifting clothes out of the drawer. "Oh, Mrs. Smithson," I began, as I turned, then stopped short, my brows lifted, my face registering, I hoped, nothing but surprise.

She said, standing squarely in the doorway, "Miss Grey?"

"Yes? I'm afraid–" I paused, and let recognition dawn, and with it puzzlement. "Wait a moment. I think–don't I know your face? You were in the Kasbah this afternoon, the café where I work, weren't you? I remember noticing you in the corner."

"That's right. My name's Dermott, Lisa Dermott." She pronounced the name Continental-fashion, *Leeza*. She paused to let it register, then added, "From Whitescar."

I said, still on that puzzled note, "How do you do, Miss–Mrs.?–Dermott. Is there something I can do for you?"

She came into the room unasked, her eyes watchful on my face. She shut the door behind her, and began to pull off her plain, good hogskin gloves. I stood there without moving, my hands full of clothes, plainly intending, I hoped, not to invite her to sit down.

She sat down. She said flatly, "My brother met you up on the Roman Wall beyond Housesteads on Sunday."

"On the Ro–oh, yes, of course I remember. A man spoke to me. Winslow, he was called, from somewhere near Bellingham." *Careful now, Mary Grey; don't overplay it; she'll know you'd not be likely to forget a thing like that.* I added slowly, "Whitescar. Yes. That's where he said he came from. We had a rather–odd conversation."

I put the things I was holding back into the drawer, and then turned to face her. There was a packet of Players in my handbag lying beside me on the dresser. I shook one loose. "Do you smoke?"

"No, thank you."

"D'you mind if I do?"

"It's your own room."

"Yes." If she noticed the irony she gave no sign of it. She sat there solidly, uninvited, in the only chair my wretched little room boasted, and set her handbag down on the table beside her. She hadn't taken her eyes off me. "I'm Miss Dermott," she said. "I'm not married. Con Winslow's my half-brother."

"Yes, I believe he mentioned you. I remember now."

"He told me all about *you,*" she said. "I didn't believe him, but he was right. It's amazing. Even given the eight years, it's amazing. I'd have known you anywhere."

I said, carefully, "He told me I was exactly like a young cousin of his who'd left home some eight years ago. She had an odd name, Annabel. Is that right?"

"Quite right."

"And you see the same resemblance?"

"Certainly. I didn't actually know Annabel herself. I came to Whitescar after she'd gone. But the old man used to keep her photographs in his room, a regular gallery of them, and I dusted them every day, till I suppose I knew every expression she had. I'm sure that anyone who knew her would make the same mistake as Con. It's uncanny, believe me."

"It seems I must believe you." I drew deeply on my cigarette. "The 'old man' you spoke of . . . would that be Mr. Winslow's father?"

"His great-uncle. He was Annabel's grandfather."

I had been standing by the table. I sat down on the edge of it. I didn't look at her; I was watching the end of my cigarette. Then I said, so abruptly that it sounded rude, "So what, Miss Dermott?"

"I beg your pardon?"

"It's an expression we have on our side of the Atlantic. It means, roughly, all right, you've made your point, now where is it supposed to get us? You say I'm the image of this Annabel of yours. Granted, I'll accept that. You and Mr. Winslow have gone to a lot of trouble to tell me so. I repeat: so what?"

"You must admit–" she seemed to be choosing her words–"that we were bound to be interested, terribly interested?"

I said bluntly, "You've gone a little beyond 'interest,' haven't you? Unless, of course, you give the word its other meaning."

"I don't follow you."

"No? I think you do. Tell me something frankly, please. Does your brother still persist in thinking that I might *actually be* Annabel Winslow?"

"No. Oh, no."

"Very well. Then you have to admit that this 'interest' of yours does go far beyond mere curiosity, Miss Dermott. He might have sent you to take a look at me, Annabel's double, once, but not more than–" I caught myself in time–"not more than that. I mean, you'd have hardly followed me home. No, you're 'interested' in quite another sense, aren't you?" I paused, tapped ash into the wastebasket, and added, "'Interested parties,' shall we say? In other words, you've something at stake."

She sounded as calm as ever. "I suppose it's natural for you to be so hostile." There was the faintest glimmer of a smile on her face: perhaps not so much a smile, as a lightening of the stolidity of her expression. "I don't imagine that Con was exactly, well, tactful, to start with . . . He upset you, didn't he?"

"He frightened me out of my wits," I said frankly. I got up from the table, and moved restlessly to the window. The curtains were undrawn. Outside, the lights and clamour of the street made a pattern two stories below, as remote as that of a coastal town seen from a passing ship. I turned my back on it.

"Look, Miss Dermott, let me be plain, please. Certain things are obvious to me, and I don't see any advantage in playing stupid about them. For one thing, I don't want to prolong this interview. As you see, I'm busy. Now, your brother was interested in me because I look like this Annabel Winslow. He told you about me. All right. That's natural enough. But it isn't just pure coincidence that brought you to the Kasbah, and I know damned well I never told him where I worked. It sticks out a mile that he followed me home on Sunday, and either he came here and asked someone where I worked, or he saw me go on for the late Sunday shift at the café, and then went back and told you. And you came next day to have a look at me . . . yes, I admit I did see you before today. How could I help noticing you, the way you stared? Well, no doubt he and you had a talk about it, and today you've followed me home. Am I right?"

"More or less."

"I told you I was being frank, Miss Dermott. I don't like it. I didn't like the way your brother talked to me on Sunday, and I don't like being watched, and I'm damned if I like being followed."

She nodded calmly, as if I had said something a little pettish, but fairly reasonable. "Of course you don't. But if you'll just be a little patient with me, I'll explain. And I'm sure you'll be interested then. . . ."

All this time she had been watching me, and there was some quality about her steady gaze that I associated with something I couldn't place. It made me feel uncomfortable, and I wanted to look away from her. Con Winslow had had the same look, only his had held a frankly male appraisal that made it more understandable, and easier to face.

She looked away at last. Her gaze shifted from me to the appointments of the shabby little room; the iron bedstead, the garish linoleum, the varnished fireplace with its elaborately ugly overmantel, the gas ring on the cracked tiles of the hearth. She looked further, as if wondering, now, whether something of me, personally, was anywhere superimposed on the room's characterless ugliness. But there were no photographs, and what books I had had with me were packed. The questing look came to rest, defeated, on the clothes untidily hanging from the drawer I had been emptying, on the handbag I had pulled open to get my cigarettes, from which had spilled a lipstick, a pocket comb, and a small gold cigarette lighter whose convoluted initials caught the light quite clearly: *M.G.*

Her eyes came back to my face. I suppressed a desire to say tartly, "Satisfied?" and said instead, "Are you sure you won't smoke?" I was already lighting another for myself.

"I think I might, after all." She took cigarette and light with the slight awkwardness that betrayed it as an unaccustomed action. She took a rapid puff at the cigarette, looked down at it as if she wondered what it was there for, then said in that flat voice of hers,

"I'll come to the main point first, and explain afterwards. You were right in saying that our interest in you was more than the normal curiosity you'd expect the likeness to arouse. You were even right—terribly right—when you said we had 'something at stake.' "

She paused, laid her cigarette carefully down in the ash tray I had placed near her on the table. She put her hands flat down on her thighs and leaned forward slightly. "What we want," she said, "is Annabel, back at Whitescar. It's important. I can't tell you how important. She must come back."

The voice was undramatic; the words, in their impact, absurdly sensational. I felt my heart give a little painful twist of nervous excitement. Though I had suspected some nonsense of this kind—and of course it *was* nonsense—all along, the knowledge did nothing to prevent my blood jerking unevenly through my veins as if driven by a faulty pump. I said nothing.

The brown eyes held mine. She seemed to think everything had been said. I wondered, with a spasm of genuine anger, why people with some obsessive trouble of their own always thought that others should be nerve-end conscious of it, too. A cruel impulse made me say, obtusely, "But Annabel's dead."

Something flickered behind the woman's eyes. "Yes, she's dead. She can't come back, Miss Grey, she can't come back . . . to spoil anything for you . . . or for us."

I watched the ash from my cigarette float and fall towards the waste-basket. I didn't look at her. I said at length, with no expression at all, "You want me to go to Whitescar. As Annabel Winslow."

She leaned back. The basket chair gave a long, gasping creak like a gigantic breath of relief. It was obvious that she had taken my apparent calmness for compliance.

"Yes," she said, "that's it. We want you to come to Whitescar . . . Annabel."

I laughed then. I couldn't help it. Possibly the laughter was as much the result of taut nerves as of the obvious absurdity of her proposal, but if there was a suggestion of hysteria in it, she took no notice. She sat quite still, watching me with that expression which, suddenly, I recognized. It was the look of someone who, themselves uninvolved, coolly assesses a theatrical performance. She had all this time been weighing my looks, my voice, my movements, my reactions, against those of the Annabel Winslow of whom she knew so much, and whom she and her brother must have spent the greater part of the last three days discussing.

I felt some nerve tighten somewhere inside me again, and deliberately relaxed it. My laughter died. I said, "Forgive me, but it sounded so absurd when it finally got put into words. Why on earth should Annabel come back? It—it's so theatrical and romantic and impossible. Impersonation—that old stuff? Look, Miss Dermott, I'm sorry, but it's crazy! You can't be serious!"

She said calmly, "It's been done."

"Oh, yes, in stories. It's an old favourite, we know that, from the *Comedy of Errors* on. And that's a point, too: it may be all right in books, but on the stage, where one can *see*, and still one's supposed to be deceived, it's absurd. Unless you do really have identical twins . . . or one person plays both parts."

"That," said Miss Dermott, "is the whole point, isn't it? We *have* got identical twins. It could be done."

"Look at it this way," I said. "It's something, you say, that has been done. But, surely, in much simpler times than these? I mean, think of the lawyers, handwriting, written records, photographs, and, if it came to the point, police . . . oh, no, they're all too efficient nowadays. The risks are too great. No, it belongs in stories, and I doubt if it's even readily acceptable there any more. Too many coincidences required, too much luck."

She nodded. Arguing with her was like battering a feather pillow. You got tired, and the pillow stayed just the same. "Yes, of course. There has to be luck, certainly, and there has to be careful planning. But it's like murder, isn't it?"

I stared at her. "Murder?"

"Yes. You only know about the ones that are found out. Nobody ever hears about the ones that get away with it. All the counting's on the negative side."

"I suppose so. But—"

"The point is that you'd not be *claiming* anything from anybody; there'd be nobody to fight you. The only person who'd lose by your reappearance is Julie, and she has enough of her own. Besides, she adored Annabel; she'll be so pleased to see you, that she'll hardly stop to think what it'll mean in terms of money. . . ."

"Julie?"

"Annabel's young cousin. She's not at Whitescar now, but she'll be coming some time this summer. You needn't worry about her, she was only ten or eleven when Annabel went away, and she'll hardly remember enough about her to suspect you. Besides, why should she? I tell you, it's not a risk, it's a certainty. Take it from me, Con and I wouldn't dare take risks, either! We've everything to lose. You wouldn't even find it nerve-racking. Apart from the daily help, and the farm hands you need hardly see, you'll be mostly with Con and myself, and we'll help you all we can."

"I don't understand. If Julie isn't there, who are you trying to—?"

"And the point about the old man is that he's never believed Annabel was dead. He simply won't have it. He'll never even question you, believe me. You can just walk in."

I was staring at her, my cigarette arrested halfway to my mouth. "The old man? Who? Who are you talking about?"

"Old Mr. Winslow, her grandfather. I spoke of him before. He thought the world of her. He kept half a dozen pictures of her in his room—"

"But surely . . . I understood he was dead."

She looked up in surprise. "Where did you get that idea? No, he's very much alive." Her mouth twisted suddenly, incongruously, into a likeness of that not-so-pleasant smile of Con's. "You might say that's the whole cause of this—situation. What made you think he was dead?"

"I didn't think. But I somehow got the impression. . . . When you spoke of 'the old man' before, you used the past tense. You said '*he was* Annabel's grandfather.'"

"Did I? Possibly. But, of course, the past tense," she said softly, "would be for Annabel."

"I see that now. Yes. But it was added somehow to an impression I got on Sunday . . . your brother said something, I forget what. . . . Yes, of course, he said—implied, I suppose, would be more accurate—that he owned the farm. No, he stated it flatly. I'm sure he did."

She smiled then, genuinely, and for the first time I saw the warmth of real feeling in her face. She looked amused, indulgent, affectionate, as a mother might look when watching the pranks of a naughty but attractive child. "Yes, he would. Poor Con." She didn't take it further, merely adding, "No, he doesn't own Whitescar. He's old Mr. Winslow's manager. He's . . . not even Mr. Winslow's heir."

"*I see.* Oh lord, yes, I see it now."

I got up abruptly, and went over again to the window. Opposite, in one of the tall, drab houses, someone came into a bedroom and switched on the light. I caught a too-familiar glimpse of yellow wallpaper with a writhing pattern of green and brown, a pink plastic lampshade, the gleam of a highly polished radio, before the curtains were twitched across the window. The radio was switched on, and some comedian clacked into the night. Somewhere a child wailed, drearily. In the street below, a woman was shouting a child's name in a wailing northern cadence.

"What do you see?"

I said, slowly, still staring out at the dark, "Not much, really. Just that Mr. Winslow—Con—wants Whitescar, and that somehow he thinks he can fix it, if I go back there as Annabel. I take it that Julie must be the heir now, if he isn't. But how on earth it's going to help Con to bring back Annabel, and put two people in the way instead of one. . . ." I finished heavily, "Oh lord, the whole thing's fantastic anyway. I can't think why I've bothered to listen."

"Extraordinary, perhaps, but not fantastic." The colourless voice behind me might have been discussing a knitting pattern. I didn't turn. I leaned my forehead against the glass and watched, without seeing them, the moving lights of the traffic in the street below. "But then, families are extraordinary, don't you think? And with all their faults, the Winslows have never been exactly dull . . . Listen for a little while longer, and you'll understand what Con and I are getting at."

I let her talk. I just leaned my head against the glass and watched the traffic, and let the soft, unemphatic voice flow on and on. I felt, suddenly, too tired even to try and stop her.

She told me the recent family history very briefly. Old Matthew Winslow (she said) had had two sons: the elder had one daughter, Annabel, who had lived with her parents at Whitescar. When the girl was fourteen, her father was killed in an accident with a tractor, and her mother died soon afterwards, within the year, of pneumonia, leaving her an orphan in her grandfather's care. The latter was then only in his early sixties, but had been for some time handicapped by arthritis, and found it heavy work to manage the place on his own. His younger son had been killed some years previously in the Battle of Britain, leaving a widow, and a month-old daughter, Julie. Matthew Winslow had immediately invited his daughter-in-law to Whitescar, but she had chosen to remain in London. She had eventually remarried, and gone out, with her small daughter, to live in Kenya. Later, when Julie was some seven years old, she had been sent back to England to school; she spent the winter vacations with her parents in Africa, but her spring and summer holidays had been passed with her grandfather at Whitescar, which she regarded as her English home.

It had not been for some time after his elder son's death that Mr. Winslow thought of offering a home and a job to Connor Winslow, his only surviving male relative. Matthew Winslow had had a nephew, who had gone to Ireland to work in a big training stable in Galway, where he had met and married a young Irish widow, a Mrs. Dermott, who had a five-year-old daughter, Lisa. A year later, Connor was born, to become the spoiled darling of his parents, and also, surprisingly, of his half-sister, who had adored him, and had never dreamed of resenting her mother's preference for the good-looking only son. But this apparently safe and happy circle had been rudely shattered when Connor was thirteen. His father broke his neck one day over a big Irish in-and-out, and exactly ten months later the inconsolable widow cheerfully married for the third time.

The young Connor found himself all at once relegated to the background of his mother's life, and kept there by an unsympathetic step-father and (very soon) by the even stronger claims of a new young family. Con's father had left no money, and it became increasingly obvious that his step-father, and now his mother, were not prepared to spare either time, or material help, on the son of the earlier marriage. So when Matthew Winslow, the great-uncle whose existence he had half forgotten, wrote out of the blue to ask Connor, then aged nineteen, to make his home at Whitescar and be trained for farm management, the boy had gone like an arrow from a bow, and with very little in the nature of a by-your-leave. If Lisa wept after he had gone, nobody knew; there was plenty for Lisa to do at home, anyway. . . .

Small wonder that Con arrived at Whitescar with the determination to make a place for himself, and stay; a determination that, very soon, hardened into a definite ambition. Security. The Winslow property. Whitescar itself. There was only Annabel in the way, and Con came very quickly to think that she had no business to be in the way at all. It didn't take him long to find out that the place, backed by Matthew Winslow's not inconsiderable private income, could be willed any way that the old man wished.

So Connor Winslow had set to work. He had learned his job, he made himself very quickly indispensable, he had worked like a navvy at anything and everything that came along, earning the respect and even the admiration of the slow, conservative local farmers, who at first had been rather inclined to regard the good-looking lad from Ireland as an extravagant whim of Matthew's; showy, perhaps, but bound to be a poor stayer. He had proved them wrong.

Matthew himself, though he had never publicly admitted it, had had the same doubts, but Con defeated his prejudices first, then proceeded to charm his great-uncle "like a bird off a tree," (so said Lisa, surprisingly). But charm he never so wisely, Con couldn't quite charm Whitescar from him, away from Annabel. "Because Con tried, he admits it," said Lisa. "The old man thought the world of him, and still does, but he's like the rest of the English Winslows, as stubborn as the devil and as sticky as a limpet. What he has, he hangs on to. He wanted her to have it after him, and what he wants, goes. The fact that she's dead," added Lisa bitterly, "doesn't make a bit of difference. If the old man said black was white he'd believe it was true. He can't be wrong, you see; he once said she'd come back, and he won't change. He'll die sooner. Literally. *And* he'll leave everything to Annabel in his will, and the mess'll take years to clear up, and the odds are that Julie's the residuary beneficiary. The point is, we just don't know. He won't say a word. But it does seem unfair."

She paused for a moment. I had half turned back from the window, and was standing leaning against the shutter. But I still didn't look at her, or make any comment on the story. I felt her eyes on me for a few moments, then she went on.

There wasn't much more. Con's next move had been the obvious one. If Annabel and Whitescar were to go together, then he would try to take both. Indeed, he was genuinely (so Lisa told me) in love with her, and an understanding between them was such an obvious and satisfactory thing to happen that the old man, who was fond of them both, was delighted.

"But," said Lisa, hesitating now and appearing to choose her words, "it went wrong, somehow. I won't go into details now—in any case, I don't know a great deal, because I wasn't there, and Con hasn't said much—but they quarrelled terribly, and she used to try and make him jealous, he says, and, well, that's only too easy with Con, and he has a terrible temper. They had a dreadful quarrel one night. I don't know what happened, but I think

Con may have said something to frighten her, and she threw him over once and for all, said she couldn't stay at Whitescar while he was there, and all that sort of thing. Then she ran off to see her grandfather. Con doesn't know what happened between them, or if he does, he won't tell me. But of course the old man was bound to be furious, and disappointed, and *he* never was one to mince his words, either. The result was another dreadful row, and she left that night, without a word to anyone. There was a note for her grandfather, that was all. Nothing for Con. She just said she wasn't coming back. Of course the old man was too stubborn and furious even to try and find her, and persuade her, and he forbade Con to try either. Con did what he could, quietly, but there was no trace. Then, a month later, her grandfather got a note, postmarked New York. It just said she was quite safe, had got a job with friends, and she wasn't ever coming back to England again. After that there was nothing, until three years later someone sent Mr. Winslow a cutting from a Los Angeles paper describing an accident in which an express train had run into a bus at some country crossing, and a lot of people had been killed. One of them was a "Miss Anna Winslow" of no given address, who'd been staying at some boarding house in the city, and who was thought to be English. We made inquiries, and they were all negative. It could have been Annabel. It would certainly be enough, with the long absence, to allow us to presume her dead. After all this time, she must be; or else she really isn't ever coming back, which amounts to the same thing, in the end." She paused. "That's all."

I turned my head. "And you? Where do you come in?"

"After she'd gone," said Lisa Dermott, "Con remembered me."

She said it quite simply. There was no hint of self-pity or complaint in the soft, flattened voice. I looked down at her, sitting stolid and unattractive in the old basket chair, and said gently, "He got Mr. Winslow to send for you?"

She nodded. "Someone had to run the house, and it seemed too good a chance to miss. But even with the two of us there, doing all that we do, it's not the slightest use."

The impulse of pity that had stirred in me, died without a pang. I had a sudden vivid picture of the two of them, camped there at Whitescar, hammering home their claims, Con with his charm and industry, Lisa with her polish and her apple pies. . . . She had called it "unfair," and perhaps it was; certainly one must admit they had a right to a point of view. But then so had Matthew Winslow.

"You see," she said, "how unjust it all is? You do see that, don't you?"

"Yes, I see. But I still don't see what you think I can do about it! You want me to go to Whitescar, and somehow or other *that* is going to help Con to become the heir, and owner. How?"

I had left the window as I spoke, and come forward to the table again. She leaned towards me, looking up under the brim of the brown hat. There was a gleam in her eyes that might have been excitement.

"You're interested now, aren't you? I thought you would be, when you heard a bit more."

"I'm not. You've got me wrong. I was interested in your story, I admit, but that was because I think your brother may be right when he says I must come originally from some branch of the same family. But I never said I was interested in your proposition! I'm not! I told you what I thought about it! It's a crazy idea straight out of nineteenth-century romance, long-lost heirs and missing wills and—and all that drivel!" I found that I was speaking roughly, almost angrily, and made myself smile at her, adding, mildly enough, "You'll be telling me next that Annabel had a strawberry mark—"

I stopped. Her hand had moved, quickly, to the telephone directory on the table beside her. I saw, then, that I had shut it over a pencil which still lay between the leaves.

The book fell open under her hand, at the page headed *Wilson—Winthorpe*. She looked at it without expression. Then her blunt, well-kept finger moved down towards the foot of the second column, and stopped there.

Winslow, Matthew. Frmr. Whitescar. . . . Bellingham 248.

The entry was marked, faintly, in pencil.

I said, trying to keep my voice flat, and only succeeding in making it sound sulky, "Yes, I looked it up. It puzzled me, because your brother had said he owned the farm. It isn't an old directory, so when you first spoke of 'the old man,' I assumed he must have died quite recently."

She didn't answer. She shut the book, then leaned back in her chair and looked up at me, with that calm, appraising look. I met it almost defiantly.

"All right, I was interested before. Who wouldn't be? After that business on Sunday . . . oh, well, skip it. Call it curiosity if you like, I'm only human. But my heaven, there's no reason why it should go further than curiosity! This—proposition you appear to be suggesting takes my breath away. No, no, I don't want to hear any more about it. I can't even believe you're serious. *Are* you?"

"Quite."

"Very well. But can you give me any conceivable reason why *I* should be?"

She looked at me almost blankly. There it was again; that merciless all-excluding obsession with their personal problems. "I don't understand."

I found that I was reaching, automatically, for another cigarette. I let it slip back into the packet. I had smoked too much that evening already; my eyes and throat felt hot and aching, and my brain stupid. I said, "Look, you approach me out of the blue with your family history, which may be intriguing, but which can really mean very little to me. You propose, let's face it, that somehow or other I should help you to perpetrate a fraud. It may mean everything to you; I don't see how, but we'll grant it for argument's sake. But why should it mean a thing to me? You tell me it'll be 'easy.' Why should I care? Why should I involve myself? In plain words, why on earth should I go out of my way to help you and your brother Con to anything?"

I didn't add, "when I don't much like you, and I don't trust him," but to my horror the words seemed to repeat themselves into the air of the room as clearly as if I, and not the tone of my voice, had said them.

If she heard them, she may have been too unwilling to antagonize me to resent them. Nor did she appear to mind my actual rudeness. She said, simply, "Why, for money, of course. What other reason is there?"

"For *money?*"

She gave a slight, summing, eloquent glance round the room. "If you'll forgive me, you appear to need it. You said so, in fact, to my brother; that was one of the reasons why we felt we could approach you. You have so much to gain. You will forgive my speaking so plainly on such a short acquaintance?"

"Do," I said ironically.

"You are a gentlewoman," said Miss Dermott, the outmoded word sounding perfectly normal on her lips. "And this room . . . and your job at that dreadful café . . . You've been over here from Canada for how long?"

"Just a few days."

"And this has been all you could find?"

"As far as I looked. It took all I had to get me here. I'm marking time while I get my bearings. I took the first thing that came. You don't have to worry about me, Miss Dermott. I'll make out. I don't have to work in the Kasbah for life, you know."

"All the same," she said, "it's worth your while to listen to me. In plain terms, I'm offering you a job, a good one, the job of coming back to Whitescar as Annabel Winslow, and persuading the old man that that is who you are. You will have a home and every comfort, a position, everything; and eventually a small assured income for life. You call it a fraud: of course it is, but it's not a cruel one. The old man wants you there, and your coming will make him very happy."

"Why did he remove the photographs?"

"I beg your pardon?"

"You said earlier that he used to keep a 'whole gallery' of this girl's photographs in his room. Doesn't he still?"

"You're very quick." She sounded appreciative, as of a favourite horse who was showing a pretty turn of speed. "He didn't get rid of them, don't worry; he keeps them in a drawer in his office, and he still has one in his bedroom. He moved the others last year, when he had one done of Julie." She eyed me for a moment. "She'll be coming up for her summer holiday before very long. You see?"

"I see why you and your brother might want to work quickly, yes."

"Of course. You must come home before Julie persuades him to be reasonable about Annabel's death . . . and to put Julie herself in Annabel's place. Whatever happens, it'll happen soon. It's doubtful if the old man'll see the year out, and I think he's beginning to realize it."

I looked up quickly. "Is he ill?"

"He had a slight stroke three months ago, and he refuses to take very much care. He's always been strong, and still, in spite of the arthritis, pretty active, and he seems to resent any suggestion that he should do less. He takes it as an encroachment. . . ." Her lips tightened over whatever she had been going to say, then she added, "The doctor has warned him. He may live for some time, but he may, if he does anything silly, have another stroke at almost any moment, and this time it might be fatal. So you see why this is so urgent? Why meeting you like that seemed, to Con, like a gift from heaven?"

I said, after a pause, "And when he's gone?"

She said patiently, "It's all thought out. We can go into details later. Briefly, all you have to do is establish yourself at Whitescar, *be* Annabel Winslow, and inherit the property (and her share of the capital) when the old man dies. I tell you, there'll be no question. Don't you see, you'll not actually be coming back to *claim* anything, simply coming home to live? With luck you'll be able to settle quietly in and establish yourself, long before there's any sort of a crisis, and by the time the old man does die, you'll have been accepted without question. Then, after a decent interval, when things seem settled, you'll turn your legacy over to Con. You'll get your cut, don't worry. Annabel's mother left her some money, which she could have claimed when she was twenty-one; it brings in a nice little independent income. You'll have that—in any case, it would look absurd if you attempted to hand *that* over. As for the main transaction, the handing over of Whitescar, that can be arranged to look normal enough. You can say you want to live elsewhere . . . abroad, perhaps . . . whatever you'd planned for yourself. In fact, you'll be able to lead your own life again, but with a nice little assured income behind you. And if 'Annabel' decided to live away from Whitescar again, leaving the place to her cousin, who's run it for years anyway, there's no reason why anyone should question it."

"The young cousin? Julie?"

"I tell you, you needn't be afraid of her. Her step-father has money, there's no other child, and she'll certainly also get a share of Mr. Winslow's capital. You'll rob her of Whitescar, yes, but she's never given the slightest hint that she cares anything about it, except as a place to spend a holiday in. Since she left school last year, she's taken a job in London, in the Drama Department at the B.B.C., and she's only been up here once, for the inside of a fortnight. All she could do, if the place was hers, would be to sell it, or pay Con to manage it. You needn't have Julie on your conscience."

"But surely—" it was absurd, I thought, to feel as if one was being backed against a wall by this steady pressure of will—"but surely, if the old man realized that he was ill, and still Annabel *hadn't* come back, he *would* leave things to Con? Or if he left them to Julie, and she was content to let Con go on as manager, wouldn't that be all right?"

Her lips folded in that soft obstinate line. "That wouldn't answer. Can't you see how impossible—ah, well, take it from me that it wouldn't work out like that. No, my dear, this is the best way, and you're the gift straight from the gods. Con believes he'll never get control of Whitescar and the capital except this way. When you've said you'll help, I'll explain more fully, and you'll see what a chance it is for all of us, and no harm done, least of all to that stubborn old man sitting at Whitescar waiting for her to come home. . . ."

Somehow, without wanting it, I had taken the cigarette, my hands fidgeting with package and lighter in spite of myself. I stood silently while she talked, looking about me through the first, blue, sharp-scented cloud of smoke . . . the sagging bed, the purplish wallpaper, the wardrobe and dresser of yellow deal, the table cloth with the geometric flowers of Prussian blue and carmine, and the stain on the ceiling that was the shape of the map of Ireland. I thought of the high moors and the curlews calling and the beeches coming into leaf in the windbreaks. And of the collie waving his tail, and the straight blue stare of Connor Winslow. . . .

It was disconcerting to feel the faint prickle of nervous excitement along the skin, the ever-so-slightly quickened heartbeat, the catch in the breath. Because of course the thing *was* crazy. Dangerous and crazy and impossible. This silly, stolid pudding of a woman couldn't possibly have realized how crazy it was. . . .

No, I thought. No. Go while the going's good. Don't touch it.

"Well?" said Lisa Dermott.

I went to the window and dragged the curtains shut across it. I turned abruptly back to her. The action was somehow symbolic; it shut us in together, storybook conspirators in the solitary, sleazy upstairs room that smelt of too much cigarette smoke.

"Well?" I echoed her, sharply. "All right. I am interested. And I'll come, if you can persuade me that it can possibly work . . . Go on. I'll really listen now."

CHAPTER THREE

Oh, the oak, and the ash, and the bonny ivy tree,
They are all growing green in the North Country.

Traditional.

IT TOOK THREE WEEKS. At the end of that time Lisa Dermott vowed that I would do. There was nothing, she said, that she or Con knew about Whitescar and Annabel that I, too, didn't now know.

My handwriting, even, passed muster. The problem of the signature had been one of Lisa's worst worries, but she had brought me some old letters, written before Annabel's disappearance, and when I showed her the sheets that I had covered with carefully practised writing, she eventually admitted that they would pass.

It was on the Thursday of the second week that Lisa appeared unexpectedly. I had moved to another boarding house immediately after our first meeting, and was using the name of Winslow—this to avoid the possibility of some later inquiry turning up a connection between Con and Lisa, and one Mary Grey. When I opened the door and showed her into my room, I thought that something was ruffling her usually stolid calm, but she took off her gloves and coat with her customary deliberation, and sat down by the fire.

"I didn't expect you," I said. "Has something happened?"

She sent me a half-glance upwards, in which I thought I could read uneasiness, and even anger. "Julie's coming, that's what happened. Some time next week."

I sat on the table's edge, and reached for a cigarette. "Oh?"

She said sourly, "You take it very calmly."

"Well, you said you expected her some time during the summer."

"Yes, but she's taking her holiday much earlier than we'd expected, and I've a feeling that the old man's asked her to come, and she's getting special leave. He doesn't say so; but I know she *had* originally planned to come in August. . . . You see what it means?"

I lit the cigarette deliberately, then pitched the dead match into the fire. (The gold lighter, with its betraying monogram, lay concealed at the bottom of a suitcase.) "I see what it might mean."

"It means that if we don't get moving straight away, Julie'll have wormed her way into Whitescar, and he'll leave her every penny."

I didn't answer for a moment. I was thinking that Con, even at his most direct, was never coarse.

"So you see, this is it," said Lisa.

"Yes."

"Con says it must mean the old man's a bit more nervous about his health than he's admitted. Apparently Julie wrote to him once or twice while he was ill, and he has written back, I know. I'm sure he must have asked her to come up early, for some reason, and he certainly seems as pleased as Punch that she can get away so soon. She said she'd be here next week, some time, but would ring up and let us know. Normally we'd have had till July or August, and anything," said Lisa, bitterly, "could have happened before then. As it is—"

"Look," I said mildly, "you don't have to hunt round for motives to frighten yourselves with. Perhaps he does just want to see Julie, and perhaps she does just want to see him. It could be as simple as that. Don't look so disbelieving. People are straightforward enough, on the whole, till one starts to look for crooked motives, and then, oh boy, how crooked can they be!"

Lisa gave that small, tight-lipped smile that was more a concession to my tone than any evidence of amusement. "Well, we can't take risks. It'll have to be this week end. You can ring up on Sunday, as we arranged. If you ring up at three, the old man'll be resting, and I'll take the call. You'd better come on Monday. Con says we can't wait any longer; you'll have to come straight away, before Julie gets here, or heaven knows what Mr. Winslow'll do."

"But, look, Lisa—"

"You'll be all right, won't you? I'd have liked another week, just to make certain."

"I'm all right. It isn't that. I was going to say that surely Con's barking up the wrong tree with Julie. I don't see how she can possibly be a danger to him, whether she's at Whitescar or not."

"All I know is," said Lisa, a little grimly, "that she's as like Annabel as two peas in a pod, and the old man's getting more difficult every day . . . Heaven knows what he might take it into his head to do. Can't you see what Con's afraid of? He's pretty sure Julie's the residuary beneficiary now, but if Mr. Winslow alters his will before Annabel gets home, and makes Julie the principal. . . ."

"Oh yes, I see. In that case, I might as well not trouble to go any further. But is it likely, Lisa? If Grandfather abandons Annabel at last, and remakes his will at all, surely now, it will be in Con's favour? You said Julie's only been to Whitescar for holidays, and she's London bred. What possible prospect—?"

"That's just the point. Last year, when she was here, she was seeing a lot of one of the Fenwick boys from Nether Shields. It all seemed to blow up out of nothing, and before anyone even noticed it, he was coming over every day, getting on like a house on fire with Mr. Winslow, and Julie . . . well, *she* did nothing to discourage him."

I laughed. "Well, but Lisa, what was she? Eighteen?"

"I know. It's all speculation, and I hope it's nonsense, but you know what a razor's edge Con's living on, and anything could happen to the old man. Once you're there, things should be safe enough: he'll certainly never leave anything to Julie over *your* head, but as it is—well, she's his son's child, and Con's only a distant relative . . . and he likes Bill Fenwick."

I regarded the end of my cigarette. "And did Con never think to set up as a rival to this Bill Fenwick? An obvious move, one imagines. He tried it with Annabel."

Lisa stirred, and dropped her eyes, but not before I had seen, quite clearly, the look which had now and then showed in those unexpressive features, and which I now recognized for jealousy; jealousy, still alive and potent, of an unhappy girl whom she had believed dead for years. And now—of Julie? "I told you," she said, "it never occurred to anyone that she was even adult! She'd just left school! Con never looked at her—I think he thought of her as a schoolgirl. Mr. Winslow certainly did; the Fenwick affair amused him enormously."

"And now she's had a year in London. She'll have probably got further than the boy-next-door stage," I said cheerfully. "You'll find you're worrying about nothing."

"I hope so. But once you're there at Whitescar, things will be safe enough for Con. Julie won't be seriously in the way."

I looked at her for a moment. "No?" I got up then, and went over to the window, where I stood looking out. There was a short silence.

"What's the matter?" asked Lisa, at length. "Nerves? You'll be all right, you know. Don't worry."

I turned back into the room. I didn't feel it necessary to explain that I hadn't even been thinking about the hazards of the proposed masquerade. I had been thinking of Julie; Julie, the unknown quantity, who might have been "seriously in the way." And for some reason the phrase had made me think of Con, and the water gleaming below us, and the smooth voice saying, *"It doesn't necessarily have to be midnight, does it, when you and I go walking at the edge of a cliff with water at the bottom?"*

I smiled at Lisa, and threw the stub of my cigarette into the fire. "And don't *you* worry," I said. "Monday, was it? I'll be there."

The approach to Whitescar was down a narrow gravelled track edged with hawthorns. There was no gate. On the right of the gap where the track left the main road stood a dilapidated signpost which had once said, *Private Road to Forrest Hall.* On the left was a new and solid-looking stand for milk-churns, which bore a beautifully painted legend, WHITESCAR. Between these symbols the lane curled off between its high hawthorns, and out of sight.

I had come an hour too early, and no one was there to meet the bus. I had only two cases with me, and carrying these I set off down the lane.

Round the first bend there was a quarry, disused now and overgrown, and here, behind a thicket of brambles, I left my cases. They would be safe enough, and could be collected later. Meanwhile I was anxious to make my first reconnaissance alone.

The lane skirted the quarry, leading downhill for perhaps another two hundred yards before the hedges gave way on the one side to a high wall, and on the other—the left—to a fence which allowed a view across the territory that Lisa had been at such pains to picture for me.

I stood, leaning on the top bar of the fence, and looked at the scene below me.

Whitescar was about eight miles, as the crow flies, from Bellingham. There the river, meandering down its valley, doubles round leisurely on itself in a great loop, all but enclosing the rolling, well-timbered lands of Forrest Park. At the narrow part of the loop the bends of the river are barely two hundred yards apart, forming a sort of narrow isthmus through which ran the track on which I stood. This was the only road to the Hall, and it divided at the gate-house for Whitescar and the West Lodge which lay the other side of the park.

The main road, along which my bus had come, lay some way above the level of the river, and the drop past the quarry to the Hall gates was fairly steep. From where I stood you could see the whole near-island laid out below you in the circling arm of the river, with its woods and its water meadows and the chimneys glimpsed among the green.

To the east lay Forrest Hall itself, set in what remained of its once formal gardens and timbered walks, the grounds girdled on two side by the curving river, and on two by a mile-long wall and a belt of thick trees. Except for a wooded path along the river, the only entrance was through the big pillared gates where the gate-house had stood. This, I knew, had long since been allowed to crumble gently into ruin. I couldn't see it from where I was, but the tracks to Whitescar and West Lodge branched off there, and I could see the latter clearly, cutting across the park from east to west, between the orderly rows of planted conifers. At the distant edge of the river, I caught a glimpse of roofs and chimneys, and the quick glitter of glass that marked the hothouses in the old walled garden that had belonged to the Hall. There, too, lay the stables, and the house called West Lodge, and a footbridge spanning the river to serve a track which climbed through the far trees and across the moors to Nether Shields farm, and, eventually, to Bellingham.

The Whitescar property, lying along the river bank at the very centre of its loop, and stretching back to the junction of the roads at the Hall gates, was like a healthy bite taken out of the circle of Forrest territory. Lying neatly between the Hall and West Lodge, it was screened now from my sight by a rise in the land that only allowed me to see its chimneys, and the tops of its trees.

I left my viewpoint, and went on down the track, not hurrying. Behind the wall to my right now loomed the Forrest woods, the huge trees full out, except for the late, lacy boughs of ash. The ditch at the wall's foot was frilled with cow-parsley. The wall was in poor repair; I saw a blackbird's nest stuffed into a hole in the coping, and there were tangles of campion and toadflax bunching from gaps between the stones.

At the Hall entrance, the lane ended in a kind of cul-de-sac, bounded by three gateways. On the left, a brand-new oak gate guarded the Forestry Commission's fir plantations and the road to West Lodge. To the right lay the pillars of the Hall entrance. Ahead was a solid, five-barred gate, painted white, with the familiar WHITESCAR blazoning the top bar. Beyond this, the track lifted itself up a gentle rise of pasture, and vanished over a ridge. From here, not even the chimney tops of Whitescar were visible; only the smooth sunny prospect of green pasture and dry-stone walling sharp with blue shadows, and, in a hollow beyond the rise somewhere, the tops of some tall trees.

But the gateway to the right might have been the entrance to another sort of world.

Where the big gates of the Hall should have hung between their massive pillars, there was simply a gap giving onto a driveway, green and mossy, its twin tracks no longer worn by wheels, but matted over by the discs of plantain and hawkweed, rings of weed spreading and overlapping like the rings that grow and ripple over each other when a handful of gravel is thrown into water. At the edges of the drive the taller weeds began, hedge-parsley and campion, and forget-me-not gone wild, all frothing under the ranks of the rhododendrons, whose flowers showed like pale, symmetrical lamps above their splayed leaves. Overhead hung the shadowy, enormous trees.

There had been a gate-house once, tucked deep in the trees beside the entrance. A damp, dismal place it must have been to live in; the walls were almost roofless now, and half drifted over with nettles. The chimney stacks stuck up like bones from a broken limb. All that had survived of the little garden was a rank plantation of rhubarb, and the old blush rambler that ran riot through the gaping windows.

There was no legend here of FORREST to guide the visitor. For those wise in the right lores there were some heraldic beasts on top of the pillars, rampant, and holding shields where some carving made cushions under the moss. From the pillars, to either side, stretched the high wall that had once marked the boundaries. This was cracked and crumbling in many places, and the copings were off, but it was still a barrier, save in one place not far from the entrance. Here a giant oak stood. It had been originally on the inside of the wall, but with the years it had grown and spread, pressing closer and ever closer to the masonry, until its vast flank had bent and finally broken the wall, which here lay in a mere pile of tumbled and weedy stone. But the power of the oak would be its undoing, for the wall had been clothed in ivy, and the ivy had reached for the tree, crept up it, engulfed it, till now the trunk was one towering mass of the dark gleaming leaves, and only the tree's upper branches managed to thrust the young gold leaves of early summer through the strangling curtain. Eventually the ivy would kill it. Already, through the tracery of the ivy stems, some of the oak boughs showed dead, and one great lower limb, long since broken off, had left a gap where rotten wood yawned, in holes deep enough for owls to nest in.

I looked up at it for a long time, and then along the neat sunny track that led out of the shadow of the trees towards Whitescar.

Somewhere a ringdove purred and intoned, and a wood warbler stuttered into its long trill, and fell silent. I found that I had moved, without realizing it, through the gateway, and a yard or two up the drive into the wood. I stood there in the shade, looking out at the wide fields and the cupped valley, and the white-painted gate gleaming in the sun. I realized that I was braced as if for the start of a race, my mouth dry, and the muscles of my throat taut and aching.

I swallowed a couple of times, breathed deeply and slowly to calm myself, repeating the now often-used formula of *what was there to go wrong, after all?* I was Annabel. I was coming home. I had never been anyone else. All that must be forgotten. Mary Grey need never appear again, except, perhaps, to Con and Lisa. Meanwhile, I would forget her, even in my thoughts. I was Annabel Winslow, coming home.

I walked quickly out between the crumbling pillars, and pushed open the white gate.

It didn't even creak. It swung quietly open on sleek, well-oiled hinges, and came to behind me with a smooth click that said *money*.

Well, that was what had brought me, wasn't it?

I walked quickly out of the shade of the Forrest trees, and up the sunny track towards Whitescar.

In the bright afternoon stillness the farm looked clean in its orderly whitewash, like a toy. From the top of the rise I could see it all laid out, in plan exactly like the maps that Lisa Dermott had drawn for me so carefully, and led me through in imagination so many times.

The house was long and low, two-storied, with big modern windows cut into the old thick walls. Unlike the rest of the group of buildings, it was not whitewashed, but built of sandstone, green-gold with age. The lichen on the roof showed, even at that distance, like patens of copper laid along the soft blue slates.

It faced onto a strip of garden—grass and flower borders and a lilac tree—whose lower wall edged the river. From the garden, a white wicket gate gave on a wooden footbridge. The river was fairly wide here, lying under the low, tree-hung cliffs of its further bank with that still gleam that means depth. It reflected the bridge, the trees, and the banked tangles of elder and honeysuckle, in layers of deepening colour as rich as a Flemish painter's palette.

On the nearer side of house and garden lay the farm; a courtyard—even at this distance I could see its clean baked concrete, and the freshness of the paint on doors and gates—surrounded by byres and stables and sheds, with the red roof of the big Dutch barn conspicuous beside the remains of last year's straw stacks, and a dark knot of Scotch pines.

I had been so absorbed in the picture laid out before me, that I hadn't noticed the man approaching, some thirty yards away, until the clang of his nailed boots on the iron of the cattle grid startled me.

He was a burly, middle-aged man in rough farm clothes, and he was staring at me in undisguised interest as he approached. He came at a pace that, without seeming to, carried him over the distance between us at a speed that left me no time to think at all.

I did have time to wonder briefly if my venture alone into the Winslow den was going to prove my undoing, but at least there was no possibility now of turning tail. It was with a sense of having the issue taken out of my hands that I saw the red face split into a beaming smile, and heard him say, in a broad country voice, "Why, Miss Annabel!"

There was the ruddy face, the blue eyes, the huge forearm bared to the elbow, and marked with the scar where the bull had caught him. Bates, head cattleman at Whitescar. *You'll know him straight away,* Con had said. But I didn't venture the name. The lessons of the past three weeks hummed in my head like a hive of bees: *Take it slowly. Don't rush your fences. Never be too sure. . . .*

And here was the first fence. *Tell the truth wherever possible.* I told it.

I said, with genuine pleasure, "You knew me! How wonderful! It makes me feel as if I were really coming home!"

I put out both hands and he took them as if the gesture, from me, was a natural one. His grip nearly lifted me from the ground. The merle collie running at his heels circled round us, lifting a lip and sniffing the back of my legs in a disconcerting manner.

"Knew you?" His voice was gruff with pleasure. "That I did, the minute you came over the top there. Even if Miss Dermott hadn't tell't us you were coming, I'd a known you a mile off across the field, lass! We're all uncommon glad to have you back, and that's a fact."

"It's marvellous to be here. How are you? You look fine, I don't think you can be a day older! Not eight years, anyway!"

"I'm grand, and Mrs. Bates, too. You'd know I married Betsy, now? They'd tell you, maybe? Aye. . . . Well, she's in a rare taking with your coming home, spent all morning baking, and turning the place upside down, and Miss Dermott along with her. You'll likely find there's tea cakes and singin' hinnies for your tea."

"Singin' hinnies?"

"Nay, don't tell me you've forgotten! That I'll not believe. You used to tease for them every day when you was a bairn."

"No, I hadn't forgotten. It was just—hearing the name again. So—so like home." I swallowed. "How sweet of her to remember. I'm longing to see her again. How's Grandfather, Mr. Bates?"

"Why, he's champion, for his age. He's always well enough, mind you, in the dry weather; it's the damp that gets at his back. It's arthritis—you knew that?—and there's times when he can hardly get about at all. And now they say there's this other trouble forby. But you'll have heard about that, too, likely? Miss Dermott said you'd telephoned yesterday and asked them to break it gentle-like to your Granda. They'd tell you all the news?"

"Yes. I—I didn't quite know what to do. I thought of writing, but then I thought, if I telephoned Con, it might be easier. Miss Dermott answered; the others were out, and, well—we had a long talk. She told me how things were, and she said she'd get Con to break it to Grandfather. I hadn't known about Grandfather's stroke, so it's just as well I didn't just write to him out of the blue. And anyway, I wouldn't have dared just walk right in here and give everyone a shock."

His voice was rough. "There's not many dies of that sort of shock, Miss Annabel."

"That's . . . sweet of you. Well, Miss Dermott told me quite a lot of the news . . . I'm glad Grandfather keeps so well, on the whole."

"Aye, he's well enough." A quick glance under puckered eyelids. "Reckon you'll see a change, though."

"I'm afraid I probably shall. It's been a long time."

"It has that. It was a poor day's work you did, Miss Annabel, when you left us."

"I know," I said. "Don't blame me too much."

"I've no call to blame you, lass. I know naught about it, but that you and your Granda fell out." He grinned, sourly. "I know what he's like, none better, I've known him these thirty years. I never take no notice of him, rain or shine, and him and me gets on, but you're too like your dad to sit still and hold your tongue. Winslows is all the same, I reckon. Maybe if you'd been a mite older, you'd 'a known his bark was always worse than his bite, but you were nobbut a bit lass at the time, and I reckon you'd troubles of your own, at that."

A short, breathless pause. "Troubles—of my own?"

He looked a little embarrassed, and stabbed at the ground with his stick. "Maybe I didn't ought to 'a said that. I only meant as everyone knew it wasn't all plain sailing with you and Mr. Con. Happen one takes these things too hard at nineteen."

I smiled. "Happen one does. Well, it's all over now. Let's forget it, shall we? And you mustn't blame Con or Grandfather either, you know. I was young and silly, and I suppose I thought I'd like to get away on my own for a bit. I didn't want to be tied down to Whitescar or—or anything, not just then, not yet; so when the time came, I just went without thinking. One doesn't think very straight, at nineteen. But now I'm back, and I'm going to try and forget I've ever been away."

I looked away from him, down towards the farm. I could see white hens ruffling in the straw of the stackyard, and there were pigeons on the roof. The smoke from the chimneys went straight up into the clear air. I said, "It looks just the same. Better, if anything. Or is that absence, making the heart grow fonder?"

"Nay, I'll not deny it's well looked after. As well every way, nearly, as in your Granda's time."

I stared at him. "As in—you talk as if that was past."

He was prodding at the earth again with his stick. "Happen it is."

"What d'you mean?"

That quick, almost surly glance upwards again. "You'll see, Miss Annabel. I don't doubt but what you'll see. Times change."

I didn't pursue it, and he turned the subject abruptly. He nodded past me, the way I had come, towards the towering woods that surrounded the site of Forrest Hall. "Now, there's the biggest change you'll find, and none of it for the better. Did she tell you about Forrests?"

"Yes." I looked back to where the crest of the ivied oak reared above the skyline, the glinting darkness of the ivy making it stand up like a ruined tower against the young summer green of the woods. "Yes, Miss Dermott told me. Four years ago, wasn't it? I thought the old gate-house looked even more dilapidated than it should. I never remember anyone living there, but at least the drive looked reasonable, and the gates were on."

"They went for scrap, after the fire. Aye, we miss the Hall, though it's not all gone, you mind. They're using some of the stable buildings over at West Lodge for poultry, and the old garden's going strong. Mr. Forrest got that going himself, with Johnny Rudd—you'll mind Johnny? He's working there still, though there's nobbut one horse in the stables. Mr. Forrest kept that one when the stud went; he's one of the old 'Mountain' lot, and I reckon Mr. Forrest couldn't bear to part, but I doubt he'll have to be sold now. He's just running wild there, and eating his head off, and there's no one can hardly get near him." He grinned at me. "You'll have to work on him yourself, now you're back."

"Me? Not on your–I mean, not any more. Those days are past, Mr. Bates."

"How's that?"

The story that Lisa and I had concocted came glibly enough. "I had a bad fall in the States, and hurt my back–nothing drastic, you know, but not a thing I'd dare risk doing again."

"That's a shame, now! I reckoned Johnny'd be rare pleased when he heard you were back. He hasn't the time to bother on wi' horses now, not at this time of year; and the colt's spoiling. Mr. Con's been along to take a hand to him, now and then, but the youngster's taken a rare scunner at him, seemingly. Won't let him near. There's naught else fit for a ride at Whitescar."

"I expect I've lost my touch, anyway."

"Eh, well," he said, "it's like we said. Things change, more's the pity. Every time I walk up this road I think on the way it was. It's sad to see the old places falling down, and the families gone, but there it is."

"Yes." Beyond the ivy-clad oak, behind a sunny tracery of treetops, I could see a chimney. The sun glinted warm on the mellow stone. There was the glimpse of a tiled roof through the boughs. A wisp of cloud, moving slowly, gave the illusion of smoke, rising from a homely fire. Then it moved on, and I saw that the roof was broken.

Bates said, beside me, so suddenly that I jumped, "You've changed. I was wrong, maybe, I didn't think you had, not that much, but now I can see."

"What can you see?"

"I dunno. It's not only that you're older. You're different, Miss Annabel, no offence." The kindly blue eyes surveyed me. "Happen you'll have had a hard time of it, out there?"

He made it sound as if the Atlantic were the water of Styx, and the lands beyond it the Outer Darkness. I smiled. "Happen I have."

"You didn't marry?"

"No. Too busy earning my keep."

"Aye. That's where it is. You'd 'a done better to stay here at home, lass, where your place was."

I thought of Con, of the lonely crumbling ruin in the Forrest woods. "You think so?" I laughed a little without amusement. "Well, I'm back, anyway. I've come back to my place now, and I expect I'll have the sense to stick to it."

"You do that." The words had an emphasis that was far from idle. He was staring at me fixedly, his eyes almost fierce in the rubicund face. "Well, I'll not keep you here talking. They'll be looking for you down yonder. But you stay here, Miss Annabel, close by your Granda—and don't leave us again."

He nodded abruptly, whistled up the collie, and strode past me up the track without looking back.

I turned down towards Whitescar.

The end of the barn threw a slanting shadow half across the yard gate. Not until I was within twenty paces of it did I see that a man leaned there, unmoving, watching my approach. Con.

If Bates had been the first fence, this was the water jump. A little embarrassment was permitted, surely, to a girl meeting, after eight years, the man from whom she'd run away.

He straightened up with the lazy grace that was so typical of him, and gave me a brilliant smile that held no trace of embarrassment whatsoever. His hand went out to the latch of the gate.

"Why, Annabel," he said, and swung the gate open with a sort of ceremony of invitation. "Welcome home!"

I said feebly, "Hullo." I was trying to see, without looking too obviously round me, if there was anyone else within earshot. The yard was apparently deserted, but I didn't dare risk it. I said, feeling perilously foolish, "It—it's nice to be back."

"You're earlier than we expected. I intended to meet you with the car. Where's your luggage?"

"I left it in the quarry. Could someone fetch it later?"

"I'll go myself. You know, you really should have let me come into Newcastle for you."

"No. I—I wanted to come alone. Thanks all the same." I found to my fury that I was stammering like a schoolgirl. I did manage to reflect that if anyone happened to be watching us, they would see merely that there was something stilted and constrained about our greeting.

I still hadn't met his eyes. He had shut the gate behind me, but I stayed standing by it, talking, still feebly and rather madly, about luggage. "Of course, you know, my main baggage is in Liverpool. I can get it sent—"

"Of course." I heard the laugh in his voice, then, and looked up. Outrageously, he was looking amused. Before I could speak again he had put out both hands and taken mine in them, smiling delightfully down at me. His voice was warm and, one might have sworn, genuinely moved. "This is wonderful . . . to see you here again after all this time. We never thought . . ." He appeared to struggle for a moment with his emotions, and added, deeply, "This is a pretty shattering moment, my dear." "*You're telling me, blast you.*" I didn't dare say it aloud, but he read it in my eyes quite easily. His own were dancing. He gave me that deliberately dazzling smile of his, then pulled me towards him, and kissed me. He must have felt my startled and instinctive resistance, because he slackened his hold straight away, saying quickly under his breath, "There are windows looking this way, Mary, my dear. I think, under the circumstances, that I'd have kissed her, don't you? Strictly cousinly and affectionate, of course?"

He was still holding my hands. I said equally softly, and through shut teeth, "And don't you think, dear cousin Connor, that she might even have hauled off and slapped your face, hard? Strictly cousinly and affectionate, of course."

I felt him shake with laughter, and pulled my hands away. "*Is* there someone watching then? Can they hear us?"

"Not that I'm aware of."

"Well, *really*—!"

"Ssh, not so loudly. You never know." He had his back to the house, and was looking down at me. "Are you really as mad as blazes at me?"

"Of course I am!"

"The occasion kind of went to my head. Forgive me."

"It's all right."

Suddenly, it seemed, we were over the water jump and moving easily into the straight. I relaxed, leaning back against the gate. We smiled at one another with a certain amount of understanding. To an observer the scene would still be perfectly in character. Even from the house, I thought, the scarlet in my cheeks could be seen quite easily; and Con stood in front of me in an attitude that might have suggested hesitation, and even humility, if one hadn't been able to see his eyes.

I said, "You should have known that I'd no intention of playing this as though I'd come back ready to fall at your feet and make it up, Con Winslow."

He grinned. "No. That would be asking a bit too much, I can see that."

"You might have thought of it before you kissed me." I leaned back against the gate and added, coolly, "Do you really want to find yourself waiting for me at the altar steps some fine morning?"

There was a startled silence. It was something, I thought, not without satisfaction, to have shaken that amused assurance. I tilted my head and smiled up at him. "Yes, it's a wonder you and Lisa didn't think of that one. It's just possible that Grandfather might think it's never too late to mend. And I might accept you this time."

Silence again, two long beats of it.

"Why, you little *devil!*" It was the first genuine feeling he had shown during the interview. "Who'd have thought—?" He broke off, and the long mouth curved. "And what if I call your bluff, girl dear? It might be the perfect ending to our little game, after all, and it's just a marvel that I never thought of it before. Sweet saints alive, I can think of a lot worse fates than ending up on the altar steps with you!" He laughed at my expression. "You see? Don't pull too many bluffs with me, acushla, or you might find them called."

"And don't get too clever with me, Con, or you'll cut yourself. I could always quarrel with you again, couldn't I? And this time, who knows, Grandfather might even throw *you* out instead of me."

"All right," said Con easily, "we've called each other's bluff, and that's that." His eyes were brilliant under the long lashes: it was obvious that, however the game went, Con was going to enjoy it to the full. The eight-years'-old tragedy was now nothing more than a counter in that same game. If it had ever touched him, it did so no longer. "We'll play it your way," he said. "I'll watch my step, really I will. I didn't mean to upset you."

"It's the only way to play it."

He still had his back to the house windows, which was just as well. His face, expressive as ever, was alight with uncomplicated excitement. "Whatever the terms—and you can set them—this is going to be the hell of a partnership, Mary Grey! You're a wonderful girl! You know, you and I have got a lot in common."

I said, just a little drily, "Why, thank you. Praise indeed."

He ignored that, or perhaps he didn't see it. "A hell of a partnership! I told you, you'll call the tune. You'll have to, if it comes to that: you'll know better than I would what a girl's reactions would be, after—well, coming back like this. I'll play it any way you say. But we'll have to play it together: it's a duet, not a duel. A duet for you and me, with Lisa turning the pages."

I wondered, fleetingly, what Lisa would have thought of the rôle so lightly assigned to her. "Very well. And to start with, kisses, cousinly or not, are out. Did you ever read *Count Hannibal?*"

"Certainly I did. And I know what you're thinking of, the bit where the hero says: 'Is it to be a kiss or a blow between us, madame?' "

"That's it. And she says: 'A thousand times a blow!' Well, that's the way it is, monsieur."

"Yes, all right. But then, if you remember what happened next—"

"He slapped her face. Yes, so he did. But that's going a bit too far, don't you think? If we just keep it calm and cousinly—"

"You're enjoying this, aren't you?"

"What?" The abruptness of the question had startled me out of laughter. I must have gaped at him quite blankly. "Enjoying it?"

"Yes. Don't pretend you're not. You're as excited as I am."

"I—I don't know. I'm certainly a bit tensed up, who wouldn't be? Hang it, I'm only human." His hand moved up to cover my wrist where it lay along the top bar of the gate. "All right, my pulse is racing. Wouldn't yours be?" I pulled the hand away from under his. "Now, we've talked long enough. When will Grandfather be around?"

"He won't be expecting you quite yet. Don't worry. Lisa says he'll wait upstairs and see you in his room after he's had his rest. Shall I show you round now, before you see him?"

"Good heavens, no. I wouldn't want to look round first, you know. People first, places later. You'd better take me in and introduce me to Lisa, and I'll see Mrs. Bates."

"You keep your head, don't you?"

"Why not? I've taken the first hurdle, anyway."

"Was I a hurdle?"

I laughed. "You? You were the water jump. No, I meant that I'd met Bates when I was on my way down from the road."

"Oh, God, yes, I'd forgotten. I saw him go up, but of course I'd no idea you were coming so early. I take it you got away with it? Good for you, you see how easy it's going to be. . . . Did you greet him by name?"

"Not till he mentioned his wife. Better safe than sorry, though I felt pretty sure, and of course the scarred arm made it a certainty."

"Where did you meet him?"

"Crossing High Riggs."

I saw his eyes widen, and laughed a little. "My dear Con, you'll have to learn not to look startled. Give Lisa some credit. Why shouldn't I recognize High Riggs? It's been called that, time out of mind."

He drew a long breath. "Fair enough. I'm learning. But it's—even more disconcerting, now that I see you actually here . . . in this setting."

"We'd better go in."

"Yes. Lisa'll be in the kitchen, and Mrs. Bates with her."

"I can smell baking, even from here. Do you suppose she'll have made singin' hinnies for my tea?"

I had spoken quite naturally, as I turned to go, but the naked shock in his face stopped me short. He was staring at me as if he'd never seen me before.

His lips opened, and his tongue came out to wet them. "You can't—I never—how did you—?"

He stopped. Behind the taut mask of shock I thought I glimpsed again what I had seen in his face at our first meeting.

I lifted my brows at him. "My dear Con, if you're beginning to have doubts about me yourself, after all this time, I *must* be good!"

The strain slackened perceptibly, as if invisible guys had been loosened. "It's only, it sounded so natural, the sort of little thing she might have said . . . And you standing there, by the yard gate. It's as if it were yesterday." He took a breath; it seemed to be the first for minutes. Then he shook his head sharply, like a dog coming out of water. "I'm sorry, stupid of me. As you say, I'll have to learn. But how in the world did you know a silly little thing like that? I hadn't remembered it myself, and Lisa wouldn't know, and it's ten to one Mrs. Bates never mentioned it to her till today, if she has even now."

"Yes, she has. Bates told me she'd be making them for my tea. He nearly caught me right out. What the dickens are they, anyway?"

"Oh, a special kind of girdle-cake." He laughed, and the sound was at once elated, and half-relieved. "So you just learned it ten minutes ago, and you come out with it as to the manner born! You're wonderful! A hell of a partnership, did I call it? My God, Mary Grey—and it's the last time I'll ever call you that—you're the girl for my money! You're a winner, and didn't I know it the minute I clapped eyes on you, up there on the Wall? If it wouldn't look kind of excessive, besides going back on our pact and making you as mad as fire, I'm damned if I wouldn't kiss you again! No, no, it's all right, don't look at me like that; I said I'd behave, and I will."

"I'm glad to hear it. And now we've been out here quite long enough. Shall we go in?"

"Sure . . . Annabel. Come along. Headed straight for the next fence; Becher's Brook this time, wouldn't you say?" His hand slid under my arm. Physical contact seemed to come as naturally to Con Winslow as breathing. "No, not that way. You ought to know they never use the front door on a farm."

"I'm sorry." I gave a quick glance round the deserted yard, and up at the empty windows. "No harm done."

"Not scared at all?"

"No. Edgy, but not scared."

The hand squeezed my arm. "That's my girl."

I withdrew it. "No. Remember?"

He was looking down at me speculatively, charmingly, still with that glint of teasing amusement, but I got the feeling that it was no longer something pleasant that amused him. He said, "Girl dear, if you only knew. . . ."

"Look," I said, "if I only knew, as you put it, I imagine I wouldn't be here at all. And we agreed to drop it all, didn't we? It's going to be quite embarrassing enough having to face you in front of Grandfather, without your amusing yourself by teasing me when we're alone."

"I only said—"

"I know what you said. And I'm saying that we'll drop the subject as from now. If I were Annabel, would you want to be reminding me of past . . . differences? Or, for that matter would you want *me* to be reminding Grandfather?"

There was a tiny pause.

"Well, well," said Con, and laughed. "All right, Annabel, my dear. A thousand times a blow. Come along into the lion's den."

CHAPTER FOUR

She can make an Irish stew,
Aye, and singin' hinnies, too . . .
North Country Song: *Billy Boy.*

WHEN CON SHOWED ME along the flagged passage, and into the kitchen, Lisa was just lifting a fresh batch of baking out of the oven. The air was full of the delectable smell of new bread.

The kitchen was a big, pleasant room, with a high ceiling, a new cream-coloured Aga stove, and long windows made gay with potted geraniums and chintz curtains that stirred in the June breeze. The floor was of red tiles, covered with those bright rugs of hooked rag that make Northern kitchens so attractive. In front of the Aga was an old-fashioned fender of polished steel, and inside it, from a basket covered with flannel, came the soft cheepings of newly hatched chickens. The black and white cat asleep in the rocking chair took no notice of the sounds, or of the tempting heavings and buttings of small heads and bodies against the covering flannel.

I stopped short, just inside the door.

At that moment, more, I think, than at any other in the whole affair, I bitterly regretted the imposture I was undertaking. For two pins I'd have bolted then and there. What had seemed exciting and even reasonable in Newcastle, simple in High Riggs, and intriguing just now in the yard outside, seemed, in this cheerful, lovely room smelling of home, to be no less than an outrage. This wasn't, any more, just a house I had come to claim for Con, or a counter in a game I was playing; it was home, a place breathing with a life of its own, fostered by generations of people who had belonged here. In the shabby Newcastle boarding house, with my lonely and prospectless Canadian life behind me, and a dreary part-time job doing nothing but stave off the future, things had looked very different: but here, in Whitescar itself, the world of second-class intrigue seemed preposterously out of place. Things should be simple in a place like this, simple and good; sunshine through flowered curtains, the smell of new bread, and chickens cheeping on the hearth; not a complicated imposture, a fantastic Oppenheim plot hatched out in a shabby bedroom with this Irish adventurer and this stolid woman with the soft, grasping hands, who, having put down the baking tray, was moving now to greet me.

They must have noticed my hesitation, but there was no one else to see it. Through a half-shut door that led to the scullery came the sounds of water running, and the chink of crockery. Mrs. Bates, I supposed. Perhaps, with instinctive tact, she had retired to let me meet the current mistress of Whitescar.

It seemed it was just as well she had, for to my surprise the stolid, ever-reliable Lisa seemed, now it had come to the point, to be the least composed of the three of us. Her normally sallow cheeks were flushed, though this may only have been from the heat of the oven. She came forward, and then hesitated, as if at a loss for words.

Con was saying, easily, at my elbow, "Here she is, Lisa. She came early, and I met her at the gate. I've been trying to tell her how welcome she is, but perhaps you'll do it better than me. She's finding it all a bit of a trial so far, I'm afraid." This with his charming smile down at me, and a little brotherly pat on the arm. "Annabel, this is my half-sister, Lisa Dermott. She's been looking after us all, you knew that."

"We've already had a long talk over the telephone," I said. "How do you do, Miss Dermott? I'm very glad to meet you. It—it's lovely to be back. I suppose I needn't tell you that."

She took my hand. She was smiling, but her eyes were anxious, and the soft hand was trembling.

She spoke quite naturally, however. "You're welcome indeed, Miss Winslow. I dare say it seems odd to you to have me greet you like this in your own home, but after all this time it's come to feel like home to me as well. So perhaps you'll let me tell you how glad everybody is to see you back. We'd—you must know, I told you yesterday—we'd all thought you must be dead. You can imagine that this is a great occasion."

"Why, Miss Dermott, how nice of you."

"I hope," she said, rather more easily, "that you'll call me Lisa."

"Of course. Thank you. And you must please drop the 'Miss Winslow,' too. We're cousins, surely, or is it half-cousins, I wouldn't know?" I smiled at her. The chink of crockery from the scullery had stopped as soon as I spoke. Through the half-shut door there came a sort of listening silence. I wondered if our conversation were sounding too impossibly stilted. If this had genuinely been my first introduction to Lisa, no doubt the situation would have been every bit as awkward. There would have been, literally nothing to say.

I went on saying just that, in a voice that sounded, to myself, too high, too quick, too light altogether. "After all, I'm the stranger here, or so it feels, after all this time, and I'm sure you've given me a better welcome than I deserve! Of course it's your home—" I looked about me—"more than mine, now, surely! I never remember it looking half as pretty! How lovely you've got it . . . new curtains . . . new paint . . . the same old chickens, I'll swear, they were always part of the furniture . . . oh, there's the old tea caddy, I'm so glad you didn't throw it out!"

Lisa had certainly never thought fit to mention the battered old tin on the mantelpiece, but, since it was decorated with a picture of George V's Coronation, they would recognize it as a safe bet. "And the Aga! That's terrific! When was that put in?"

"Five years ago." Lisa spoke shortly, almost repressively. Con was watching me with what seemed to be amused respect, but Lisa, I could see, thought I was jumping a bit too fast into that attentive silence from the scullery.

I grinned at her, with a spice of mischief, and moved over to the hearth. "Oh lord, the old rocking chair . . . and it still creaks. . . ." I creaked it again, and the sleeping cat opened slitted green eyes, looked balefully at me, and shut them again. I laughed, almost naturally, and stooped to stroke him. "My welcome home. He looks a tough egg, this chap. What happened to Tibby?"

"He died of old age," said Con. "I buried him under your lilac tree."

"He'd have died of middle-age long before that, if I'd had my way." Lisa was back at the table, scooping hot rolls off the tin on to the baking sieve.

She seemed relieved to be back in action. She didn't look at Con or me. "The place for cats is in the buildings, and they know it."

"You didn't try and keep *Tibby* outside?"

"Tibby," said Con cheerfully, "was so hedged about with the sanctity of having been your cat, that he was practically allowed to live in your bedroom. Don't worry about Tibby. He got even Lisa down in the end, and lived his life out in the greatest possible honour and luxury."

I smiled and stroked the cat's ears. "Not like Flush?"

"Flush?" This was Lisa. I caught the sudden quick overtone of apprehension, as if she had caught me speaking without the book.

Con grinned at her. "Elizabeth Barrett's dog. When Elizabeth bolted, early one morning, just like Annabel, her father is said to have wanted to destroy her little dog, as a sort of revenge."

"O—oh . . . I see."

He looked at me. "No, Annabel, not like Flush. Revenge wasn't . . . our first reaction."

I let it pass. "And this one?" I said. "What's his claim to the best chair in the kitchen?"

"Tommy? That fat, lazy brute?" Lisa was patently feeling the strain. A conversation about cats at this juncture was, obviously, the last straw in irrelevance. Lisa's Teutonic thoroughness wanted to get on with the task in hand, lay the next brick or so, and slap a few more solid lies in to mortar the brand-new structure together. She said, almost snappily, "Heaven knows I throw him out often enough, but he will come in, and I haven't had the time today to shift him."

Con said lazily, "His personality's stronger than yours, Lisa my dear." He, apparently, shared my belief that the bricks of deception could be perfectly well made with the smallest straws of irrelevance. He took a roll off the rack and bit into it. "Mmm. Not bad. They're eatable today, Lisa. I suppose that means Mrs. Bates made them?"

His sister's forbidding expression broke up into that sudden affectionate smile that was kept only for him.

"Oh, have some butter with it, Con, do. Or wait until tea time. Won't you ever grow up?"

"Isn't Mrs. Bates here?" I asked.

Lisa shot me a look, three parts relief to one of apprehension. "Yes. She's through in the scullery. Would you like—?"

But before she could finish the sentence the door was pushed open and, as if on a cue, a woman appeared in the doorway, a round squat figure of the same general shape as the Mrs. Noah from a toy ark, who stood on the threshold with arms in the traditional 'akimbo' position, surveying me with ferocious little boot-button eyes.

Lisa led in hastily, "Oh, Mrs. Bates, here's Miss Annabel."

"I can see that. I ain't blind, nor yet I ain't deaf." Mrs. Bates' thin lips shut like a trap. The fierce little eyes regarded me. "And where do *you* think you've been all this time, may I ask? And what have you been a-doing of to yourself? You look terrible. You're as thin as a rail, and if you're not careful you'll have lost all your looks, what's left of 'em, by the time you're thirty. America, indeed! Ain't your own home good enough for you?"

She was nodding while she spoke, little sharp jerking movements like one of those mandarin toys one used to see; and each nod was a condemnation. I saw Con flick an apprehensive look at me, and then at his sister. But he needn't have worried; Lisa's briefing had been thorough. *She adored Annabel, cursed her up hill and down dale, wouldn't hear anyone say a word against her; had a frightful set-to with Mr. Winslow after she ran away, and called him every tyrant under the sun. . . . She's frightfully rude—plain-spoken she calls it—and she resents me, but I had to keep her; Bates is the best cattleman in the county, and she's a marvellous worker. . . .*

"A fine thing it's been for us, let me tell you," said Mrs. Bates sharply, "thinking all this time as you was lost and gone beyond recall, but now as you *is* back, there's a few things I'd like to be telling you, and that's a fact. There's none can say I'm one to flatter and mince me words, plain-spoken I may be, but I speak as I find, and for anyone to do what you gone and did, and run off without a word in the middle of the night—"

I laughed at her. "It wasn't the middle of the night, and you know it." I went up to her, took her by the shoulders and gave her a quick hug, then bent and kissed the hard round cheek. I said gently, "Make me welcome, Betsy. Don't make it harder to come home. Goodness knows I feel bad enough about it, I don't need you to tell me. I'm sorry if it distressed you all, but I—well, I was terribly unhappy, and when one's very young and very unhappy, one doesn't always stop to think, does one?"

I kissed the other cheek quickly, and straightened up. The little black eyes glared up at me, but her mouth was working. I smiled, and said lightly, "And you must admit I did the thing properly, dreadful quarrel, note left on the pincushion and everything."

"Pincushion? What did you ever want with a pincushion? Never did a decent day's work in your life, always traipsing around after horses and dogs and tractors, or that there garden of yours, let alone the house and the jobs a girl ought to take an interest in. Pincushion!" She snorted. "Where would you be finding one of them?"

"Well," I said mildly, "where did I leave it?"

"On that mantelpiece as ever was, *which* well you remember!" She nodded across the kitchen. "And when I come down that morning I was the one found it there, and I stood there fair pussy-struck for five mortal minutes, I did, afore I dared pick it up. I knew what it was, you see. I'd heard you and your Granda having words the night before, *and* I heard you go to your room just after, which well you know I did. I didn't never think to have the chance to tell you this, but I folleyed you along, Miss Annabel, an' I listened outside your door."

I was very conscious of Con just at my shoulder. I said quickly, "Betsy, dear—"

I saw Con make a slight, involuntary movement, and thought: he doesn't want me to stop her; he thinks I'll learn something from all this.

He needn't have worried, she had no intention of being stopped until I had heard it all.

"But there wasn't a sound, not of crying. Just as if you was moving about the room quiet-like, getting ready for your bed. So I thought to meself, it's only a fight, I thought, the old man'll be sorry in the morning, and Miss Annabel'll tell him she won't do it again, whatever she done, riding that Everest horse of Mr. Forrest's maybe, or maybe even staying out too late, the way she has been lately, and the old man not liking it, him being old-fashioned that way. But I thinks to meself, it'll be all right in the morning, the way it always has been, so I just coughs to let you know I'm there, and I taps on the door and says: 'I'm away to bed now, Miss Annabel,' and you stopped moving about, as if I'd frightened you, and then you come over to the door and stopped inside it for a minute, but when you opened it you still had all your things on, and you said 'Good night, Betsy dear, and thank you,' and you kissed me, you remember, and you looked so terrible, white and ill, and I says, 'Don't take on so, Miss Annabel,' I says, 'there's nought that doesn't come right in the end, not if it was ever so,' and you smiled at that and said 'No.' And then I went off to bed, and I never heard no sound, and if anyone had tell't me that next morning early you'd up and go, and stay away all these years, and your Granda fretting his heart out after you, for all he's had Mr. Con here, and Julie as is coming this week, *which* she's the spitting image of you, I might say—"

"I know. Lisa told me. I'm longing to meet her." I touched her hand again. "Don't upset yourself any more. Let's leave it, shall we? I—I've come back, and I'm not going again, and don't be too angry with me for doing what I did."

Lisa rescued me, still, I gathered, trying to bring the straying runner back on course. "Your grandfather'll be awake by now. You'd better go up, he'll want to see you straight away." She was reaching for her apron strings. "I'll take you up. Just give me time to wash my hands."

I saw Mrs. Bates bridle, and said, smoothly enough, "Don't trouble, Lisa. I—I'd sooner go up by myself. I'm sure you'll understand."

Lisa had stopped halfway to the sink, looking irresolute, and rather too surprised.

Mrs. Bates was nodding again, with a kind of triumph in the tight compression of her mouth. Con took another new roll, and saluted me with a tiny lift of the eyebrow as he turned to go. "Of course you would," he said. "Don't treat Annabel as a stranger, Lisa my dear. And don't worry, Annabel. He'll be so pleased to see you that he's not likely to rake up anything painful out of the past."

Another lift of the eyebrow on this masterly *double-entendre* of reassurance, and he was gone.

Lisa relaxed, and seemed to recollect something of her lost poise. "I'm sorry." Her voice was once more even and colourless. "Of course you'll want to go alone. I was forgetting. It isn't every day one gets a—an occasion like this. Go on up now, my dear. Tea'll be ready in half an hour. . . . Mrs. Bates, I wonder if you would help me with the tea cakes? You're a much better hand at them than I am."

"Which is not to be wondered at, seeing as how I'm north country bred and born, *which* no foreigner ever had a good hand with a tea cake yet," said that lady tartly, but moving smartly towards the table.

Lisa had stooped again to the oven. Her back was towards us. I had to say it, and this was as good a moment as any. "Betsy, bless you, singin' hinnies! They look as good as ever!"

Lisa dropped the oven shelf with a clatter against its runners. I heard her say, "Sorry. Clumsy," in a muffled voice. "It's all right, I didn't spill anything."

"You don't think," said Mrs. Bates crisply, "that them singin' hinnies is for you? Get along with you now, to your Granda."

But the nod which went along with the briskly snapping voice said, quite plainly, "Don't be frightened. Go on. It'll be all right."

I left the kitchen door open behind me.

It was obvious that no questions of identity were going to rouse themselves in the minds of Mrs. Bates and her husband; but the real ordeal was still ahead of me, and if there were ever going to be questions asked, my every movement on this first day was going to be important.

So I left the door open, and was conscious of Lisa and Mrs. Bates watching me as I crossed the flagged back lobby, pushed open the green baize door which gave on the front hall, and turned unhesitatingly to the right before the door swung shut behind me.

"It's a very simple house," Lisa had said. "It's shaped like an L, with the wing shorter than the stem of the L. The wing's where the kitchens are, and the scullery, and what used to be the dairy, but all the dairy work's done in the buildings now, so it's a laundry house with a Bendix and an electric ironing machine. There's a baize door that cuts the kitchen wing off from the main body of the house.

"It's not the original farmhouse, you know, it's what you might call a small manor. It was built about a hundred and fifty years ago, on the site of the old house that was pulled down. You'll find a print of the original farmhouse in Bewick's *Northumberland;* that was a square, grim-looking sort of building, but the new one's quite different, like a small country house, plain and sturdy, certainly, but graceful too . . . The main hall's square, almost an extra room . . . a wide staircase opposite the front door . . . drawing room to one side, dining room to the other with the library behind; that's used as an office . . . your grandfather's bedroom is the big room at the front, over the drawing room. . . ."

As the baize door shut, I leaned back against it for a moment, and let myself pause. It could not have been more than three-quarters of an hour since I had met Bates in High Riggs, but already I felt exhausted with sustained effort. I must have a minute or two alone, to collect myself, before I went upstairs. . . .

I looked about me. The hall had certainly never been built for an ordinary farmhouse. The floor was oak parquet, and the old blanket chest against the wall was carved oak, too, and beautiful. A couple of Bokhara rugs looked very rich against the honey-coloured wood of the floor. The walls were plain ivory, and there was a painting of a jar of marigolds, a copy of the Sartorius aquatint of the Darley Arabian, and an old coloured map of the North Tyne, with *Forreft Hall* clearly marked, and, in smaller letters on a neat segment of the circle labelled *Forreft Park*, I identified *Whitefcar*.

Below the map, on the oak chest, stood a blue ironstone jug, and an old copper dairy pan, polished till its hammered surface gleamed like silk. It was full of blue and purple pansies and wild yellow heartsease.

Whitescar had certainly not suffered from Lisa's stewardship. I reflected, in passing, that Lisa had been wrong about Mrs. Bates. Mrs. Bates by no means disliked her; her attitude of armed neutrality was a faint reflection of the ferocious affection she had hurled at me. Anyone who could keep a house as Lisa had had almost certainly won Mrs. Bates' loyalty, along with as lively a respect as a Northumbrian would care to accord a "foreigner."

I went slowly up the wide oak staircase. The carpet was moss-green and thick; my feet made no sound. I turned along the landing which made a gallery to one side of the hall. At the end of it a window looked over the garden.

Here was the door. Oak, too, with shallow panels sunk in their bevelled frames. I put out a finger and ran it silently down the bevel.

The landing was full of sunlight. A bee was trapped, and blundering, with a deep hum, against the window. The sound was soporific, dreamy, drowning time. It belonged to a thousand summer afternoons, all the same, long, sun-drenched, lazily full of sleep. . . .

Time ran down to nothing; stood still; ran back. . . .

The moment snapped. I turned, with a sharp little movement, and thrust open the casement beside me. The bee bumbled foolishly about for a moment or two, then shot off into the sunlight like a pebble from a sling. I latched the window quietly behind it, then turned and knocked at the door.

Matthew Winslow was wide awake, and watching the door.

He lay, not on the bed, but on a broad, old-fashioned sofa near the window. The big bed, covered with a white honeycomb quilt, stood against the further wall. The room was large, with the massive shiny mahogany furniture dear to the generation before last, and a thick Indian carpet. The windows were charming, long and latticed, and wide open to the sun and the sound of the river at the foot of the garden. A spray of early Albertine roses hung just outside the casement, and bees were busy there. For all its thick carpet, cluttered ornaments, and heavy old furniture, the room smelt fresh, of sunshine and roses on the wall.

On a small table beside the bed were three photographs. One was of Con, looking dramatically handsome in an open-necked shirt, with some clever lighting throwing the planes of his face into relief. Another, I guessed, was Julie; a young, eager face with vivid eyes and a tumble of fair, fine hair. I couldn't see the third from where I stood.

But all this was for the moment no more than a fleeting impression. What caught and held the eye was the figure of the old man reclining against the cushions on the sofa with a plaid rug across his knees.

Matthew Winslow was a tall, gaunt old man with a thick mane of white hair, which had once been fair. His eyes, puckered now and sunken under the prominent brows, were grey-green; now the edges of the iris had faded, but the eyes still looked bright and hard as a young man's. His mouth, too, was hard, a thin line between the deep parallels that drove from nostril to jaw line. It would have been, for all its craggy good looks, a forbidding face, had it not been for a gleam of humour that lurked somewhere near the corners of mouth and eyes. One would certainly not, at first glance, take Matthew Winslow for a man who needed to be guarded from anything. He looked as tough as pemmican, and nobody's fool.

In response to his gruff summons I had entered the room, and shut the door quietly behind me. There was a pause of complete stillness, in which the buzzing of the bees among the pink roses sounded as loud as a flight of aircraft.

I said, "Grandfather?" on a note of painful hesitation.

His voice was harsh when he spoke, and the words uncompromising, but I had seen him wet his lips and make the attempt twice. "Well, Annabel?"

There was surely, I thought confusedly, some sort of precedent for this, the prodigal's return? *He ran, and fell on his neck, and kissed him. . . .*

Well, Matthew Winslow couldn't run. That left me.

I went quickly across the room and knelt down beside the sofa, and put my hands on his lap, on top of the plaid rug. His thin hand, with its prominent, blue-knotted veins, came down hard over mine, surprisingly strong and warm.

In the end it was easy to know what to say. I said quite simply, "I'm sorry, Grandfather. Will you have me back?"

The hand moved, holding mine together even more tightly. "If I said no," said Grandfather crisply, "it would be no more than you deserve." He cleared his throat violently. "We thought you were dead."

"I'm sorry."

His other hand reached forward and lifted my chin. He studied my face, turning it towards the light of the window. I bit my lip and waited, not meeting his gaze. He said nothing for a long time, then, as harshly as before, "You've been unhappy. Haven't you?"

I nodded. He let me go, and at last I was able to put my forehead down on the rug, so that he couldn't see my face. He said, "So have we," and fell silent again, patting my hand.

Out of the corner of my eye I could see Con's portrait, the fine mouth just moving into that smile of his, full of challenge, and something that was more than mischief; an exciting, and, yes, a dangerous face. Well, Con, it was done now, all behind me, the burned boats, the Rubicons. We were over Becher's Brook, the Canal Turn, the lot, and into the straight. Home.

Con's eyes watched. What good would it do now to lift my head and say, "Your beloved Con's betraying you. He's paying me to come and pretend I'm your granddaughter, because he thinks you'll die soon, and he wants your money, and your place." And something in me, some little voice I'd never listened to before, added, "And once he's made certain of that, I wouldn't give twopence for your life, Grandfather, I wouldn't really. . . ."

I stayed where I was, not speaking.

The old man said nothing. The bees had gone. A small bird flew into the roses by the open window; I heard the flirt of its wings, and the tap and swish of the twigs as it alighted.

At length I lifted my head, and smiled at him. He removed his hands, and looked at me under the thrust of his brows. If there had been any sign of emotion in his face, it had been banished now.

"Get a chair." He spoke abruptly. "And sit where I can see you."

I obeyed him. I chose an upright chair, and sat correctly and rather primly on it, knees and feet together, back straight, hands in lap, like a small girl about to recite her catechism.

I thought I saw a glimmer of appreciation in his eyes. "Well?" he said. Without moving, he seemed all at once to sit up straighter, even to tower over me. "You've got a lot of talking to do, girl. Supposing you start."

CHAPTER FIVE

> Some men has plenty money and no brains, and some men has plenty brains and no money. Surely men with plenty money and no brains were made for men with plenty brains and no money.
>
> —From the Notebook of the Tichborne claimant.

"WELL?" said Lisa softly, like an echo.

She was waiting at the foot of the stairs. A shaft of sunlight through the hall window dazzled along the edge of the copper bowl of pansies. She had her back to the light, and I couldn't see her expression, but even in the one softly uttered word I could hear some of the trembling uncertainty she had showed in the kitchen. "How did it go off?"

I had paused when I saw her waiting, and now came reluctantly down the stairs.

"All right. Far better than I'd have expected."

She gave her withdrawn, close-lipped smile. It was as if, with this quiet lying-in-wait, these careful whispers, she was deliberately putting me back where I belonged; inside a dusty little cell of conspiracy, able to share my thoughts and hopes only with herself and Con, bound to them in a reluctant but unbreakable intimacy.

She said, "I told you there was nothing to be afraid of."

"I know. But I suppose conscience makes cowards of us all."

"What?"

"Nothing. A quotation. Shakespeare."

She looked faintly resentful, as she had in the kitchen when Con and I had seemed to be moving too fast for her. Perhaps the quotation irked her, or the realization that I hadn't come from Grandfather's room bursting with confidences; or perhaps she didn't like to be reminded that I had once had a conscience. At any rate she slammed the door of the conspirators' cell hard on me once again. "You're very literary today. You want to be careful. It isn't in character."

I smiled. "I've had plenty of time to settle down and improve my mind abroad."

"Hm. He didn't—he wasn't suspicious at all?"

"No." I spoke a little wearily. "It's exactly as you and Con foretold. There's no reason why he should be. It never even entered his head."

She pursed her lips with satisfaction. "Well, what did happen?"

My mind went back to the scene upstairs. Well, they couldn't buy everything.

I said slowly, "You can have the main outlines, if you like. I told him where I'd been since I left here, and how I'd been living. You know we'd arranged to tell the simple truth about that, as much as possible."

"Did he say much about . . . the trouble? The reason why you went?"

"Nothing that need concern you. I just tried to make it clear that, whatever had happened in the past, nothing in the world would persuade me to —well, to take up with Con again." I saw the look in her face, and added smoothly, "That, of course, was to protect Con and myself. It was quite possible, you know, that Grandfather was nursing some hopes of a reconciliation. I had to insist that there could never be anything between Con and myself except—" I hesitated—"you might call it armed neutrality."

"I see. Yes, that would have been—" she stopped. That conspirators' look again. "I'm sure you're right. There was nothing more? Nothing about the—the future?"

"Nothing at all."

She looked about her. "Well, you can't say much more just now, that's obvious. He'll be coming down soon. Later tonight, when we're alone, you can tell me all that was said."

"Make my report? No," I said gently.

Her mouth opened, with as much surprise as if I had struck her. "What d'you mean? You surely don't think that you can—"

"You probably wouldn't understand what I mean. But let's put it like this. I've a difficult rôle to play, and the only way to play it is to *be* it, to live in it, breathe it, think it, try to dream it. In other words, not to have to keep stepping out of Annabel's skin to remember that I'm just someone pretending to be Annabel. I can't act this thing in a series of little scenes, Lisa, with commentaries to you and Con in the intervals. If there's anything vital, or if I should want your help, believe me, I won't hestitate to come to you. But the biggest help you can both give me is simply to forget all that's happened in the last three weeks, and think of me, if you can, just as Annabel, come back to take my accustomed place in my own home. If you keep asking me questions, jerking me back out of my part into the part of Mary Grey, impostor . . . Well, then, Lisa, some day I may get my parts mixed up, and go wrong. And I could go very wrong indeed, very easily."

I paused, and added, lightly enough, "Well, there it is. Forget Mary Grey. Forget she ever existed. Believe me, I'm right. This is the only way to take it."

She said doubtfully, "Well, yes, but . . ."

I laughed. "Oh, Lisa, stop looking at me as if you were Frankenstein, and the monster had just got away from you! I'm only talking common sense! And you've only to remember that Con and I are mutually committed, even to the extent of signing those deadly little 'confessions' for each other to keep, just in case. I've no doubt Con keeps mine next to his skin, day and night. Call it remote control if you like, but it's there! Even if Annabel Winslow *is* home again, at least you know that she's got to bat on Con's side this time!"

"I—well, yes, of course. Forgive me, I didn't really doubt you, but this afternoon has been disconcerting, to say the least. You . . . you're so very *good* at this. I've been the one to be nervous."

"I assure you, I'm quaking inside! It's all right. I won't double-cross you, you know, Lisa, even if I dared."

"Dared?"

I didn't answer, and after a moment her eyes dropped. "Well, that's that, then. And you're quite right. I'll try and do as you say, and forget it all, unless there's anything urgent. But it certainly doesn't look as if you're going to need much help, my dear. If you got away with that—" A movement of her head towards the upper landing completed the sentence for her.

"Well, I did. Now let's forget it. Did you say something about tea?"

"I was just going to make it."

"Do you want any help?"

"Not on your first day home."

"Then I think I'll go upstairs for a little. Am I in my old room?"

She smiled. "Yes. D'you mind using the nursery bathroom? You'll be sharing it with Julie."

"Of course not. Does she know about me?"

"Yes. She rang up last night, to say she'd be here on Wednesday, and Mr. Winslow told her about you. That's all I know."

"Wednesday . . ." I paused with a foot on the lowest stair. "Ah well, that gives us two more days. Oh, Lisa, I forgot, my cases—"

"Con brought them in just now, and took them up."

"Oh? It was good of him to get them so quickly. I'll see you at tea, then. Where d'you have it?"

"When I'm alone, in the kitchen as often as not. But for today, the drawing room. Your grandfather'll be down, I expect. Did he say?"

"Yes. He—he wants to show me round the place himself after tea."

The brown eyes held mine just a moment longer than was necessary.

"Of course," said Lisa, abandoning comment with what looked like an effort, "he would want to do that. Naturally. Well—I'll see you later."

I turned and went back upstairs. I could see her watching me as, unhesitatingly, I took the left-hand passage past the head of the gallery.

Yours is the second door. . . . It was a pleasant room, with a long latticed window like Grandfather's, and the same Albertine rose nodding outside it. There was a wide window seat, covered with chintz in a pretty, Persian-looking pattern of birds and flowers and trellis work, done in deliberately faded colours. The same chintz appeared for curtains and bedspread. The furniture was plain deal, white-painted; originally it would speak of "nursery," but now a new coat of paint made it merely cottagy and very charming. The floor was of polished boards with a couple of rugs, and the walls and ceiling were plain ivory white.

Con had dumped my baggage on the floor near the foot of the bed. He had also thoughtfully brought up my handbag, which I must have left in the kitchen, and this lay on the bed.

I wasn't prepared to cope with unpacking yet. I picked up the handbag and carried it across to the window seat. I sat down, opened the bag, and took out my cigarettes.

As I shook one loose from the pack, I glanced at the door. There was a key in the lock. So far, so good. I had a feeling that I was going to need frequent doses of privacy to recover from the rounds of a game which, though so far it had proved a walk-over, might well get stickier as time went on.

I put the cigarette in my mouth, and felt in the little mirror-pocket in my bag where I had carried a flat book of matches. It wasn't there. My fingers met merely a slip of paper. Surely, I thought, irritably, I had had one? I had been smoking in the bus coming from Newcastle . . . I pulled the bag wider to look for it. I saw it immediately, then, a little scarlet book labelled *Café Kasbah*, tucked deep in the pocket on the other side of my bag, where I kept bills and shopping lists and oddments of that sort.

I lit the cigarette slowly, and sat contemplating the bag, open on my lap. Now that I had noticed it, there were other signs. The top had come loose on one of my lipsticks; the few papers that I carried were shuffled hastily back into their places as I didn't think I had put them; the slip of paper where I had scribbled down the Whitescar telephone number, which had been among the other papers, was pushed into the mirror compartment where normally the matches were kept. Whoever had scrabbled hastily through my handbag had taken few pains to cover his tracks.

Con? Lisa? I grinned to myself. What was it they called this kind of thing? Counter-espionage? That, I was sure, was how it would rank in Lisa's mind. Whatever you called it, it was surely a little late, now, for them to be checking on my *bona fides*.

I went quickly through what was there. The telephone number; it was natural enough that I should have scribbled that down; numbers change in eight years. A bus time table, acquired that day on my way here. The receipt for my lodgings near the Haymarket, also received that morning. That was all right; it was addressed to "Miss A. Winslow."

Then I hesitated, with it in my hand. Was it all right, after all? It was admittedly unlikely that Grandfather would ever see it, or check on it if he did, but both Con and Lisa had visited me there. It was better out of the way. I crumpled the paper up, and threw it into the empty fireplace. I would burn it before I went downstairs.

I turned over the other papers. A few shopping chits; a couple of used bus tickets; a folded paper of pale green. . . .

I picked it out from among the others, and unfolded it. "*Passenger Motor Vehicle Permit . . . Mary Grey . . .*" and the address near Montreal. There it lay, clear as a curse, the Canadian car permit; the owner's licence that you carry daily, yearly, and never even see, except when the time comes round to renew it. . . .

Well, I thought, as I crumpled it in my hand, Con and Lisa must realize what an easy mistake this had been to make. I wondered, not without amusement, how on earth they would manage to warn me about it, without having to confess that they had searched my belongings. At least they could not also have searched my cases; the key hung on a chain round my neck, and there it was going to stay. . . .

From somewhere outside I heard Lisa calling, and Con's voice in reply. I heard him cross the yard towards the house. There was a low-voiced colloquy, then he went back towards the buildings.

I got up, and set a match to the crumpled bill in the fireplace, then carefully fed the car permit into the flames. I picked up the poker, and stirred the burned fragments of paper till they flaked and fell away to nothing, through the bars of the grate. Then I went back to the sunny window, picked up my half-smoked cigarette, and sat for some minutes longer, trying to relax.

The window looked out over the small front garden. This was a simple square bounded by low sandstone walls, and sloping slightly towards the river. From the front door a gravel path, weedy and unraked, led straight to the white wicket gate that gave on the river bank and the bridge that spanned the water. The path was bordered by ragged hedges of lavender, under which sprawled a few hardy pansies and marigolds. Behind these borders, to either side, the unkempt grass reached back to what had once been the flower beds.

Here was confusion indeed. Lupins had run wild, all the gay colours faded back to their pristine blue; peonies crouched sullenly under the strangling bushes of fuchsia and flowering currant, and everywhere ivy, bindweed, and rose-bay willow herb were joyously completing their deadly work. At first glance, the riot of colour might deceive the eye into thinking that here was a pretty garden still, but then one saw the dandelions, the rampant rose bushes, the docks in the rank grass under the double white lilac tree. . . .

Beyond the far wall, and the white wicket, was a verge of sheep-bitten grass, and the wooden bridge that was Whitescar's short cut to town. From the other end of the bridge the track wound up through the trees that crowded the far bank, and vanished eventually into their shadow.

My eye came back, momentarily, to the tangled garden. Two blackbirds had flown into the lilac tree, quarrelling furiously. The great heads of milky blossom shook and swayed. I could smell lilac from where I sat.

(*Annabel's garden. She planted it all. Remember to ask Con what's in it . . . if he knows.*)

He had not known.

I leaned to stub out my cigarette on the stone sill outside the window frame.

It was time to go down. Act Two. Back into the conspirators' cell with Con and Lisa.

I found myself hoping passionately that Con wouldn't be in to tea.

He wasn't, and it was still, it seemed, going to be easy. Grandfather came down a little late, opening the drawing room door on me discussing amiably with Lisa what had happened to various neighbours during my long absence, and thereafter acted more or less as though the eight years' gap had never been.

After tea he took me outside, and led the way towards the farm buildings. He walked fairly rapidly, and held his gaunt body upright apparently without effort. With the westering sun behind him, shadowing the thinned, bony face, and making the grey hair look blond as it must once have been, it wasn't difficult to see once more the active, opinionated, quick-tempered man who had done so much through his long life to make Whitescar the prosperous concern it now was. I could see, too, why Con—in spite of the old man's favour—walked warily.

Grandfather paused at the yard gate. "Changed much?"

"The farm? I—it's hard to tell."

A quick look under the jutting white brows. "What d'you mean?"

I said slowly, "Oh, some things, yes. The new paint, and—that wall's new, isn't it? And the concrete, and all that drainage. But I meant—well, I've been gone a long time, and I suppose I've lived so long on a memory of Whitescar, that now it's bound to look strange to me. My picture of it—my imagined picture, I mean—has become almost more real than the thing itself. For one thing," I laughed a little, "I remember it as being always in sunshine. One does, you know."

"So they say. I'd have thought you'd be more likely to remember it the way you left it. It was a vile day."

"Yes. I went before it was fully light, and you can imagine what it looked like. Rain and wind, and the fields all grey and flattened. I remember how awful that one looked—at least, was it in corn that year? I—I forget."

"Turnips. But you're quite right. The corn was badly laid everywhere that year."

"The odd thing is," I said, "that I hardly really remember that at all. Perhaps the psychologists would say that the rain and wind, and that grey early morning, were all mixed up in my mind with the misery of leaving home, and that I've allowed myself to forget it." I laughed. "I wouldn't know. But all the years I was away, I remembered nothing but sunshine . . . fine, lovely days, and all the things we used to do . . . childhood memories, mostly." I paused for a little. "I suppose you could say that my actual memories of home got overlaid, in time, with dream-pictures. I know that, after a few years, I'd have been hard put to it to give a really accurate description of . . . this, for instance."

I gestured to the tidy yard, the shadowy cave of the barn, the double stable doors with the tops latched back to the wall.

"If you'd even asked me what sort of stone it was built of, I couldn't have told you. And yet, now that I'm back, I notice everything. Tiny things that I must have taken for granted all my life, and never really seen before."

"Hm." He was staring at me fixedly. There was neither gentleness nor affection, that I could see, in the clear grey-green gaze. He said abruptly, "Con's a good lad."

I must have sounded slightly startled. "Yes, of course."

He misunderstood the wariness of my manner, for his voice had a harsher note as he said, with equal abruptness, "Don't worry. I'm not harking back to that business eight years back. You've told me you had your reasons, and I've accepted that."

I said nothing. I saw him glance sideways at me, then he added testily, as if I had been arguing, "All right, all right. We've said all there is to say. We'll drop it now. But apart from things that are over and forgotten, Con's a good lad, and he's been a son to me this last eight years."

"Yes."

Another of those bright, almost inimical glances. "I mean that. I'd have done badly without him for a long time now, and this last year or two, it'd have been impossible. He's more than made up for what's past. He's put everything he knows into the place."

"Yes. I know."

The white brows jutted at me. "Well? Well?"

I smiled at him. "What do you expect me to say, Grandfather? It's quite true. I left you, and Con stayed. If you're making something of it, go right ahead, I'm listening."

There was a little silence. Then he gave a short bark of laughter. "You don't change," he said. "So you've come back to quarrel with me, have you?"

"Grandfather darling," I said, "no. But I don't quite see what you're getting at. You're trying to tell me how wonderful Con is. All right; I'll give you that. He's been telling me himself. But you can't blame me for being a bit wary. Eight years ago, all this would have been leading up to a spot of match-making. I hoped I'd made it clear that that was impossible."

"Mm. So you said, but one never knows how much one can believe a woman, especially when she starts talking all that claptrap about love turning to hate, and so forth."

"I said nothing of the sort. I don't hate Con. If I felt strongly about him at all, I couldn't have come back while he was still here, could I? I told you how I felt; indifferent, and more than a bit embarrassed. I'd give quite a lot not to have had to meet him again, but since he's here, and not likely to go . . ." I smiled a little. "All right, Grandfather, let it pass. I had to see you, and it'd take more than Con to keep me away. Now, you don't usually hand out compliments for the fun of the thing. You're leading up to something. What is it?"

He chuckled. "All right. It's this. You always knew Whitescar would be yours when I died, didn't you? Should have been your father's, and then it would have been yours."

"Yes. I knew that."

"And had it occurred to you that I might have made other arrangements during the time you were away?"

"Well, of course."

"And now that you've come back?"

I turned half to face him, leaning against the gate, just as I had leaned to talk to Con earlier that day. "Come to the point, Grandfather dear."

The old eyes peered down at me, bright, amused, almost malicious. For some reason I was suddenly reminded of Con, though there was no outward resemblance whatever. "I will. It's this. They'll have told you I'm not expected to live a great while—no," as I made some movement of protest, "don't bother. We all know what this confounded condition of mine means. Now, you cleared out eight years ago, and, for all we knew, you were dead. Well, you've come back." He paused. He seemed to be waiting for a reply.

I said steadily, "Are you accusing me of coming back for what I think I can get?"

He gave his sharp crack of laughter. "Don't be a fool, girl. I know you better than that. But you *would* be a fool if you hadn't thought about it, and wondered where you'd stand. Have you?"

"Of course."

He gave a nod, as if pleased. "That's a straight answer, anyway. And I'll be straight with you. Look at it this way. You walked out eight years ago; Con stayed. Do *you* think it right that you should just walk back like this, after the work that Con's put into this place meantime—and that fool Lisa Dermott for that matter—and just scoop it all up from under his very nose?

Would you call that fair? I'm hanged if I would." His head thrust forward suddenly. "What in thunder are you laughing at?"

"Nothing. Nothing at all. Are you trying to tell me that you've left everything to Con and Lisa?"

Again that glint of mischief, that could have been malice. "I didn't say that. And don't you go letting them think it, either. I'm not dead yet. But is there any reason that you can think of why I shouldn't?"

"None at all."

He looked almost disconcerted, staring at me under his white brows. I realized then what the fleeting likeness had been between him and Con; it was a matter of expression, nothing else; an impression of arrogance, of deliberately enjoying a moment of power. Matthew Winslow was enjoying the situation just as much as Con, and for allied reasons. He liked the power that it gave him.

He said testily, "I wish I knew what the devil there was in all this to laugh at."

"I'm sorry," I said. "I was thinking of Con. 'The engineer hoist with his owne petard.' "

"What? What are you talking about, girl?"

"It was a quotation," I said, helplessly. "I'm sorry, Grandfather. I'm serious, really I am."

"You'd better be. Quotation, indeed. You've been wasting your time abroad, I can see that. Some modern rubbish, by the sound of it. Well, what were you thinking about Con?"

"Nothing, really. Aren't you going to tell him that you've made a will in his favour?"

"I didn't say I had. And I forbid you to speak to him about it. What I want is to get things straight with you. Perhaps I should have left it till you'd been home a bit longer, but as it happens, I've been thinking a good deal about it lately. You knew Julie was coming up here?"

"Yes. Lisa told me."

"I wrote and asked her to come as soon as she could, and the child tells me she can get leave straight away. When she comes, I want to get things fixed up. Isaacs—do you remember Isaacs?"

"I—I'm not sure."

"The lawyer. Nice chap. I'm sure you met him."

"Oh, yes, of course. I remember now."

"He's coming on Friday, and then again next week. I suggested the twenty-second."

"The twenty-second? That's your birthday, isn't it?"

"Good God, fancy your remembering." He looked pleased.

"Lisa's planning a party, she told me, since we'll all be here, Julie too."

"Yes. A family gathering. Appropriate." He gave that dry, mischievous chuckle again.

I tilted my head and looked up at him, all amusement gone. "Grandfather—"

"Well?"

"At this—appropriate—family gathering—" I paused—"do you intend to tell us all where we stand?"

"A nice, old-fashioned gathering of the vultures round the old man's bones? How do you think I like all this talk of what's to happen after I'm dead?"

I grinned at him. "You started it, and you told me to be a realist. But, look, Grandfather—" I fought not to let my voice sound too urgent—"if you do intend to—to make Con your heir . . . would you tell him so? Please?"

"Why the devil should I?"

"It—it would make things easier for me."

"Easier for *you?* What d'you mean?"

"Only that he—well, he'd resent me less. You can't blame Con for being a realist, too, can you? You must know he'll have had expectations."

"If he has," said Grandfather drily, "then he's an optimist." He caught my expression, and laughed. "What I do with my property's my own affair, Annabel, and if I choose to allow people to confuse themselves, that's their funeral. Do I make myself clear?"

"Very clear."

"Good. You'll gather that I intend to keep my affairs to myself."

"Yes. Well, you've a perfect right to."

There was a pause. He seemed to be choosing his words, but when he spoke, it was bluntly enough, "You know I always wanted you to marry Connor."

"Yes, I know. I'm sorry, Grandfather."

"It always seemed to me the best answer."

"For Whitescar; yes, I see that; but not for me. And not really for Con, Grandfather. Honestly, it wouldn't work. Ever." I smiled. "And it does take two to make a match, you know. I don't think you'll find Con in the same mind as he was eight years ago."

The old eyes were suddenly very sharp and shrewd. "Not even if Whitescar went with you?"

"Of course not!" But I was disconcerted, and showed it. "Don't be so mediaeval, Grandfather!"

He still peered down at me, bright-eyed. "And if it went with Connor?"

"Is that a threat, or a bribe?"

"Neither. You've shown me how little effect it would have. I'm thinking about your future, if the place were Con's. Would you stay?"

"How could I?"

"Is that meant to be a pistol at my heart?"

"Good heavens, no. You don't have to worry about me. I'd have Mother's money."

"And Whitescar?"

I was silent.

"Wouldn't you care?"

"I—I don't know. You've just pointed out that I can hardly expect to walk straight home after eight years."

"Well, that's true enough. I'm glad you seem to have faced it. I shan't be here for ever, you know."

"I know. But at least I can be here as long as you are."

He snorted. "Soft soap, child. That'll get you nowhere. And don't glare at me like that, it cuts no ice! So you expect me to cut you right out, do you, leave Julie to her own devices, and hand the place lock, stock and barrel, to young Connor? That it?"

I pushed myself upright, away from the gate.

I said, "Grandfather, you always were insufferable, and you were never fair in all your born days. How the devil do you expect me to know what you plan to do? You'll do as the mood takes you, fair or no, and Con and I can take what comes, charm we never so wisely." I added, "That was another quotation. And don't say I've been wasting my time again, because that's from the Psalms."

Grandfather's face never changed, but something came behind the eyes that might have been a grin. He said mildly, "Don't swear at me, Annabel my girl, or old as you are, I'll soap your mouth out."

"Sorry." We smiled at one another. There was a pause.

"It's good to have you back, child. You don't know how good." He put a hand to the latch of the gate. "Come down to the river meadows. There's a yearling there you'll like to see."

We went down a lane between hedgerows whispering with budding meadowsweet. The hawthorn was rusted thickly over with bunches of dried flowers hardening to fruit.

At the end of the lane a gate opened on a field deep with buttercups and cuckoo-flowers. A grey mare moved towards us, swishing her tail, her sides sleek and heavy. From the shade of a big beech a yearling watched us with eyes as soft and wary as a deer.

"He's a beauty."

"Isn't he?" There was satisfaction and love in the old man's voice. "Best foal she ever dropped. Forrest kept a three-year-old out of her by the same sire, but they'll make nothing of him. Yes, she's a grand mare; I bought her from Forrest three years ago, when the stud was sold up. Give over, Blondie, give over, now." This to the mare, who was pushing at his chest with her muzzle as he opened the gate and held it for me. "Come through. The grass is dry enough. You'll have to find some better shoes for this tomorrow."

I followed him into the field. "What's wrong with the three-year-old?"

"What? Oh, Forrest's horse? Nothing, except that nobody had time to do anything about him. Only kept him out of sentiment, I suppose, as he's one of the old 'Mountain' lot. Everest got him; you'll remember Everest? He's gone to the Chollerford stud now; getting long in the tooth, the old devil, but his get's as good as it ever was; look at that yearling. And Forrest's colt could be a winner, too, if they'd time to school him. Rowan, they called him." He chuckled, and clapped the mare's neck. "By Everest, out of Ash Blonde here."

"Rowan? Another name for Mountain Ash?"

"That's it. Sort of nonsense Forrest always went in for with his names. You knew the stud was gone?"

"Oh, yes. What have you called this one? You said he was the same breeding."

"We haven't named him yet. That'll be for his owners."

The mare threw her head up to avoid his caressing hand, and swerved a little, flicking her tail pettishly. She pricked her ears at me, and reached out an inquiring muzzle.

I said, ignoring it, "He's sold, then?"

"Yes. I'm afraid you'll find nothing here to ride now. Blondie's heavy at foot, as you can see, and the youngster'll be away next month." He laughed. "Unless you try your hand with Forrest's three-year-old. I've no doubt he'd let you if you asked him."

The mare was pushing close to me. The yearling, looking interested, was coming to join her. From behind me, some way along the lane, I heard footsteps approaching. I backed away from the mare's advance until I was right up against the gate. She pushed her head at me again, and breathed gustily down the front of my dress.

I said breathlessly, "Asked who?"

"Forrest, of course. What the devil's the matter with you, Annabel?"

"Nothing. What should be the matter?" The footsteps were nearer.

Grandfather was regarding me curiously. "You're as white as a sheet! Anyone'd think you were afraid of the mare!"

I managed a little laugh. "Afraid of her? How absurd! Here, Blondie. . . ." I put out a hand to her. I hoped he wouldn't see how unsteady it was. The mare was nibbling the buckle of my belt. The yearling had come right up to her shoulder, and stood staring. Any minute now he would close in too. . . .

I looked away from Grandfather's curious, puzzled stare, and said quickly, "I thought Mr. Forrest was in Italy."

"He's coming back some time this week, so Johnny Rudd tells me. They didn't expect him quite yet, but I imagine the sale of the place in Italy went through quicker than he'd expected."

I gave the mare's head a shove away from me. I might as well have shoved an elephant. I said, unsteadily, "I—I understood he'd left for good. I mean, with the Hall gone, and—and everything—"

"No, no. He's planning to settle at West Lodge now, Johnny tells me, with the Rudds to look after him. He came back last year to clear up the rest of the estate, and he and Johnny set to work and got the old gardens going; I believe that's what he plans to do now."

"Yes, Con did say—"

Con's voice, from beyond the bend in the lane, called, "Uncle Matthew? Annabel?"

"Here!" called Grandfather.

The mare was nibbling at my frock, and, retreating from her advance, I was pressed so hard against the gate, that the bars bit into my back. Grandfather gave a quick little frown. "Annabel—"

"I thought as much!" Con said it, mercifully, from just behind me. "I might have known you'd bring her straight down here!"

He must have summed up the situation at a glance as he rounded the bend in the lane: Grandfather, his attention divided between the yearling and my own odd behaviour; myself, backed against the gate, chattering breathlessly, and trying, with patently unsteady hands, to stop the mare from blowing lovingly down the breast of my frock.

I saw the flash of amusement in Con's eyes, and then he had leaned over the gate beside me, handed off the importunate mare with one strong thrust and a "Give over, now," that sent her swerving straight away, ears flattened and tail switching. The yearling threw up his lovely head and veered after her. As I relaxed, Con pushed open the gate and came through.

Grandfather, fortunately, was watching the yearling as it cantered away into the shade of the trees. "Moves well, doesn't he?" he said fondly.

"He's a little beauty," agreed Con.

"Little?" I said shakily. "He looks enormous!"

A flicker in Con's eyes showed me the ineptitude of this remark for someone who was supposed to have lived and breathed horses for most of her life. Then he covered up as smoothly as a practised actor, the amusement warming his voice so faintly that only I would hear it. "Yes, he's pretty well-grown, isn't he, seeing he's barely a year old. . . ." And he plunged easily off into technicalities with Mr. Winslow, no doubt to give me time to recover my poise.

Presently Grandfather said, "I was telling Annabel that she'll have to see Forrest about some riding if she wants it."

"Forrest? Oh, is he back?"

"Not yet. Some time this week. Johnny Rudd told me they didn't look for him before autumn at the soonest, but apparently he's sold the villa, and he's coming back to live at West Lodge."

Con was leaning on the gate beside me. He sent a slanting look down at me, with a lurking smile behind it. "That's a bit of luck, Annabel. He'll let you ride the Mountain colt."

I was still shaken, but I had no intention of letting Con amuse himself further at my expense. I said immediately, with every evidence of enthusiasm, "Do you really think he would? That's wonderful!"

Con's eyes widened. Grandfather said shortly, "Of course he would, unless you've lost your touch completely! Want to come across and look at him now?"

"I'd love to."

"Can't it wait?" said Con. "You look tired."

I looked at him, slightly surprised. "I'm all right."

Con straightened up with that lazy grace of his that looked deliberate, but was in reality as natural as breathing. At the movement, slow though it was, the mare, who was grazing near, rolled a white-rimmed eye and moved away.

"Doesn't like you, does she?" said Matthew Winslow. "Come along then, my dear. Coming, Con?"

Con shook his head. "No, I've a lot to do. I really only came down to see if you'd come up into the seventeen-acre and take a look at the cutter for me. She's been running rough, and I don't seem to be able to get to the bottom of the trouble. I could take you up in the car."

"The cutter? Good God, can't you put that right without running to me?" But the old man had stopped and turned, looking far from displeased. "Well, in that case—" He looked at me. "Some other time, perhaps? Unless you go along there yourself? He's at grass, two fields along from the bridge, you know the place, beyond the wood."

"Yes," I said, "I know it. I'll go now."

My one desire was to get away, to be alone, not even to have to walk back to the house in their company. But even as I spoke, half-turning to go, I saw a shade of what looked like genuine anxiety on Con's face.

I realized then, suddenly, that his timely appearance on the scene had not been a matter of chance. He had not come down to see about the repair of the cutter, and then stayed to tease me; his coming had been a deliberate rescue bid. He had guessed that I had been brought down to the paddock; guessed, too, what might be happening there, and that the prolonged interview with Grandfather might be too much of a strain. He had come down solely to get me out of it, to draw Mr. Winslow off. In all probability there was nothing wrong with the cutter at all. . . .

And if, once here, he had been unable to resist teasing me a little, it was no more than he was entitled to, under the circumstances. He was standing now with grave patience, listening to a crisp lecture on the incompetence of a young man who could not, in twenty seconds, diagnose and correct every fault in every piece of machinery in use on the estate.

Well, fair was fair. I wouldn't worry him further. I interrupted the lecture. "I don't think I will go, after all. I'll go back to the house. I—I've done enough for today."

Matthew Winslow looked at me, still with that crinkle of puzzlement round his eyes. "Something *has* upset you, child. What is it?"

Suddenly, absurdly, I wanted to cry. "Nothing truly. Nothing. Con's right. I'm tired." I made a little gesture. "It's been wonderful playing the prodigal returning, and everyone's been so kind . . . too kind. But, you know, it's terribly exhausting. I feel as if I'd been back a year already, things have crowded in so fast."

We were back in the lane. As Con pulled the gate shut behind me, he took my arm as if in reassurance.

"Of course it's a strain. We all understand that. You should go in now, and rest till supper."

He spoke, as before, gently. I saw Grandfather glance quickly from his face to mine, and back again. It must be obvious to anyone that Con's solicitude was quite genuine, and I knew the reason for it, but I wasn't going to have Matthew Winslow leaping to the wrong conclusion. I withdrew my arm and said quickly,

"I think I will." Then I turned to the old man. "Have you still got the cribbage board?"

His face lightened to a grin. "Of course. You remember how to play?"

"How could I forget?" (*"She used to play with him often: it's an old-fashioned game; you know it? Good. . . ."*) I added, "I also remember that you owe me a vast sum of money, Grandfather."

"Nonsense. I always beat you."

"Ah, well," I said cheerfully, "I've improved, in eight years. I'll win your house and lands off you yet, so watch your step!"

At his dry little chuckle I felt Con stiffen beside me. He said abruptly, "Well, you'll not be playing tonight, at all events, I hope?"

"No, no. The child will want an early night. Besides, I'll probably stay up in the seventeen-acre with you. How are you getting on there?"

Con answered him, and the two of them talked across me as we walked slowly back towards the yard where the car stood. Con's manner with his great-uncle was charming; relaxed and easy and familiar, but with just the hint of a deference which obviously flattered the old man, coming from someone as vital and as capable as Con, to a man who, for all his deceptive appearance of power, was a frail husk that the first chill wind might blow away.

Grandfather was saying, "Nonsense! I can give you a hand when we've got the cutter running properly."

Con gave him that flashing, affectionate smile. "You'll do no such thing. Come along, by all means, and bully us, but I'm afraid that's all we'll let you do!"

"You coddle me. I'm not senile yet, and I won't be treated like a girl."

Con grinned. "Hardly that. In any case, the girl's going to work, once she's got herself run in again! Can you drive a tractor—still, Annabel?"

"I dare say I might manage, even if I have rather lost my touch with horses," I said evenly.

We had reached the gate of the main courtyard. Grandfather climbed, a little stiffly, into the big Ford that stood waiting there. Con shut the car door on him.

In the distance, from the fields beyond High Riggs, came the steady, smooth whirr of the grass cutter. Unless I was very much mistaken, there was nothing wrong with it at all. As Con shut the car door and turned, his eyes met mine. There was a smile in them. He said, "Over to me," very softly, and then, "*Do* you drive a tractor, by the way?"

"I have done."

"And," said Con, "a car?"

I studied him for a moment, then I smiled. He had earned it, after all. I said, "I had a car in Canada; I've just burned the permit, and I don't know where my licence is, but that doesn't mean a thing. I dare say I'd qualify for a British one, if I needed to."

"Ah," said Con. "And now, if you wouldn't mind shutting the gate behind us . . . ?"

CHAPTER SIX

" 'Tis down in yonder garden green,
Love, where we used to walk,
The finest flower that ere was seen
Is wither'd to a stalk."

Ballad: *The Unquiet Grave.*

SUPPER WITH LISA AND GRANDFATHER was not the ordeal I had feared it might be. The old man was in excellent spirits, and, though he was in something of a "do you remember" vein, and Lisa's eyes, under their lowered lids, watched us both overanxiously, it went off smoothly enough, with no hitch that I could see. Con wasn't there. It was light late, and he was at work long hours in the hayfield while the weather lasted.

Shortly after supper Grandfather went into the office to write letters, and I helped Lisa wash up. Mrs. Bates went off at five, and the girl who helped in the kitchen and dairy had gone home when the milking was over. Lisa and I worked in silence. I was tired and preoccupied, and she must have realized that I didn't want to talk. She had made no further attempt to force a tête-à-tête on me, and she didn't try to detain me when, soon after nine o'clock, I went up to my room.

I sat there by the open window, with the scent from the climbing roses unbearably sweet in the dusk, and my mind went round and round over the events of the day like some small creature padding its cage.

The light was fading rapidly. The long flushed clouds of sunset had darkened and grown cool. Below them the sky lay still and clear, for a few moments rinsed to a pale eggshell green, fragile as blown glass. The dusk leaned down slowly, as soft as a bird coming in to brood. Later, there would be a moon.

It was very still. Close overhead I heard the scratch and rustle of small feet on the sloping roof tiles, then the throaty murmur as the pigeons settled back again to sleep. From the garden below came the smell of lilac. A moth fluttered past my cheek, and a bat cut the clear sky like a knife. Down in the neglected garden-grass the black and white cat crouched, tail whipping, then sprang. Something screamed in the grass.

I brushed the back of a hand impatiently across my cheeks, and reached for a cigarette. Round the side of the house, in the still evening, came the sharp sounds of a door opening and shutting. A man's footsteps receded across the yard, and were silenced on turf somewhere. Con had been in for a late meal, and was going out again.

I got up quickly, and reached a light coat down from the hook behind the door. I dropped the packet of cigarettes into the pocket, and went downstairs.

Lisa was clearing up after Con's meal in the kitchen. I said quickly, "I'm going out for a walk. I–I thought I'd take a look round on my own."

She nodded, incuriously. I went out into the gathering dusk.

I caught him up in the lane that led down to the river meadow. He was carrying a coil of wire, and hammer and pliers. He turned at the sound of my hurrying steps, and waited. The smile with which he greeted me faded when he saw my expression.

I said breathlessly, "Con. I had to see you."

"Yes." His voice was guarded. "What is it? Trouble?"

"No–at least, not the kind you mean. But there's something I have to say. I–I had to see you straight away, tonight."

I was close to him now. His face, still readable in the thickening dusk, had stiffened almost into hostility, arming itself against whatever was coming. So much, I thought, for Con's co-operation; it was fine as long as you stayed in line with him, but the moment he suspected you of deviating. . . .

"Well?" he said.

I had meant to start reasonably, quietly, at the right end of the argument I had prepared, but somehow the abrupt, even threatening, sound of the monosyllable shook my resolution into flinders. Womanlike, I forgot reason and argument together, and began at the end.

"This can't go on. You must see that. It can't go on!"

He stood very still. "What do you mean?"

"What I say! It'll have to stop! We were mad, anyway, even to have thought of starting it!" Once begun, it seemed I couldn't check myself. I had had more of a shaking that day than I cared to admit, even to myself. I stumbled on anyhow, growing even less coherent in the face of his unresponding silence.

"We–we'll have to think of some other way–something to tell Grandfather–I'm sure we can think something up! You must see there's no point in my staying, now, you must see! Even if I could have got away with it–"

I heard him breathe in sharply. "*Could have* got away with it? Do you mean he's found you out?"

"No, no, *no!*" I heard my voice rising, and checked it on a sort of gulp. We were near the gate where we had been that afternoon. I took a step away from him, and put out a hand to the gate, gripping it hard, as if that might steady me. I said, shakily, "Con . . . look, I'm sorry–"

His voice said coldly, behind me, "You're hysterical."

Since this was undoubtedly true, I said nothing. He put the tools and wire down beside the hedge, then came up to the gate beside me. He said, as unpleasantly as I had ever heard him speak, "Getting scruples, my dear, is that it? A little late, one feels."

His tone, even more than what his words implied, was all the cure my nerves needed. I turned my head sharply. "Does one? I think not!"

"No? Think again, my pretty."

I stared at him. "Are you trying to threaten me, Connor Winslow? And if so, with what?"

It was almost dark now, and he was standing with his back to what light there was. He had turned so that he was leaning his shoulders against the gate, seemingly quite relaxed. I felt, rather than saw, his look still on me, watchful, intent, hostile. But he spoke lightly.

"Threaten you? Not the least in the world, my love. But we're in this together, you know, and we work together. I can't have you forgetting our . . . bargain . . . quite so soon. You're doing splendidly, so far; things have gone even better than I dared to hope . . . *and* they're going to go on that way, darling, till I—and you, of course—get what we want. Fair enough?"

"Oh, quite."

The moon must be rising now beyond the thick trees. I could see the first faint glimmer on the river. The sky behind the black damask of leaf and bough was the colour of polished steel. The mare, grazing thirty yards away, had lifted her head and was staring towards us, ears pricked. Under the eclipsing shadow of hedgerow and tree she gleamed faintly, like some palladic metal, cool and smooth. The yearling was beside her, staring too.

I regarded Con curiously, straining my eyes against the dark. "I wonder . . ."

"Yes?"

I said slowly, "I wonder just how far you would go, to get what you wanted?"

"I've sometimes wondered that myself." He sounded amused. "You'd maybe be surprised what you can bring yourself to do, little cousin, when you've never had a damned thing in your life but what you could make—or take—with your own two hands. And what's wrong with that, anyway? A man who knows he can—" He broke off, and I thought I saw the gleam of a smile. "Well, there it is, girl dear. I'm not going to be sent on my travels again . . . fair means if I can, but by God, I'll see foul ones if I have to!"

"I see. Well, we know where we are, don't we?" I brought the packet of cigarettes out of my coat pocket. "Smoke?"

"Thanks. You smoke too much, don't you?"

"I suppose I do."

"I knew you'd more sense than to panic at the first hint of something you didn't like. What is the trouble, anyway? I've a light. Here."

In the momentary flare of the match I saw his face clearly. In spite of the light words, and the endearments with which he was so lavish, I could see no trace of liking, or even of any human feeling, in his expression. It was the face of a man concentrating on a job; something tricky, even dangerous, that called for every ounce of concentration. Me. I had to be got back into line.

The match went out. I thought I must have been mistaken, for his voice when he spoke was not ungentle. "Supposing you tell me exactly what's upset you? Something has, hasn't it? What was it? The horses this afternoon? You looked like seven sorts of death when I came down."

"Did I?"

"You know, you don't have to go near Forrest's horse if you don't want to."

"I know I don't—and incidentally, thank you for coming to my rescue." I leaned back against the gate beside him, and drew deeply on my cigarette. "I'm sorry I started this at the wrong end, and scared you. I don't have to tell you, I hope, that I'm not planning to let you down. I—I've had a hell of a day, that's all, and I was letting it ride me. I'll try and explain now, like a reasonable human being, which means not like a woman."

"You said it, honey, not me. Go ahead; I'm listening."

"It's true, though, that I did want to talk to you about altering our plans. No, wait, Con; the point is, things have changed."

"Changed? How? Since when?"

"Since I had my talk with Grandfather down here this evening."

"I . . . thought there had been something." I heard his breath go out. "I told you, you looked like death. I thought it was that fool of a mare."

"The point is, Con, that all this may have been for nothing. It shook me, rather. I—I think he's going to leave Whitescar to you anyway."

"*What?*"

"That's what he said."

"*He said so?*"

"Almost. I'll swear that's what he meant. Did you know that his lawyer, his name's Isaacs, isn't it?—is coming down here on Friday?"

"No, I didn't know." He sounded dazed. His voice was blurred at the edges.

"Well, he is. Julie gets here on Wednesday, and Mr. Isaacs comes on Friday. Grandfather didn't say anything definite, but he hinted like mad. I've a feeling he wants to have some sort of family gathering on his birthday, and he's asked the lawyer here before that, so it's a fairly reasonable guess that it's to be about his will. He said 'I want to get things fixed up.' "

He moved sharply, and the gate creaked. "Yes, but this *is* only a guess! What about Whitescar? What did he actually say?"

"Not very much, but—Con, it's all right. I wouldn't have mentioned it to you, if I wasn't sure. I'll swear that's what he means to do. Oh, no, he didn't quite commit himself, not in so many words, even to me. But he was as definite as he'd ever be."

"How?"

"Well, he reminded me first of all that Whitescar had always been promised to Annabel. 'It should have been your father's, and then it would have been yours.' "

" 'Would have been?' " he asked, sharply.

"Yes. Then he began to praise you. You'd been a son to him, he couldn't have done without you—oh, all sorts of things. He really does recognize your place here, Con. Then he said, would it be right if I were allowed simply to walk back home, and claim Whitescar over your head. Yes, over your head. 'Would you call that fair? I'm hanged if I would!' Those were his very words."

"My God, if you're right!" he breathed. "And Julie? Did he say anything about her?"

"Nothing you could be clear about. He wouldn't even say definitely that he intended to tell us all on the twenty-second, and when I tried to pin him down—asked flat out if he was remaking his will in your favour—he just wouldn't give a straight answer. I couldn't press it, you know what he's like. He seems to like to keep people guessing, doesn't he?"

"He does, damn him!"

He spoke with such sudden, concentrated viciousness, that I stopped with my cigarette halfway to my lips. I was reminded sharply, shockingly, of the charming way he had talked to the old man that afternoon. Oddly enough, I thought that both attitudes were equally genuine.

I said gently, "The thing is, Con, don't you see, he's old? I think he *minds* not being able to do things the way he used to. He's always been—well, I've gathered he's a pretty dominating type, and now his property and his money's the only kind of power he's got left. That's why he won't commit himself; I don't think he realizes just how unfair he's being to younger people . . . to you, anyway. He just thinks—quite rightly—that it's his property, and he'll play Old Harry with it if he wants to. But he's made up his mind now. He must have, since he's sent for Mr. Isaacs."

I could see Con's cigarette smouldering unheeded between his fingers. He hadn't stirred. I got the impression that only the essentials of what I'd been saying had got through.

He said painfully, as if the readjustment of ideas was somehow a physical effort, "If he's made a decision, it's happened since you got here . . . or rather, since he knew you were coming back. He went to the telephone soon after Lisa broke the news to him. I remember her telling me so. It must have been to get hold of Isaacs." He lifted his head. "My God, but you must have got this the wrong way round! Why should he send for him now, *except to cut me out and include you in?*"

"He isn't doing that. Be sure of that. I tell you, he kept asking me, harping on it almost, if I thought it was fair for me to walk straight home after eight years and expect to take up as I left off. That was almost the very phrase he used. Yes, he asked flat out if I thought I ought to be allowed to walk straight home and scoop Whitescar from under your nose, after all the work you'd put into it."

"Did he, by God?" A long breath, then he laughed, a sharp exultant crack of sound. "And what did you say?"

"Well, I thought it would be less trouble if I just said no. I may say he seemed surprised."

"And well he might! Annabel would never have parted with a penny piece to me, and what's more, she'd have seen that he didn't, either!"

"Well," I said, "she could have learned sense in eight years, couldn't she? Found out what really mattered most?"

"You call that sense? Letting her rights go, for want of a fight?"

"'Rights?' Annabel's? What about Mr. Winslow's? Hasn't he as much 'right' to leave his own property any way he pleases?"

"No."

"Oh? Well, I'm not breaking any lances with you over Annabel. You've staked a claim of your own, and I won't argue with that, either. In any case, it looks very much as if you're going to get what you want."

"Do you know something?" said Con slowly. "You're a very much nicer person than Annabel ever was."

"Good heavens, why on earth? Because I encouraged Grandfather to give you the poor girl's property?"

"No. Because I honestly believe you want me to have it. And not just for the 'cut' you'll stand to get, either."

"Don't you believe it. I'm as mercenary as hell," I said cheerfully.

He ignored that. "You said she 'might have learned sense in eight years,' and found out what really mattered. What really does—to you?"

I knew he couldn't see my face, but all the same, I looked away. I said shortly, "I'm a woman. That should answer it."

Through the ensuing silence I heard a horse's steady cropping, now quite close at hand. At the bottom of the pasture the river glimmered. Something drifted across like a shadow, shimmering at the edges, shapeless and quiet as a ghost. The yearling, moving up nearer, beside his mother.

I had just had time to realize how Con could have interpreted my last remark, when he spoke again, mercifully ignoring it, and coming sharply back to the matter in hand.

"And there really was nothing more about Julie?"

"Nothing." I dropped my cigarette, and trod it out. "Well, there it is. I think it's true. For one thing, he told me not to tell you anything about it."

I caught the gleam of a grin. "Did he now?"

I said tartly, "And don't just accept it as if you expected me to let him down automatically. I wouldn't have told you if—if I hadn't wanted to ask you to change our . . . plans."

He didn't follow this up. He seemed to have a truly remarkable power of only attending to what he wanted to. He was saying thoughtfully, "I can't quite understand it, if it's true. Ironic, isn't it, how our little conspiracy has turned out? I find you, import you into Whitescar at great trouble and some risk, expose myself and my ambitions to your uneasy female conscience . . . and all for nothing. He'd have left it to me all along." His cigarette went fizzing down into the damp grass. "Funny, you'd have expected it to act the other way. I mean, it seems absurd to have kept you in his will all these years, in spite of me, only to cut you out when you actually do turn up. I—well, I don't get it. I wish I understood."

"I think I do. I think—how shall I put it?—he's been keeping a sort of dream alive all these years, almost in spite of what he suspected to be the truth. You've all insisted that Annabel was dead, and, being who he is, and also because he must know you wanted Whitescar, he simply got stubborn about it. He's hung on to his dream and his belief out of sheer obstinacy, even though probably in his heart he's known it wasn't true . . . and perhaps, partly, to keep some sort of hold over you, too. Yes, I think that might have come into it. . . ." I paused. "Well, now I've come back; he finds he was right all along. But also, mark you, he finds himself facing the *reality* of the dream that he's been using as a threat to stop you getting too sure of yourself. He's kept telling you that he'll leave the place to Annabel, come what may. Well, now she's here, having pretty well demonstrated that she doesn't give much of a damn for Whitescar, disappearing for eight years without a trace. You, on the other hand, have proved yourself the obvious legatee. So he's had to make his mind up in a hurry; and he's going to do, at last, what he knows he ought to have done all along."

"You may be right. It's illogical enough to be likely."

"What's more," I said, "there's one thing I'm pretty sure of."

"What's that?"

"I think you've been a residuary beneficiary all along. Maybe with Julie, maybe not. I think that, underneath it all, he's believed Annabel was dead. He's obstinate enough to have left her name as his heir, but it's my belief he's expected you to inherit any time these last few years. But my coming home has given him a jolt. He's realized he's got to do something quickly, and make it stick."

"You might be right. My God, you might be right."

"I don't see why not."

"If only we knew where Julie comes in."

"Yes, Julie's the unknown quantity. Did you hear when I told you he sent for her? He did invite her, as Lisa thought. He wrote to her. Did you know?"

"No." I heard the twist to his voice. "You see? You've been back here—twelve hours, is it? and, claim or no claim, he tells you more than he'd tell me in twelve months."

"Con, please. Don't tear yourself up so."

I spoke quite without thinking. Unexpectedly, he laughed, and his voice lightened. "All right, darling, what the hell. We'll wait and see, and pray you're right. And irony or no, I still say you're my lucky star!"

"I don't know about that. If I'd never come, your luck would have still been in. You'd have got what you wanted the way you've got everything else; just as you said, with your two hands." I half turned towards him. In spite of myself, my voice tightened. "Con . . . you still haven't heard what I came to say."

"What else? Oh lord, you're still upset, and now you feel it's all been for nothing. Is that it? Or are you beginning to worry in case I get what I want without you, and don't keep my side of the bargain? Relax, honey.

I'll keep it, never fear. You'll get your cut, just the same." I heard the smile in his voice. "I'd not trust you else, sweetie, you could do me too much damage."

"No, I'm not worried about that. I'd do you no harm. I only want to go. I told you, didn't I?"

"Go?"

"Yes. Cut right out. Leave. Straight away."

He said blankly, "You're—crazy!"

"No. It's obvious that I'm not needed any more, so—"

"Now look—"

"No, Con, listen to me, please! It's true that you *might* have got all this without my coming at all, or, on the other hand, my coming may have forced the decision on Grandfather. We weren't to know which way he'd decide. The game was worth playing, as far as it went. But now it isn't necessary. We've seen that. And since I'm not needed here any more, I really would rather go. No, please don't be angry; you know I'd never have let you down if I'd been needed, but I'm not. I—I want to go. Don't ask me to explain any more, I can't, you'd only laugh at me for—for scruples or something, and I couldn't take it, not tonight. Won't you just accept the fact—?"

"I'll accept nothing!" We were back where we had been, with enmity sharp and open between us. "If it's your conscience that's bothering you, for heaven's sake forget it! You've just found out that you're not robbing anyone after all—you're not even going to have to hand Annabel's share of Whitescar over to me! You came into this with your eyes wide open, and if this is the way you intend to react after one day, then I can only say it's turned out better for you than you deserve!" He paused, and added, more pleasantly, "Now relax, for pity's sake. You're hurting nobody, and the old man's as pleased as a dog with two tails to have you here."

"I know, but—"

"And how could you walk out now? Tell me that. What d'you think people—let alone Mr. Winslow—would say? What possible excuse could there be, short of the truth?"

"It's simple enough. I've only to go to Grandfather tonight and tell him that I came back to see him, but that on second thoughts I can see how silly it was of me to come . . . because of you, I mean. After all, Con, he can't expect me to find it easy to be with you again, can he? He'll accept that; he might even think I'm sulking because of his decision to leave Whitescar to you."

I waited a moment, but he didn't speak. I turned to face the gate, gripping the top bar hard with both hands. "Con, it's best, really it is. It'll work. The luck's running our way; today's proved it. We'll think up what to say to Grandfather, then I'll go, tomorrow. I can stay in Newcastle till Wednesday—it'd look queer if I didn't stay to meet Julie—and I can come for Grandfather's birthday. Then I'll go to London. I can always come back if—if he's ill or anything." My voice was going out of control again. I stopped and took a steadying little breath that caught somehow in my throat, and must have sounded like a sob. "You—you can't want me here, Con. Can't you see, if I go, it'll do you nothing but *good?* If I go straight away again, now, that'll clinch it as far as Grandfather's concerned, surely? He'd never leave me anything at all, not even money. You'd get the lot, you and Julie."

He had made a quick movement in the dark. His hand came down over mine in a kind of pounce, and gripped it hard against the bar. "Stop this!" He spoke sharply. "You're hysterical. Think, can't you? What the hell's the matter with you tonight? You know quite well this is nonsense. If you go now, what sort of questions d'you think will be asked? Then heaven help us both, and Lisa too."

"I don't see how they could find out—"

"Another thing. There's no possible excuse you could give for going now. You'd see that, if you'd behave like a reasonable human being instead of a hysterical girl."

"I told you—"

"Oh, don't be a fool." He sounded exasperated, and thoroughly angry. "When you came back here—you, Annabel, I mean—you must have known you'd have to face me. If, after twenty-four hours, you decide you can't 'take' me any more, what's Mr. Winslow going to think? He's no fool. He's going to assume that I've made myself objectionable—made another pass at you . . . raked up the past and upset you . . . something, anyway—and this time he mightn't be prepared to forgive me. No."

"Oh. Yes. Yes, I do see that. Well, we could think of something else—"

"I tell you, *no!* For one thing, we still don't know for certain about the terms of this will, or even if there *is* to be a new will. Even if you're right, do you think I want him cutting you right out, as he certainly would if you left tomorrow?"

I stared painfully at the shadow beside me. "What do you mean?"

"My dear little conscience-stricken nitwit, do you think I want to see him splitting his capital two ways instead of three? If you stay, I get your share as well as my own. If you go, I go halves, if I'm lucky, with Julie . . . I'm talking about money now. I need the money to run the place. It's as simple as that." His hand moved over mine, holding it hard down on the bar. "So, darling, you'll stay. You'll go on playing the sweet repentant prodigal. And you'll play it till you collect at least Annabel's rightful share of what money's going. Is that clear?"

"No."

"Girl dear, do I have to give it to you in a children's comic strip? I can't put it any clearer. And in any case, it doesn't matter. You'll do as I say."

"No."

Silence.

I said shakily, "I didn't mean I didn't understand. I just meant no."

For a moment I thought his stillness would explode into violent anger. I could feel it running through his wrist and hand into mine. Then the tension changed in quality. He was peering at me, as if he would pierce the dusk to read my face.

He said slowly, "You still haven't told me the reason for all this. Now, supposing you do. . . . Well? Something's scared you, and badly, hasn't it? No . . . not the horses; something important. . . . And I'd give a lot to know just what. . . ."

His voice had altered completely. The anger had vanished, and in its place was only a kind of curiosity; no, more than that; a kind of speculation.

Where his anger had failed to frighten me, it was absurd, now, suddenly, to be afraid. I said hurriedly, "Nothing's scared me. It's just . . . I told you, I've had a rather ghastly day . . . I'm sorry, I—oh, don't ask me any more questions, *please!* I—I've done quite a lot for you today. Do this for me. We *can* think of some way, I know, if you'll only help. . . ."

For the first time, I touched him of my own volition. I reached my free hand and laid it over his, where it held mine over the bar of the gate.

Then, suddenly, the moon was there, swimming up behind the treetops into a milky sky, and the shadows of the trees bored toward us, blue and hard as steel, across grass awash with silver.

I could see his face clearly, bent to mine. The expression of his eyes was hidden; the moonlight threw back a glint from their curved, brilliant surfaces, hiding everything but an impression of blackness behind. I was again sharply aware of that terrifying single-track concentration of his. The bright, blank eyes watched me.

Then he said, quite gently, "You mean this? You really want to give it up, and go?"

"Yes."

"Very well, my dear. Have it your own way."

I must have jumped. He smiled. I said, incredulously, "You mean, you'll help me? You'll let me go—give it up, and you'll just wait and see . . . fair means?"

"If that's the way you want it." He paused, and added, very kindly, "We'll go straight in now, and tell your grandfather that you're not Annabel at all. We'll tell him that you're Mary Grey of Montreal, an enterprising tramp on the make, who wanted a peaceful niche in life in the Old Country, and a spot of assured income. We'll tell him that the three of us, Lisa, myself and you—all of whom he trusts—have plotted this thing against him, and that we've been laughing at him all day. I don't know what passed between you in his bedroom this afternoon, but I imagine that he might be quite sensitive about it, don't you? . . . Yes, I thought so. And when we've assured him, at the end of this long, happy day, that Annabel's as dead as mutton for all we know, and has been this last five years. . . . Do you see?"

The horses moved nearer, cropping the long grass. Through the hanging trees the river glittered in the growing moonlight. Across it a heron lumbered up on to its wings, and flapped ponderously downriver.

Eventually I said, "Yes. I see."

"I thought you would."

"I should never have started it."

"But you did. With your eyes open, sweetie."

"It would kill him, wouldn't it? Whatever sort of scene . . . I mean, if we told him, now?"

"Almost certainly. Any shock, any sudden strong emotional reaction, such as anger, or fear. . . . Oh yes, I think you can be sure it would kill him. And we don't want him dead—yet—do we?"

"Con!"

He laughed. "Don't worry, sweetheart, that's not the plan at all. I only said it to wake you up to the, er, realities of the situation."

"To frighten me, you mean?"

"If you like. If I want something badly enough, you know, I get it. I don't count small change."

I said, before I thought, "I know that. Don't think I haven't grasped the fact that you once tried to murder Annabel."

A long, breathless pause. Then he straightened up from the gate. "Well, well. You *have* put two and two together and made five, haven't you? Well, go on believing that; it'll keep you in line. . . . That's settled, then. We carry on as planned, and you, my lovely, will do as you're told. Won't you?"

"I suppose so."

His hand was still over mine. The other hand came up under my chin, and lifted my face to the moonlight. He was still smiling. He looked like every schoolgirl's dream of romance come true.

I moved my head away. "Don't, Con. Let me go."

He took no notice. "Don't hold this against me, honey, will you? I've said some pretty hard things to you, but—well, you know as well as I do what's at stake, and it seemed the only way. I'm not worrying really that you'll let me down when it comes to the push. . . . This was bound to happen; I was expecting it. It's reaction, that's all. It's a highly emotional set-up, and you've taken more than enough for one day. So we'll forget it, shall we? You'll feel fine in the morning." His hand touched my cheek, and he gave a little laugh. "You see how right I was to choose a nice girl? That conscience of yours does give me the slightest advantage in this mutual blackmail pact of ours, doesn't it?"

"All right. You've made your point. You're unscrupulous and I'm not. 'Vantage to you. Now let me go. I'm tired."

"Just a minute. Do you think the blackmail would run to just one kiss?"

"No. I told you this afternoon—"

"Please."

"Con, I've had enough drama for one day. I'm not going to gratify you by struggling in your arms, or whatever. Now let me go, and let's call the scene off."

He didn't. He pulled me nearer to him, saying, in a voice nicely calculated to turn any normal woman's bones to pulp, "Why do we waste our time quarrelling? Don't you know yet that I'm crazy about you? Just crazy?"

"I've gathered," I said drily, "that you've your very own way of showing it, as a rule."

His grip slackened. I thought, with satisfaction: that's spoiled your routine, anyway. But it hadn't quite thrown him out of gear. He gave a little laugh that managed to make what I had said an intimate joke between us, and drew me closer once more. His voice sank to a murmur, somewhere near my left ear. "Your hair looks like melted silver in this light. Sure, and I'm–"

"Oh, Con, don't!" How, short of cruelty, could one get through? I added, a little desperately, "Con, I'm tired–"

Then, even as Con himself had rescued me that afternoon, rescue came. The grey mare, who had been browsing her way, unnoticed, steadily nearer and nearer the gate, suddenly lifted her beautiful head, and thrust it between us, blowing gustily, and still chewing. A froth of grass stains went blubbering down the front of Con's white shirt.

He swore lamentably, and let me go.

The mare rubbed her head hard against me. Trying not to laugh, I ran a hand up to her forelock, and with the other hand held her gently by the muzzle, keeping her head away from Con. I said, shakily, "Don't be angry! She–she must have been jealous."

He didn't answer. He had taken a pace away from me, to pick up the tools and the coil of wire.

I said quickly, "Please don't be angry, Con. I'm sorry I've been a fool tonight, but I was upset."

He straightened, and turned. He wasn't looking angry. His face held no expression whatever, as he regarded me and the mare.

"So it appears. But not, apparently, by the horses."

"The–oh, well," I said, pushing the mare's head to one side, and coming away from the gate, "I told you it wasn't that, didn't I? And she's awfully gentle really, isn't she?"

He stood there, looking at me. After a moment or two he said in a curiously dry, abrupt tone, "Well, so long as you know just where you are."

"Oh yes," I said wearily, "I know just where I am."

I turned away and left him standing there in the lane, with the fencing wire in his hand.

The path to Forrest Hall looked as if nobody had been that way for a hundred years.

I don't remember consciously deciding to take it: I only wanted to get away from Con, and not to have to encounter Lisa for a little while longer. I found myself, with no clear idea why I had come this way, walking rapidly away from the house, along the river path that led towards the Hall.

The moss was silent underfoot. To my left, the sliding sparkle of the water lit the way. Big trees edged the path, lining the river bank. The track was ribbed with the shadows of their trunks, thrown slanting by the moon. Now last year's beech-mast crackled under my feet, and I thought I could smell lime blossom, until the path led me up to the high wall that girdled

Forrest, and there the neglected overgrowth crowded in, with its stronger scents of ivy and rotting wood and wild garlic and elder flowers.

Set deep in the tangle was the gate leading through into the Hall grounds. The elder bushes, and the ivy cascading over the wall, had almost hidden it from sight. It creaked as I pushed it, and opened crookedly on one hinge.

It was darker in the wood, but here and there, in some chance patch of moonlit sky framed by the branches, burned a star, sparkling blue-white, like frost. The air was still, and the vast trees kept quiet their tangled boughs. The river made all the sound there was.

You could easily have missed the summerhouse if you didn't know where it was. It stood a little back from the path, under the trees, and rhododendrons had run wild up the bank in front of it, until its entrance showed only as a gaping square of blackness behind the other shadows. I had gone straight by it when an owl, sweeping past me low down, like the shadow of a flying cloud, startled me into turning. Then I saw the hard edge of the moonlight on the tiles of the roof. A flight of shallow steps, blurred by moss, led up through the bushes.

I paused for a moment, looking at it. Then I left the path, and made my way up the steps, pushing aside the sharp leaves of the rhododendrons. They were as stiff as leather, and smelt bitter and narcotic, of autumn and black water.

The summerhouse was one of those once-charming "follies" built by some eighteenth-century Forrest with a taste for romance. It was a small, square pavilion, open in front, and pillared with slender Ionic columns of peeling plaster. The floor was marble, and round the three sides ran a broad seat. A heavy, rustic-seeming table still stood in the centre of the floor. I touched it with an exploratory finger. It felt dry, but thick with dust, and, I suspected, birds' droppings. In the sunlight of high summer, with the bushes trimmed back, and the view of the river, and cushions on the benches, the place would be charming. Now it was a home not even for ghosts. Pigeons would nest there, and perhaps a blackbird or two, and the owl in the roof. I left it and went down the steps to regain the path.

There I hesitated, half inclined, now, to go back. But the events of the day still pressed on me, and the woods were quiet and fresh. If they were not full of comfort, at least they offered solitude, and a vast indifference.

I would go on, I thought, a little further; as far as the house. The moonlight was strong, and even when the path turned (as it soon did) away from the river, I could see my way fairly easily.

Presently the timber thinned again, and the path shook itself free of the engulfing rhododendrons, to skirt a knoll where an enormous cedar climbed, layer upon layer, into the night sky. I came abruptly out of the cedar's shadow into a great open space of moonlight, and there at the other side of it, backed against the far wall of trees, was the house.

The clearing where I stood had been a formal garden, enclosed by artificial banks where azaleas and berberis grew in a wild tangle. Here and there, remains of formal planting could be seen, groups of bushes and small ornamental trees, their roots deep in the rough grass that covered lawns and flower beds alike. Sheep had grazed the turf down to a close, tufted mat, but underneath this, the formal patterning of path and lawn (traced by their moon-slanted shadows) showed clear. At the centre of the pattern stood a sundial, knee-deep in a riot of low-growing bushes. At the far side of the garden, a flight of steps mounted between urns and stone balustrading to the terrace of the house.

I paused beside the sundial. The scent of the small, frilled roses came up thick and sweet, and mixed with honeysuckle. The petals were wet, and the dew was heavy on the grass where I stood.

The shell of the house gaped. Behind it, the big trees made a horizon, against which the moon sketched in the shapes of the broken walls and windows. One end of the house, still roofed and chimneyed, thrust up looking almost intact, till you saw the forest through the window frames.

I crossed the damp, springy grass towards the terrace steps. Somewhere an owl hooted, and a moment later I saw it drift past the blind windows, to be lost in the woods beyond. I hesitated, then slowly climbed the steps. Perhaps it was here that I would find the ghosts. . . .

But they were not there. Nothing, not even a wisp of the past, stirred in the empty rooms. Peering in through the long windows, I made out the shapes of yesterday. . . . The drawing room—a section of charred panelling, and the wreck of a door, and what remained of a once lovely fireplace. The library, with shelves still ranked against the two standing walls, and a damaged chimneypiece mounted with what looked like a coat of arms. The long dining room, where a young ash sapling had thrust its way up between broken floor boards, and where ferns hung in the cracks of the wall. . . . On an upper landing, one tall window had its lancet frames intact, standing sharply against the moonlight. For a moment it seemed as if the leaded tracery was there still, then you could see how the ferns grew in the empty sockets, with a plant of what might in daylight show to be wild campanula, its leaves and tight buds as formal as a design in metal.

No, there was nothing here. I turned away. The weedy gravel made very little sound under my feet. I paused for a moment at the head of the terrace steps, looking back at the dead house. The Fall of the House of Forrest. Con's mocking words came back to me, cruelly, and, hard after them, other words, something once read and long forgotten. . . .

Time hath his revolutions, there must be a period and an end of all temporal things, finis rerum, an end of names and dignities, and whatsoever is terrene, and why not of De Vere? For where is Bohun? Where's Mowbray? Where's Mortimer? Nay, which is more and most of all, where is Plantagenet? they are intombed in the urnes and sepulchres of mortality . . .

Magnificent words; far too magnificent for this. This was no noble house ruined, no Bohun or Mowbray or Mortimer; only the home of a line of successful merchant adventurers, with a purchased coat of arms, that had never led a battle charge; but they had built something here of beauty and dignity, and cared for it, and now it had gone; and beauty and dignity had gone with it, from a world that was content to let such things run through its fingers like water.

There was a movement from the bushes at the edge of the clearing; the rustle of dead leaves underfoot, the sound of a heavy body pushing through the thicket of shrubs. There was no reason why I should have been frightened, but I jerked round to face it, my heart thudding, and my hand on the stone balustrade grown suddenly rigid. . . .

Only a ewe with a fat lamb nearly as big as herself, shoving her way between the azaleas. She saw me, and stopped dead, head up, with the moon reflecting back from her eyes and from the dew on her clipped fleece. The lamb gave a startled cry that seemed to echo back into the woods and hang there for ever, striking the sounding board of their emptiness. Then the two of them vanished like clumsy ghosts.

I found that I was shivering. I walked quickly down the steps and across the clearing. As I hurried under the layered blackness of the cedar, my foot struck a cone as solid as a clock weight, and sent it rolling among the azaleas. A roosting blackbird fled out of the bushes with a clatter of alarm notes that set every nerve jumping, and jangled on and on through the trees like a bell that has been pulled and left swinging.

It brought me up short for the second time. I was just at the entrance to the river path, where it plunged out of the moonlight into the wood.

I took half a step forward towards those shadows, then paused. I had had my hour of solitude; enough was enough. I had a home of a sort, and it was time I went back to it.

I turned aside to where the main drive entered the clearing, then hurried down its wide avenue, past the banked rhododendrons, past the ruined gatehouse and the ivy tree, till I reached the painted gate marked WHITESCAR, and the well-kept road beyond it.

CHAPTER SEVEN

Alang the Roman Wall,
Alang the Roman Wall,
The Roman ways in bygone days were terrible to recall . . .

Norman Turnbull: *Northumbrian Song.*

JULIE ARRIVED just before tea on a drowsy afternoon. Everywhere was the smell of hay, and the meadowsweet was frothing out along the ditches. The sound of the distant tractor was as much a part of the hot afternoon as the hum of the bees in the roses. It made the sound of the approaching car unnoticeable, till Lisa looked up from the table where she and I had been slicing and buttering scones for the men's tea, and said, "There's a car just stopped at the gate. It must be Julie." She bit at her lower lip. "I wonder who can be bringing her? She must have got Bill Fenwick to meet her train."

I set down my knife rather too carefully. She gave me one of her thoughtful, measuring looks. "I shouldn't worry. This'll be nothing, after the rest."

"I'm not worrying."

She regarded me a moment longer, then nodded, with that little close-lipped smile of hers. In my two-days' sojourn at Whitescar, Lisa seemed to have got over her odd fit of nerves. Indeed, she had taken my advice to her so much to heart that sometimes I had found myself wondering, but only momentarily, if she really had managed to persuade herself that I was Annabel. At any rate she seemed to have adopted me as genuine; it was a sort of protective colouration for herself.

"I'll go out and meet her," she said. "Are you coming?"

"I'll let you meet her first. Go ahead."

I followed her down the flagged passage to the back door, and waited there, just in the door's shadow, while she went out into the sunlight.

Julie was at the wheel of an open car, a battered relic almost as old as she was, carefully hand-enamelled a slightly smeared black, and incongruously decorated in dazzling chrome—at least, that was the impression one got—with gadgets of blatant newness and dubious function. Julie dragged ineffectually at the hand brake, allowing the car to slide to a stop at least four yards further on, then hurled herself out of the door without even troubling to switch off the engine.

"Lisa! What heaven! We've had the most *sweltering* run! Thank God to be here, and I can smell new scones. How's Grandfather? Has she come? My dear, you don't mind Donald, I hope? It's his car and he wouldn't let me drive because he says I'm the world's *ghastliest driver*, but he had to at the end because I wouldn't get out and open the gates. I asked him to stay—I hope you don't mind? He can have the old nursery and I'll do every *stroke* of the work myself. *Has* she come?"

She had on a white blouse, and a blue skirt belted tightly to a slim waist with a big leather belt the colour of new horse chestnuts. Their simplicity did nothing to disguise the fact that they were expensive. Her hair, which was fair and fine, shone in the sun almost as pale as cotton floss, and her eyes were grey-green, and very clear, like water. Her face was tanned golden, and her arms and legs, which were bare, showed the same smooth, amber tan. A heavy gold bracelet gave emphasis to one slim wrist.

She was holding Lisa's hands, and laughing. She hadn't kissed her, I noticed. The ecstasy of welcome was not personally for Lisa, but was so much a part of Julie's own personality that it sprang, as it were, unbidden. Fountains overflow. If people are near enough, the drops fall on them, sparkling.

She dropped Lisa's hands then, and turned, with a swirl of her blue skirt, towards the man whom I now noticed for the first time. He had been shutting the yard gate behind the car. Now, before responding to Julie's hail of "Donald! Come and meet Lisa!" he walked quietly across to where the car stood, with her chrome glittering in the sun as she shook to the vibrations of the engine. He switched the engine off, took out the key, put it carefully into his pocket, and then approached, with a slightly diffident air that was in startling contrast to Julie's ebullience.

I found later that Donald Seton was twenty-seven, but he looked older, having that rather solemn, withdrawn look that scholarship sometimes imposes on the natural reserve of the Scot. He had a long face, with high cheekbones, and eyes set well under indecisively marked brows. The eyes were of indeterminate hazel, which could look shallow or brilliant according to mood. They were, indeed, almost the only indication that Donald Seton ever varied his moods. His face seldom changed from its rather watchful solemnity, except to let in, like a door opening on to bright light, his rare and extremely attractive smile. He had fine, straight hair that refused discipline, but tumbled forward in a thick mouse-brown thatch that showed reddish lights in the sun. His clothes were ancient and deplorable, and had never, even in their fairly remote past, been "good." They reminded me somehow of his car, except that his person was not ornamented to a similar extent. He was the kind of man who would, one felt, have stigmatized even the most modest band of Fair Isle as "a bit gaudy." He looked clever, gentle, and about as mercurial as the Rock of Gibraltar. He made a most remarkable foil for Julie.

She was saying, with that same air of delighted improvisation, "Lisa, this is Donald. Donald Seton. Darling, this is Lisa Dermott; I told you, she's a kind of cousin, and she's the most *dreamy* cook, you've no idea! Lisa, he can stay, can't he? Where have you put *her*?"

"Well, of course he may," said Lisa, but looking faintly taken aback. "How do you do? Have you really driven Julie all the way up from London? You must both be tired, but you're just in time for tea. Now, Mr.—Seton, was it?—"

"Didn't Grandfather *tell* you?" cried Julie. "Well, really, and he's always jumping on me for being scatterbrained! I *told* him on the phone that Donald was bringing me! Why, it was the whole *point* of my coming now, instead of August, or almost, anyway. Donald's the most terrific big bug in Roman Remains, or whatever you call it, and he's come to work up at West Woodburn where there's a Roman camp—"

"Fort," said Mr. Seton.

"Fort, then, isn't it the same thing? Anyway," said Julie eagerly, "I thought if I came *now*, I'd be up here when he was, *and* be here for the birthday party Grandfather's talking about, and anyway, June's a heavenly month and it always rains in August. *Has* she come?"

For once, Lisa's not very expressive face showed as a battleground of emotions. I could see relief at Julie's gay insouciance about her reasons for coming to Whitescar and the birthday party; avid curiosity and speculation about Donald; apprehension over the coming meeting between Julie and myself; pure social embarrassment at having another visitor foisted on her without notice, and a swift, house-proud calculation that she would manage this, as she managed everything. Besides—I could see her assessing the smile Julie flung at Donald—it might be worth it.

"Of course we can put you up, easily," she said, warmly, for her. "No, no, it doesn't matter a bit, there's always room, and any friend of Julie's—"

"It's very good of you, but I really wouldn't dream of putting you to the trouble." Mr. Seton spoke with a quiet lack of emphasis that was as definite as a full stop. "I've explained to Julie that I'll have to stay near my work. I'll be camping up there on the site, when the students come, but for a night or two, at any rate, the hotel expects me."

"Ah, well," said Lisa, "if that's what you've arranged. But of course you'll stay and have tea?"

"Thank you very much. I should like to."

"That's *absurd!*" cried Julie. "Donald, I *told* you, it would be *much* nicer staying here. You don't have to do the polite and refuse just because Grandfather forgot to tell Lisa you were coming, for goodness' sake! As a matter of fact I may have forgotten to tell Grandfather, but then I was so excited about Annabel and then it was three minutes and it's a call box in my digs and you know Grandfather's always been as mean as stink about reversing the charges. Anyway, Donald, darling, you can't *possibly* camp at West Woodburn, it's the *last* place, and I've seen that site of yours; there are *cows*. And you've got to escape your dreary old Romans sometimes, so obviously you'll stay here. That's settled, then. Lisa I can't bear it another moment. Where *is* she?"

I hadn't moved from the shadows of the passage. But the fraction before Julie turned, Donald, looking past her shoulder, saw me standing there. I had been prepared for surprise, shock, even, in the recognition of everyone who had known Annabel before, but the startled amazement in Donald Seton's eyes jolted me, until I realized that, to him, I was a ghost of Julie. The look went, banished from his eyes immediately, but I wondered just what he had seen; a Julie grown older, thinner; not greyer, that would have been absurd, but somehow greyed? The eight years were dry in my throat, like dust.

Julie had seen me. I saw her eyes widen, then the same look spring in them.

I came out into the sunlight.

"*Annabel!*"

For a moment she stayed poised, as it seemed, between welcome and something else. The moment hung suspended for ever, like the wave before it breaks. I thought, Lisa was wrong, this is the worst thing yet: I can't bear it if she hates me, and God knows, she may be the one to have the right.

"Annabel *darling!*" said Julie, and dived straight into my arms and kissed me. The broken wave washed over me; the salt drops tingled and smarted in my eyes. She was laughing and hugging me and holding me away from her and talking, and the moment slid past with all the other moments, and was gone.

"Annabel, you *devil*, how *could* you, it's been such *hell*, and we were so unhappy. Oh, I could kill you for it, I really could. And I'm so thankful you're not dead because now I can *tell* you. That's the worst of people dying, they get away. . . . Oh lord, I'm not crying—these must be those tears of joy they always shed like *mad* in books, only I've never believed them. . . . Oh, it's terrific, it really is! You've come back!" She gave me a little shake. "Only *say* something, darling, for pity's sake, or I *will* think you're a ghost!"

I noticed that Donald had turned away, tactfully, to examine the side of the Dutch barn. Since this was made of corrugated iron, it could hardly be said to provide an absorbing study for an archaeologist; but he seemed to be finding it quite fascinating. Lisa had withdrawn a little behind Julie, but she was watching unashamedly.

I looked at Julie, feeling suddenly helpless. What was there to say, after all?

I cleared my throat, smiled uncertainly, and said the only thing that came into my head. "You—you've grown."

"I suppose I have," said Julie blankly.

Then we both laughed, the laughter perhaps a little high and overpitched. I could see Lisa looking at me with her mouth slightly open. It came to me suddenly that she was staggered and dismayed at the ineptitude with which I was playing this scene; all the more feeble since she had seen the way I dealt with Grandfather. As far as it was possible for me to do so at that moment, I felt amused. Of course there was nothing to say. Here, at least, Lisa was a bad psychologist. What did she expect me to do? Make a charmingly social occasion out of this? My part in the scene had been far more convincing than she knew.

The next second, uncannily, Julie was echoing my thought. "You know, isn't it silly? I've noticed it before, about meeting anyone one hasn't seen for a long time. You long and long for the moment, like mad, and then, when it comes, and you've got the first hullos said, there's nothing whatever to say. All that comes later, all the *where have you been and how did you get on* stuff. For the moment, it's quite enough to have you here. You do understand, don't you?"

"Of course. I'm just thanking heaven you do. I—I can't think of much in the way of conversation, myself." I smiled at her, and then at Donald, now gravely waiting on the outskirts of the conversation. "I'm still English enough to regard tea as a sort of remedy for any crisis. Shall we go in and have it? How do you do, Mr. Seton?"

"Oh lord, I'm sorry," said Julie, and hastily made the introduction. "Only for pity's sake call him Donald, everybody does, at least, everybody he *likes*, and if he doesn't like them, he never speaks to them at all, which comes to the same thing."

I laughed as I shook hands with him. "It sounds a marvellous way of getting along."

"It works," said Donald.

"Oh," said Julie, at my elbow, "Donald has his very own way of getting through life with the minimum of trouble to himself."

I glanced at her quickly. Nothing in Donald's expression showed me whether this was intended to have a sharp edge to it, or anything in Julie's, for that matter. She looked very lovely and gay, and she was laughing at him.

She thrust an arm into mine. "Where's Grandfather? Surely he's not up in the field in this weather? It's far too hot."

"He's lying down. He does every afternoon now."

"*Does* he? I mean, does he *have* to?"

Lisa had gathered Donald up, so to speak, and, with the usual polite murmur about washing his hands before tea, was shepherding him ahead of us towards the house.

I said, "It's only a precaution. He has to be careful. He might be risking another stroke if he did anything too energetic, or had any sort of an upset. So gently with him, Julie. I think my coming back has been a bit of a strain, but he's taken it remarkably well."

"And Con?" The sideways glance was disconcertingly shrewd.

I said lightly, "He's taken it very well, too." I wondered, by no means for the first time, how much the eleven-year-old Julie had known about her cousin's disappearance. "You'll see him later. I imagine he'll take his tea up in the field with the men."

"Are you going to take it up? I'll help if you like, or we can make Donald come and carry everything—you don't exactly look as if you ought to be hiking loads around in this heat, if I may say so. What on earth have you been doing to yourself, you look so thin, and your figure used to be heaven, at least *I* thought so, which might mean anything, because when I was eleven my ideal was the Angel Gabriel and they're not supposed to have figures anyway, are they?"

"Julie! At least you didn't piffle on at that rate when you were eleven, or if you did, I don't remember it! Where on earth did you learn?"

Julie laughed. "Donald."

"That I don't believe."

"Well, he never speaks at all unless it's necessary, so I have to do enough for two on one person's wits. Result, half my talk is piffle, whereas Donald's silence is a hundred per cent solid worth. Or would it be two hundred per cent? I never know."

"I see."

"And there was you."

"I?"

"Yes. Nobody could piffle quite so well. The stories you used to make up. I can still remember them, and the funny thing is, a lot of them seemed somehow more real than you, or at any rate they seemed the realest part of you."

"Perhaps they were."

She gave me a swift look as we went into the house, and squeezed my arm. "When you look like that you break my heart."

"I don't see why."

"You look unhappy, that's why. Whenever you're not actually smiling. It's just a look you have. It's not like you . . . I mean, you weren't like that before."

"I meant, I don't see why you should worry over the way I feel."

"Don't you?"

"No. Why should you care what happened to me? I lighted out regardless, didn't I? And now I come back, like a ghost to trouble sleep. Why should you care?"

The grey-green eyes were open and candid as a child's. "Because I love you, of course," said Julie, quite simply.

The passage was dim after the glare of the sun. I was glad of this. In a moment I said, lightly, "Better than the Angel Gabriel?"

She laughed. "Oh, he stopped being top hit years ago. Much better."

In a way, Julie's homecoming was as exacting as my own.

Mrs. Bates was, inevitably, lying in wait in the kitchen: "And very nice it is to see you, Julie, and very smart you're looking, quite London, I'm sure. A real shame I call it, the way they make you work at the B.B.C.—not a chance to come up and see your poor Granda, *not* to mention others as I could name what would have liked a sight of you any time this past year. And was that your young man that went through with Miss Dermott? 'Not official?' And what does that mean, may I ask?"

Then there was Con, who came down unexpectedly from the hayfield, ostensibly impatient to welcome Julie, but curious, I knew, to see who had driven her down.

It was amusing to watch the meeting between him and Donald. We were quietly settled, waiting for Mrs. Bates and the tea cart, when Con walked in. He had presumably conformed by washing his hands, but he was still in his working clothes—old breeches, and a white shirt, short-sleeved and open at the neck. He brought with him, into the rather charmingly old-fashioned room, the smell of sunshine and hay, and—it must be confessed—a faint tang of horses and outdoor, sunbaked sweat. He looked magnificent.

He greeted Donald with none of the curiosity that I knew he was feeling. If he had been wondering about Julie's new escort as a potential threat to his own position, the worry, I could see, was dispelled as soon as he entered the room, and saw the unobtrusive figure sitting quietly in the old-fashioned chintz-covered chair by the fireplace. I could also see, quite well, that he was pleased—as Donald rose to greet him—to find himself the taller of the two by at least three inches. The contrast between the two men was certainly remarkable, and I saw an odd expression in Julie's eyes as she watched them. Lisa's face, for once, was much more transparent; one almost expected to hear from her the proud, contented clucking with which the mother hen regards the swan that she has just personally hatched. The only person in the room who seemed unconscious of Con's overwhelming physical splendour was Donald. He greeted the other man serenely, and then turned back to resume his conversation with me.

Grandfather came in then, followed immediately by Mrs. Bates with the tea. The old man was using a stick, which I hadn't seen him do before, and I thought he looked more finely drawn than usual, with a waxy tinge to the skin.

"Grandfather, it's lovely to see you!" Julie, as she rose to greet him, gave him a fond, anxious look. "How are you?"

"Hm. You've controlled your anxiety remarkably well, haven't you? How long is it since you were here? Twelve months?"

"Only ten," said Julie. "Grandfather, this is Donald Seton. He's a London friend of mine who drove me up, such luck, and he's going to be up here all summer, working at West Woodburn."

"How d'ye do? Good of you to bring the child. Glad you could stay to tea. Working at West Woodburn, eh? What sort of work?"

As Donald answered, I noticed that Con, ostensibly talking to Julie, was listening carefully. Mrs. Bates, lingering beside Lisa, hadn't taken her eyes off Donald.

"Thank you, Mrs. Bates," said Lisa, pouring tea. "That's everything, I think . . . Annabel, I wonder if you'd help hand the cups?"

"Let me, please," said Donald quickly, getting to his feet. Con slanted a lazy look up at him, and stayed where he was.

Lisa—with great restraint—poured tea for Julie and Grandfather before she attended to Con, but when she did come to Con's cup, I noticed that she not only put sugar in, but even stirred it, before giving it to Donald to hand to him. Donald carried it across with no change of expression, and Con took it without even looking away from Julie, who was telling some story or other which involved a lot of laughter.

Mrs. Bates had made no move to go, but busied herself rather ostentatiously, handing scones. The little black eyes had never left Donald.

"London, eh?" This came as soon as he left his chair, and was detached, so to speak, from Grandfather's orbit. "So you've come up north for the summer, from what I hear?"

"Yes."

"And what d'you think of the North?" This in the tone of a champion throwing down a rather well-worn glove. "I suppose you Londoners think we've not even got electric light in these parts yet?"

"Haven't you?" said Donald, startled into a vague glance at the ceiling.

I said quickly, "Mrs. Bates regards all Londoners as ignorant southerners who think the Arctic Circle begins at Leeds, or something."

"One wonders," put in Julie from the sofa, "if they mayn't be right, sometimes. Not this year, it's been heaven *everywhere*."

"Even here?" said Grandfather, rather drily.

I saw a glance pass, like a spark across points, between Con and Lisa I said quickly, "Betsy, dear, Mr. Seton isn't a southerner, really; he's from Scotland."

"Oh?" She appeared only slightly mollified. "I've never been up in them parts. But you *live* in London, like?"

"Yes, I've got rooms there. But I usually spend the summer somewhere out on a—well, in the country. This year I'm at West Woodburn."

"For the whole summer?" I hoped the calculating glance that Mrs. Bates shot at Julie wasn't as obvious to him as it was to me. But she underlined it. "How long are *you* staying, Julie?"

"Mm?" Julie had been laughing at some remark of Con's. "Who, me? As long as I can. I've got three weeks."

"Mrs. Bates," said Lisa, "there's the telephone, I think. Do you mind? . . . I'm sorry, Mr. Seton, but she's been a member of the family for so long, and of course she's known Julie since she was very small . . . I think she puts all Julie's friends into the same age group."

"And that," said Julie cheerfully, "stays at about thirteen plus. Donald doesn't mind, do you, darling?"

"Not in the least." Mr. Seton, who had, during the cross-examination, been handing sandwiches and scones round with unruffled good humour, now sat down, and took one himself. Somehow, I noticed, the stand of sandwiches and cakes had finished up in a position midway between his chair and mine, and within easy reach of both. No mean strategist, I thought, watching him finish his sandwich, and quietly take another. They were very good; I had made them myself.

"Now," said Grandfather, who, being a Winslow male, obviously thought it was time he was back in the centre of the stage, "about this Roman camp at West Woodburn. . . ."

"Fort, actually," said Donald.

"Fort, then. Habitancium, isn't that the Roman name for it?"

"Habitancum." Donald took another sandwich in an absent sort of way, while managing to keep a keenly interested gaze fixed on his questioner. "That's the name on the various inscriptions that have been uncovered. There are no other references, and the place is named solely from the inscriptions, so, in fact," that sudden, charming smile, "your guess is as good as mine, sir."

"Oh, Ah. Well, what I want to know is this—"

But Mrs. Bates, laden with more scones, and big with news, re-entered the room briskly.

"The way things gets around in these parts is like magic, it is that. Here's Julie only been at home five minutes before her young man's ringing her up on the phone. He's waiting." She slapped the plate of scones down on the tea cart, and stared pointedly at Julie.

The latter looked blank for a moment, then I saw the faintest tinge of pink slide up under her skin. "My—young man?"

"Aye," said Mrs. Bates a little sourly. "Young Bill Fenwick from Nether Shields. Saw you pass, he says, when they was working up near the road."

"Young Fenwick?" said Grandfather. "Nether Shields? What's this? What's this?"

"I've no idea." Julie spoke airily, setting down her cup. "Did he say it was for me?"

"He did, and well you know it. Never talked about anyone else since last time you were here, and if you ask me—"

"Oh, Mrs. Bates, *please!*" Julie, scarlet now, almost ran out of the drawing room. Mrs. Bates gave a ferocious nod that was aimed somewhere between Grandfather and Donald. "He's a nice lad, Bill Fenwick is, but he's not for the likes of her, and *that's* the truth and no lie!"

"Mrs. Bates, you really mustn't—" began Lisa.

"I speak as I find," said that lady tartly.

"Hm," said Grandfather. "Pity you find such a lot. That'll do, now, Betsy. Go away."

"I'm going. Enjoy your teas, now, I made those scones meself. You'll not get the likes of *them* in London," with a nod at Donald, "*nor* in Scotland, neither, let me tell you. Now, did I see that cat come in or did I not?"

"Cat?" said Lisa. "Tommy? Oh no, surely not, he's never allowed in here."

"I thought I seed him run past when I opened the door."

"Nonsense, Betsy, you're imagining things." Grandfather was poking about testily under the sofa with his stick. "There's no cat in here. Don't make excuses, now, just go away, do. The scones are excellent. Perhaps you'll get Julie to bring the hot water in, when she's finished her telephone call?"

"All right," said Mrs. Bates, unoffended. "There's nobody can say I can't take a hint as well as anyone." But, pausing at the door, she fired her last shot. "Mr. Forrest, too, did I tell you? He's back already. Didn't expect *him* till Friday, but he's flown. Maybe *he'll* be on the phone soon." And, with a chuckle, she disappeared.

There was a pause.

"Ah, well," said Con, reaching out a lazy hand, "the scones are worth it."

"Hm," said Grandfather, "she's all right. Trust Betsy with my last half-penny, and that's a thing you can't say of many, nowadays. Now, Seton, where were we?"

"Habitancum," said Con, "just about to start digging."

"Ah, yes. Well, what are you going to find? Tell me that? If there's anything worth finding round here, I wish you digging Johnnies would find it at Whitescar. No likelihood of *that*, I suppose?"

I saw a sudden look of surprise flicker over Donald's face, to be followed by what looked like rather furtive embarrassment. Grandfather, drinking tea, hadn't noticed, but Con had. I saw his eyes narrow momentarily in a speculative look. Then I saw what was hidden from anyone else in the room. Donald's hand, with a portion of ham sandwich, had been hanging down over the arm of his chair while he talked. The skirts of his armchair almost touched the floor. From under the edge of this crept a stealthy, black and white paw, which once again patted the edge of the ham sandwich.

"There's nothing marked hereabouts on any existing map," said Donald, now serenely ignoring this phenomenon, "but that's not to say there *was* nothing here, of course. If you start turning up Roman coins with the plough, sir, I hope you'll send straight for me." As he spoke, he had returned the sandwich to the plate, and then his hand went, oh, so idly, over the arm of the chair, holding a substantial portion broken off. The paw flashed out and took it, not too gently. Tommy, it appeared, had had to learn to snatch what bits he got.

"And how long are you to be here?"

"Possibly until August, on this particular job."

"I doubt," said Con with a grin, "if we'll be doing much ploughing before you go, then."

"No?" said Donald, adding, apologetically, "I'm afraid I'm very ignorant. Your, er, Mrs. Bates was perhaps not so far out in her judgment of Londoners."

"Well," said Grandfather, "if you can tell wheat and barley apart, which I've no doubt you can, then you'll be one up on me and Connor—I wouldn't know a Roman inscription from a whisky advertisement, and neither would he."

Con's protest, and my "Are you sure?" came simultaneously, and everyone laughed. Into the laughter came Julie, so blandly unconcerned, and so fussily careful of the hot-water jug she was carrying, that the attention of everyone in the room switched straight to her with an almost audible click. It was all Con could do, I knew, not to ask her outright what Bill Fenwick had had to say.

"Julie?" Old Mr. Winslow had no such inhibitions. "What did the boy want?"

"Oh, nothing much," said Julie airily, "just how was I, and how long was I here for, and—and all that."

"Hm. Well, now, let's have a look at you, child. Come and sit by me. Now, about this job of yours. . . ."

Conversation began to flow again, Con and Lisa both listening with some interest to Julie's account of her first year's work at Broadcasting House. Beside me, the skirts of Donald's chair began to shake in a frustrated fashion. I said gently, "Won't you have another sandwich, Mr. Seton? These are crab. They—er, they go down rather well."

I saw the glimmer in his eyes as he took one. Half a minute later I saw the paw field a piece, very smartly, and, in a matter of three-quarters of a second, come out for more. Tommy, flown with good living, was getting reckless.

"You're not eating anything," said Lisa to me. "Have another sandwich. There's one left—"

Even as she turned to look, the paw shot out, and the last of the crab sandwiches vanished, whole, from the plate on the bottom tier of the cart.

"I'm so sorry," said Donald, blandly, to me. "I took it myself. Have a macaroon."

CHAPTER EIGHT

"O wherefore should I tell my grief,
Since lax I canna find?
I'm stown frae a' my kin and friends,
And my love I left behind."

Ballad: *Baby Livingston.*

JULIE AND I went out together that evening. Lisa's eyes followed us to the door, but she said nothing. Donald, not to be moved from his decision, had driven off to West Woodburn soon after tea. Grandfather, whom the heat was tiring, I thought, more than he would admit, had gone early to bed. Con had not come in again. No doubt he would come back at dusk for a late supper. The sound of the tractor wound on and on through the soft evening into the dusk.

Though it would have seemed the natural pilgrimage to take her to see the mare, I had had enough of the lane. We went the other way, through the garden towards the wicket gate and the river path that led towards West Lodge. In the half-light the rank borders looked and smelled heavy with flowers. The swifts were out, and flying high. Their screaming was thin and ecstatic, and exciting, like all the sounds that one feels one is not meant to hear: the singing of the grey seal and the squeak of a bat and the moaning of shearwaters under the ground at night on the wild sea's edge.

Now that we were alone together there still seemed curiously little to say. She had told the truth when she said that the major things of life had no need to be talked over. I supposed that for her the return of the idolized cousin from the dead was one of these. Never by word or look had she betrayed any consciousness that my advent might make the least difference to her future. It might not even have occurred to her . . . but it soon would; it must. If it didn't occur to her, it might occur to Donald.

We had been filling up the eight years' gap—I with completely truthful reminiscences of my life in Canada, and Julie with a lively and (it is to be hoped) libelous account of the year she had spent in the Drama Department at Broadcasting House.

". . . no, *honestly*, Annabel, it's gospel truth!"

"I don't believe it. It sounds as if you wouldn't even know what 'gospel' means."

" 'Good tidings.' "

"Heavens!"

"I thought that'd shake you," said Julie complacently.

"I suppose you got that from Donald too?"

" 'All good things–?' I expect so." Her voice had abruptly lost its sparkle.

I looked at her. "He's very nice," I said, tentatively.

"Yes, I know." She spoke without enthusiasm. She had picked a dead dry stalk of last year's hedge-parsley, and switched it idly through the buttercups that lined the river path where we walked.

"You mustn't mind Mrs. Bates, Julie. Marrying and burying are meat and drink to her."

"I know. I don't mind. I suppose I did let her jump to conclusions, rather."

"Here's the boundary. Shall we go on?"

"No. Let's find somewhere to sit."

"The stile will do. It's quite dry."

We climbed the two steps of the stile and sat side by side on the broad cross-bar, facing away from the house. It was another quiet evening, and the trees that edged the meadows were still in the dusky air. The path had left the river some way to our right; along it, here, the willows streamed untrimmed, their long hair trailing in the water.

I said, "You know, I'm afraid I jumped to conclusions about Donald. I was hoping they were correct."

"Were you?"

I laughed. "I fell for your Donald, from a great height."

Her face came alight for a moment. "One does. That's how it happened, with me. He's such a–a poppet. Even when I'm a bit foul to him, like today, he's just the same. He's–oh, he's so *safe*. . . !" She finished on a note that sounded more despondent than anything else, "And I do adore him, I do, really."

"Then what's wrong?"

"I don't know."

I waited.

She extended a sandalled foot, and regarded it. "It's true; I do want to marry him. And most times I want nothing better than to marry him *soon*. And then, sometimes, suddenly . . ." A little pause. "He hasn't asked me, actually."

I smiled. "Well, you've got three weeks."

"Yes." She dimpled, then sighed. "Oh, Annabel, it's all such *hell*, isn't it? If only one could *tell!* Like *that*, the way they do in books, but when it comes to the real thing it's actually quite *different*. I mean–"

"I wouldn't have thought you need worry quite so hard. You've loads of time, after all. You're only nineteen."

"I know." Another sigh, and a despondent silence.

I said, after a minute, "Would you rather talk about something else? You don't need to tell me anything you don't want to."

"Oh, but I do. In a way it was one of the things I was so longing to see you again for. I thought you'd know, you see."

"My dear," I said helplessly.

"Oh, I know you don't know him yet. But when you do—"

"That wasn't what I meant. I meant why the blazes should you imagine I could be of any help to you? I—I made a pretty fair mess of my own life, you know."

I half expected the routine and automatic response of kindness and reassurance, but it didn't come. She said immediately, "That's why. It isn't the people who've had things their own way who—well, who get wisdom. And they haven't the time to think about what life does to other people, either. But if you've been hurt yourself, you can imagine it. You come alive to it. It's the only use I can ever see that pain has. All that stuff about welcoming suffering because it lifts up the soul is rot. People ought to avoid pain if they can, like disease . . . but if they have to stand it, its best use might be that it makes them kinder. Being kind's the main thing, isn't it?"

"Julie, I wouldn't know. I've never got these things straight with myself yet. And on a rainy day I find I believe quite different things from on a fine one. But you might be right. Being cruel's the worst thing, after all, so kindness might be the best. When you come to think about it, it covers nearly everything, doesn't it? One's whole duty to one's neighbour."

"And the other whole duty?"

"My dear, I don't even pretend to know what that duty is. My duty to my neighbour will have to do. Maybe it'll count."

She had reached out an idle hand to the bush beside her, and broken off a small spray of hawthorn blossom, not yet dead. The milky heads hung bunched; I could smell their thick, sleepy scent. She twisted the stem between her fingers, so that the flowerheads swung out and whirled like a tiny roundabout. She seemed all at once very young and uncertain as she hesitated, apparently on the brink of some confidence.

I spoke almost nervously. "Julie."

"Mm?" She seemed absorbed in the twirling flowers.

"Julie—don't ask me about it now, but . . . well, just keep quiet for the moment about the state of affairs between you and Donald, will you? I mean, if people want to jump to conclusions, like Betsy, let them."

The flowers stopped twirling. She turned her head, her eyes wide and surprised. "Heavens, why?"

"I'm sorry. I can't explain. But if you've really made up your mind to have Donald when he asks you—and if you can't make him do so in the next three weeks, I wash my hands of you—well, quarrel with him all you like in private, but don't let other people see you having too many doubts."

"Honey!" To my relief she sounded amused. "Is this Aunt Agatha's advice to young girls, or do you really mean anyone special when you say 'other people'?"

I hesitated. I believe that at that moment I very nearly told Julie the whole story. But I said, merely, "You might say I meant Grandfather. I think this stroke he's had has frightened him, rather, and he's fretting a bit about the future—our future."

She sent me a glance that was all at once adult and wise. "*My* future, do you mean, now that you've come home?"

"Yes. You know what men of his generation are like, they think there's really nothing but marriage . . . I know you're still very young, but I—I know he'd like to think of your being settled with someone like Donald. I'm sure he liked him, too. So—don't rock the boat too much, Julie, at any rate not while you're here."

"The boat? Mr. Isaacs and all?" She laughed suddenly. "I *thought* there was something in the wind! Don't you start worrying about that, Annabel, good heavens, all *I* want is to get on with my own life in my own way, and I think—I *think*—that includes Donald!" She dropped a hand over mine where it lay on the bar. "But don't you ever go away again. Promise?"

I said nothing, but she took this for assent, for her hand squeezed mine softly, and then withdrew. She added, cheerfully now, "All right, I won't rock any boats. All the storms of my love-life shall be—passed? blown? raged? waged?—up at the Roman camp."

"Fort."

"Oh lord, yes. I *must* learn to be accurate about the more important things of life. Fort. Look, there's Mr. Forrest's horse, over there, like a shadow. He looks awfully quiet. Don't you love the way everyone shakes their heads over him and says 'He won't be easy to school'?"

"I do rather. But I expect it's true. Blondie's foals do have that reputation."

"Do they?"

"Didn't you know? And Grandfather tells me this one is by Everest."

"By Everest? Oh, I see, you mean that's the name of the father?"

"The sire, yes. Don't you remember him? He was a bit of a handful, too, like all the old 'Mountain' lot." I glanced at her, amused. It seemed that Con had been right; this was not Julie's *métier*. She had shown the same cheerful ignorance in the drawing room over tea, when the talk had turned on the affairs of Whitescar. Grandfather had noticed; I had seen him eyeing her; and Con had noticed, too. And now she had made it obvious that she realized my return would deprive her of her place here; she had also made it apparent that she didn't care. She wasn't only making things easy for me: I was sure it was true. For Julie, this place was a holiday, no more. I felt a real rush of relief, not only for my conscience' sake, but because Con could now bear no grudge against her. What sort of grudge, or what shape that grudge would take, I hadn't yet allowed myself to guess at.

She was holding the flowers close to her face, watching Rowan with the uncritical admiration of complete ignorance.

"He's lovely, isn't he?" she said dreamily. "Like something in a book.

And the field smells like heaven. Pegasus, in the Elysian fields. He ought to have a manger of chalcedony and a bridle of pearl."

"Have you the faintest idea what chalcedony is?"

"Not the faintest. It sounds wonderful. Have you? It ought to be like marble shot with fire and gold. What is it?"

"Something looking a bit like soap, the healthy kind. As big a let-down as jasper, anyway. The gates of Paradise are made of that, according to Revelation, but really it's the most—"

"Don't tell me! Let me keep my gates of jasper just as I've always seen them! Is this what the New World does to you? Have a heart, won't you? And admit that he *ought* to have a manger made of fire and gold and cedar wood and turquoises at *least!*"

"Oh, yes," I said. "I'll give him that."

The horse was grazing steadily along the hedge where a tall guelder-rose broke the yard-high barrier of hawthorn. His shoulders brushed the pale saucers of bloom, and, through the leaves, the growing moonlight touched him here and there, a dapple of light shifting over moving muscle; then a sudden liquid flash from the eye as he raised his head to stare.

I heard him blow a soft greeting through whickering nostrils. He seemed to eye us uncertainly for a moment, as if he might come forward, then he lowered his head again to the grass. "I thought he was coming," said Julie breathlessly. "They all used to, to you, didn't they? Will you help school him? Johnny Rudd says he'll be the very devil, he won't let anyone near him in the stable, and he's next to impossible to catch in the field."

"He sounds a useful sort of beast," I said drily.

She laughed. "What a way to speak of Pegasus! You can't deny he's a beauty."

"No, he's that all right. What colour is he in daylight?"

"Red chestnut, with a pale mane and tail. His name's Rowan. Aren't you going in to speak to him?"

"I am not. This isn't my night for charming wild stallions."

"It seems a dreadful pity that all the horses had to go. It must have been a dreadful wrench for Mr. Forrest—though I suppose it would only come as a sort of last straw, considering everything else that had happened."

"Yes."

There was a little pause. Then Julie said, with a curious soft abruptness, her eyes still on the horse, "You know, you don't have to pretend with me. I know all about it."

The dusky trees, the shapes of hawthorn, the ghost of the grazing horse, all seemed to blur together for a moment. I didn't speak.

"I—I just thought I'd let you know I knew," said Julie. "I've known all along. Have you . . . have you spoken to him yet?"

The confusion in my mind blurred again, swung into another shape. I said, "Have I—what do you mean? Spoken to whom?"

"Mr. Forrest, of course."

Silence again. I couldn't have spoken if I'd tried. Before I could grope for words, she looked at me again, fleetingly, sideways, and said, like a nice child who confesses to something that she may be punished for, "I'm sorry. But I did want to tell you that I knew all the time. I knew that you and Mr. Forrest were lovers."

I said, "Oh dear sweet *heaven*."

"I'm sorry." She repeated the words with a kind of desperation. "Perhaps I shouldn't have told you I knew. But I wanted you to know. In case it was difficult or—or anything. You see, I'm on your side. I always was."

"Julie—"

"I didn't spy on you, don't think that. But I saw you together sometimes, and people don't always notice a kid of eleven hanging about. I was always around, all that spring and summer, during the holidays and I knew you used to leave letters in the ivy tree at the old Hall gate. I thought it wonderfully romantic. But I can see now that it must have been pretty awful. For you, I mean. You were younger than I am now."

My hands were pressing down hard to either side of me on the bar of the stile. "Julie . . . you . . . we . . . I didn't . . ."

"Oh, I know there wouldn't ever be anything *wrong*. I mean, really wrong. . . ."

Let her talk, I thought, let her tell me just what she saw, what she knew. At worst she might only remember having drifted like a shadow round the edges of romance. Romance? Adam Forrest? *Con?* The two names burned in front of me, as if they had been branded in the bars of the stile. . . .

"You couldn't help it. One can't help who one falls in love with." Julie was offering this shabby cliché as if it were the panacea still sealed all glittering in its virgin polythene. "It's what one does about it that matters. That's what I meant when I said I knew you'd had a bad time; I mean, if one falls in love with a married man there *is* nothing to do, is there?" It seemed that, to Julie, falling in love was an act as definable and as little controlled by the will, as catching a disease in an epidemic. That there came a moment when the will deliberately sat back and franked the desire was as foreign to her as the knowledge that, had the will not retreated, desire would have turned aside and life, in the end, have gone as quietly on.

"One can only go away," said Julie. "It's all there is to do. I knew why you'd gone, and I thought it marvellous of you. Do you know, I used to cry about it?"

I said, in a very hard, dry voice, "You needn't have done that."

She gave a little laugh. "Oh, it wasn't all tragedy to me at that age. It was sad, yes, but beautiful too, like a fairy tale. I used to try and make up happy endings to myself in bed, but they could never really work, because they meant that she—his wife, I mean—would have to die. And even if she *was* awful, it's always cheating, in a story, to kill off the person who prevents the happy ending. And I suppose I did see it more as a story, in those days, than as something that was really happening to people I knew. Was it so very dreadful, that time?"

"Yes."

"I've sometimes wondered, since," said Julie, "if life isn't just a little too much for all of us. Sometimes one thinks . . . oh well, never mind. You don't mind my having told you? I rather wanted you to know I knew. That was all. We won't speak of it again if you like."

"It doesn't matter. It's over."

She looked almost shocked. "Over?"

"My God, Julie, what d'you expect? One can't tear a great hole in one's life pattern and expect the picture to be unspoiled till one chooses to come back and finish it. One can't fit straight back into the space one left. Nor does one want to. Of course it's over!"

"But I thought–"

I said, and I could hear myself how nerves had sharpened my voice, "Do you seriously think I'd have *dreamed* of coming back if I'd known he was still here?"

"*Didn't* you know?"

"Of course I didn't! I thought I'd made very sure he wasn't, or I'd never have come, except perhaps just a flying visit to see Grandfather again, and make things up with him. But as for coming here to stay . . . *No.*"

"But–" her voice sounded all at once as frankly disappointed as a child's –"but it's not the same now, is it? I mean, now that you *have* come, and he *is* here, and . . ." The sentence trailed off.

"You mean because Crystal Forrest's dead?" I said flatly.

I heard her give a little gasp. "Well . . . yes."

I laughed. "Poor Julie. Your happy ending at last. I'm sorry."

"Annabel–"

"Forget it, darling. Oblige me by forgetting it. And remind me one day to thank you for forgetting it as far as Con and the rest are concerned. I'd have rather hated them to know. Con has his own–theories–as to why I left."

Her voice was suddenly mature, and curious. "You dislike Con. Why?"

"Heaven knows. And 'dislike's' the wrong word. Say I distrust him. Julie . . ."

"Mm?"

"Just what, exactly, did you know about me and–about me and Adam?"

"Only what I told you. I knew you met, and I knew you wrote quite regularly, and put the notes in the hole in the ivy tree. And I think I knew that it–it was a hopeless passion–what are you laughing at?"

"I'm sorry. Your vocabulary. Go on, it was a hopeless passion . . ."

"All right," she said without rancour. "I suppose I do read all the wrong books. But *you're* taking this the wrong way. I believe you really don't care any more."

"No."

"Ah, well." It was a sigh almost of disappointment. "I'd hoped it would come right in the end. You see, everybody knew they were unhappy, him and his wife, I mean. You couldn't ever tell what *he* was thinking, but she didn't try very hard to pretend, did she? I mean, it got sort of painful when they were anywhere together in public. Even I noticed, though I was only a kid. It's true, isn't it?"

"Yes."

"But there wasn't ever any talk of their separating. Everybody used to say they ought to divorce, but that he wouldn't divorce her money."

"They would."

"Yes. And of course I thought it was so obvious that he would fall in love with you. Anybody would."

"Julie, my love, you and I ought to be fairly careful how we compliment one another on our looks in public."

She grinned. "True enough. All the same, between ourselves, you were pretty smashing at nineteen. Confess!"

She was laughing at me in the light of the rising moon. I looked at her appraisingly. "I'm beginning to think I must have been."

"You're nice, aren't you?" she said naïvely. "Well . . . I still can't help having the feeling that I oughtn't to talk to you about it, for fear of making you unhappy, but still . . . I've wondered since, money or no money, why he didn't divorce her. She wasn't an R.C., so it can't have been that. *Could* it have been the money, Annabel? I'm not being foul, but after all, he couldn't ever have kept Forrest going–"

"I doubt if he cares that much about Forrest." I realized as soon as I had spoken how oddly my reply was framed, but she didn't notice.

"Then why? Why did they stay together? Why was she so filthy to him, almost as if he'd done something dreadful? It wasn't you, because it was going on for years before that. Why?"

"How could I know? He–he never discussed it." Then, out of nowhere, came a guess like a certainty, "She had no child."

"I–see," said Julie, slowly. "And he . . . ?"

"Some men take life itself as a responsibility. Maybe that was it. Maybe he took her unhappiness as his. How could he leave her? You can't leave people who have nothing else."

"You know," she said, "you talk about it all as if it was sort of remote, just a story about someone else."

"That's what it feels like," I said. "Look, why don't we go in? Come along, you're yawning like a baby. You've had a long journey today, and you must be tired. There'll be plenty of time to talk. Is Donald coming down tomorrow?"

"I expect so."

"I'm looking forward to meeting him again. Tell me all about him tomorrow. I seem to have kept you on my affairs tonight, but we'll forget them, as from now, shall we?"

"If that's the way you want it."

"That's the way I want it."

"Okay." She yawned again, suddenly and unashamedly, like an animal or a child. "Oh lord, I *am* sleepy. No need to drink mandragora to sleep out the great gap of time my Donald is away." She giggled. "Funny how he simply will not fit into any romantic context."

"Maybe you're safer that way, considering the kind of thing you appear to read."

"Maybe. Oh Annabel, it *is* so good to have you here. Did I say?"

"Yes. Thank you, Julie. Sleep well."

"Oh, I shall. But this ghastly hush is *devastating* after London, and if that blasted owl starts up I shall shoot it, I swear I will, even if it *is* a mother with seven starving babies in the ivy tree."

"That sort of owl has three."

She unlatched the garden gate and pushed it open. "You always did know everything about everything."

"Oh no, Julie! You make me sound like some ghastly Nature Girl hob-nobbing with the owls, and charming wild horses, and flitting about the woods at night—" I stopped.

If Julie had noticed she made no sign. "Aren't you coming in?"

"Not yet. It's a lovely night, and I'm not tired. Nature Girl on the prowl. Good night."

"Good night," said Julie.

CHAPTER NINE

The wind doth blow to-day, my love,
And a few small drops of rain;
I never had but one true-love;
In cold grave she was lain.

Ballad: *The Unquiet Grave.*

IF YOU STOOD on the low piece of crumbling wall that enclosed the trunk, you could just reach your hand into the hole. I held on to the writhen stems of the ivy with one hand and felt above my head into the hollow left by some long-decayed and fallen bough.

I put my hand in slowly, nervously almost, as I might have done had I known that Julie's owl and seven mythical young were inside, and ready to defend it, or as I might have invaded a private drawer in someone's desk. The secret tryst; Ninus' tomb; the lovers' tree; what right had a ghost there, prying?

In any case there was nothing to pry into. Whatever secrets the ivy tree had held in the past, it was now only a tree, and the post box was an empty hole, the bottom cracked and split, its fissures filled with crumbling touchwood as dry as tinder. Some twigs and rotting straw seemed to indicate that a starling had once nested there. The ivy, brushing my face, smelt dark and bitter, like forgotten dusty things.

I climbed down from the wall and wiped my hands on my handkerchief.

Beside me, skirting the ruins of the gate-house, the neglected avenue curled away into the shadows. I turned my head to look where, in the strong moonlight beyond the blackness cast by the trees, the white gate glimmered. I could almost make out the neat black letters on the top bar: WHITESCAR. I made a half-movement in that direction, then checked myself. *If it be now, 'tis not to come.* Well, let it be now.

I put away my handkerchief, and walked quickly past the ruined gate-house, up the silent mosses of the drive, towards Forrest Hall.

The moon was fuller tonight, and it was later. The skeleton of the house stood up sharply, with the dramatic backcloth of trees cutting its lines and angles, and throwing into relief the tracery of the bare windows. One or two sheep grazed among the azaleas. The little tearing sounds they made, as they cropped the grass, sounded loud in the windless air.

I could smell the roses and honeysuckle that smothered the sundial. I went slowly down the moss-furred steps, and over the grass towards it. The dial was covered with a thick mat of leaves and tendrils. I picked one of the tiny chandeliers of the honeysuckle and held it to my face. The long stamens tickled, and the scent was thick and maddeningly sweet, like a dream of summer nights. I dropped it into the grass.

I sat down on the lowest step where the pediment jutted into the encroaching grass, and pushed aside the trailing honeysuckle with gentle hands, till the shaft of the sundial lay bare. The moonlight struck it slantingly, showing the faint shadows of carving under the soft rosettes of lichen.

I scratched a little of the moss away, and traced the letters with a slow, exploratory finger.

TIME IS. TIME WAS. . . .

Another line below it. No need to trace that out.

TIME IS PAST. . . .

It didn't need the startled swerve of a ewe ten yards away, or the rustle and patter of small hoofs retreating, to tell me that I had been right. He had come, as I had guessed he would.

My hands were pressed flat on the dry mosses. I could feel the blood in them jump and beat against the chill of the stone. I waited for a moment, without moving, crouched there on the step of the sundial, my hands hard against the stone.

Well, let it come. Get it over with. Learn just where you stand. *If it be not now, yet it will come.*

I turned slowly round, and, as stiffly as a puppet on strings, got to my feet.

He was standing not twenty yards away, at the edge of the wood. He was just a shadow under the trees, but it could be no one else. He had come, not by the drive, but up the path from the summerhouse.

I stood without moving, with the moon behind my shoulder, and my back to the sundial. I think that I had a hand on it still, as if for support, but oddly enough, the emotion that struck at me most vividly at the sight of him was that of relief. This was the worst thing that had happened, and I had had no time to be ready for it; but now it had come, and it would get over. Somehow, I would find the right things to say. . . .

It seemed a very long time before he moved. The moonlight fell strongly on him as he came forward, and even at that distance I could see that he was staring as if he had seen a ghost. His features were blanched and dramatized by the white slanting light, but even so it was apparent that some violent emotion had drained his face to a mask where the flesh seemed to have been planed from the strong-looking bones, leaving it a convention, as it were, of planes and angles, lights and shadows. The eyes looked very dark, and the brows made a bar of black across them. I could see the deeply incised lines down his cheeks, and the thin line of a mouth schooled to reserve or patience. But when his lips parted to speak, one saw all at once how thin the defences were. His voice sounded vulnerable, too, half hesitating. This was a man who was by no means sure of his reception. And why should he be? Why indeed?

He spoke at last, in a half-whisper that carried no expression. "Annabel?"

"Adam?" Even as I said it, I thought the name sounded exploratory, tentative, as if I'd never used it before.

He had stopped a yard or so away. There was a pause, painfully long. Then he said, "I came as soon as I knew."

"Did you expect to find me here?"

"I didn't know. I thought . . . I don't know what I thought. Does it matter? You came."

"Yes," I said, "I—I had to see you."

I found that I had braced myself for his response to this, but he made none. His voice was so flattened and expressionless that it sounded barely interested. "Why did you come home?"

"Grandfather's ill. He—he may not have long to live. I had to see him again."

"I see." Another pause. That flat, empty voice again. "You never told me you were coming."

He might have been talking to a stranger. Between lovers there are such situations, so highly charged that words are absurd; but then lovers have their own language. We had none. Adam Forrest's love was dead, and there was nothing to say.

I answered him in the same way. "I didn't know you were still here. I only heard it by chance, the other night, from something Grandfather said. I'd understood you lived permanently in Italy now. In fact, when I came back to England, I'd no idea that your—" I stopped, swallowed, and finished stupidly on a complete *non sequitur*, "I didn't even know that Forrest Hall had gone."

"You never did have much regard for logic, did you? What you started to say was that you didn't know that Crystal had died."

"I—"

"Wasn't it?"

"Yes. I—I hadn't heard. I'm sorry."

He acknowledged this with a slight movement of the head, and let it go. He was standing perhaps six feet away. The moonlight fell between us, slantingly, from behind my left shoulder. The angled shadows it cast made his expression difficult to read. They also, which was more important, made it possible for him to see me clearly. But he was watching me steadily, without moving, and the close unwavering regard was discomforting.

He said slowly, "Are you trying to tell me that if you had known—that I was here at Forrest, I mean, and free—you would not have come back?"

Behind me the edge of the sundial, rough with dried lichen, bit into my hands. Was this, after all, easier than I had imagined, or was it worse? His voice and face gave nothing away. There was nothing to indicate that he cared, any more than I did. Why should he? Eight years was a long time. I said, almost with relief, "Yes. Just that."

"I see." For the first time the steady gaze dropped, momentarily, then came back to me with a jerk. "But you came tonight to meet me?"

"I told you. I came, hoping you'd come along. I had to see you. After I found out last night that you were coming back from Italy, that you still lived here, I knew I—well, I couldn't just wait around and meet you in public."

"That was nice of you." The flat voice held no irony.

I looked away. Beyond the massed shadows of the forsaken garden, the house stood up, raw-edged and broken. "Your home," I said, not very evenly, ". . . I'm sorry about that, too, Adam. That sounds a bit inadequate, but what can one say? It's been a bad time all round, hasn't it? You must have been very unhappy."

For the first time his face changed. I saw the ghost of a smile. "You say that?"

I stirred. Easy? This was intolerable. Heaven knew I had dreaded the interview, and heaven knew I could hardly have expected to get through it more smoothly than this. I had expected questions, recriminations, anger even . . . anything but this calm, dead voice and steady stare that (since the moment when I had turned momentarily into the moonlight to glance up at the house) had narrowed sharply as if he were only just bringing me into focus.

I stood away from the sundial and began to rub my scored palms together.

"I must go." I spoke hurriedly, nervously, looking down at my hands. "It's late. I—I can't think that we have anything more to say. I—"

"Why did you go?"

The question came so suddenly that, although it was softly spoken, I looked up at him, startled. He was still watching me with that steady, unreadable stare. "You know," he said, "you can't simply walk out like this. I would have thought we had a very great deal to say. And I'd like to go right back to the beginning. Why did you go like that?"

"You know why I went!" I could hear how my voice shook, edged with nerves, but I couldn't control it. I tried to thrust him back again, off the dangerous ground. "Don't let's go back over it, please! I—I couldn't stand it! That's all over, you know that as well as I do. It was over eight years ago, and it—it's best forgotten. *Everything's* best forgotten . . ." I swallowed. "I've forgotten it, I truly have. It's as if it had happened to someone else. It—it doesn't seem to mean anything to me any more. People change, you know. In all that time, people change. You've changed yourself. Can't we . . . just *leave* it, Adam? I didn't come to see you tonight because I hoped . . . because I wanted—" I floundered desperately for words—"I knew you'd feel just the same as I do, now. I only came tonight so that we could—we could—"

"Agree that it was forgotten? I know, my dear." His voice was very gentle. There was no reason why I should have to bite my lips to keep the tears back, or why I should have to turn sharply aside and jerk a spray from the yellow rose, and be twisting it round and round in my fingers. This was nothing to me, after all. "You don't have to worry," he said. "I shan't torment you. There's someone else, isn't there?"

"No!" I hadn't meant to say it quite like that. I saw his brows lift a fraction.

"Or has been?"

I shook my head.

"In eight years?"

I looked down at the bruised rose in my fingers. "No. It's not that. It's only—"

"That people change. Yes. I understand. You've changed a good deal, Annabel."

I lifted my head. "Have I?"

His mouth twisted. "So it would seem. Tell me; do you—or perhaps I should say *did* you—intend to stay at Whitescar, now that you're back?"

At least here was a safe and easy path. I scuttled down it breathlessly, talking too fast. "I hadn't really made any firm plans. I told you I only came to see Grandfather. Until I got here, up North, I mean, I had no idea he was so frail. You knew he'd had a stroke? Actually, I'd decided to come back and see him before I knew of that. I hadn't been sure if he—if they'd want me back at Whitescar, but I wanted to see him if he'd let me. I didn't know what the situation would be, but he's been very kind." I hesitated. "They all have. I'm glad I came back. I'd like to stay till . . . as long as Grandfather's here. But afterwards . . ." I stopped.

"Afterwards?"

"I don't think I'll stay afterwards."

A pause. "And the place? Whitescar?"

"There'll be Con."

I was unwinding the split and twisted rose stem with great care. A thorn had drawn blood on my thumb. I stared unseeingly at the tiny black gout of blood that blobbed and split glossily over the flesh. I didn't know he had moved until his shadow slithered forward a pace, slantingly, and fell across the grass beside me.

"You'd leave Whitescar to Connor Winslow?"

I smiled. "I may have to."

"Don't beg the question. You know what I mean. If the place were yours, would you stay?"

"No."

"Has that decision anything to do with me?"

I swallowed. "You know it has."

Quite suddenly, his voice came alive, the way flesh does after frostbite. He said, "You came back because you thought I had gone. When you found I was still here, you decided to go again. You make things very clear, Annabel."

I said, as steadily as I could, "I try to. I'm sorry."

There was a pause. He spoke almost as if he were reasoning quietly with me about something that didn't matter very greatly. "You know, I've regretted everything I said and did that night, far more bitterly than you could have done. I doubt if I'll ever quite forgive myself. Not only for losing my head and saying all that I said to you that last time we met, but for ever having allowed things to . . . get to the stage they did. You were very young, after all; it was I who should have known better. The sort of life I led with Crystal was no excuse for—for losing my head over you, when I could do nothing but hurt you."

"Don't, please, there's no need—"

"Don't think I'm trying to excuse myself for the way I spoke and acted that last night. I'd just about come to the end—or so I thought; except that, of course, one never does." He took in his breath. "So I finally lost my head, and begged you—bullied you—to go away with me, away from Whitescar and Forrest, and to hell with everybody, including my wife. And you refused."

"What else could I do? Look, there's no need to go back over this. I've told you it's best forgotten. It should never even have started. We should have realized where it would take us."

"That's what you said then, that night, isn't it? True enough, of course, but as far as I was concerned, much too late. I remember that you even promised to keep out of my way." He gave a brief smile that was more like a grimace. "So then," he said, "I told you that, if you weren't prepared to do as I asked, I never wanted to see you again. Oh no," at my involuntary movement, "I suppose I didn't put it quite so crudely, but I dimly remember a good many wild and whirling words, to the effect that either you would have to leave the neighbourhood, or I would, and since I was tied to Forrest and to my wife . . ." He drew in his breath. "But heaven help me, Annabel, I never dreamed you'd go."

"It was better. You must see it was better."

"Perhaps. Though I wonder, looking back. No doubt, in the end, I'd have behaved like a reasonable mortal, and we could have found some . . . comfort. Fundamentally, I suppose, we're both decent human beings, and you, at least, kept your moral sense intact. Then, six years later . . ." He paused, and seemed to straighten his shoulders. "Well, there it is. You were young, and I behaved badly, and frightened and hurt you, and you went. But you're older now, Annabel. Surely you must understand a little more than you did then, about the kind of life I led with Crystal, and the reasons why I was driven to act the way I did?"

"I do, oh, I do. It isn't that. Please don't think I—I'm bearing a grudge or—or anything. This, the way I feel now, has nothing to do with what happened then, try and believe that." I added, quietly, "Whatever was said or done, it's over, eight years over. There was nothing to forgive . . . and now, let's pretend there was nothing to remember, either. Let it go, Adam. From now. It's better not to talk about it any more. Good night."

I turned quickly away from him, but his shadow moved again across the turf, this time with something like a pounce. His hand caught at my arm, and, almost before I realized what was happening, he had pulled me round to face him.

"Wait. Listen. No, I can't let you go like this. You've got to listen to me. It's only fair."

"I don't see that—"

"If you'd rather wait till you're less upset, I'll let you go now. But I've got to see you again."

I said breathlessly, trying to pull away from him, "No!"

"What do I have to do? Grovel?"

"Adam, I've been trying to explain—"

"My God," he said, "what did I do that made you hate me so?"

"I don't, I don't! I told you."

"Then stay one minute, and listen. Look, Annabel, don't cry. It's all right. Just let me—wait just one minute, and let me tell you . . . You've told me it's all over for you; you don't love me. Very well, I'll accept that. Don't worry, I'll accept it. My God, how can I expect anything else? But you can't imagine that I'll just retire quietly to West Lodge and do nothing about it, can you?"

Somewhere, far off behind the cedar tree, the owl hooted. I said waveringly, "Do nothing about what?"

"About trying to see you again." His other hand came up now, and he had me by both arms, lightly, holding me a little away from him. "You see," he said, "there's still one thing that we haven't made plain. It isn't over for me."

I felt myself stiffen, and so must he have done, for he went on quickly, "No, all right, I've told you I'll accept the fact that you want to forget the past. But there's still the future, my dear, and you've told me there's no one else; you can't expect me to stand by and do nothing, now that you've come home." He smiled suddenly, and for the first time there was warmth and even lightness in his voice. "And I owe you a courtship, don't I? We'll have no more clandestine romance, my love! No more notes sneaked into the old ivy tree, no more damned chilly moonlit meetings in the summer-house, with the rhododendron leaves sopping wet, and you fussing about bats getting into your hair!" He shook me gently, and his smile widened. "No, this time I'll woo you properly, by daylight, according to the book. I'll even start by calling on your grandfather–"

"*No!*" This time he must have felt the genuine shock of panic that kicked through me, jerking me rigid against the light clasp of his hands. Here was something I hadn't thought of. I had come to meet him tonight, with no very clear idea of what would be said, but only with the knowledge that the eight-years'-past love affair must, somehow, be kept from Con. Eight years was a long time, and it hadn't for a moment occurred to me that passion might be still there, smouldering, ready to flare up–into danger. It had seemed so easy: all I had had to do, after all, was to tell Adam Forrest the simple truth–that I did not care for him; that the past was dead and buried, and that I wanted it to remain so.

Then, the interview once over, the friendly, civil good-byes of long-estranged lovers given . . . I had hoped, more, known, that betrayal would not come from this direction. Yet here it was: after the days of smooth, too-easy masquerading, here, where it had been least expected, was danger.

Desperately I tried to marshal my thoughts. But the only coherent thing that came to me was that Con must not know. I had a sudden vision of his face as he had looked at me, down in the lane beside the meadowsweet . . . and behind him, Lisa's watchful, toffee-brown eyes.

"Please," I said shakily, "you mustn't do that. You mustn't come to Whitescar. Promise me that you won't come to Whitescar!"

"My dear, all right." He had dropped his hands when I spoke, and was staring at me now, the smile gone, and a deep crease gathering between his brows. "Just as you wish. Heaven knows I don't want to tease you. I'll promise anything you like, except not to try to see you again. You can't ask me to go quietly away and do nothing, knowing you're there at Whitescar. For one thing, we're bound to meet, and I–" the flicker of a smile again–"am bound to see that that happens as often as possible. But don't worry. I think I understand the way you feel, and I'll respect it . . . only you mustn't deny me the chance of trying to change it, now that we're free."

"Free?" The visions crowded in again, Con, Lisa, Grandfather, Julie . . . I said, bitterly, "Which of us is ever free?"

"My dear–"

The very quietness of his insistence was terrifying. Something that could have been panic mushroomed up inside me and burst into words I had never meant to say. "You mean, now that *you're* free! You mean you think you can dismiss me when it's convenient–forget me for eight years–and then, when I come back, just calmly expect to take up where you left off? You like to keep your mistresses in your own time, is that it? 'It isn't over for you—'" I mimicked him, cruelly. "No, I dare say not! Now that you're home for good, and your wife's dead, no doubt it'll suit you to have me around! Well, it doesn't suit me! How much plainer do I have to be? I've tried to put it kindly, but you won't take it. It's over. *Over*. So will you please, please, *please*, let me go and leave me alone?"

Even in that uncertain light, I saw the change in his face, and stopped, half afraid. Then my thoughts steadied. There was danger here; I must not forget that. Whatever happened, whatever I told him, whether or not I tried to go on with the masquerade, there was danger. Why not take the risk, and get it over now? Everything ought only to have to die once. Adam Forrest had gone through all this years ago; he mustn't be allowed to start it again, and for nothing. There was only one way to prevent that. Con had shown me how to play my cards, after all.

But for the moment I could find no way to do it. I stood silent, staring at him.

Then the decision was taken from me. He spoke so pat on my thoughts that he might have been taking a cue. "If it weren't absurd," he said, very slowly, "if it weren't something so crazy as to sound like black magic . . . I'd have said you couldn't be Annabel. Even in eight years, I wouldn't have thought you'd change so much."

I drew a sharp little breath, and choked over it, then I said quickly, and perhaps too loudly, "That's silly! Who else could I be?"

"That," he said, even more slowly, "is what I'm wondering."

I suppose the interview had got through what poor defences I had had. I simply stood there, and stared at Adam Forrest, with a curious sense of drifting, of destiny. Those dark gods who watch over the moonlit trysts of lovers had helped, cajoled, and then betrayed me to this final irony. I made no attempt to speak, just stared at Adam Forrest, and watched the thing dawning, incredulously, in his face.

Even when he took a rapid step that brought him within a foot of me, I didn't move. He said slowly, "I must be going mad. It can't be possible. It can't." He put out his hands and turned me round, quite gently, to face the moon. I didn't meet his eyes. I looked down, shutting my lips tightly to stop them trembling. There was a long pause.

Then he dropped his hands again, and turned away abruptly. He took several rapid strides away from me, and I thought he was going to leave me there and then, and wondered in a brief moment of panic where he was going, but he stopped suddenly, and stood for a few seconds with his back to me, looking at the ground.

Then he turned, churning his heel in the grass, and came back. His face looked quite impassive.

"Is this true?"

I hesitated painfully. The moment stretched like a year. Then I saw that the hesitation had answered for me. I nodded without speaking.

"You're not Annabel Winslow?"

I cleared my throat and managed to say, steadily enough, even with a kind of relief, "No, I'm not Annabel Winslow."

"You're . . . not . . . Annabel." He said it again, the sharpness of his questions blurred now into bewilderment.

This time I said nothing. The irrational feeling of escape, of relief, persisted. The flooding moonlight; the backcloth, as motionless and silent as paint, of the ruined house and towering trees; the little sundial with its sharply etched shadow thrown beside our own, these lent the scene an air of complete unreality. We were not people who ate and worked and talked through the sunlit days: we were beings from a fantasy world, creatures of a moonlit stage, living only by our passions, able to talk about love and death and pain, only in the subtle and rarefied voices of poetry. This was the world of the doomed black sail, the enchanted cup, the swallow flying through the casement with the single gold hair in his beak. We were Pervaneh and Rafi, floating like ghosts through the night-time garden, and to us the death of love would come as poetry; not fear, and quarrelling, the grimy commonplaces of the station platform, the unanswered telephone, the letter gone astray, the years of dragging loneliness. . . .

The moonlight struck the sundial as sharply as the sun. Time was.

I was still facing the light. He had come close to me again, and was scrutinizing my face. "You look like her, you move like her. But your voice is different . . . and there's something else. . . . Don't ask me what. But it's . . . extraordinary. It's beyond reason."

I said gently, "But it's true."

He gave a little laugh that had no relationship with mirth. "You've spent a lot of time tonight assuring me of various truths. At least this one is the easiest to accept." He half turned away, and thrust the tangle of tendrils aside from the dial's face. "Who are you?"

"Does that matter?"

"Probably not. But it matters a great deal why you are here, and why you're doing this—whatever it is you are doing. At least you don't seem to be trying to hedge. You might as well tell me the lot; after all, I have every right to know."

"Have you?"

He turned his head as if in exasperation. "Of course. You must know a good deal about my affairs, or you wouldn't have been here to meet me tonight. Who told you? Annabel?"

"Annabel?" I said blankly.

"Who else could it have been?" He had turned back to the sundial, and appeared to be tracing out the figures with a forefinger. His voice was abrupt. "Tell me, please. Where you met her, what happened, what she told you. What you know of her."

"It wasn't that!" I cried. "It didn't happen like that! I never met Annabel! It was Julie who told me!"

"Julie?"

"Yes. Oh, don't worry, she didn't know anything, really, about you and Annabel; but she'd seen you meet and talk in the wood, and she knew about the post box in the ivy tree. She saw Annabel put a letter in there one day, and take another out. She–she just thought it was a perfectly natural and very romantic way of conducting a love affair. She never told anyone."

"I see. And just what has she told you?"

"Only this–about the meetings and the ivy tree. She wanted me to know she knew. She–she rather imagined I'd be wanting to see you again, straight away."

"Hm." He had turned back to the sundial, and seemed absorbed in chipping a flake of moss away with a fingernail. "A bit of luck for you, wasn't it? That she knew, and told you? Otherwise you'd have been a little startled at our first meeting." A piece of moss came away, and he examined the inch or so of bronze beneath it with great care. "Are you sure that was all Julie told you? I'm not suggesting that she deliberately played the spy; she was only a child at the time, and would hardly realize what was going on. But one doesn't like to think that anyone, least of all a child–"

"Honestly, there was nothing else."

"Yet you played your part so very well." His voice, now, had an edge to it that would have engraved the bronze dial he was fingering. "I find it hard to believe that you knew so little. Perhaps Connor Winslow found out somehow–"

"No!" I said it so sharply that he glanced at me, surprised. "At least, he's said nothing to me. He hardly mentions you." I added, lightly, "I'm a very good actress, of course; you'll have guessed that. I merely played to the cues I got. It wasn't difficult. After all, it's what one expects to have to do when one's involved in this kind of game. If you think back over what was actually said, you'll find that I merely played your service back. All the *statements* were made by you."

He dropped the flake of moss on to the dial. It fell with a tiny rustling click. I saw him straighten as if with relief, but he still sounded grim. "Oh yes, you'd have to be clever. But not, it appears, quite clever enough. The sudden appearance of a lover must have been something of a shock. I grant you courage, too; you did very well. . . . And now, please, back to my question. Who are you, and what is this 'game' you say you're playing?"

"Look," I said, "I've told you the truth and played fair with you. I do assure you I needn't have let you guess. I'm not going to harm anybody, I'm only out to do myself a bit of good. Can't you let it go . . . at any rate till you *see* me harming someone? Why should it concern you, what goes on at Whitescar?"

"You ask, why should it concern me? You come back here posing as Annabel, and ask why it should concern me?"

"Nobody knows about you and her except Julie, and I've already told Julie that we're not–"

"That's not the point." The words snapped. "Don't hedge. What's your name?"

"Mary Grey."

"You're very like her, but of course you know that." A long look. "The thing doesn't seem possible. Mary Grey. My God, this sort of thing doesn't happen outside the pages of fiction! Am I seriously to believe that you have somehow got yourself into Whitescar, and are masquerading as Annabel Winslow?"

"Yes."

"Why?"

I laughed. "Why do you think?"

There was a silence. He said, not pleasantly, "Funny, you don't look venal."

"Try earning your living the hard way," I said. "You never know how you'll turn out till you've been down to half a dollar and no prospects."

His lips thinned. "That's true enough."

"Oh, yes, I forgot. You do know. You work for your living now, and hard, too, they tell me. Well, didn't you mind having to spoil your hands?"

"I—beg your pardon?" He sounded considerably startled, I couldn't imagine why.

"Wouldn't *you* perhaps have taken a chance to step into some easy money, if the chance came, and it did no harm?"

"I did once. But they'll have told you about that, too. And how can we expect to calculate what harm we do? Who's briefing you?"

The question came so sharply that I jumped. "What?"

"You couldn't do this on your own. Someone's briefed you and brought you in. Julie, I suppose, wanting to spoil Connor's chances?"

I laughed. "Hardly. Con himself, and his sister."

He stared at me unbelievingly. "Con? And Lisa Dermott? Do you really expect me to believe that?"

"It's true."

"Connor Winslow bring back 'Annabel' to cut him out of what he expects? Don't take me for a fool; he'd as soon slit his own throat."

"I'm not cutting Con Winslow out."

"No. Julie, then?" His voice hardened.

"No. Annabel herself."

"Annabel's dead." Only after he had spoken them, did he seem to hear the words, as if they had been said by someone else. He turned his head almost as if he were listening, as if he expected to hear the last heavy syllable go echoing through the woods, dropping, ripple by ripple, like a stone through silence.

"Mr. Forrest, I'm sorry. . . . If I'd known—"

"Go on." His voice was as hard and sharp as before. "Explain yourself. You say Connor has brought you in to impersonate Annabel, in order to cut Annabel out of her rights in Whitescar land. What sort of a story is that, for heaven's sake?"

"It's simple enough. Grandfather has refused to believe she's dead, and he's refused to alter his will, which leaves everything to her. As things stand now, Whitescar goes to Annabel, with reversion to Julie. I think it seems pretty obvious that in the end Grandfather would have done the sensible thing, admitted that Annabel must be dead, and willed the place to Con; in fact, I think he intends to do just that. But he's ill now, really ill; and you know him, he may play about with the idea, just to torment people, until it's too late. Con *might* have got Whitescar anyway, after some sort of legal upheaval, because I'm pretty sure Julie doesn't want it, but he'd only get a proportion of Grandfather's money along with it, not enough for what he'd want to do."

"I . . . see."

"I thought you might."

"And just what do you get out of it?"

"A home, at the moment. That's a new thing for me, and I like it. A competence."

"A competence!" he said, explosively. "Why, you lying little thief, it's a small fortune!"

I smiled. If the interview had seemed unreal at first, when the ghosts and dreams of passion had hung between us, how infinitely less real it was now, with me standing there, hands deep in pockets, looking composedly up at Adam Forrest, and talking about money. "Be realistic, won't you, Mr. Forrest? Do you really see Con Winslow bringing me in out of sweet charity, and watching me pocket all the money that goes to Annabel?"

"Of course. Stupid of me." He spoke as if he were discussing the weather. "You hand the major part to him, and are allowed to keep your 'competence.' How very neat, always assuming that there's sufficient honour among thieves . . . Where did you meet Connor Winslow?"

I said evasively, "Oh, he saw me one day. I had a job in Newcastle, and I came out to this part of the county one Sunday, for a day out, you know, a walk. He saw me, and thought, as you did, that I was his cousin come back. He followed me, and found out who I was, and we talked." I didn't feel it necessary to go into details of the three weeks' planning; nor did I bother to tell him that I had, to begin with, opposed Con's plan myself.

"And hatched this up between you?" The contempt in his voice was hardly veiled. "Well, so far, I gather, you've been completely successful . . . as why shouldn't you be? The thing's so fantastic that you'd be almost bound to get away with it, given the nerve, the information . . . and the luck."

"Well," I said, calmly enough, "it seems the luck's failed, doesn't it?"

"Indeed it does." His voice was gentle, calculating. He was watching me almost with hatred, but I could forgive him that, remembering how he had betrayed himself to me. He said slowly, "Yes, you've been clever. I don't know how easily you managed to deceive the people at Whitescar, but, after Julie had talked to you, you must have realized you couldn't hope to get away with such a deception with me. You must have gone through quite a bad moment when you heard that your erstwhile lover was coming home."

"Quite a bad moment," I said steadily.

"I'm glad to hear it. But you kept your head, clever Miss Grey. You had to risk seeking me out here and talking to me; you didn't dare wait to meet me for the first time in public. So you took the chance, and came. Why didn't you go to the summerhouse?"

"The summerhouse? Do you mean that little pavilion along the other path, in the rhododendrons? I didn't realize that had been your meeting place, till you told me so yourself."

"It would hardly have been here," he said drily, with a glance at the blank and staring windows.

"I did realize that. But this seemed the obvious spot to wait. I—I thought if you came at all, you'd come this way to look."

"Yes, well, I came. So far, you've been right every way, Miss Grey. But now, what happens? You're taking this remarkably calmly, aren't you? Do you really imagine that I won't blow the whole thing sky-high on you?"

I thrust my hands down into my pockets again. I said coolly, "I have no idea what you'll do. It's quite possible that tomorrow you'll turn up at Whitescar, and tell Grandfather what you've learned tonight. You'll tell him that she's dead after all, and that all these years Con has been nursing his resentment, and planning to take Whitescar . . . and looking forward to Grandfather's death. And you might add for good measure that Julie's thinking of marrying, and that her husband's job will take her away from Whitescar."

There was a silence. Adam Forest said unemotionally, "You bitch."

"I thought you'd see it my way." (Con, smiling at me in the lane, his voice soft in the whisper that conspirators, and lovers, use. Yes, Con had taught me how to play it.) "It's really better for everyone the way it is, isn't it?" I finished, gently.

"Whether a thing is right or wrong doesn't depend on how many people it hurts. This is wrong."

I said suddenly, violently, "How the hell dare you sit in judgment on me, Adam Forrest?"

He jumped. I saw his eyes narrow on me suddenly, then he relaxed with a queer little sigh. "Then what about Julie? I can't see that it's 'better' for her. This criminal arrangement of yours may suit everyone else, including old Mr. Winslow, since it means keeping him in a false paradise until he dies. But what about Julie?"

"Julie has money of her own. So has this man of hers, and he's way up in his profession."

"That," said Adam Forrest gently, "is hardly the point."

"It's the point unless you do propose to—what's the phrase we crooks use?—blow the gaff."

He was giving me that appraising, narrow stare again. "I could, you know. In fact, I must."

"You'd find it very difficult to convince Grandfather. Con and Lisa did a very good job of briefing, and I'm well dug in. And Julie would just laugh at you."

There was another of those silences. He didn't stir, but I felt the hair prickle along my skin as if I had expected a blow.

When he spoke, his voice sounded quite normal, friendly, almost. "You speak like an American."

"Canadian, actually." I was surprised and wary. "It's one of my assets, of course, as an impersonator. *She* went to the States, and, according to *my* story, from there to Canada."

"To come from Canada, Miss Grey, one needs a passport." He laughed suddenly, not a nice sound. "Yes, I thought that would get through to you. Nobody else thought of it?"

I said hoarsely, "Why should they? They accepted me without question. You don't usually ask to see people's papers, unless there's some doubt."

"That," he said pleasantly, "is just what I mean. And I shouldn't destroy it, my dear. They're terribly easy to trace."

I drove my fists down, and held them steady.

"Mr. Forrest–"

"Well?"

"What are you going to do?"

"What do you think?"

"I don't think you quite understand, you know. Grandfather–"

"I understand perfectly. You and Connor are trading on his age and sickness. That's quite clear. But it's Julie I'm thinking about–Julie, and my own constitutional dislike of seeing anyone get away with this kind of damned lie. If I did agree to hold my tongue now, it would be purely for old Mr. Winslow's sake. But if he dies–"

I said violently, "How much of a fool can you be? If he dies before he remakes his will, and you throw Annabel back into her grave, what do you suppose would happen to Julie?"

This time the silence was electric. The night was so still that I heard my own heart beats, and I thought he must hear them, too. Ten miles off, a train whistled for a crossing.

As if it had been a signal to wake us both, he said, "Don't be absurd." But his voice had slackened with uncertainty.

"I meant it, oddly enough. I think I know Con Winslow a little better than you do."

"That's very probable," he spoke with (I thought) a quite undue dryness. "If this–fantasy–is true, do I take it that you expect to stay on in safety at Whitescar?"

"I'll face that when the time comes."

"You think he'll marry you? Are you playing for that, too?"

"Look here–!" I began, hotly, then stopped and bit my lip. It was an obvious conclusion, after all. "I am not," I said clearly, "anything to Con Winslow, or he to me . . . except accomplices."

"I beg your pardon." His apology was surprisingly prompt, and sounded genuine. "Then am I to take it that you are protecting Julie . . . for a 'competence'?"

"You can take it how you like. I've assured you that no one will be harmed by what I'm doing, but I don't expect you to believe me. Why should you? I can only beg you to keep out of what doesn't concern you . . . at least until you see wrong being done."

He said, all at once sounding very tired, "I don't understand you."

"Why should you? But I mean what I say, remember that. And I'm telling you the truth about this. I'm playing this game for my own advantage, that's obvious; I saw a chance to get out of poverty and hard work, to grab what they call a place in the sun, and I took it. It's wrong, I admit that; I'm unscrupulous, I admit that. But I'm not *bad*, and I wouldn't do it if anyone was going to suffer for it. Believe me, they'll have plenty, and the little I'll get will mean a lot to me, and nothing to any of them."

He said, angrily, "That's immoral nonsense. It's also quite beside the point."

"I know that." I laughed. "But all the same, you think about it, Mr. Forrest. This is one of those cases where to do the right thing will be to do nothing but harm. So let well alone, will you? Stifle your conscience, and keep away from Grandfather. It's none of your business, after all."

"If I could believe you. If I knew what you were playing at."

"Don't worry about that, or about my future. It has nothing to do with you."

He let out a breath like a sigh. "No. All right. I'll keep out of it, for a while, at least. But watch your step . . . Annabel." As I caught my breath, he added, roughly, "If I'm to play your game, or even watch from the sidelines, I can hardly call you 'Miss Winslow.' "

"Then you will . . . play my game?" I said breathlessly.

"I think so. Though heaven knows why. Let's say I'll go away and think about it, and hold a watching brief. But I promise you that if I plan to —what was it?—'blow the gaff,' I'll warn you first."

I said huskily, "I don't know why you should do this for me."

"Nor do I," he said wearily. "But . . . be careful."

"I intend to. And I—I'm sorry I said those things to you."

"What things?"

"About your dismissing Annabel and then wanting to take up your—your love affair again. It was unkind, but—well, I was scared. You must see that I'd have said anything to . . . make you let me go."

"Yes, I see."

I hesitated. "Good night . . . Adam."

He didn't answer. I turned away and left him.

Just before the dark leaves of the rhododendrons hid him from me, I thought I heard him say "Good night."

CHAPTER TEN

"Why should not I love my love?
 Why should not my love love me?
Why should not I speed after him,
 Since love to all is free?"

Traditional.

THE DAYS went by, warm and cloudless. Haymaking was in full swing, and the mown fields smelled Elysian, lying in ribbed gold under a blue sky. Wild roses tumbled anyhow through all the hedges, and Tommy, the fat black and white cat, startled everyone by confounding the experts and having seven kittens.

And Adam Forrest did nothing.

I had got the passport away to the bank, which made me feel a little better, but it was a day or two after that moonlit meeting before I stopped watching the road between West Lodge and Whitescar. When two days, three days, passed with no sign from him, I began to think that perhaps, having "thought it over," he had decided to take me at my word and, for Grandfather's sake, to hold his tongue and await developments. I had not seen him again, though Julie had once or twice persuaded me to walk through the river meadows to look at the horse, Rowan; and I had gone, realizing that, whatever Adam Forrest's intentions, I might as well behave as normally as possible, and naturally Julie expected my interest in the colt to be intense.

I had made no further attempt at confidence with Julie, and she had offered none, but I could not help suspecting that all was still far from well between her and Donald Seton. How far her own feelings were settled, it was impossible to guess. She was young, volatile, perhaps a trifle spoiled, but from what little she had said to me—perhaps because she *had* said so little—I believed her affections to be seriously engaged. I had, on my first sight of Donald, decided that here was a man one could both like and respect; since then he had been down to Whitescar two or three times, and I had liked him better each time, though I thought I could see the cause of the tension that appeared to exist, if not between the two of them, then in Julie's mind. I could see that his quietness, his steady reserve, might appear daunting and even formidable to a nineteen-year-old extrovert accustomed to the easy and outspoken admiration of the young men of her own London set. Still waters might run deep, but at nineteen one can hardly be expected to appreciate the fact.

The complaint she had made in jest, on that first evening, had its foundations firmly in the truth. Donald Seton would not "fit into any romantic context." And Julie, for all her gay sophistication, was young enough still to want her love affair sprinkled with stardust, and vulnerable enough to be hurt by a reserve which she must mistake for indifference, or at best a reluctance to pursue. Donald was, in other words, a disappointment. Liking, affection, comradeship, all growing steadily from the first seed of love—these were not what Julie, at nineteen, was looking for. Not happiness, but intensity, was what she craved. As a lover, the quiet Scot by no means measured up to the standards of Julie's favourite reading, or (more immediately) to those of the unhappy man who, eight years ago, had left notes for his mistress in the old ivy tree. Poor Julie, if she only knew. . . . I found myself hoping, with quite startling fervour, that Donald would emerge soon from his Roman preoccupation, and *speak*.

Meanwhile, he called at Whitescar in the evenings, after work had packed up, and, on one occasion, Julie went up to West Woodburn to see what was going on there, and even, possibly, in a genuine attempt to learn something about the job.

Although in this, it seemed, she was not successful, it did appear as if Donald had moved at least a little of the way towards her. He had brought her back in the evening, and stayed to dinner, listening silently and in apparent amusement to her lively—and malicious—account of the way he occupied his time.

"Sitting in a hole," said Julie, "my *dears*, I mean it, sitting all day at the bottom of a little pit, scraping away at *mud*, and with a thing the size of a teaspoon! Nothing but mud, *honestly!* And every spoonful preserved as if it was the Grand Cham's jewels. I never was so disillusioned in my life!"

"No gold coins? No statues?" I asked, smiling.

"My dear, I think there was a Roman bootlace."

Donald's eyes twinkled. "That was our big day. You mustn't expect excitement all the time."

She opened her lips, and then shut them again. I thought her smile was brittle. I said quickly, "Just what are you doing, anyway?"

"Only a preliminary bit of dating."

"Dating?" Grandfather looked up from his cheese.

I saw Donald glance at him, in that diffident way he had, and affirm that this was genuine interest and not mere civility, before he replied. "Yes, sir. It does consist, as Julie says, of just scratching at the earth. We've dug a trial trench through the wall and rampart of the fort, and we're going down layer by layer, examining the successive ramparts, and whatever debris—in the way of pottery shards and so on—comes to light as we work down. In that way, we can determine what building was done in the fort at different times. Eventually it sorts itself out into a picture of the general history of the place, but at present—" the glimmer of a smile at her—"Julie's quite right. It's nothing but scraping at earth, and must seem deplorably dull."

"*You* seem to find it terribly absorbing, anyway," said Julie. I don't think she had meant the words to have an edge, but they sounded almost pettish, like the retort of a piqued child.

Donald didn't appear to notice. "Well," he said, "it's like most jobs, I suppose, masses of dull routine most of the time; but the good moments, when they come, can be pretty exciting."

"Oh?" said Julie, then suddenly laughed, with an attempt at her normal sparkle of good humour. "Well, for goodness' sake tell us when that's likely to happen, and we'll all come and watch! At *least*–" this to me–"he's coming up out of the mud on Wednesday. Did I tell you? *And* so am I. We're going into Newcastle, to the Royal."

"The theatre? How lovely. But, darling, Wednesday . . . it's Grandfather's birthday, had you forgotten? We're making rather an occasion of it, since we're all here–"

"Oh yes, I know, that's why we're going to the matinée. Donald says he can usually only manage Saturdays, but there weren't any seats left, and it's John Gielgud's new play, and I simply *cannot* miss it. So Donald's sneaking off Wednesday, after lunch, and we're going. Grandfather knows, and we'll be back in good time for the party. Donald's staying for that, too."

"Very sensible of him. I know Lisa's got something wonderful laid on, but she won't tell me what it is."

Lisa smiled, but rather absently. I knew she was fidgeting until she could get out of the dining room and back to the kitchen, where she could start to prepare Con's supper. When he worked late, she gave him this in the kitchen at whatever hour he came in, and I knew that, for her, this half-hour, when she had him to herself, was the peak of her day.

"Look," Donald was saying, in that pleasant, unemphatic voice of his, "it's very nice of you to have asked me, but I hadn't realized it was a family party. I think perhaps I'd better say–"

"Now, don't go crying off," said Grandfather. "We'll be thankful to have you. Never known a family gathering yet where the presence of a stranger didn't do a lot of good. Families are usually pretty damned grim when they get together, especially Winslows. We'll have to behave ourselves if you're here."

Donald laughed. "Well, if you put it like that. . . ."

"I do indeed. Anything I have to say to the family as such can be said in three minutes precisely, on the way to bed." The fierce, faded old eyes went round the table, lingering momentarily on Con's empty chair. "And better so. There's been too much talk already, and I can't stomach post mortems before I'm dead."

The sheer unfairness of this took my breath away, and I saw Julie open her eyes wide. Donald, to whom these last remarks had been addressed, said rather faintly, "Oh, quite."

I rescued him. "Then we'll see you on Wednesday? That'll be nice. What's the play, Julie?"

Julie, her face lighting, her pique forgotten, plunged happily into an account of it, unaware of the fact (or perhaps uncaring) that she was betraying with every word how far her heart lay from Whitescar and the quiet island of Forrest Park. I saw Grandfather watching her, an odd expression on his face. Ah well, I thought, this was best. I stole a glance at Lisa, to see if this was being stored up for Con, but she was looking at her watch, and murmuring something about coffee in the drawing room.

"Well," said Grandfather, a little drily, as he pushed back his chair, "enjoy yourselves."

"We will, be sure of that! But till then," said Julie, dimpling at Donald, "I'll let you get on with your mudlarking in peace, and put in a bit of work for Con instead. In any case, I think haymaking's more fun, and far more profitable to the human race."

"Very probably," said Donald equably.

Sure enough, Julie spent the next two or three days in the hayfield, driving the tractor for Con.

Here I watched her rather more anxiously. It was just possible that Julie (provoked, restless, and already slightly bored with the country holiday that wasn't answering its purpose), was hoping to try out the age-old romantic device of making Donald jealous. She had two strings to her bow: Bill Fenwick from Nether Shields, who came over now and again, ostensibly to "give a hand" in the hayfield when he could be spared from home, but in reality, it was obvious, for a chance to be near Julie; and Con. Bill I dismissed without a thought, except to hope that he would not be hurt; but Con was a different proposition. He was not a man who could be used in this sort of way, or in any sort of way that he didn't initiate. Besides, he was extremely attractive, and older and more sensible girls than Julie had rebounded before now into far less exciting arms. And if Con suddenly decided that three-thirds of the Winslow money was even better than two, and seriously turned his attention to Julie. . . .

I need not have worried. At any other time, I suppose, Con would have flirted with her as a matter of course, a purely automatic reaction, as instinctive as that of a cock bird displaying to the female; but, just at present, Con had more important things on his mind. Mr. Isaacs, the lawyer, had been duly summoned to see Grandfather, and had spent Friday morning closeted with him in his office. The old man had said nothing whatever about this interview, but had allowed it to be known that Mr. Isaacs would call again in a few days' time, that is, on the morning of his, Grandfather's, birthday. The inference was obvious, and, to my eyes, the effect on Con was obvious, too. The tension in him had increased perceptibly in the last few days; he was quieter than usual, and seemed edgy and strained. We saw very little of him; he rarely even ate with us, but spent all his time in the hayfield, working with an energy and fierce physical concentration that were remarkable, even for him. This was partly, I thought, due to a genuine passion for hard work, partly to work off the tension he was feeling, and partly, also, to keep out of old Mr. Winslow's way. The die was cast, one way or the other; it seemed likely that it was cast in Con's favour, and Con was taking no risks.

In this he may have been wise. Since the lawyer's visit, there had been a perceptible change, too, in Grandfather. Where Con had grown tense and wary, turning that diamond-hard concentration of his on his job, old Mr. Winslow became daily more difficult and less predictable, prone to sudden irritabilities, and even (what was new in him) fits of vagueness and absence of mind. The continued hot weather seemed to trouble him. He was very easily tired, but as he did less, so his fretfulness increased, and it seemed, wherever possible, to be directed at Con. His decision now finally made, it was as if the abdication of that will-to-power, which had been his driving force, had slackened something in him. He even seemed, physically, to have grown smaller. Where before he had been formidable, he now seemed merely fretful, and his resentful nagging at Con (over matters which previously he had been quite content to leave to the younger man) were the grumblings of a pettish old man, no longer the storms of a tyrant.

For me, it was something of a relief to find myself abruptly removed from the centre of attention. Con was, for the moment, no longer concerned with me, and Lisa had accepted me completely. What jealous thoughts she may have originally had of me, she had transferred to Julie, who (to do her justice) had done nothing to deserve them. Me, she seemed even to like; I had the odd feeling that, in her stolid, brother-centred way, she was even grateful for my presence at Whitescar, where Mr. Winslow persisted in regarding her as something of a stranger, a sort of paid-housekeeper-cum-poor-relation; Mrs. Bates with a slightly jealous Northern caution; and Con himself with a casual affection that took everything, including the most detailed personal service, completely for granted.

Meanwhile, the heat increased, charging the air with thunder, adding this threat to the other perceptible weights in the air. Day by day the great soap-sud clouds built up their slow thunder towers in the southwest. The trees hung heavily, as if themselves exhausted by the heat, and the sky was a deep, waiting blue.

And Con kept quiet, and watched the clouds, and drove himself and the men like galley slaves to clear the fields before the weather broke. . . . And with that same cold preoccupation, and for a closely analogous reason, he watched Grandfather.

Wednesday came, still without the threatened thunderstorm. The air felt a little lighter, as a small breeze had sprung up, though without shifting the towering, beautiful clouds. But the sense of oppression (or was it foreboding?) seemed to have lifted.

Mr. Isaacs came just before midday, and Grandfather took him straight into the office. I gave them ten minutes, then went to the dining room to get the sherry.

As I crossed the hall, Julie came downstairs, pulling on her gloves.

I paused. "Why, hullo! Are you going now? My, my, don't you look wonderful!"

This was true. She was wearing crisp cotton, the colour of lemon ice, and her gloves were white. The pale, shining hair was brushed into an elaborate and very attractive style that had been thought up at least two hundred miles from Whitescar. Over one arm she carried a little coat of the same material as the frock.

I said: "Ve—ery nice! But why so early? I thought Donald couldn't get away till after lunch?"

She tugged the second glove into place, pushing the heavy gold bracelet higher up her wrist with a sharp little movement that looked almost savage. "Donald," she said crisply, "can't get away at all."

"What?"

"He rang up an hour ago to say that he couldn't go, after all."

"Oh, Julie, no! Why?"

Her careful composure shivered a bit, like cat ice wrinkling under the wind. Her eyes were stormy. "Because he doesn't think what *I* want to do matters a damn, that's why!"

I threw a glance towards the office door. "Come into the dining room. I was just going to take Mr. Isaacs and Grandfather some sherry. . . ." In the dining room I said, "Now come off it, honey. Why can't he come? What's happened?"

"Somebody's turned up from London, that's why. Some beastly man from the Commission, who's working with Donald, and Donald says he'll have to stay and see him. He says—oh, what's it matter, anyway? I didn't listen. It's always the same, I might have known. The one time he *did* say he'd leave his precious blasted Romans—"

"Julie, he'd come if he could. He can't help it."

"I know! Oh, it isn't *that!* It's just—oh, it's just *everything!*" cried Julie. "And he sounded so *calm* and *reasonable*—"

"He always does. He would in a fire. It's a habit men have; they think it calms us, or something."

"Well, but he seemed to think *I* ought to be reasonable, too!" said Julie, furiously. "How dumb can you get? . . . Annabel, if you laugh, I'll kill you!" She gave a reluctant grin. "Anyway, you know *exactly* what I mean."

"Yes, I know. I'm sorry. But you're not being fair to Donald, are you? The man's got a job to do, and if something crops up that has to be attended to—"

"Oh, I know, I know! I'm not as silly as all that. But he knew how *foully* disappointed I'd be. He needn't have sounded just as if he didn't even *mind* not going out with me."

"He wouldn't mean to, you know. He's just not the type to spread himself all over the carpet for you to trample on. He'd be as sorry as the next man, but he—well, he just hasn't got the gift of the gab."

"No, he hasn't, has he?" Her voice was genuinely bitter. She had turned aside to pick up the jacket from the chair where she had thrown it.

"My dear—"

"It's all right. I dare say I'm being stupid about it, but I can't help that. It would be different if he'd ever—if I knew—" she sounded all at once very young—"if I was sure he cared."

"He does care. I'm sure he does."

"Then why the hell doesn't he *say* so?" cried Julie explosively. She snatched up her coat. "Oh, what's the *use?*"

"Is he still coming to dinner tonight?"

"He said he'd try. I said he could please himself."

"Oh, Julie!"

"Oh, I didn't just say it like *that.* I was really quite nice about it." She gave me a wavering smile. "Almost reasonable . . . But if he *knew* what hellish thoughts were churning away inside me. . . ."

"It's often a good thing they don't."

"They? Who?"

I grinned. "Men."

"Oh, *men,*" she said, in accents of loathing. "*Why* are men?"

"I give you three guesses."

"The most harmless answer is that there'd be nothing whatever to do if there weren't any, I suppose."

"There'd be nothing whatever, period," I said.

"Well, you've got something there," said Julie, "but don't ask me to admit it for quite some time. Oh, Annabel, you've done me good. I must go now; there's the car."

"Car?"

She gave me a little sideways look under her lashes. "I told you I wasn't going to miss this play. I'm going with Bill Fenwick."

"I see."

"And just what do you see?"

I ignored that. "But surely the play's going to open in London soon? You'll see it there?"

"That," said Julie, "is not the point."

"No, quite. Donald couldn't get away, so you rang up Bill Fenwick, and asked him to take you? That it?"

"Yes," she said, with a shade of defiance.

"And *he* dropped everything, and promptly came?"

"Yes." She eyed me. "What's wrong with that?"

"Nothing at all," I said cheerfully. "I hope they've finished leading for the day at Nether Shields, that's all."

"Annabel," said Julie, warmly, "are you trying to be a pig?"

I laughed. "I was, rather. Never mind me, honey, go and enjoy your play. We'll be seeing you at dinner. And, Julie—"

"What is it?"

"If Donald does come, don't make it too obvious that you're a bit fed up with him, will you? No—" as she made a little movement of impatience—"this isn't Advice from Aunt Annabel. What's between you and Donald is your affair. I was thinking of something quite different . . . I'll explain later. There's no time now . . . but come and see me when you get in, will you? I've something to tell you."

"Sure," said Julie.

The front door shut behind her. I found the sherry glasses, and a tray, but as I set the decanter on this, the office door opened, and Grandfather came out.

He was making for the baize door that led to the kitchen lobby, but, hearing the chink of glass, he stopped, turned, and saw me through the open door of the dining room. He seemed to hesitate for a moment, then abruptly to make up his mind. He came into the room, and shut the door quietly behind him.

"I was just going to bring you some sherry," I said. "Were you looking for me?"

"I was going to get Betsy Bates and that girl Cora to witness my signature," he said, in a dry, rather harsh voice.

"Oh." I waited. He stood just inside the door, his head bent and thrust forward, staring at me under his brows.

"Child–" He seemed not quite to know what he had come to say.

"Yes?"

"I've taken you at your word."

I tried not to let him see the relief that swept through me. "I'm glad of that."

"I believe you are."

I said earnestly, "It's right, Grandfather, you said yourself it was only right and fair. It's best for everyone–Con, me, the place, your peace of mind."

"Julie?"

"And Julie," I said steadily. "Julie loves this place, don't think she doesn't, but can you see her running it?"

He gave his little bark of laughter. "Frankly, no. Must confess I've wondered, though, with young Fenwick in the offing–"

I said quickly, "There's nothing in that. It's Donald Seton, and you know he lives in London when he's not on field work."

"Hm. Gathered there was something in the wind. Not quite senile yet. Decent sort of fellow, I thought. Gentleman, and so on. Only thing is, he doesn't look as if he's got a penny to his name."

I laughed. "His clothes and car? That's affectation, when he's out on a dig. I'll bet he's formal enough in London. He makes eighteen hundred a year, rising to two thousand five hundred, and his family's got money."

"How the devil d'you know?"

"Julie told me. She looked him up."

"Good God," said Grandfather, impressed. "Girl's got sense, after all." He gave a curious little sigh, and then smiled the tight, lipless smile of the old. "Well, that's that, isn't it? All settled. But I don't mind telling you, I haven't liked it. Boy's all right, don't think I don't know it, but not m'own flesh and blood. Not the same. Young people don't understand that nowadays, but it's true. A bit too much of the damned foreigner about Connor sometimes."

"Foreigner?" I said blankly.

"Irish," said Grandfather. I thought of Donald, and smiled to myself, but he didn't see. He was looking past me, out of the window. "If your father, or Julie's, had lived, it would have been a different matter."

"Yes," I said gently.

The old eyes came back to me. "You and Connor should have made a match of it. Should still. I'm not raking up the past, but after what's been between you—"

"I told you, it would never have worked."

"Not then, no. Too much of the Winslow in both of you, perhaps. But now . . . say what you like, the onlooker sees most of the game. I still think it would be the best thing. For the place, for Connor; yes, and for you. Never a woman born yet, that wasn't the better for a husband. Don't just stand and smile at me, child. Come here."

I went and stood in front of him. He put up a hand, and held it against my cheek. It was cool and very dry, and felt as light as a leaf. "It's made me very happy, your coming back. Don't think for a moment that you're not my favourite, because you are."

"I always did say you were never fair in your life."

"I've left you some money," he said gruffly. "A good sum, and Julie, too. I want you to know."

"Grandfather, I—"

"It's settled. We'll have neither thanks nor argument. I've done what I think fair, in spite of what you say about me. Tell you just how it stands. It's tangled up in a lot of lawyers' nonsense, but it amounts to this: Whitescar goes to Connor, with the house, stock, implements, the lot. I take it you won't contest that? Or Julie?"

"No."

A grin. "Doubt if you could, anyway. Isaacs' wrapped it all up in legal jargon, with reasons stated. Seems you have to stop anyone being able to say, later on, that you were cranky when you made the will. So there it is, all laid out: Whitescar goes as an acknowledgment of Connor's 'devoted work,' for which I've so far made 'inadequate recompense.' True enough. Well, there it is. Then we come to the recompense for you."

"For me? What have I ever done, except run away?"

"Recompense for losing Whitescar. Should have been yours. Handed over your head to Connor."

"Oh." I waited, helplessly.

"The money," said Grandfather. He had a hand on the table, and was leaning on it. He sent me a look up under the white brows, a pale counterfeit of his old, bright glance, but recognizably the same. "I've divided it into three. A third goes to Julie, outright. It's all she ever expected, and I doubt if she'll quarrel with Con over Whitescar. If she marries this man of hers, she'll be well enough found. The other two-thirds I've left in trust, to pay your income for life."

"In—trust?"

"That's what I said. Worked it all out with Isaacs as the best way. I want you repaid for losing Whitescar, and I want to see you well provided for. But I don't want the money to leave the land outright. You said you'd not stay here when I'd gone; remember? So it's left in trust for your lifetime. After your death it comes back to Connor absolutely, or to his heirs. On the other hand, if Connor should die before you, without issue, then Whitescar becomes yours, and the money along with it, absolutely. I take it, if he were gone, you'd look after the place . . . ? Good girl." His hand lifted. "No, wait, I haven't finished. There's one thing more. If you should marry Connor—"

"Grandfather—"

"If you should marry Connor, and live at Whitescar, the money becomes yours then, absolutely. Clear?"

"Y—yes."

The only really clear thing was the old man's determination to tie the money to Whitescar; and me, along with it, if he could, to Con. The wrong end of the shotgun, with a vengeance. Dazedly I tried to assess the probable results of what he had just told me. "But . . . *two*-thirds for me, and a third for Julie? What about Con? If I don't—I mean—" I floundered, and stopped. It was no use insisting; let him keep his dream.

"I've left him a little, and Lisa, too."

"But, Grandfather—"

"My good girl—" he was suddenly irritable—"anyone would think you were trying to get rid of every penny piece to Connor! Are you mad? If the place comes to him over the heads of you and Julie, he can hardly expect much more! It'll not be easy for him, with only a small capital to back him, but he'll have all the liquid assets of the place, and he'll make out."

He stopped, breathing rather hard. I noticed all at once how heavily he was leaning on his hand. He pulled a handkerchief, rather fumblingly, from his breast-pocket, and touched it to his mouth. "Con's a good lad, and a clever lad; he's not afraid of work, and the land's in good heart. I think it's fair enough, all round."

"Darling, of course it is! More than fair! And now let's stop thinking about it; it's done, let's all forget it, and you forget it, too." I grinned at him. "You know I can't stomach these post mortems."

He patted my cheek. "Dear child," he said, and went abruptly out of the room.

What it cost Con in self-command I shall never know, but he did not come in to luncheon. The lawyer left immediately afterwards, and Grandfather retired to rest. I had promised Lisa to go into Bellingham that afternoon to do some shopping. She was already busy with preparations for dinner, but had refused to allow me to help her "because," she said simply, "I enjoy special occasions, and I'm selfish; but you shall do the table if you like."

I laughed. "All right, I've no quarrel with that. If I'm to be allowed to eat your cooking without having to work for it, that's okay by me."

"Oh, you can wash up," said Lisa placidly, adding, with that spice of malice that was never far away, "Julie can help you."

The shopping did not take long, and I caught the four o'clock bus back from Bellingham, which put me down at the head of the lane. I assembled my rather awkward collection of packages and set off downhill.

When I reached the mouth of the disused quarry where, on that first day, I had left my luggage, I saw a car standing there, an old car with too much chrome winking too brightly in the sun. Donald's car.

I picked my way in at the rutted entrance of the quarry. Donald was there, pipe in mouth, hands deep in trouser pockets, his head tilted back, apparently surveying the high wall at the back of the quarry. This was of sand-coloured stone, darkened with weathering, and here and there fissured red with iron. It was a big quarry, deep and narrow, consisting of several sections opening out of one another, partitioned off by jutting walls of rock. The cliff tops were crested with woods, whose crowding trees had sown seedlings broadcast, so that every ledge and tumble of rock was hung with green, and young oaks thrust golden frilled leaves above the brambles and foxgloves that hid the edges of the quarry floor. It must have been decades since any stone had been taken out of here.

Donald turned when he heard my footsteps, took the pipe out of his mouth, and smiled.

"Why, hullo."

"Hullo." I added, a little awkwardly, with a gesture of the basket and parcels in my hands, "I saw your car, and yielded to temptation. You were coming down to Whitescar, weren't you?"

"If I hadn't been," said Donald diplomatically, "I should be now."

I laughed. "You could hardly do anything else. I've an awful nerve, haven't I?" I hoped that my glance at his suit, which was, for once, impeccably formal, had not been too obvious. "But surely, you're coming to dinner?"

I thought he looked uncertain. I added, quickly, "Julie said you weren't quite sure if you could manage it after all, but we're hoping you will. It'll be worth it, I promise you. There were rumours about duckling."

"I'm sure it will. Miss Dermott's a wonderful cook. Well, if you're sure I haven't put things out—"

"Of course you haven't. We were all hoping you'd manage to get away. Julie'll be delighted. She's out just now; she went into Newcastle after all; but she'll be back in time for dinner."

"Did she? Then she won't miss the play. I'm glad. Did her cousin take her?"

"Con? No. Bill Fenwick. Have you met him?"

"Not yet. Would you like to put your parcels in the car?" He moved to open the door and take them from me.

"Thanks very much." I handed them over with a sigh of relief. "There. At least that's one way of ensuring that you do come to dinner. I only hope I'm not taking you down too early."

"No; I wasn't going straight there, as it happens; I want to go over and see Mr. Forrest, so I'll take you down via Whitescar, and—" he grinned—"it'll be very nice to have someone to open the gates."

"Fair enough. And there's an extra one now; one of the cattle grids is damaged, and you have to use the gate." I added, curiously, for his eyes had returned to the quarry face, "What interests you here? This is a geologist's sort of thing, not an archaeologist's, surely?"

"Oh, sure. But there is something interesting. This is the local sandstone, the building stone you'll see they've used for all the old houses hereabouts, and most of the walls, too. It's an old quarry. I've been asking about it, and I'm told it stopped working in 1910. I'd like to find out when it started, how far back there are any records of it."

"I can tell you one thing, though it may be only legend. This is supposed to be the quarry that Whitescar came out of, and I suppose Forrest too, though Whitescar's older. At any rate the first workings here must be at least four hundred years old."

"Older than that, by far." He smiled. "The quarry was here long before Whitescar was built. When you come to think about it, it is more likely that the place got its name from a quarry—a white scar—that was already a well-known landmark, *before* they took the stone out to build the house."

"It could be, I suppose. Is this a guess, or can you tell, somehow?" I looked vaguely at the overgrown rock around us.

"I can tell." I saw, suddenly, a spark of excitement in the deep hazel eyes. "Come and tell me if you see what I see. Over here, and watch your feet. There are bits of old iron and stuff lying around still. The oldest end of the quarry's along here, and it's flooded. I'll go first, shall I?"

We picked our way through the foxgloves, and the buds of ragwort, where loose stones and shards of rusting iron made going dangerous. A rabbit bolted out of a clump of nettles, and dived out of sight down an unlikely looking crevice.

"A nice fat one," said Donald, watching it.

"Were you thinking of the cooking pot, and Lisa's arts?"

"I was not. I was thinking about myxomatosis."

"Oh. Seeing the rabbits coming back, you mean?"

"Yes, the destructive little devils. But will you ever forget seeing them hobbling about, dying and in pain, and having to kill them, and not quite knowing how, and being afraid one wouldn't manage it cleanly the first time? One got sickeningly good at it, in the end. It may be the wrong thing to say to a farmer's daughter, but I'm pleased to see them back, nice and fat and immune, and I hope they eat every blade of grass belonging to the brutes who deliberately gave them the disease. . . . But of course you won't remember it. You weren't here, I keep forgetting. You seem so much a part of the scene at Whitescar. It's a lovely place, isn't it?"

"Do you know," I said, "I'm quite aware that that was a *non sequitur*, but it was also a compliment."

He looked surprised. "Was it?" He seemed to consider. "Yes, I've got it. So it was. Well, I didn't see it, but if I had I would have meant it."

"Fair enough." I laughed. "Except that *then* you'd never have said it."

He smiled slightly. "Probably not. The curse of Scotland, the padlocked tongue." But his eyes weren't amused.

I said, before I thought, "Maybe. But is it any worse than the curse of Ireland; the tongue without a latch, even, let alone a lock?"

He grinned then, spontaneously, and I knew he was thinking as I was, too late, about Con. But all he said was, "Or the curse of England; the double tongue?"

I laughed. "Ah well, it makes life pleasanter, doesn't it? Do you like living in the South?"

"Very much. I've good rooms in London, and my work takes me out as much as anyone could want."

"Do you think you'd want to settle permanently in London?"

We had clambered over a ridge of fallen stones, jammed by time into a bank of solid clay. Below us, round in another angle of the quarry, I could see water.

He stopped. He still had his pipe in his hand. It had gone out. He examined it carefully, but absently, as if he was not quite sure what it was. Then he stuffed it into his pocket. "You mean if I married Julie?"

I hadn't been ready for quite such direct dealing. "Yes. Yes, I did mean that. Perhaps I shouldn't have—"

"If I married Julie, I should still have to go where my work was," said Donald bluntly, "and it won't always be at West Woodburn." He looked at me. "Are you trying to tell me that she'll want to come and live here?"

"No."

"Ah. Well, I didn't altogether get the impression that she was wedded to the place."

"She's not." I hesitated, then added, equally bluntly, "Nor likely to be."

He looked at me sharply. Beside me a tuft of silvery hairgrass had fluffed into a lace of pale seeds. I ran my fingers through them, and then regarded the handful of tiny particles. I took a breath and plunged on. "You know, I wouldn't dream of saying this sort of thing to you, if it weren't important. You may think I'm speaking out of turn, and if so, I hope you'll forgive me."

He made the slight, indescribable sound that, in the North, manages to express assent, deprecation, interest, dissent, apology—anything at all that the listener cares to read into it. It sounds like "Mphm," and you can conduct whole (and perfectly intelligible) conversations with that one sound, anywhere north of the Tyne. As a contribution from Donald, it was unhelpful.

I opened my hand and let the seeds drift down on to the clay. "Have you said anything to Julie yet?"

He said quite simply, "No. It's been—so quick, you see . . . eight weeks since we met, that's all. I don't mean that *I'm* any the less sure, but I don't know if she . . . well, she's so young."

"She's nineteen. Nowadays girls know their own minds at nineteen."

"Do they?" I caught a slight hesitation in his manner then, and wondered if he had been suddenly reminded of another nineteen-year-old, eight years ago at Whitescar. He said, "I rather thought Julie had given every indication of not knowing."

"Bill Fenwick? He's a very nice boy, I think, but I assure you, you needn't worry about him."

"I wasn't thinking about Bill Fenwick."

"What do you mean, then?"

"Connor."

"*Con?*" I stared for a moment, then said flatly, "If you'd asked me, I'd have said she didn't even like him."

He had taken out his pipe, and was filling it again, more, I thought, for something to fidget with than because he wanted to smoke. He glanced up across it, and I thought his look sharpened. "I should have thought he was the very sort of chap a girl would be bound to fall for."

"Oh, lord, lord, he's attractive," I said impatiently. "You might say devastating. But Julie's never shown any signs of falling for him, and she's had plenty chance to . . . Goodness knows, if she wasn't susceptible to sheer blazing good looks like Con's at fifteen or sixteen, then she probably never will be. You forget, she was brought up here; she probably thinks of him like a brother . . . and not a particularly favourite one."

"You think so? I'm not very knowledgeable about these things. It just seemed to be so likely, and so . . . suitable."

"Suitable? I doubt it! Anyway, Julie's not a nitwit, and she's had plenty of time to fall for Con if she was ever going to, instead of which . . ." I paused, and brushed a finger idly over a tight purple thistle top. "Things are a little—difficult—just now at Whitescar. I can't quite describe why . . . it's a sort of emotional climate. . . ."

"I know," he said, surprisingly. "Everyone seems a little too much aware of what other people are doing."

"You've felt it? Then you know what I mean. It's partly to do with my coming back, and Grandfather's stroke, and his making a new will . . . oh, and everything. But it's rather horrid, and definitely unsettling. I know Julie's feeling it, and I'm so afraid she'll do something just plain silly. If it weren't for that, I'd be quite happy to settle back, and depend on her good sense and good taste, but just at present . . ." My voice trailed off, awkwardly.

"Do you know," said Donald, "whether you meant it or not, that was a compliment?"

I glanced at him. He looked amused, relaxed, confident, calmly pressing the tobacco down into the bowl of his pipe. I suddenly realized that I had been tempering the wind to a fully grown and completely self-possessed lamb. I had underrated Donald, and so (I thought with amused relief) had Julie.

I took a little breath of relief. Then I grinned maliciously. "Think nothing of it. That was my double tongue. How do you know I meant you?"

His eyes twinkled. "It never occurred to me that you could mean anyone else. That's one of the blessings of being a Scot, a profound and unshakable conviction of your own worth."

"Then hang on to that, and forget about Con," I said. "Heavens above, what's got into me? Donald, don't ask me why, and blame me for an interfering so-and-so if you like, but I wish to goodness that you'd simply *ask* the girl!"

He sent me that sudden, transforming grin. "It'll be a pleasure. Now, come along, and be careful down this slope, there may be loose bits. Here, take my hand. That's it."

"Goodness, that water's deep, isn't it?"

"It is that. Round here now. It's all right, you can walk on the edge, the rock's safe."

The water lay still and billiard-green in the shadow of the ledge where we stood. The edges of the pool were as sharply quarried as those of a swimming bath. On two sides the water was held in by a right angle of the high cliff; at the side where we stood, the quarry was floored with flat, bare rock, as smooth as concrete, which dropped squarely away in front of us to the water level some four feet below.

Here the water was in shadow, oil-green, slightly opaque, and somehow dangerous-looking, but where the sunlight struck it, it was lucid with grass-green colour streaked with weed, and beneath the surface the planes of quarried rock showed clearly, coloured according to their depth, green-gold and gold-jade, like peaches drowned in chartreuse.

"Look." He pointed down through the water towards one of the slanting slabs of stone that showed like a buttress shoring up the side of the pool. "Do you see that bit of rock?"

"The one that's lying on a slant? Yes. It looks as if it had been shaped, doesn't it? Such a nice, regular oblong."

"It has been shaped." Something in his voice made me look at him. He said, "Look at it again. Don't you see the marks?"

I peered down. "I . . . think so. I can't be sure. Do you mean what looks like a sort of rough scoring, diagonally across the block? That's not artificial, surely?"

"I think it was. Those marks would be sharply scored originally; chisel marks. That block's been under water a long time, and even still water will smooth out a stone surface, given time."

I stood up and looked at him. "Given time?"

"I don't know how long, because I don't know when this part of the quarry was flooded. But those stones down there were quarried about two thousand years ago."

"Two thou—" I stopped short and said, rather blankly, "You mean the *Romans?*"

"That's my guess. About two thousand years ago they opened a quarry here. Later, possibly much later, the 'white scar' among the woods was re-opened and worked again. Perhaps the Roman workings were already flooded; at any rate, new ones were started, and the original ones left to the weather. And now, this year, with this dry spring, and the drought, the water level sinks a couple of feet just when I chance to be poking about in this part of the world, and I see the stones. That's how things happen."

"Is it—is it important? Forgive me, I'm terribly ignorant, but what does it tell you, apart from the fact that they got building stone from here, for the Wall?"

"Not for the Wall. Hardly, when they were driving that along the whin sill anyway. They quarried the stone for the Wall on the spot."

"For the fort at West Woodburn, then? Habitancum, where you're working?"

"The same applies. There's stone there. They dug the local stuff whenever they could, of course, to save time and transport."

He seemed to be waiting, eyeing me in amiable expectation. It was a moment or two before the very simple conclusion presented itself.

"Oh! Yes, I get it. But, Donald, there's nothing Roman hereabouts, is there? At least, I've never heard of anything, and surely, if there were, the one-inch map would have it marked?"

"Exactly," said Donald.

I stared at him stupidly for a moment or two. "I . . . see! You think there *may* be something? Some unknown Roman work?"

He pushed his pipe down into a pocket, and turned away from the water's edge. "I've no idea," he said, "but there's nothing to stop me looking, is there? And now, if you're ready, I'll be taking you down to Whitescar, and then I'll get along and see Mr. Forrest, and ask his leave to go poking around in his policies."

CHAPTER ELEVEN

"I cannot get to my love if I wad dee,
The water of Tyne runs between him and me."

North Country Song.

WHEN WE got to the farm, it was to find a slightly distracted Lisa watching for me with some tale of disaster that involved a cream trifle, and Tommy, the black and white cat.

"And I'll wring his neck if he comes near the dairy again," she said, violently for her.

I said mildly, "We've got to remember he's eating for eight."

"Nonsense," said Lisa, "he had them days ago. Oh, I see what you mean. Well, even if he *is* feeding seven kittens, and let me tell you if only I can find them I'll drown the lot, that's no excuse for taking the whole top off the trifle I'd made for your grandfather's birthday dinner."

"Just a minute," said Donald, "no doubt I'm not just at my best today, but who has taken the trifle?"

"That beastly Tommy."

"The black and white cat? The fat one I—the one who was in to tea the other day?" Donald liked cats, and had made friends with them all, even the little half-wild tortoiseshell that lived like a wraith under the henhouse.

"That's the one. And not so fat either, now he's had his kittens, but after half the trifle and a pint of cream—"

I said helplessly, seeing Donald's expression, "It's all right. Nature has not suspended her laws, not yet. Everyone was wrong about Tommy—except that marmalade brute from West Lodge, at least I suppose it was him, because now that Tommy's unmasked he's the only tom for miles. Oh lord, I'm getting muddled too. And poor Tommy's figure wasn't due to incontinence—at least, not of the kind we'd thought; it was just kittens. Seven of them."

"And Annabel saw them in the loft, and didn't tell me till next morning, and by that time the brute had shifted them, and he's too sly to let us see him going to feed them." Lisa slapped a bucket down on the kitchen table.

"You wouldn't really drown them? All?" Donald spoke in the carefully non-committal voice of the man who would sooner die stuck full of arrows than seem to be soft-hearted over an animal.

"I certainly would, and Tommy too, if he gets in the dairy again."

"You can't change a personal pronoun overnight," I said apologetically, to Donald. "I'm afraid Tommy won't even decline to Thomasina. He'll be Tommy till the end of his days."

"Which are not," said Lisa, "so far distant, though even I have not the heart to have the brute put down, and leave those wretched kittens to starve to death somewhere. But if I find them before they're too big, they'll certainly have to drown. Did Mr. Seton say he was going over to West Lodge now? Annabel, would you be an angel and go across with him as far as the gardens, and get some strawberries? I rang up, and Johnny Rudd said he'd keep them for us. They should be ready, so hurry back, if you don't mind; we'll have them all to pick over."

Something must have shown in my face, for I saw her recollect herself for the first time for days. She must have forgotten that I had not yet been across to the gardens.

I saw her eyes flicker with a moment of calculation, and then she turned to Donald, but he spoke first. He must have seen something too; he saw more than one thought, I reflected; but of course he put my hesitation down to simple physical causes.

"Annabel's tired. Look, I can easily drop in at the market garden for you. You go past it to get to the Lodge, don't you?"

I said, "It's all right, Donald, thanks all the same. I'm not tired, and if you've to see Mr. Forrest at the Lodge, time will be getting along by the time you manage to get away, and besides, you don't want to have to hurry. I'll come along with you now, if I may, and walk straight back with the strawberries by the short cut, and then we can get on with hulling them. I'd like to see Johnny Rudd, anyway. He'll be in the garden?" This to Lisa.

"Yes." Her eyes were on me. "You haven't seen him since you came back, have you? His hair's going grey now, but he hasn't changed much. He's the only one who'll still be working there by this time; he said he'd wait if he could. The two boys go off at five. But if Mr. Forrest should be in the garden—"

"Oh, did I tell you?" I said. "I saw him the other day."

"Did you?" The question only just missed being too sharp. "To speak to?"

"For a moment. I forgot what we talked about, but I thought he'd changed, rather a lot." I picked up the basket. "I'll be as quick as I can," I said.

What had been the old walled kitchen garden of Forrest Hall lay beside the stables, about a quarter of a mile from the West Lodge, where Adam Forrest now lived.

Even here some pomp remained from the once palmy days of the Forrests. The entrance to the stableyard—now worked as a small farm—was a massive archway, with shields bearing the same heraldic beasts that flaunted their improbable attitudes on the gateposts at Forrest Hall. Over the arch stood the old clock tower, with a gilded weather vane over it. Trees crowded close on the other side of the lane, and the river glittered just beyond them. The road was rutted and green with weeds, its verges deep in wild flowers, but the cobbles of the yard, glimpsed through the archway, were sparkling clean, like the shingle on a seaswept beach. A little way off, beyond a clump of laburnum and copper beech, the chimneys of West Lodge glinted in the sunlight. Smoke was rising from one of them. Life at Forrest Park had shifted its focus.

Beyond the stableyard stretched the twelve-foot-high wall of the kitchen garden. There was a wrought-iron gate set into it.

"This one?"

"Yes."

Donald stopped the car, and I got out.

"Now, don't bother about me. It's just as quick taking the cut back across the fields. I'll go that way."

"If you're sure—"

"Quite sure. Thanks for the lift. I'll see you at dinner."

The car moved off. I pushed the gate open.

The last stretch of the lane had been deep under trees. Now, I walked through the gate, between two massive yews, and into a brilliance of sunshine that made me blink and narrow my eyes.

It wasn't only the brightness, however, that gave me pause. Here, the contrast with the moonlit derelict at Forrest was both striking and disturbing. In this garden, filled with sun and warmth and scent inside its four high walls, everything, at first sight, was as it might have been in the eighteenth-century heyday of the place.

All along one wall was the glass, and under it I could see the peaches and apricots and grapes of a more luxurious age, still carefully pruned and trained, and beneath them the homely forests of tomatoes and chrysanthemum seedlings, and the occasional splashes of colour that meant hydrangeas or begonias coming into flower for the market. Along the other three walls were the espaliered fruit trees. The fruit, small, green and shining, crowded thickly on the boughs against the warm sandstone.

Down the centre of the garden went a broad walk of turf, beautifully cut and rolled, and to either side of this was a flower border, spired and splashed and shimmering with all the colours of an English June; lupins, delphiniums, peonies, poppies, irises, Canterbury bells, all held back by lavender swags of catmint, and backed by a high rustic trellis where climbing roses held up their fountains of bright flowers. At the far end of the walk, at the focal point, as it were, of the vista, I could see the basin of some disused stone fountain, with a couple of bronze herons still on guard over what had been the pool. This was set round with flagstones, between which were clumps of lavender, rosemary, thyme and sage, in a carefully planned confusion as old as the garden itself. They must have left the old herb garden, I thought, and this one avenue of flowers. The rest was all order and usefulness—peas and beans and turnips and potatoes, and regimented fruit bushes. The only other thing that spoke of the glory that had departed was a tall circular structure in one corner of the garden, a dovehouse, *columbarium*, with honeysuckle and clematis running riot over its dilapidated walls. The pegged tiles of its roof sagged gently over the beams beneath, as canvas moulds itself to the supporting ropes. The tiles showed bronze-coloured in the sunlight, their own smoky blue overlaid and softened by the rings of that lovely lichen that spreads its amber circles, like water-lily leaves, over old and beautiful things. The dove-doors had decayed, and looked like empty eye sockets; I saw starlings fly out.

But elsewhere all was order. Not a weed. I reflected that if Adam Forrest and Johnny Rudd kept all this themselves, with the help of a couple of boys, I could hardly taunt him with not understanding the meaning of labour. The place must be killing work.

At first I couldn't see anyone about at all, and walked quickly up the grass walk, towards the greenhouses, peering through the rose trellis to right and left. Then I saw a man working among raspberry canes over near one of the walls. He had his back to me, and was stooping. He was wearing faded brown corduroys, and a blue shirt, and I could see an old brown jacket hung near him over a stake. He had dark hair with grey in it.

He didn't seem to hear my approach, being intent on fastening a bird net back securely over the canes.

I stopped on the path near him. "Johnny?"

He straightened and turned. "I'm afraid—" he began, then stopped.

"You?" For the life of me I couldn't help sounding unbelieving. This was certainly the Adam Forrest I had met and spoken with a few nights ago, but now, facing him in the broad glare of the afternoon, I could see how different he was from my remembered picture of him. What I had seen on that last, almost dreamlike meeting had been something like seeing a sequence from a film taken years ago, when he had been ten, no, fifteen years younger. Some unreality of the night had lent itself to him: I remembered the fine planes of his face, the smoothness of skin young in the moonlight, the darkness of hair and eyes dramatized in the drained light. In the moonlight he had seemed merely tallish, well enough built, and had moved easily, with that air of self-confidence that goes with strength—or with inherited wealth. Now, as he straightened in the sunlight to face me, it was as if the film had spun along swiftly, and the actor had, with skilful make-up, confirmed the passage of years. His hair, which had been very dark, was showing grey; not gracefully, at the temples, but in an untidy flecking all over, like the dimming of dust. The fine structure of strong bone couldn't be altered, but there were lines I hadn't seen by moonlight, and he was thinner than the size of his frame should have allowed. Before, he had been conventionally dressed, and I had noticed neither the cut nor the quality of his clothes; but now the light showed up a shabbiness that—so unconsciously he wore it—must have been part of every day. Some part of my mind said that of course it was only common sense to wear rough clothes for a rough job, but another part, that I had not known existed, linked the shabbiness with the lines on his face, and the greying hair, and winced away from them with a pity I knew he didn't want, and that I had no right to feel. I noticed that he was wearing gloves, and remembered my taunt about his hands, and was sorry.

He smiled at me, narrowing his eyes against the sun. They were grey-blue, and puckered at the corners. He spoke easily, as if there could be no constraint between us.

"Hullo. Were you looking for Johnny Rudd? I'm afraid he's gone."

"I came for some strawberries. The cat's been at the trifle, and it's Grandfather's birthday, so Lisa rang up with an S.O.S., and Johnny said he'd try to save some."

"Then he'll have left them up in the packing shed. Come and see."

We walked up the path together. I saw him eyeing me, as curious as I had been, no doubt, to see what the daylight showed.

I said, "Have you met Julie's young man? Donald Seton?"

"No. Why?"

"He came across with me just now, to see you about something, but he thought you'd have finished for the day, so he went along to the Lodge."

"Oh? What's it about, d'you know?"

"Yes, but I'll leave him to tell you himself." I caught his quick look, and smiled a little. "Oh, don't worry, it's nothing personal. You're still quite safe."

We had reached a door in the wall behind the greenhouses, which led to the workrooms of the place—boiler room, potting houses, cold frames. He stopped with his hand on the knob, and turned. I noticed all at once that his eyes looked tired, as if he didn't sleep well. "Safe? *I?*"

"Indeed, yes. If you're not an accessory after the fact, I don't know what you are. You never came after that passport. You never came across to Whitescar, and tried to trip me up and catch me out in front of Grandfather, as no doubt you think you could easily have done. You've done nothing. Why?"

"I don't know. I honestly don't know." He hesitated, as if to say something more. Then, instead, he merely turned, and pushed the door open for me. "This way, now; leave the door, it's all right; Seton may come looking for me. Is Julie with him?"

"No. She's gone into Newcastle with Bill Fenwick."

He shot me a look. "That troubles you. Why?"

"Because Con won't like it one bit," I said crisply, "and Con is a . . . creature of impulse."

"That's absurd." He said it as he had done before, but with just a shade less conviction.

"Any situation bordering on violence is absurd—until it suddenly breaks, and then, *wham*, there you are, in the middle of something you'd thought only happened in the Sunday Press."

"What about this man who's here—Seton, was it?"

"That's different. He'll take her away from Whitescar, and they'll live in London, and spend half the year in a tent somewhere, digging. Con's all for that, as you may imagine—and the further away, the better. Uzbekistan, for instance, or the Desert of Lop, if the Romans went there, I wouldn't know."

"Does she want to go?"

"Pining to," I said cheerfully. "Don't worry, I've practically fixed it. I told you I'd look after Julie." I caught his eye, and laughed. "What is it?"

"This—crazy business; and I'm as crazy as any part of it. That's what comes of working by instinct instead of sense; I suppose women do it every day, but I'm not accustomed to it, and I dislike it. There's nothing to assure you that you're still rational. Look at the situation: I'm not sure who you are; I'm not sure what you're doing; I'm certain it's wrong; but for some reason I'm prepared to let you do it."

"I told you who I was, and what I was doing."

"Yes, you did. You were honest, as far as that went. And you've got me into a position where I seem to be condoning what you do, even though I'm damned if I do more. I suppose it's because I think rather a lot of old Mr, Winslow, and oddly enough, I'd trust you over Julie, who seems to me to be the only other person who matters. I confess I'd wondered, before you came, just what the set-up would be at Whitescar, when Mr. Winslow died. You say you're 'looking after' her interests. Well, as long as Julie comes to no harm, I don't much care how you and Connor fight it out the rest of the way. If you can get it, I shan't grudge you your 'competence.' "

"You needn't worry; you can trust me over Julie."

He sighed. "The odd thing is that I believe you, and for that alone I deserve to be behind bars as an accessory, just as soon as you are. Here's the packing shed. Come and see if Johnny's left your strawberries."

The shed was big and cool, its basic smell, of geraniums and damp peat, dizzily overlaid by that of a tank crammed full with sweet peas. It was as orderly as the garden: there were shelves of plant pots and boxes, in graded sizes; printed labels in rows (probably in alphabetical order); raffia hanging in loops that looked as if they would never dare tangle or snap; and two or three pairs of clean cotton gloves on a hook beside the window.

I watched Adam Forrest with some awe as he crossed the shed and reached down a pair of these. There were two punnets of strawberries on a bench to the left of the window. "Enough, do you think?" he asked.

"I think so."

"There may be a few more ripe, in the bed by the dovehouses. I can pick them, if you've time to wait."

"No, don't trouble. I'm sure there'll be enough, and I promised to get back quickly. Dinner's at half-past seven, and we'll have them to pick over. Look, I brought a basket. We can tip them all in together, and you can keep the punnets."

"It comes cheaper that way," agreed Adam gravely.

I gaped at him for a second, for some absurd reason more embarrassed than at any time in our too rapidly intimate relationship. Lisa hadn't mentioned money; I had none with me, and hadn't thought about it till now. I said, stammering, "I—I'm afraid I can't pay for them now."

"I'll charge them," said Adam imperturbably. He reached for a notebook, and made a jotting on a meticulously columned page headed "Winslow." He caught my eye on him, and grinned, and suddenly, in the shadowed shed, the years fell away, and there was the lover of the moonlit tryst, the actor of that early film. I caught my breath. He said, "Whitescar runs an account. They don't seem to have time to grow any vegetables there themselves . . . I doubt if anybody has even touched the garden—" he shut the book and returned it neatly to its place—"since you left. Careful! You're spilling those! What did I say to make you jump?"

"You know quite well. You did it deliberately. You . . . got under my skin."

"That makes two of us," said Adam; at least, that's what I thought he said, but he muttered it under his breath, and the words were swallowed as he turned his head quickly to the door, adding aloud, "I suppose this is Mr. Seton?"

"Oh . . . hullo, Donald. Yes, Mr. Forrest's still here. Mr. Seton, Adam. . . ."

The men exchanged greetings. Donald said, "You got your strawberries?"

"I did. Your dinner's safe. I told Mr. Forrest you wanted to see him, Donald, but I managed to keep quiet about the reason."

"You needn't have done that." He turned to Adam. "I don't know if

Annabel told you, sir, but I'm an archaeologist; I'm attached to the Commission—the Royal Commission on Historical Monuments—and just at present I'm in charge of the work being done up at West Woodburn."

"I had heard that excavating has started there," said Adam. "Just what are you hoping to do?"

"Well, the Commission's job is to list and describe all existing Roman monuments, with maps and photographs and so on. It's worked on a county basis, and I'm one of the team assigned to Northumberland. . . ."

I had got the strawberries all tipped into my basket, but lingered a little, interested to hear the outcome of what Donald had to say. He gave Adam a very brief account of the work he was engaged on, and then passed, with an admirably Scottish economy of time and words, to the business of the moment.

When he described how he had seen the "Roman stones" in the quarry, it was obvious that he had caught Adam's interest. "And you think it likely, if that quarry *was* originally Roman, that there may be some Roman buildings near by?"

"Fairly near, at any rate," said Donald. "There's nothing remarkable about the rock itself—the quarried rock—if you follow me. If it were marble, for example, you might expect it to be worked, even if it had to be carried long distances; but this kind of sandstone is the common local stone. If the Romans did start a quarry there, then they would do so for pure reasons of convenience. In other words, they were building locally."

"I see," said Adam. "And am I right in thinking that there's nothing recorded hereabouts? I've never read of anything, though I've always been interested in local history."

"Quite right. There's nothing nearer than the camp at Four Laws, and, since that's on Dere Street, the materials for building it would certainly be taken from somewhere on the road, not right across country from here. So it did occur to me that, if the quarry was started here, in the peninsula, when the same stone occurs all along the ridge above the river—and is rather more get-at-able there—it did occur to me to wonder if whatever was built was built on the peninsula itself."

"Somewhere in Forrest Park?"

"Yes. I wanted to ask your permission to have a look round, if I may."

"With the greatest of pleasure. I'm afraid the Forestry Commission acres are out of my jurisdiction, but the meadowland, and the Hall grounds, by all means. Go where you like. But what exactly will you be looking for? Surely anything there was will be deep under several feet of earth and trees by now?"

"Oh yes. But I did wonder if you could help me. Can you remember if there's anything else in the way of a quarry, anything that might be an overgrown pit, or artificial bank—you know the kind of thing?"

"Not at the moment, but I'll think it over. The only pit I can think of is the old icehouse near the Forrest gate-house. That's dug deep into the earth under the trees, but that can hardly—wait a minute!"

He broke off, his brows knitted in an effort of memory. I watched him half-excitedly, Donald with the utmost placidity. Doubtless he was very much better aware than I was that "discoveries" rarely, if ever, come out of the blue.

"The icehouse," said Adam. "Mentioning the icehouse struck a chord. Wait a minute, I can't be sure, but somewhere, some time, when I was a child, I think . . . I've seen something at Forrest. A stone . . . Roman, I'll swear." He thought a moment longer, then shook his head. "No, it's gone. Could it have been the same ones, I wonder, that I saw? The ones in the quarry?"

"Not unless there was a very dry season, and you probably wouldn't have noticed them unless they were even nearer the surface than they are now. Wouldn't you say so, Annabel?"

"Certainly. And anyway, nobody but an expert could possibly have guessed those *were* Roman. They looked quite ordinary to me, and to a child they'd mean nothing at all."

"That's true. You can't remember anything more, sir? What made you think it was Roman stone? Why the icehouse? What is the icehouse, anyway?"

"A primitive sort of refrigerator. They usually built them somewhere in the grounds of big houses, in the eighteenth century," said Adam. "They were big square pits, as a rule, dug somewhere deep in the woods where it was cool. They had curved roofs, with the eaves flush with the ground, and a door in one end, over the pit. People used to cut the ice off the lake—there's a small pool beyond the house—in winter, and store it underground in layers of straw, to bring out in summer. The one at Forrest's in the woods near the old gate-house."

"Then you may have seen this thing there, surely? It was quite usual for later builders to lay hands on any Roman stones they could, to use again. They were good blocks, well shaped and dressed. If there were a few left stacked in the old quarry, above water level, a local eighteenth-century builder may well have taken them and—"

"The cellars!" said Adam. "That was it! Not the icehouse, we weren't allowed in; it wasn't safe, and it was kept locked. We weren't allowed in the cellars, either, but that was different; they were at least accessible." He grinned. "I thought there was something surreptitious and candlelit about the memory, and it also accounts for the fact that we never mentioned it to anyone. I'd forgotten all about it until this moment. Yes, I'm fairly sure it was in the cellars at Forrest. I can't remember any more than that, except that we were rather intrigued for the moment, as children are, by the carving on the stone. It was upside down, which made it harder to make out what it said, even if we could have—"

"What it *said?*" Donald's voice was sharp, for him.

Adam looked surprised. "Yes. Didn't you say the stones were carved? There was some sort of lettering, as far as I remember, and a carving of some kind . . . an animal."

"I said 'chiselled,' not 'carved,'" said Donald. "If you're right, it sounds as if you may have seen an inscription. All I saw were the ordinary tooling marks on the stone, the marks made by dressing with chisels. Like this. . . ." He fished in his inside pocket, and came out with a thick wad of papers. There seemed to be (besides a wallet, several dozen letters and a driver's licence) an Ordnance Survey map of the North Tyne, and a thin booklet of what looked like—but surely could not be—logarithms. Donald looked at them vaguely, selected an old envelope, on which I distinctly saw a postmark two years old, and restored the rest to his pocket.

Adam handed him a pencil. "Thanks. This," said Donald, drawing with beautiful economy and accuracy on the dog-eared envelope, "is something like the stones I saw."

He handed the paper to Adam, who studied it. "I see. No, that doesn't convey anything to me; I'd never have known that was Roman . . . not even now, let alone at ten years old. Well, the obvious thing to do is to go and look, isn't it? This is really rather exciting. If it turns out to be an inscription of the Ninth Legion or something, will Forrest's fortune be remade?"

"Well," said Donald cautiously, "you might get it on to T.V. . . . The house is a ruin, isn't it? Is it still possible to get into the cellars?"

"I think you'll find you can get down. I don't have to tell you to watch yourself, I'm not sure what sort of condition the place is in. But you may certainly go just where you like. Look, I'll make you a plan."

He reached to the nearby shelf for a paper—it looked like an invoice form—and spread it on the bench. Donald handed back the pencil. I came to Adam's elbow to look. He drew a couple of lines, then, with a subdued exclamation of irritation, pulled off the cotton gloves, dropped them on the bench beside him, and picked the pencil up again. "I can't write in them. Do you mind?"

"Mind?"

Then I saw. His hands were disfigured, most horribly, it must have been by burns. The skin was white and dead-looking, glassed like polythene, and here and there were puckered scars that showed purple; the shape of his hands, like the other bone structure, had been beautiful, but the injuries had distorted even that, and made them hideous, things to shock. Things to hide, as, until now, he had hidden them. This was something else that the romantic moonlighting had not revealed.

I must have made some small sound, some little gasp of indrawn breath. Adam's pencil checked, and he looked at me.

I suppose most people stared like that, sick and shocked, for a moment or two, then looked quickly away, saying nothing, talking of something else, pretending not to have seen.

I said, "Adam, your hands, your poor hands. . . . What did that to your hands?"

"I burned them."

The fire at Forrest. His wife. *The bed was alight by that time. He managed to drag the bedclothes off her, and carry her downstairs. . . .*

He had reached one of those terrible hands for the discarded gloves. He hadn't taken his eyes off my face. He said gently, "I'll put them on again. I'm sorry, I forgot you wouldn't know. It's rather a shock, the first time."

"It—it doesn't matter. Don't, for me . . . I—I've got to go." I reached blindly for the basket. I could feel the tears spilling hot on to my cheeks, and couldn't stop them. I had forgotten all about Donald, till I heard him say "Here" and the basket was put into my hands. I said shakily, "I've got to hurry back. Good-bye," and, without looking at either of them, my head bent low over the basket, I turned and almost ran out of the packing shed.

I was conscious of the silence I had left behind me, and of Adam, straightening abruptly, the pencil still in his hand, staring after me.

CHAPTER TWELVE

Go with your right to Newcastle,
And come with your left side home;
There will you see these two lovers. . . .

Ballad: *Fair Margaret and Sweet William.*

AS IT TURNED OUT, there were more than enough strawberries for supper. Julie didn't come back.

The dinner, though delicious, could hardly be said to be festive. It was as if all the accumulated tensions of the last days had gathered that evening at the dining table, building slowly up like the thunderheads that stood steadily on the horizon outside.

Con had come in early, rather quiet, with watchful eyes, and lines from nostril to chin that I hadn't noticed before. Grandfather seemed to have recruited his energies with his afternoon rest; his eyes were bright and a little malicious as he glanced round the table, and marked the taut air of waiting that hung over the meal. It was his moment of power, and he knew it.

If it had needed anything to bring the tensions to snapping point, Julie's absence provided it. At first it was only assumed that she was late, but, as the meal wore on, and it became apparent that she wasn't coming, Grandfather started making irritatingly frequent remarks about the forgetfulness and ingratitude of young people, that were intended to sound pathetic, but only managed to sound thoroughly bad-tempered.

Con ate more or less in silence, but a silence so unrelaxed as to be almost aggressive. It was apparent that Grandfather thought so, for he kept casting bright, hard looks under his brows, and once or twice seemed on the verge of the sort of edged and provocative remark with which he had been prodding his great-nephew for days.

I drew what fire I could, chattering shamelessly, and had the dubious satisfaction of attracting most of the old man's attention to myself, some of it so obviously affectionate—pointedly so—that I saw, once or twice, Con's glance cross mine like the flicker of blue steel. Afterwards, I thought, when he knows, when that restless, torturing ambition is stilled at last, it will be all right; everything will be all right. . . .

As Grandfather had predicted, Donald's presence saved the day. He seconded my efforts with great gallantry, making several remarks at least three sentences long; but he, too, was unable to keep his eyes from the clock, while Lisa, presiding over a magnificent pair of duckling *à la Rouennaise*, and the strawberries hastily assembled into whipped cream *Chantilly*, merely sat unhelpfully silent and worried, and, in consequence, looking sour.

The end of the meal came, and the coffee, and still no Julie. We all left the dining room together. As Con pushed back his chair, he said abruptly, "I'm going to telephone Nether Shields."

"What the devil for?" asked Grandfather testily. "If the girl chooses to forget, let her be."

"She's not likely to have forgotten. I'm afraid there may have been an accident."

"Then what's the use of telephoning Nether Shields? If they knew anything, they'd have rung us up. The girl's forgotten. Don't waste your time."

"I'll ring, all the same," said Con, and left the room abruptly. Grandfather's gaze as he watched him was bright and sardonic.

To forestall what comment he might make, I said quickly, "If she did forget, she may have gone back to supper with Bill Fenwick."

"Nonsense," said Grandfather roundly, and stumped out of the dining room.

In the drawing room Lisa poured coffee, her attention stolidly on the cups. Grandfather mercifully relapsed into silence, fidgeting with his fingers, and forgetting to drink his coffee. Donald was still watching the clock, though I suspected that his motives had altered somewhat. I'd have given a lot, myself, to go for a long, long walk, preferably several miles away from Whitescar.

"If anything has happened to that child—" began Grandfather, at length.

"Nothing will have happened," I said. "You'd have heard if there'd been an accident. She'd have rung up . . . or someone else would. Don't worry, it'll be all right. She'll turn up soon."

"If a tire burst when they were miles from anywhere—" Donald put in a comforting oar—"that could delay them."

"As long as this? It's nine o'clock."

"Mphm," said Donald.

I glanced anxiously at Grandfather. The bright malice had faded. He looked his age, and more, and the hand with which he pushed aside his untasted coffee was shaking a little.

Con came back into the room.

"Nothing," he said tersely. "Mrs. Fenwick knew Julie was due back here for dinner. Bill said he'd be home by seven. No sign."

"I told you it was no use telephoning!" Grandfather almost snapped it. "But you know best, as usual."

Con took the coffee which Lisa had stirred and handed to him. "It was a chance," he said, mildly enough. "And I thought it might save you worrying."

"You're very solicitous of others, all of a sudden, aren't you, Connor? Why so anxious? Because you want to see the family all assembled together? Lisa tell you what I said at luncheon, eh?"

It was unforgivable enough, especially in front of Donald, but normally it would hardly have worried anyone. Con's reaction was indicative, uncomfortably so, of the pressure that had been building up behind the quiet, sealed front.

He went rather pale, and put down his coffee half-drunk. He didn't even look where he was setting the cup, but put it blindly down on what would have been vacancy, if Lisa had not quietly taken it out of his hand. For a moment he and Grandfather stared at one another, and I waited, with a sort of horror, for the valves to blow.

Then Con said, "If I'm wanted, I'll be in the field," and turned his back on his great-uncle. "Good night, Seton." Quietly still, but like one escaping to a freer, purer air, he went out of the room.

Unexpectedly, Grandfather chuckled. "Good lad," he said, with a sort of fierce approval, then turned a ghost of his old, charming smile on Donald. "I warned you, didn't I? You'll have to forgive us for thrusting our family squabbles on you."

Donald returned some sort of polite reply, and, thereafter, the conversation trickled back into fairly normal channels. But half an hour went by, and still there was no sign of Julie, nor did the telephone ring. I must have shown how worried I was, and Grandfather took to saying, at shorter and shorter intervals, "Where on earth can the child have got to?" or alternatively, "Why the devil couldn't she have telephoned?" until I could see it was getting across even Donald's admirable nervous system. I wasn't surprised when, almost too soon for civility, he rose to his feet, and said he thought he had better be going.

No one made any attempt to stop him. Lisa got up with rather too patent relief, and let him carry the coffee cups out to the kitchen for her.

I followed. "I'll come back in a minute, Lisa, when I've done the gate for Donald. Leave them for me: you said you would."

It was dusk in the lee of the big barn, where Donald had parked his car. When I reached it, I couldn't see him. Puzzled, I paused beside the car, peering around me into the shadows.

Then I heard a soft step, and turned swiftly. Donald came very quietly round the end of the barn, from the direction of the stableyard. Seeing me waiting beside the car, he stopped abruptly, and even in that light I could see he was out of countenance. I stared at him, completely at a loss for words. He looked like a man who has been caught out in a dubious act.

There was one of those ghastly pauses, then he smiled. "It's all right, I haven't been hiding the silver behind the barn. I've been visiting friends."

"Friends?" I said, blankly.

He laughed. "Come and see."

I followed him into the yard, where he pushed open the half-door of the empty stable. The interior smelled sweet and dry, of hay and horses. Opposite the door was a big loose-box, the bars down now, since Blondie had gone out to grass. Donald switched on the light, and led the way into the loose-box. There was an iron manger running the breadth of it, deep, and half full of clean straw. I supposed the hens laid there sometimes.

"Here," said Donald softly, "meet the family."

I leaned over the manger. Deep in the straw was a nest, but not of eggs. Seven kittens, some days old, still blind and boneless, all sleeping soundly, lay curled together in a tight, furry mass, black and white and ginger. Donald put down a gentle hand to touch the warm fur. As he did so, a wraith, black and white, jumped on to the iron manger at his elbow, purred softly, and slid down beside the kittens. There was a wriggling, and butting, and readjusting of fur, then Tommy settled down, eyes slitted and happy, paws steadily kneading the rustling straw.

"How on earth did you find them?" I whispered.

"Tommy showed me tonight, when I got back from West Lodge."

"Well, I'll keep your secret. Nobody'll come in here, while the horses are out. . . . Did you really have to leave so early?"

"I thought I'd better."

"Mm, yes, I see what you mean." We left the darkened stable quietly, and walked back to the car. Beside it, I hesitated for a moment, then turned quickly to him. "Look, Donald, don't worry."

"Aren't you worrying?"

"Well, one can't help it, can one? But nothing'll have happened. Depend on it, they've forgotten, and stayed out to a meal, or something."

"It seems unlikely."

"Well, perhaps the car *has* broken down."

"Mphm," said Donald.

"Why don't you wait? They really ought not to be long."

"No, thanks, but I won't. Did I remember to thank Miss Dermott for the supper?"

"You thanked her very nicely. No, I'll do the gate."

"Oh, thank you. . . ." But he lingered, a hand on the car door. He seemed about to say something, then I thought he changed his mind. What he did say, rather tentatively, was, "Nice chap, Forrest."

"Yes."

"He seems interested in this quarry. He says he'll come over himself tomorrow, and hunt up that stone in the cellar with me."

"I hope you'll find it. Does it sound to you as if it could be the real thing?"

"That's impossible to tell, but I think it may well be, if only because he's kept that strong impression, all these years, that it was Roman. He thinks there must have been at least one or two words that he and his sister would have recognized as Latin, even at the age of nine or ten." He grinned. "He reckons that an EST or a SUB would have been about their limit at the time. Let's hope he's right."

"It's terribly exciting, isn't it?"

"At best," said Donald cheerfully, "it'll probably simply say 'Vote for P. Varro as quarry foreman. Shorter hours and longer pay.' "

I laughed. "Well, good luck to it, anyway."

"Would you care to come along tomorrow afternoon and help in the hunt?"

"No, thanks, I won't. I—I have things I've got to do."

"Mphm," said Donald. This time it seemed to signify a vague agreement. He hesitated again, and suddenly I found myself wondering if Julie had told him anything about Adam.

I glanced up at him. "I'm sorry I was upset this afternoon. Did he—did he mind, d'you think?"

"He didn't seem to." Donald spoke so quickly that I realized that this was exactly what he had been wanting to say, and hadn't liked to broach the subject, even to bring me comfort. "He said nothing. I'm sure he'd understand. I shouldn't worry."

"I won't," I said. "Good night, Donald."

"Good night."

The car's engine started with a roar, and the ancient vehicle jerked forward. I saw Donald lift a hand as he passed me, then the car grumbled its way off into the dusk towards High Riggs and the top of the hill.

The washing-up was done, and we were back in the drawing room, Lisa with some mending for Con, myself playing a rather abstracted game of cribbage with Grandfather, when at length we heard a car enter the yard. Almost before it had drawn to a halt, one of its doors slammed; there was a short pause, and, faintly, the sound of voices, then the car moved off again immediately, and high heels tapped quickly across the yard to the kitchen door. We heard Julie cross the kitchen lobby and push open the green baize door to the hall. Then the hasty steps tapped their way across the hall, and were on the carpeted stairs.

Grandfather put his cards down with a slam, and shouted, "Julie!"

The flying steps stopped. There was a pause.

"*Julie!*"

She came slowly down the stairs again, and crossed the hall to the drawing-room door. With another part of my mind I heard the car's engine receding over the hill.

The drawing-room door opened. Julie stood there for a moment before she came in. Her eyes went swiftly round the room, and came to rest on Grandfather. Her hair was ruffled from the ride in the open car; her colour was high, and her eyes shone brilliantly. She looked very lovely; she also looked like the conventional picture of the young girl fresh from her lover's embrace, confused by the sudden light and the watching eyes. For a moment I wondered, with a sinking heart, if I had been wrong, and her interest in Bill Fenwick was serious, but then—I'm not quite sure how, except that Julie and I were so much alike—I knew, with relieved certainty, that the confused brilliance of her glance was due, not to love and embarrassment, but to sheer temper.

I saw Lisa's plump hands check in their work, and the sock she was mending sink slowly to her lap, as she stared at Julie with what looked like speculation.

"Julie!" Grandfather sounded angry. "Where have you been? We've spent the whole evening waiting and watching for you, and worrying in case anything had happened. Heaven knows I don't expect you to remember anything as completely unimportant as your grandfather's birthday, but I do think—"

"I'm sorry, Grandfather." Her voice was tolerably composed, but I saw how white her hand was on the doorknob. "I—we meant to get back. I didn't forget—there was an accident."

"An accident?" The old man's hands had been flat on the table among the cards. I saw them twitch, like a puppet's hands pulled by strings threaded through the arms.

I looked up quickly. "I take it nobody's hurt?"

She shook her head. "No, it was a silly thing. It wasn't Bill's fault. We weren't going fast—it was in the speed limit area, and Bill really was driving quite slowly. Somebody backed out of a garage straight into us."

"Was Bill's car damaged?"

"Yes. The door panel was dented, and he'd hit the front wheel, and Bill was afraid he'd knocked it out of true, and bent the track rod, or whatever you call it, but he hadn't. Then there was all the fuss, and the police—" she swallowed—"you know how it is; and then we had to get the car back to a garage and let them see what the damage was, and Bill had to arrange to take it back later to have it done. I—we couldn't help it, really we couldn't."

"Of course you couldn't," I said. "Look, honey, have you had supper? Because—"

"You could have telephoned," said Grandfather sharply. I noticed he was breathing hard, and the thin fingers twitched among the fallen cards.

"I'm sorry," said Julie again, but with something too sharp and driven-sounding in her voice. Outside, the yard gate clashed, and I saw her jump. "I know I should have, but I didn't think of it till we were on the way home. You—you know how it is, with everything happening, and Bill's car, and the other man being foul about it, and telling all sorts of lies to the police, only they *did* believe Bill and me . . ." Her voice quavered and she stopped.

Grandfather opened his mouth to speak, but I forestalled him. "She'd be too upset to think about it, Grandfather. You know what even the smallest of accidents is like; it shakes you right to pieces. Well, it's lucky it's no worse." Then, to Julie, "We thought it might be something like this; we knew you wouldn't have skipped the party unless something *had* happened. Look, my dear—" I got to my feet—"it's obvious you've had a shaking. I think you should get yourself straight upstairs to bed. I'll bring you something to eat; there's plenty left. . . . That was a wonderful meal you missed —Aylesbury ducklings, and strawberries straight off the straw. Tommy ate the trifle."

"Did he?" said Julie uncertainly. "Lisa, really, I'm terribly sorry, but—"

Lisa said, "Donald Seton was here." It was impossible to tell, from her composed, colourless tone, whether or not she was actuated by deliberate malice.

The result was the same. Julie bit her lip, stammered, and looked ready to cry. "Here? I—I didn't think he was coming."

I said gently, "I met him when I was on my way back from Bellingham. His London colleague had left early, and he was free, so I told him we were expecting him. He'd obviously been hoping to come, anyway," I smiled. "He'd changed into a very respectable suit."

"He left some time ago," said Lisa. "We thought he would wait to see you, but he said he had to go."

Julie turned to look at her, but vaguely, as if she wasn't really seeing her. I said, as lightly as I could, "I hope this all happened *after* the play? You saw that all right?"

"Oh, yes. It—it was wonderful."

"Then I expect, when you've had a rest," I said briskly, "you'll vote it was worth it, accident or no. Now, darling, I really think—"

The baize door opened and swung shut on a *whoosh* of air. Con came quickly across the hall, to pause in the open doorway behind Julie.

He had changed back into his work clothes before he had gone up to the field, and in breeches and open-necked shirt he looked tough, and also extremely handsome. And this for the same reason as Julie. He, too, was in a flaming temper, and it didn't need much gazing in the crystal ball to guess that the pair of them had just had a monumental row.

Julie never even turned her head on his approach. She merely hunched one shoulder a little stiffly, as if he were a cold draught behind her, and said to Lisa, on a strained, high note, "Did Donald say anything?"

"What about?" asked Lisa.

"No, Julie," I said.

Grandfather's hand scuffed irritably at the cards on the table in front of him. "What's all this? What's all this? Young Seton? What's he got to do with it?"

"Nothing," said Julie. "Nothing at all!" Her voice went thin and high. "And nor has Con!" She flung him a glance over her shoulder, about as friendly as a volley of swan-shot.

"Con?" Grandfather's eyes went from one to the other. "Con?" he repeated querulously. "Where does Con come into this?"

"That's just it!" said Julie, dangerously. "He doesn't, for all he seems to think he's the master here, and I'm answerable to him! Can you *imagine*–?" She checked herself, and went on in a voice that trembled insecurely on the edge of self-control, "Just now, as we came back, Bill had to stop the car for the gate at High Riggs–you know the grid's broken, and you've to use the gate–well, Con saw fit to come over, and asked me where the hell I'd been, (I'm sorry, Grandfather, but I'm only saying what *he* said) and why was I so late, and, as if that wasn't bad enough, he started pitching into Bill! As if it had been Bill's fault! Even if it *had*, it's not *your* business–" swinging on her cousin–"to start anything like that! What put *you* in such a howling temper, for heaven's sake? Speaking to Bill like that, swearing and everything, making a fool of me . . . and I'll be very surprised if he shows his face here again! He was furious, and I don't blame him! I had to apologize for you! How do you like *that?*"

"You know, Connor," said Grandfather, mildly enough, "you ought not to have done this. Julie's explained it to us. It wasn't young Fenwick's fault that–"

"That's not the *point!*" cried Julie. "Don't you *see?* Even if it *had* been Bill's fault, or mine, it's *none of Con's business!* If I choose to stay out all *night*, that's *my* affair!"

"And mine," said Grandfather, with sudden grim humour.

"All right," said Julie, "yours! But not Con's! He takes too dashed much on himself, and always did! It's time someone said something. It's been going on for years, without anyone noticing, and now this–*this* sort of thing –is the last straw as far as I'm concerned! Being ticked off like a naughty child in front of Bill Fenwick, and all because–" she mimicked Con's voice –"it was 'vital we should all have been here tonight, and now Great-Uncle Matthew's as mad as fire!'" She swung back on Con. "So what? I've explained to him, and that's all there is to it. Why should you make it your business? You're not the master here yet, and as far as *I'm* concerned you never will be!"

"Julie!" I said sharply. "That's enough!"

They ignored me. Grandfather thrust his head forward, his eyes intent under scowling brows. "And just what do you mean by that?"

"Just," said Julie, "that this is my home, and Con–why, Con doesn't even *belong* here! And I'm beginning to think there isn't room for both of us, not any more! If I'm to be able to go on coming here–"

Grandfather slammed the cards down on the table in front of him. "And now, perhaps you'll let me speak! What you appear to forget, all of you, is that this is *my* house . . . still! Oh, I know you think I'm old, and sick, and that I'll go at any moment; I'm not a fool, that may be true, and by heaven, from the sort of scene you've made tonight, you appear to be eager to see the last of me! No, keep quiet, you've said enough; you've had a shaking, and I'll excuse you for that reason, and we'll say no more, but let me make this clear; this is my house, and while I'm alive I'll expect civil conduct in it—or you, Julie, and you, Connor, can both of you go elsewhere! And now I'm going to bed." And he put shaky hands to the arms of his chair.

Julie said raggedly, on a sob, "I'm sorry, Grandfather. I—I am a bit shaken up, I guess. I didn't mean to upset you. I don't want any food, Annabel. I'm going upstairs."

She turned past Con as if he didn't exist, and ran out of the room.

Con hadn't moved. It wasn't until that moment, when we were all looking at him, that I realized that, since he had come in, he hadn't spoken. His face seemed to have emptied even of anger, and gone blank. His eyes looked unfocussed.

"Well?" said Grandfather, harshly. "What are you waiting for?"

Con turned on his heel without a word, and went back across the hall. The baize door whispered itself shut behind him.

I stooped over Grandfather's chair. "Darling, don't upset yourself. Julie's a bit strung-up tonight; she's more shaken than she knows . . . and Con . . . Con's been working far too hard, you know he has, and I guess he's tired. It wasn't very sensible of him to tackle Julie, but if they hadn't both been a bit edgy, it wouldn't have come to anything. I expect they'll apologize in the morning."

He looked up at me, almost vaguely, as if the effort of that last speech had exhausted him. He looked very old, and tired, and almost as if he didn't quite know who I was. He said, muttering it to himself rather than to me, "Always the same. Always the same. Too highly strung, that's what it is, your mother always said so; and Julie's the same. History repeats itself." The faded eyes focussed on me then. "Annabel. Should have married Con in the first place, as I wanted. Settled the pair of you. Settled this. I'm going to bed."

I bent to help him rise, but as soon as he was on his feet he shook me off almost pettishly. "I can manage, I can manage. No, don't come with me. I don't want a pack of women. And that goes for you, too, Lisa. Good God, d'you think I can't see myself to bed?"

He went to the door. I thought, he really is old; the tallness, and the sudden flashes of energy are what deceive us. . . . Something closed round me that might have been loneliness, or fear. . . .

He went out. Lisa and I were left looking at one another.

I remember thinking, with something like a shock, one forgets she's there; she heard all that; she heard what was said to Con. . . .

She had put her work composedly away. For all she showed it, the scene might never have taken place. As she moved towards the door, I said quickly, "He meant it, you know. I wouldn't upset him by saying anything else."

"I wasn't going to. I'm going to bed. Good night."

It didn't even seem strange at the time that it was Lisa who should go unconcernedly upstairs, and I who should look for Con.

He was in the kitchen, sitting in the rocking chair by the range, pulling on his gumboots. His face still wore that blind, shuttered look that was so unlike him. He glanced up briefly, then down again.

I said, "Con, don't pay any attention. She's upset because she and Donald quarrelled, and she missed seeing him tonight. She didn't mean a thing. She doesn't really think those things, I'm sure."

"It's my experience," said Con woodenly, thrusting his foot down into the boot and dragging it on, "that when people are upset they say exactly what they do think. She was quite startingly explicit, wasn't she?"

I said, without quite realizing what I was saying, "Don't let it hurt you."

"Hurt me?" He looked up again at that. The blue eyes held an odd expression; something puzzled, perhaps, along with a glitter I didn't like. Then he smiled, a deliberately charming smile that made goose-pimples run along my spine. "You can't know how funny that is, Annabel, my sweet."

"Well, my dear," I said calmly, "funny or not, try to see the thing in proportion. I don't know if anyone told you, but Julie and Bill Fenwick were involved in a sort of minor accident tonight. That's what made her late, and distressed her so much. Bill, too—his car was damaged, so he wouldn't be in too sweet a mood. It'll blow over."

"What makes you explain to me?" He stood up and reached for the jacket that hung on the back of the door. "It's none of my business. I don't belong here. Lisa and I are only the hired help."

"Where are you going?"

"To the buildings."

"Oh, Con, it's late. You've done enough. Aren't you tired?"

"Flaked out. But there's something wrong with the cooler, and I'll have to get it put right." That quick, glittering look again. "I suppose even Julie would be content to let that be my business? Or would it be interfering too much with the running of her home?"

"Con, for pity's sake—"

"Sweet of you to come and bind up the wounds, girl dear, but I assure you they don't go deep."

"Are you sure?" His hand was already on the door latch. I said, "Listen. I ought not to tell you, but I'm going to. You've no need to worry any more."

He stopped, as still as a lizard when a shadow falls across it. Then he turned. "What d'you mean?"

"You do belong here. You've made your place . . . the way you said . . . with your two hands; and you do belong. That's all I—ought to say. You understand me. Let it go at that."

There was a silence. The shutters were up again in his face. It was impossible to guess what he was thinking, but I should have known. He said at length, "And the money? The capital?" Silence. "Did he tell you?"

I nodded.

"Well?"

"I don't know if I ought to say any more."

"Don't be a fool. He would have told us all, himself, tonight, only that damned girl made a scene."

"I still don't think I should."

He made a movement of such violent impatience that I was startled into remembering the perilous volcano-edge of the last few days. I had gone so far; let us have peace, I thought.

He was saying, savagely, in a low voice, "Whose side are you on? By God, you've had me wondering, you're so thick with Julie and the old man! If you've started any thoughts of feathering your own nest—! How do I know I can trust you? What right have you got to keep this to yourself?"

"Very well. Here it is. It comes out much as you'd expected, except that, nominally, very little of the capital comes to you."

"How's that?" His gaze was brilliant now, fixed, penetrating.

"He's divided it between Julie and me, except for a small sum, which you get outright. He didn't say how much that was. With you inheriting the property over our heads, he thought that was only fair." I went on to tell him what Grandfather had said to me. "The major part is divided into three, as we'd expected, with two-thirds of it nominally mine. That can be passed to you, just as we planned." I smiled. "Don't forget the blackmail's mutual."

He didn't smile back. He seemed hardly to be listening. "Julie. Will she fight the will? She'll have grounds."

"I'm sure she won't. She doesn't want the place."

"No, she just thinks I should be out of it." He turned away, abruptly. "Well, since the boy's not afraid of hard work, he'd better go out and get on with it, hadn't he?"

"Con, wait a minute—"

"Good night."

He went. I stayed where I was for a moment, frowning after him. For heaven's sake, I thought, suddenly irritable, did I have to add to the tangle by feeling sorry for Con as well? Con was perfectly capable of taking care of himself; always had been; had always had to be . . . I shook myself impatiently. Con, let's face it, was a tough customer. Keep that straight, and keep out of it. . . .

I went slowly upstairs, and stood on the landing for a few moments, wondering if it would be better to see Julie now, or wait till morning.

I had tried to set Con's mind at rest, with no very conspicuous success; had I the right to give Donald's confidence away, in an attempt to do the same for Julie? More urgent still was the other problem; how much to tell her of the truth about my own situation. Something had to be told her, I knew that; I hadn't yet decided how much, but it was imperative that she should be made to realize, a little more clearly, the kind of person Con was, and of what he was capable.

I hovered there for some time, between her door and my own, before it occurred to me that, by seeing her now, I could probably kill two birds with one stone: if her mind were cleared with regard to Donald, she would happily leave the Whitescar field open for Con. Let us have peace. . . .

I went to the door of her room and knocked softly. There was no reply. No light showed under the door, or from the adjacent bathroom.

She could surely not be in bed yet? I tapped again and said softly, "Julie; it's me, Annabel."

No answer. As I stood, irresolute, I heard a soft step in the passage beside me. Lisa's voice said, calmly,

"She's gone."

I looked at her blankly. "What?"

She smiled. "'History repeats itself,' he said, didn't he? She's run out on us."

"Don't be absurd!" I was so shocked that I said it very angrily. She only shrugged, a slight uncaring gesture of the heavy shoulders.

"I found her room empty. Look."

Reaching past me, she pushed the door open, and switched on the light. For a second it felt like an intolerable invasion of privacy, then I saw that, indeed, the bedroom was deserted. Julie had made no attempt to get ready for bed. Even the curtains were undrawn, and this emphasized the vacant look of the room.

"Look," repeated Lisa. I followed her pointing finger, and saw the pretty high-heeled sandals tossed anyhow on the floor. "You see? She's changed into flat ones."

"But she may not have gone *out*."

"Oh yes, she has. Her door was standing wide when I came upstairs, and then I saw her from my window. She went over the bridge."

"Over the bridge?" I went swiftly to the window. The moon was not yet strong, and the narrow footbridge that led from the garden gate could barely be seen in the diffused lights from the house. "But why?" I swung round. "Lisa, you *were* joking, weren't you? She can't possibly really have–oh, no!" This as I pulled open the wardrobe door. "Her things are here."

"Don't worry. She won't have gone far. No such luck."

So the scene in the drawing room had gone home. I shut the wardrobe door with a sharp little click. "But where can she have gone? If she only wanted to escape–go for a moonlight walk–surely she'd have gone into the river meadows where you can see your way, or along towards Forrest Hall?"

"Heaven knows. Why worry about a silly girl's nonsense? She'll have run off to cry on her young man's shoulder, as likely as not."

"But that's ridiculous!"

She shrugged again. "Girls are fools at nineteen."

"So they are."

"In any case, I saw her go."

"But it's miles to West Woodburn!"

Something sharpened for the first time in her gaze. "West Woodburn? I was thinking of Nether Shields."

"Good heavens," I said impatiently, "Bill Fenwick never came into it, poor chap! I thought you understood that, when you prodded her about Donald Seton tonight."

"I didn't know. I wondered." Her voice was as composed and uninterested as ever.

Something I didn't yet recognize as fear shook me with a violent irritation. "Wherever she's gone, I don't much care for the idea of her wandering about the countryside at this time of night! If it *was* either West Woodburn or Nether Shields, you'd think she'd have taken the car!"

"When Con has the key in his pocket?"

"Oh. No, I see. But if she'd waited to see me—"

"And with you," said Lisa, "talking to Con in the kitchen?"

I stared at her for a moment, uncomprehendingly. Then I said, "For goodness' sake, Julie couldn't be so stupid! Do you mean to say she thought I was ganging up on her? With Con? Just how young and silly can you get?"

My sharp exasperation was partly induced by the fact that I hardly understood my own motives in following Con to the kitchen. When Lisa laughed, suddenly and uncharacteristically, I stared at her for a moment, blankly, before I said slowly, "Yes, I see that that's funny."

"What did you say to Con?"

"Nothing much. I wanted to apologize for Julie, but he was in a hurry."

"A hurry?"

"He was on his way out."

The toffee-brown eyes touched mine for a moment. "Oh?" said Lisa. "Well, I shouldn't wait up. Good night."

Left to myself, I crossed again to the window. There was no sign of movement from the garden, or the river path. I strained my eyes for the glimpse of a light coat returning through the trees. Down to my right I could see the reflection of the lights from the byres where Con was working, and hear the hum of machinery. The garden below me was in darkness.

I believe I was trying to clear my mind, to think of the problem as it now faced me—Julie and Donald, Con and Lisa—but for some reason, standing there staring into the dark, I found I was thinking about Adam Forrest's hands. . . . Some seconds later I traced the thought to its cause; some memory of that first sunlit evening when I had seen the cat pounce in the long grass, and some creature had cried out with pain and fear.

There had been bees in the roses, then; now it was the steady hum of machinery that filled the darkness, unaltering, unfaltering in its beat. . . . *History repeats itself*, Lisa had said.

Something tugged at the skirts of my mind, jerked me awake. A formless, frightening idea became certainty. Julie, running to change her shoes, seizing a coat, perhaps, creeping softly downstairs, and out . . . Con, in the kitchen, hearing the door, seeing her pass the window . . . Then, the girl running along the river in the dark, up the steep path where the high bank shelved over the deep pool . . . that pool where the rocks could stun you, and the snags hold you down. . . .

He was on his way out, I had said, and Lisa had given me that look. *Well, I shouldn't wait up.*

The machinery ran smoothly from the byre. The lights were on.

I didn't wait to grab a coat. I slid out of the room, and ran like a hare for the stairs.

CHAPTER THIRTEEN

"O where hae ye been, my handsome young man?"

Ballad: *Lord Randal.*

I DIDN'T EVEN LOOK to see if Con were in the buildings after all. The something that had taken over from my reasoning mind told me he wouldn't be. I had no time to make assurance double sure. I ran across the yard, and down the narrow river path towards the bridge. The wicket at the end of the bridge was standing open, its white paint making it insubstantial in the dusk, like a stage prop.

It was really only a few minutes since Julie had left the house. Con would hardly have had time to go up-river as far as the stepping stones at the end of the lane, where he could cross, and wait to intercept her on the path above the pool. But the impression of haste that he had given in the kitchen stayed with me as a spur. I ran.

The path sloped up steeply, runged like a ladder with the roots of trees. The ground was dry and hard. Above me the trees hung in still, black clouds, not a leaf stirring. It was very dark. I stumbled badly, stumbled again, and slowed to a walk, my outstretched hands reaching for the dimly seen, supporting stems of the trees. Julie would have had to go slowly, too; she could not have got so very far. . . .

I thought I heard a movement ahead of me, and suddenly realized what in my fear I hadn't thought of before. There was no need for silence here. If it were Con, and he knew I was coming, it might be enough.

I called shrilly, "Julie! Julie! Con!"

Then, not far ahead of me, I heard Julie cry out. It wasn't a scream, just a short, breathless cry, almost unvoiced, that broke off short as if she'd been hit in the throat.

I called her name again, my own cry echoing the same sound of fear and shock, and ran forward as fast as I dared, through the whipping boughs of alder and hazel, and out into the little clearing above the pool.

Julie was lying on the ground, at a point where the path skirted the drop to the pool. She lay half on her back, with one arm flung wide, and her head at the brink of the drop. I saw the loose fall of her hair, pale in the moonlight, and the still paler blur of her face. Con was beside her, down on one knee. He was stooping over her to take hold of her.

I cried, "Julie! No!" and ran out from under the trees, only to stop short as a shadow detached itself from the other side of the clearing, and crossed the open space in four large strides. Before Con could so much as turn his head, the newcomer's hand shot out, and dragged him back from Julie's body. There was a startled curse from Con, which was swallowed up in the sounds of a brief, sharp struggle, and the crashing of hazel bushes.

After the first moment of paralyzing shock, I had run straight to Julie. Her eyes were shut, but she seemed to be breathing normally. I tried quickly, desperately, straining my eyes in the dimness, to see if there were any bruises or marks of injury on her, but could find none. Where she had fallen, though the ground was hard, there was a thickish mat of dog's mercury, and her head lay in a spongy cushion of primrose leaves. I pushed the soft hair aside with unsteady gentle fingers, and felt over her scalp.

Her rescuer trod behind me. I said, "She's all right, Adam. I think she's only fainted."

He sounded breathless, and I realized that he, too, had heard the cries, and come running. The noise that I had made must have masked his approach from Con. "What's going on?" he demanded. "Is this your cousin Julie? Who's the man?"

I said shortly, "My cousin Con."

"Oh." The change in his voice was subtle but perceptible. "What's he done to her?"

"Nothing, as far as I know. I think you've probably jumped the gun a bit. Is there any way of getting water from the river?"

"Are you trying to tell me—?"

"Be quiet," I said, "she's coming round."

Julie stirred, and gasped a little. Her eyes fluttered and opened fully, dark and alive where her face had been a sealed blank. They turned to me. "Annabel? Oh, Annabel. . . ."

"Hush now, it's all right. I'm here."

Behind me came the crash and rustle of hazel boughs. Julie said, "Con—"

"It's all right, Julie, nothing's going to happen. Mr. Forrest's here with us. Lie quiet."

She whispered, like a child, "Con was going to kill me."

I heard Adam draw in his breath. Then Con's voice said, rather thickly, from behind us, "Forrest? What the hell was that in aid of?"

He was on his feet, not quite steady, perhaps, with his shoulder against a tree. He put the back of a hand up to his mouth. "What the bloody hell do you think you were doing? Have you gone mad?"

Adam said quietly, "Did you hear what she said?"

"I heard. And why you should choose to listen to crap of that sort, without—"

"I also heard her cry out. Don't you think that perhaps it's you who've got the explaining to do?"

Con brought his hand away from his face, and I saw him looking down as if he could feel blood on it. He said violently, "Don't be a damned fool. What sort of story's that? Kill her? Are you crazy, or just drunk?"

Adam regarded him for a moment. "Come off it. For a start, you can tell us why she fainted."

"How the devil do I know? She probably thought I was a ghost. I hadn't spoken a damned word to her, before she went flat out on the path."

I said to Julie, "Is this true?"

The scarcely perceptible movement of her head might have meant anything. She had shut her eyes again, and turned her face in to my shoulder. Con said angrily, "Why don't you tell them it's true, Julie?" He swung back to the silent Adam. "The simple truth of the matter is, Julie and I had words tonight, never mind why, but some pretty hard things were said. Afterwards I found out that she'd been involved in a car accident earlier in the evening, and I was sorry I'd made the scene with her. I'd seen her go flying out of the house, and I knew how upset she'd been when she went upstairs earlier . . . Annabel, blast it all, tell him this is true!"

Adam glanced down at me. "Apart from Con's feelings," I said, "to which I've never had a clue, it's quite true."

"So," said Con, "it occurred to me to come across and intercept her, and tell her I was sorry for what had happened, only no sooner did she see me in the path than she let out a screech like a frightened virgin, and keeled clean over. I went to see what was the matter, and the next thing was you were manhandling me into that damned bush. Don't worry, I'll take your apologies for granted, I suppose it was quite natural for you to think what you did. But *you*—" he addressed Julie on a scarcely conciliatory note—"it's to be hoped you'll see fit to stop making these damned silly accusations, Julie! I'm sorry I scared you, if that's what you want me to say, and I'm sorry if you've hurt yourself. Now for pity's sake try to get up, and I'll help Annabel take you home!"

But as he came towards us, Julie shrank a little against my shoulder. "Keep away from me!"

Con stopped. Adam was standing between him and Julie, and, though I couldn't see his expression, I realized he was at something of a loss. The situation seemed to be hovering uncertainly between melodrama and farce. Then Con said, on a note of pure exasperation, "Oh, for God's sake!" and turned on his heel and left the clearing. We could hear him, unhurrying, making his way downstream towards the bridge.

The silence in which he left the three of us was the silence of pure anticlimax. I had a strong feeling that, whatever had happened tonight, Con Winslow had walked off with the honours of war.

Adam started to say something then, I think to ask Julie a question, but I cut across it. "That can wait. I think we'd better get Julie back to the house. Con told you the truth; she's had a shock tonight, and now a bad fright, and the sooner we get her to bed the better. Can you get up, my dear?"

"I think so. Yes, I'm all right."

Between us, Adam and I helped her to her feet. She still seemed dazed, and was shivering a little. I pulled her coat close round her. "Come on, darling, can you walk? We must get you back. Where were you going, anyway?"

"To Donald, of course." This in the tone of one answering a very stupid question.

"Oh. Well, you'll see him tomorrow. Come along now, and don't worry, you're all right with Adam and me."

She responded to my urging arm, and went forward across the clearing, but so uncertainly and slowly that Adam's arm soon came round over mine to support her.

"I'd better carry you," he said. "It'd be quicker."

"I'm too heavy," protested Julie, still in that small, shaky voice quite unlike her own.

"Nonsense." He took her up into his arms, and quite unselfconsciously she put her own round his neck and held on. I went ahead of them to hold back the swinging branches, and, when we got to the bridge, opened the gate and held it. Con, even in his anger, had taken the trouble to shut and latch it.

The back door was standing open. The kitchen was dark, and the house seemed quiet. At least, I thought, snapping on the light, there was no sign of Con.

Adam paused inside the door, to say a little breathlessly, "Shall I take her straight upstairs? I can manage."

Julie lifted her head, blinking in the light. "I'm all right now. Really I am. Put me down, I'm fine."

He set her gently on her feet, but kept an arm round her. I was thankful to see that, though still pale, she didn't look anything like as drawn as she had seemed in the dead light of the moon. She managed a little smile for Adam. "Thanks very much for . . . everything. I'm sorry to be a nuisance. All right, Annabel, I'll go to bed, but may I just sit down a minute first and get warm?"

I said, "Put her in the rocking chair near the stove, Adam. I'll get some brandy. Would you like a drink?"

"Thank you. Whisky, if you have it."

When I brought the drinks in, Julie was in the rocking chair, leaning back as if exhausted, but looking every moment more like her usual self. Adam stood by the table, watching me. At the sight of his expression, my heart sank.

"Mix your own, will you, Adam?" I said. "Here you are, honey."

"I loathe brandy," said Julie, with a healthy flicker of rebellion.

"You'll take it and like it." I lifted the cover off the stove, and slid the kettle over the hot plate. "*And* a hot-water bottle in your bed, and some soup or something just as soon as I get you there." I glanced at Adam. "It's no wonder she fainted; the silly little ass wouldn't have any supper, and all this on top of a mishap to the car she was in, and a mad quarrel with Con. Julie, there's some of tonight's soup left over. Can you take it? It was very nice."

"As a matter of fact," said Julie, showing signs of abandoning the rôle of invalid, "I should adore it."

"Then finish your brandy while I put the soup to heat, then I'll take you up to bed."

Adam, if he heard this very palpable hint, gave no sign. As I brought the pan of soup in, he was saying to Julie, "You're beginning to look a little better. How do you feel?"

"Not a thing wrong with me, except hunger."

"You didn't hurt yourself—give yourself a knock or anything—when you fell?"

"I—I don't think I can have. I can't feel anything." She prodded herself experimentally, and then smiled up at him. "I think I'll live."

There was no answering smile on his face. "Then can you tell us now," he asked, "why you said that your cousin was going to kill you?"

I set the soup pan on the stove with a rap. "I don't think Julie's fit to talk about it now. I saw what happened, and—"

"So did I. I also heard what she said." His eyes met mine across Julie's head. They were as hard as slate, and his voice was inimical. I saw Julie look quickly from the one to the other of us, and even, in that moment, spared a flicker of pity for a child's dead romance.

"You seem uncommonly concerned," he said, "to stop her telling her story."

"You've heard what happened," I said steadily, "and there's nothing to be gained by discussing it now. If we talk much longer there's a chance we'll disturb Grandfather, and he's had more than enough upset for one night. I know that most of what Con told you was true, and almost certainly the last bit was, as well. Julie saw him, got a sudden fright, and fainted. I'm fully prepared to believe that's just what happened."

"I'm sure you are," said Adam, and I saw Julie turn her head at his tone.

"For heaven's sake!" I said crudely. "You're surely not *still* trying to make out it was attempted murder!"

I heard Julie take in a little breath. "Annabel—"

"It's all right, darling, I know you said it, but you didn't know just what you were saying. He'd half scared you to death, looming up like that through the trees. Now, if you're ready—"

"Will you please let your cousin speak for herself?" said Adam.

I looked at him for a few moments. "Very well. Julie?"

Julie looked doubtfully up at him. "Well, it's true," she said. Her voice held a puzzled uncertainty that was uncommonly convincing. "I know I *said* he was trying to kill me, and I—I think I must really have thought so, for a moment, though why, I can't quite tell you." She broke off and knitted her brows. "But actually, it happened just as Con said, and Annabel. . . . I'm not lying, Mr. Forrest, really I'm not. He—he never touched me. I know it sounds silly, but I'm sure I'd never have fainted if it hadn't been for the car accident, and then not having anything to eat . . . and then when I saw him, suddenly, like that, in the dark—" she gave a tremulous smile—"and, let's face it, I *was* feeling a bit wary of him, because I'd said some pretty foul things to him, and . . . well, that's all I remember."

I said, "Do you want Mr. Forrest to telephone the police, and report what happened?"

"Police?" Her eyes widened. "What on earth for?"

"In case it happens to be true that Con meant to kill you."

"*Con?* Annabel, how crazy can you get? Why, you don't really think—?"

"No, honey, no. But I think that's the way Mr. Forrest's mind's working. He threw Con into a bush."

"*Did* you?" Julie sounded shocked, then, lamentably, began to giggle. "Oh dear, thank you very much, but—poor Con! Next time he really *will* try to murder me, and I don't blame him!"

I didn't dare look at Adam. I said hurriedly, to Julie, "Darling, it's time you went upstairs, and don't make a *sound*. Adam, I'm most desperately sorry you've had all this—oh, my dear sweet *heaven*, the soup!"

It was hissing gently down the sides of the pan on to the top of the spotless stove. "Oh, Lisa's stove, and you should *never* let soup boil! It just shows—" as I seized a cloth and swabbed madly at the enamel—"that you shouldn't mix cooking and high drama. All this talk of murder—Adam, I'm *sorry*—"

"Think nothing of it." His face was wooden. "I'd better go." He turned to Julie. "Good night. I hope you'll feel quite all right in the morning." Then to me, "I hope my ill-advised attempts to help haven't made the soup quite undrinkable."

The door shut very softly behind him.

"Annabel!" said Julie. "Do you think he *meant* to be nasty?"

"I'm quite certain he did," I said.

The cooler-house was clean, shining and empty. The floors had been swilled some time earlier, and were not yet dry; they gleamed under the harsh, strong light from the unshaded bulbs. Aluminum shown coldly, and enamel glared white and sterile. The machinery hummed, and this, since there was nobody in sight, gave the place an even barer, emptier appearance.

I stepped over a twist of black hosepipe, and looked through an open door into the byre. There, too, the lights glared on emptiness.

"Con?"

No reply. I crossed the wet floor and threw the switch over. The machinery stopped. The silence seemed to surge in, frightening, thick, solid. Somewhere a tap dripped, an urgent rapping on metal. I went back to the door of the byre and reached for the light switch. My steps sounded incredibly, frighteningly loud, and so did the snap of the switch as I clicked it off. I turned back into the cooler-house.

Adam came quietly in and stood there, just inside the doorway. I stopped dead. My heart began to jerk. I must have looked white with fatigue, and as guilty as sin. I said nothing.

After a while he said, "Covering up?"

"What?"

"For your accomplice. You knew what I meant, didn't you?"

"I suppose I did."

"Well?"

"Look," I said, striving to sound no more than reasonable, "I know what you think, but, believe it or not, we told you the truth! For goodness' sake, don't try to take this thing any further!"

"Do you really think I can leave it there, after tonight?"

"But nothing *happened* tonight!"

"No, because I was there, and possibly because you were, too."

"You surely can't think that I—!" I checked myself. "But you heard what Julie told you."

"I heard what you persuaded her to say. I also heard her say that Con was going to kill her."

"She admitted she had nothing to go by! She was scared of him, and got a sudden fright—what's the use of going over and over it! You can see for yourself how seriously Julie's taking it now!"

"She trusts you. That's something I find particularly hard to take. She's another fool, it seems, but she at least has the excuse of being young, and knowing nothing against you."

I looked at him rather blankly.

He gave a tight little smile. "I only mean that Julie has no reason not to trust you, whereas I had, being merely a fool 'sick of an old passion.' Well, that's over. You can't expect to take any more advantage of my folly, now."

"But I've *told* you—"

"You've told me very loud and clear, you and Con. And Julie has echoed you. You showed a touching family solidarity. All right, you can tell me three more things. One, why Connor went across the river at all."

"He explained that. He was going—"

"Oh yes, I forgot. He was going to apologize to her, wasn't he?" The irony bit. "Well, we'll skip that. Now tell me why he left the machinery running while he did so? I heard it; it was going all the time, and the lights were on. Odd, wouldn't you say? A careful type like that, who shuts gates behind him even when he's just been chucked into a bush and accused of murder?"

"There's—there's nothing in that. Maybe someone else was here."

"Who else, at this time of night? No one's here now. But we'll skip that, too. The third thing is, why did you follow Julie yourself?"

"Well, obviously, I didn't like the idea of her going out alone like that when she was so upset."

"Did you know Connor had gone to intercept her?"

"No, of course not! The lights were on in the byre, anyway. I thought he was working here."

"Then why," said Adam, "did you cry out—sounding so frightened, at that—as you ran up through the wood?"

"I—I heard her scream. Of course I was frightened!"

"You called out before she made a sound."

"Did I? I must have wanted to stop her, make her wait for me."

"Why, in that case, did you call 'Julie, Julie! *Con!*' "

Silence.

"So you did expect him to be there?"

"I thought he might be."

"And you were frightened."

"Yes," I said, "yes, yes, yes! And don't ask me why, because I've told you before! It was you who said it was absurd when I told you Con might be violent."

"I know I did. I thought you were exaggerating. Which is one of the reasons I so stupidly believed you, when you said you could look after Julie. Well, now we know better."

"Listen, Adam–"

"I've done enough listening. Look at this from my point of view. You told me you're in some racket or other which will turn out right in the end. You persuaded me to keep out of it, God knows how, but you did. Now, tonight, this happens. Because I chanced to be there, no harm was done. But you admit that Connor may have intended to do harm. That he may be dangerous."

"I've always admitted that."

"Very well. But the time has come for me to stop trusting you, you must see that. In the first place, I had no reason to, except that . . . I had no reason to. Now after this–" a gesture took in the sterile, gleaming shed, and the now silent machinery–"I have less than none."

I said, after a pause, "Well? I can't stop you. What are you going to do? Telephone the police? Tell them Con tried to frighten Julie to death? Even if you had some sort of case–which you haven't; even if Julie would charge Con–which she won't; even if you had me as a witness–which you haven't, what could you prove? Nothing, because there *is* nothing to prove. All you'd achieve would be a howling scandal, and Grandfather laid out, and all for nothing."

"I might count it an achievement to have made the police take a look at you."

"At me?" For a moment I regarded him blankly. "Oh, *that*."

It must have been obvious that I genuinely hadn't realized for a moment what he was talking about. I thought he was disconcerted, but he said steadily, "I promised I'd warn you. Here's the warning, now. I'll give you twenty-four hours, as from now, to make your break with Connor, and leave. I don't care what story you tell, or what excuse you offer, but you must break this thing up, and go. And don't imagine that, in the event of Mr. Winslow's death, you can come back. I promise you that if 'Annabel' is a legatee in his Will, and turns up to lay claim to a single penny of it, I'll have you investigated so thoroughly that you won't see the outside of Durham Gaol for ten years. And what will happen to Connor and his sister, I neither know nor care. Good night."

"Adam!"

He paused in the doorway, and looked back.

"Adam—" Rigid self-control made my voice colourless almost to stupidity. "Wait just a moment. Don't go. Listen—"

"I've done enough listening." In the harsh light his face was as hard as stone, and as strange. There was nothing in it but weariness and contempt. "I'm afraid I'm no longer in the mood to play this extraordinary game of yours. I meant what I said, Miss Grey. Good night."

In the silence after he had gone, the tap dripped, a small, maddening sound, like a reiterated note on a harpsichord, a little out of tune.

I found I was leaning against the chilly metal of the cooler. I felt cold, with a sweating, empty slackness, like someone who has just vomited. My brain felt bruised, and incapable of any thought except a formless desire to get to bed, and sleep.

"Well, by God!" said Con, just behind me.

Even then, I turned slowly, and stared at him with what must have been a blank and stupid look. "Where were you?" Then, my voice tautening, "How much did you hear?"

He laughed, and lounged out of the inner shed into the light. He looked quite composed, even overcomposed, and his eyes were brilliant and his expression confident. His mouth was cut a little at the corner, and a graze showed swollen, but it only served to lend him a sort of extra rakish attraction.

He came close to me, and stood there, hands deep in pockets, swaying backwards and forwards on his heels, graceful and collected. "Oh, I kept my distance! I thought that Forrest and I hadn't much to say to one another, girl dear. And I thought that maybe you'd handle him a bit better than I could. And it seems I was right, me jewel. Was it you switched the engines off?"

"Yes. As an alibi for murder it wasn't bad, on the spur of the moment, Con."

The brilliant eyes narrowed momentarily. "Who's talking about murder now?"

"I am. You switched the engines on, and the lights, so that they could be seen and heard from the house, and then you ran upstream and across the stepping stones, and met Julie in the clearing."

"And if I did?" The bright eyes were narrow and dangerous. He had stopped swaying. Suddenly I realized what I should have known even before he came so near. He was drunk. I could smell whisky on his breath. "And if I did?" he said gently.

"Adam was right. You did mean to kill her there, Con."

There was a little silence. His eyes never wavered. He said again, softly, "And if I did?"

I said steadily, "Only this, that if you thought I'd stand for anything like that, you must be a fool and an imbecile. Or don't you think at all? What sort of person d'you think I am? You said yourself not long ago that you knew I was straight, heaven help us, because otherwise you'd have been too scared of my trying to twist you in what we're doing. Well, you blundering criminal fool, did you really think I'd see you kill Julie, and not send the whole works sky-high, myself included?"

He was laughing now, completely unabashed. "All right, me darlin', murder's off the cards, is it? But you know, I'm not the fool you make me out to be. You weren't supposed to know anything about it. Oh, you might have suspected all you liked in the morning, when her poor drowned body came up on the shingle, but what could you prove? You'd have kept quiet, and held your grandpa's hand, wouldn't you?"

"Oh, my God," I said, "and to think I felt sorry for you tonight, because you were so much alone."

"Well," said Con cheerfully, "there's no harm done, is there, except a little keepsake from Forrest." He touched his cheek. "Did you manage to shut the bastard up after all?"

"I don't know."

He had begun to rock on his heels again. Somewhere behind the brilliant gaze was amusement, and wariness, and a speculation that for some reason made my skin crawl.

"'Adam,' wasn't it, now? How do you come to be calling him 'Adam,' girl dear?"

My heart gave a jerk that sickened me. I said, and was relieved to find that my voice sounded nothing but normal, and very tired, "That was one thing you and Lisa slipped up on. They must have got to Christian names. When I went today to get the strawberries, he called me 'Annabel' . . . And now I'm going in. I can't talk to you tonight. I'm tired, and you're in the wrong kind of mood. Sufficient unto the day. You're luckier than you deserve that nothing's happened; and I can't even guess what Adam Forrest'll do tomorrow, but, just at the moment, I don't care."

"That's my girl." He spoke a little thickly. Before I realized what he was doing, his hands came out and he took me by the shoulders. His eyes between the beautiful lashes were sapphire-blue and laughing, and only slightly liquid with drink. "It's beautiful you are, acushla, did you know?"

"I could hardly avoid it, with Julie in front of me all day."

His teeth showed. "Good for you. But you take the shine out of Julie, bejasus and you do. Look, now—"

I stood stiffly under his hands. "Con, you're drunk, and you're getting maudlin, and I loathe this stage Irishry anyway. If you think you can plan to murder Julie, and then bat off and drink yourself stupid, and then come and blarney me with a lot of phony Irish, you can damned well think again. And—" this as he moved, still smiling, and his hands tightened—"if you try to kiss me, that'll be another slap on the jaw you'll get, so I'm giving you fair warning."

His hands slackened, and dropped. He had flushed a little, but he still smiled. I said levelly, "Now, for heaven's sake, Con, get to bed and sleep it off, and pray to every saint in heaven that Adam Forrest chooses to hold his tongue. And take it from me, this is the last time I cover up any single thing for you. Good night."

As I reached the doorway I looked back. He was standing looking after me with an expression I could only read as amusement and affection. He looked handsome and normal and quite sober and very nice.

He smiled charmingly, "Good night, Annabel."

I said shortly, "Don't forget to put the light out," and went quickly across the yard.

CHAPTER FOURTEEN

I wrote a letter to my love,
And on the way I lost it;
One of you has picked it up,
And put it in her pocket.

Traditional.

I HARDLY SLEPT that night. I lay, it seemed for hours, watching the wheeling moonlight outside the open curtains, while my mind, too exhausted for sleep, scratched and fretted its way round the complications of this absurd, this crazy masquerade.

I suppose I dozed a little, for I don't remember when the moon went down and the light came. I remember realizing that the dark had slackened, and then, later, a blackbird fluted a piercing stave of song alone in the cold dawn. After he fell silent there was a deep hush, for the space of a long breath, and then, suddenly, all the birds in the world were chattering, whistling, jargoning in a mad medley of sound; the dawn chorus. I found myself smiling. It was an ill wind, indeed, that blew no good.

My moment of delight must have worked like the Ancient Mariner's spontaneous prayer, for soon afterwards I fell deeply asleep. When I looked at the window again it was full daylight, and the birds were singing normally in the lilacs. I felt wide awake, with that floating bodiless calm that sometimes comes after a night of scanty sleeping. I got up, and went over to the window.

It must be still very early. The dew was thick, grey almost as frost, on grass and leaf. The air smelled thin and cool, like polished silver. It was very still, with the promise of close and thundery heat to come. Far away, from the direction of West Lodge, I heard a cock crow thinly. Through a gap in the trees to my left I saw the distant glint of chestnut, where the Forrest colt moved, cropping the wet grass.

Sometimes, I think, our impulses come not from the past, but from the future. Before I had even clearly thought what I was doing, I had slipped into narrow grey trousers and a pale yellow shirt, had dashed cold water on my face, run a comb through my hair, and was out of my room, sliding downstairs as quietly as a shadow. The house slept on, undisturbed. I tiptoed out through the kitchen, and ten minutes later, bridle in hand, I was letting myself in through the gate of the meadow where Rowan grazed.

I kept clear of the gap in the trees, so that, even if someone else were awake at Whitescar, I couldn't be seen. I moved quietly along under the hedge, towards the horse. He had raised his handsome head as soon as I appeared, and now watched intently, ears pricked forward. I stopped under the guelder-rose, where there was a gap in the hedge and a couple of railings. I sat on the top one and waited, dangling the bridle. The panicles of guelder-rose, thick-coloured as Devonshire cream, spilled dew onto my shoulder, chilly through the thin shirt. I rubbed the damp patch, and shifted along the railing, so that the early sunshine struck my shoulders.

Rowan was coming. He paced forward slowly, with a sort of grave beauty, like a creature out of the pages of poetry written when the world was young and fresh, and always just waking to an April morning. His ears were pricked so far forward that the tips almost met, his eyes large and dark, and mildly curious. His nostrils were flared, and their soft edges flickered as he tested the air towards me. The long grass swished under his hoofs, scattering the dew in bright, splashing showers. The buttercup petals were falling, and his hoofs and fetlocks were flecked gold with them, plastered there by the dew.

Then he was a yard away, pausing, just a large, curious hardly broken young horse staring at me with dark eyes that showed, at the edge, that unquiet hint of white. I said, "Hi, Rowan," but I didn't move.

He stretched his neck, blew gustily, then came on. Still I didn't move. His ears twitched back, forward again, sensitive as snails' horns, as radar antennae. His nostrils were blown wide, puffing sweet breath at my legs, at my waist, at my neck. He mouthed my sleeve, then took it in his teeth and tugged it.

I put a hand on his neck, and felt the muscles run and shiver along under the warm skin. I ran the hand up to his ears, and he bent his head, blowing at my feet. My hand slipped up to the long tangled forelock, and held it. I slid slowly off the fence bar, and he didn't try to move away, but put his head down and rubbed it violently up my body, jamming me back against the railings. I laughed at him and said softly, "You beauty, you love, you lovely boy, stand still now, quiet now . . ." and then turned him, with the hand on his forelock, till his quarters were against the railings, and his forehand free. Then with my other hand, still talking, I brought the bit up to his muzzle.

"Come along now, my beauty, my darling boy, come along." The bit was between his lips and against his teeth. He held them shut against it for a few seconds; I thought he was going to veer away, but he didn't. He opened his teeth, and accepted the steel warm from my hand. The bit slipped softly back into the corners of his mouth, and the bridle slid over his ears; then the rein was looped round my arm and I was fastening the cheek strap, rubbing his ears, between his eyes, sliding my hand down the springy arch of his neck.

I mounted from the top of the fence, and he came up against it and stood as if he had done it every day of his life. Then he moved away from it smoothly and softly, and only when I turned him towards the length of the field did he begin to gather himself and dance, and bunch his muscles as if to defy me to hold him. I'm not, in fact, quite sure how I did. He went at a canter, that lengthened too quickly towards a gallop, to the far corner of the long meadow, where there was a narrow wicket giving on the flat grass of the river's edge. He was biddable enough at the wicket, so that I guessed that Adam Forrest had taken him this way, and taught him his manners at the gates. But, once through the wicket, he danced again, and the sun danced and dazzled too, down through the lime leaves, and the feel of his bare back warm and shifting with muscle between my thighs was exciting, so that I went mad all at once, and laughed, and said, "All right, have it your own way," and let him go; and he went, like a bat out of hell along the flat turf of the river's edge, with that smooth lovely motion that was as easy to sit as an armchair; and I wound my right hand in his mane and stuck on like a burr to his withers with too-long-disused muscles that began to ache before long, and I said, "Hi, Rowan, it's time we got back. I don't want to get you in a lather, or there'll be questions asked. . . ."

His ears moved back to my voice, and for a second or two after I began to draw rein, he resisted, leaning on the bit, and I wondered if I could manage to check and turn him. I slackened the bit for a moment to break his stride, and, as it broke, pulled him in. He came sweetly, ears flickering back to me, and then pointing again as he turned. I sang to him, mad now as the morning, "Oh, you beauty, you beauty, you love, home now, and steady. . . ."

We had come the best part of a mile, round the great curve of the river that led to West Lodge. I had turned him just in time. The chimneys of the Lodge were showing above the nearer trees. I spared a glance for them as the horse wheeled and cantered, sober and collected now, back along the river. His neck was damp, and I smoothed it, and crooned to him, and he flowed along smoothly and beautifully, and his ears twitched to my voice, and then, halfway to his own meadow, I drew him to a walk, and we paced soberly home as if he was a hack hired for the day, and bored with it, and there had been no few minutes of mad delight there along the sward. He arched his neck demurely and fiddled with the bit, and I laughed at him and let him have it, and when we came to the wicket he stopped and moved his quarters round for me to reach, as gentle and dainty as a dancer.

I said, "All right, sweetheart, that's all for today," and slid down off him and ducked under his neck to open the wicket. He pushed through, eager now for home. I turned to shut the wicket, and Rowan wheeled with me, and then snorted and threw up his head, and dragged hard at the rein I was holding.

I said, "Steady, beautiful! What's up?" And looked up to see Adam Forrest a yard away, waiting beside the wicket, watching me.

He had been hidden from me by the thick hawthorn hedge, but of course he would have heard Rowan's hoofs, and seen us coming from some way off. He was prepared, where I was not. I actually felt the colour leave my face, and stood stock still, in the act of latching the gate, like a child in some silly game, one hand stiffly held out, the other automatically holding the startled horse.

The moment of shock snapped, and passed. The wicket clicked shut, and Adam came forward a pace and took Rowan's bridle from me. I noticed then that he had brought a bridle himself; it hung from a post in the hedge beside him, and there was a saddle perched astride a rail.

It seemed a very long time before he spoke. I don't know what I expected him to say; I know that I had time to think of his reactions as well as my own; to imagine his resentment, shame, anger, bewilderment.

What he said was merely, "Why did you do it?"

The time had gone past for evasions and pretences; in any case Adam and I had always known rather too well what the other was thinking. I said merely, "I'd have thought that was obvious. If I'd known you were still at Forrest I'd never have come. When I found I had to face you, I felt caught, scared—oh, anything you like, and when you wouldn't just write it off and let me go, I suppose I got desperate. Then you decided I was an impostor, and I was so shaken that on the spur of the moment I let you go on thinking it. It was—easier, as long as I could persuade you to keep quiet about me."

Between us the horse threw up his head and fidgeted with the bit. Adam was staring at me as if I were some barely decipherable manuscript he was trying to read. I added, "Most of what I told you was true. I wanted to come back, and try to make it up with Grandfather. I'd thought about it for some time, but I didn't think he'd want me back. What kept me away was the worst kind of pride, I know; but he's always rather played power-politics with money—he's terribly property-conscious, like a lot of his generation—and I didn't want to be taunted with just coming back to claim my share, or to put in my claim for Mother's money." I gave a little smile. "As a matter of fact, it *was* almost the first thing he said to me. Well, there it was, partly pride, partly not being able to afford the passage . . . and, apart from all those considerations, there was you."

I paused. "But after a bit I began to see things differently. I wanted desperately to come back to England, and I wanted not to be . . . completely cut off from my home any more. I didn't write; don't ask me why. I suppose it was the same impulse that makes you turn up unexpectedly, if you have to visit a house where you're not sure of your welcome; warning them gives people too much time to think of excuses, and be wary; whereas once you're on the doorstep they've got to welcome you. Maybe you don't know about such things, being a man, but I assure you it's quite commonly done, especially if you're a person who's never sure of their welcome, like me. And as for you, I—I thought I might be able to keep out of your way.

I knew that . . . things . . . would be long since over for you, but I thought you'd understand why I felt I had to come back. If I had to meet you, I'd manage to let you know I'd only come on a visit, and was going to get a job elsewhere."

Rowan jerked his head, and the bit jingled. Adam seemed unconscious of the movement. I went on, "I'd saved a bit, and when Mrs. Grey—my last employer—died, she left me a little money, three hundred dollars, along with a few trinkets for keepsakes." I smiled briefly, thinking of the gold lighter, and the car permit left so carefully for Con and Lisa to find. "She was a cripple, and I'd been with her quite a time, as a sort of housekeeper-chauffeuse. I was very fond of her. Well, with the three hundred dollars, and my savings, I managed to pay for my passage, with something left over. I came straight up to Newcastle from Liverpool, and got myself a room, and a temporary job. I waited a day or two, trying to nerve myself to come back and see how things were. Of course, for all I knew, Grandfather was dead. . . ."

Half absently I stooped and pulled a swatch of grass, and began to wisp the horse. Adam stood without moving; I had hardly looked at him. It was queer that when a part of your life, your very self, was dead, it could still hurt you, as they say a limb does still, after it has been cut off.

"I hadn't wanted to make too many inquiries, in case Con somehow got to hear of it. I'd even taken my rooms in the name of my late employer, Mrs. Grey. I didn't know what to do, how to make my approach. I wanted to apply to the lawyers for Mother's money, you see, only I wasn't sure if I dared risk Con's finding out I was home. Well, I waited a day or two, wondering what to do—"

"Just a minute." Adam, it seemed, was listening, after all. "Why should you not 'dare' let Connor know you were home?"

I ran the wisp along Rowan's neck, and said briefly, "He tried to kill me one night, along the river, just near where we found him with Julie."

He moved at that. "He *what?*"

"He'd wanted to marry me. Grandfather wanted it, too. You knew that. Con hadn't a hope then—or so he thought—of getting the property any other way, so he used to—to harry me a bit. Well, that night he threw a bit of a scene, and I wasn't just in the mood for it; I wasn't exactly tactful, and I made it a bit too clear that he hadn't a hope, then or ever, and . . . well, he lost his temper and decided to get rid of me. He chances his arm, does Con." I lifted my eyes, briefly, from my task. "That's how I guessed, last night, that he'd have gone to find Julie. That's why I followed her."

"Why did you never tell me?"

His tone was peremptory, proprietorial, exactly as it might have been eight years ago, when he had had the right.

"There was no chance. It happened the last night I was here. I was on my way home, after I'd left you in the summerhouse. You remember how late it was. You know how I always used to go over the river by the stepping stones, and then home by the path and the bridge, so no one would know

I'd been to Forrest. It was just as well I bothered, because that night I ran into Con."

"Oh, my God."

"That was the—the other reason why I ran away. Grandfather took his part, you see. He'd been angry with me for months because I wouldn't look at Con, and there'd been scenes because he'd found I was staying out late, and I'd lied once or twice about where I'd been. He—I suppose it was natural, really—he used to storm at me, and say that if I ever got into trouble, I could go, and stay away. . . ." I smiled a little. "I think it was only talk and temper; it was a bit hard on Grandfather, being saddled with an adolescent girl to look after, but of course adolescents take these things seriously. When I got home that night, after getting away from Con, I was pretty nearly hysterical. I told Grandfather about Con, and he wouldn't believe me. He knew I'd been out somewhere, and suspected I'd met somebody, and all he would say was 'where had I been?' because it was late, and he'd sent Con to find me himself. I think he just thought Con had lost his head and had been trying to kiss me, and all I was saying about murder was pure hysteria. I don't blame him, but there was a . . . pretty foul scene. There's no point in raking it all up; you can imagine the kind of things that were said. But you see why I ran away? Partly because of what had happened between you and me, and because I was scared stiff of Con . . . and now because Grandfather was taking his part, and I was afraid he and Con would start ferreting about, and discover about you. If Crystal had found out . . . the way she was just then. . . ."

Rowan put his head down, and began to graze with a jingling of metal. I paused, leaning one hand against his neck. "Well, you understand why I was afraid to come back to Whitescar, even now. If Con *had* been in charge here, alone, I'd never have dared, but once I found that Grandfather was still alive, and still playing at power-politics between me and Con and Julie, and that Julie might be exposed to exactly the same sort of danger as I had been . . ."

"And that I had gone."

"And that you had gone," I said steadily, "I knew I'd have to come back here. It would still have been a pretty sticky thing to attempt, in the teeth of Con and Lisa, and not being sure of Grandfather's reception of me, but then Con himself appeared like Lucifer out of the blue, and presented me with what looked like a nice, peaceful, Connor-proof homecoming. I rather grabbed at it. I only planned, you see, to stay here as long as Grandfather lived."

"I begin to see. How did you fall in with Connor?"

"I took a risk which I shouldn't have taken, and went to take a look at Whitescar. I didn't even get out of the bus, just went along the top road from Bellingham to Chollerford, one Sunday. I got out at Chollerford, to get the bus along the Roman Road. I—I wanted to walk along the Wall, to—to see it again."

Nothing in his face betrayed the fact that lay sharply between us; that it was on the Wall that he and I, sometimes, by chance—and oh, how carefully calculated a chance!—had met.

I said steadily, "Con saw me. He waited his chance and followed me. He recognized me, of course, or thought he did. When he came up on me I was startled, and scared stiff, and then I saw he was just doubtful enough for me to pretend he'd made a mistake. So I gave him the name I'd been using, and got away with it." I went on to tell him, then, of the interview on the Wall, and the subsequent suggestions that were made to me. "And finally, when I realized that Con was fairly well 'in' with Grandfather, and that he and Lisa had it in for Julie, and that Grandfather himself had had a stroke . . . Well, I thought to myself, this is one way of getting home with Con not lifting a finger to stop me. So I agreed. And it went off well enough, until I found that you *were* still here. . . ."

He said with sudden impatience, "That horse isn't sweating. Leave that alone. We'll turn him loose."

He began to unbuckle the cheek strap, adding, with as much emotion as if he were discussing the price of tomatoes, "Go on. When did you find I was still here?"

"Grandfather mentioned it, quite casually, the first evening. I'd managed to chisel a bit out of Con and Lisa, about the fire, and your taking Crystal to Italy, and then Vienna, and the nursing homes and everything, and her death, but you know Con, he's interested in nothing but himself, and I didn't dare press too much about you and your affairs. When I heard from Grandfather that you hadn't gone permanently, it gave me a shock. I went that night to Con and said I wanted to back down. He—threatened me. No, no, nothing like that, he just said what was true, that it had gone too far, and that a hint of the 'truth' would shock Grandfather. Of course I knew I'd told Grandfather nothing but the truth, but for all they get across one another, he thinks the sun rises and sets in Con, and it would have finished him to know what sort of a swine Con is—can be. It still would. I realized that I'd have to stay, but the thought of having to meet you was . . . terrifying. I went over to Forrest that night, the night before you came."

"To lay the ghosts?"

"I suppose so. But the next night . . . I knew you'd come, I don't know how."

You always did. . . . Nobody had said the words. He wasn't looking at me; he was sliding the bridle off, over Rowan's ears. The horse, his head free, flung it up and sideways, and swerved away from us, thrusting out into the sunlight at a trot. Then he dropped his head, and began to graze again. Adam looked down at the bridle in his hands as if he wasn't quite sure what it was, or how it had got there. Then he turned, and hung it with great care beside his own. "And when I came, you found it easier to let me think you—that Annabel was dead."

"Wasn't she?" I said.

He turned then, and for the first time we really looked at one another. "Why should you have thought so? After you'd gone, when you'd had time to think . . . there'd been so much . . . you must have known I . . ." His voice trailed away, and he looked down at his feet.

I felt something touch me, pierce almost the armour of indifference that the hurt of eight years back had shelled over me like nacre. It was not enough to have learned to live with the memory of his cruelty and indifference; I had still to care.

I said, hardly enough, "Adam, eight years ago, we quarrelled, because we were unhappy, and there was no future unless we did the sort of harm we had no right to do. I told you, I don't want to go back over it. But you remember as well as I do, what was said."

He said roughly, "Oh God, yes! Do you think I haven't lived through every minute of that quarrel since? Every word, every look, every inflection? I know why you went! Even discounting Con and your grandfather, you'd reason enough! But I still can't see why you never sent me a single word, even an angry one."

This time the silence was stretched, like a shining thread that wouldn't snap. The sun was strong now, and fell slanting over the eastward hedge to gild the tops of the grasses. Rowan rolled an eye at us, and moved further away. The tearing sound as he cropped the grass was loud in the early-morning stillness.

When I spoke, it was in a voice already heavy with knowledge; the instinct that sees pain falling like a shadow from the future. "But you had my letter."

Before he spoke, I knew the answer. The truth was in his face. "Letter? What letter?"

"I wrote from London," I said, "almost straight away."

"I got no letter." I saw him pass his tongue across his lips. "What did it . . . say?"

For eight years I had thought of what I would have liked to say. Now I only said, gently, "That if it would give you even a little happiness, I'd be your mistress, and go with you wherever you liked."

The pain went across his face as if I had hit him. I saw him shut his eyes. He put up a hand to them; it was disfigured and ugly in the clear sunlight. He dropped it, and we looked at one another.

He said, quite simply, as if exhausted, "My dear, I never even saw it."

"I realize that now. I suppose I should have realized it then, when I got no answer. I should have known you'd not have done anything quite so cruel."

"Christ," he said, without violence, "I think you should."

"I'm sorry. It never even occurred to me that the letter might have gone astray. Letters don't, as a rule. And I was so unhappy, and alone, and—and *cut off* . . . girls aren't at their most sensible at such times. Adam, don't look like that. It's over now. I waited a few days; I—I suppose I'd really only gone to London to wait for you; I'd never intended, originally, to go abroad. But then, when I telephoned—did she tell you I'd telephoned?" At his expression, I gave a little smile. "Yes, I telephoned you, too."

"Oh, my dear. And Crystal answered?"

"Yes. I pretended it was a wrong number. I didn't think she'd recognized my voice. I rang again next day, and Mrs. Rudd answered it. She didn't know who I was; she just told me the house was shut, and that you and Mrs. Forrest had gone abroad, indefinitely. It was then that I—I decided to go right away. I went to a friend of mine who was emigrating. I had some money. I went along to look after her children, and—oh, the rest doesn't matter. I didn't write to you again. I—I couldn't, could I?"

"No." He was still looking like someone who has been mortally hurt, and hasn't known it till he sees the blood draining away into the grass. "No wonder you said what you did, the other night. It seems there's even more than I thought, to be laid at my door."

"You couldn't help it, if a letter went astray! It was hardly—*Adam!*"

His eyes jerked up to mine. "What is it?"

I licked my lips, and said, hoarsely, "I wonder what did happen to that letter? We're forgetting that. I said a minute ago, letters just don't go astray, not as a rule, not for eight years. Do you suppose—" I wet my lips again—"*she* took it?"

"*Crystal?* How could—oh my God, no, surely? Don't look like that, Annabel, the damned thing's probably lying in some dusty dead-letter office somewhere on the Continent. No, my dear, she never knew. I'll swear she never knew."

"Adam, you can't be sure! If she did—"

"I tell you she didn't know! She never gave any sign of knowing! And I assure you, that if she could have found a whip like *that* to use on me, she'd have used it."

"But when she got so much worse—"

"She was no worse than neurotic for years after you went away. It was only after the fire—after I'd taken her to Florence—that you could have called her really 'mentally ill,' and I had to take her to Vienna. She never once, in all that time, mentioned any sort of suspicion of you."

"But Adam, you don't know—"

"I know quite well. Stop this, Annabel!"

"Adam, no one's ever told me—how did Crystal die?"

He said harshly, "It was nothing to do with this. You can take my word for it. For one thing, no letter turned up among her papers after her death, and you can be sure she kept everything there was."

I said, "Then she *did* kill herself?"

He seemed to stiffen himself like a man lifting a weight, only able by stark courage to hold it there. "Yes."

Another of those silences. We were standing so still that a wren flew on to a hazel close beside me, chattered a stave of shrill and angry-sounding song, then flew away. I was thinking, without drama, well, here was the end of the chapter; all the threads tied up, the explanations made. There was nothing more to say. Better say good-bye, and go home to breakfast, before tragedy dissolved in embarrassment, and the lovers who had once been ready to count the world well lost should find themselves talking about the weather.

The same thought showed momentarily in Adam's face, and with it, a sort of stubborn resolution. He took a step forward, and the maimed hands moved.

I said, "Well, I'd better be getting back before Con sees I've been on Rowan."

"Annabel–"

"Adam, don't make me keep saying it's finished."

"Don't make me keep saying it isn't! Why on earth d'you think I found myself trusting you against all reason and judgment, *liking* you–oh God, more than liking you–if I hadn't known in my blood who you really were, in spite of that bag of moonshine you handed to me so convincingly?"

"I suppose because I was like her."

"Nonsense. Julie's the image of what you were, as I knew you, and she never makes my heart miss a single beat. And tell me this, my dear dead love, why did you cry when you saw my hands?"

"Adam, no, you're not being fair!"

"You care, don't you? Still?"

"I . . . don't know. No. I can't. Not now."

He always had known what I was thinking. He said sharply, "Because of Crystal?"

"We'll never know, will we? It'd be there, between us, what we did."

He said, grimly, "I could bear that. Believe me, I made my reparations." He turned his hands over, studying them. "And this was the least painful of them. Well, my dear, what do you want to do?"

"I'll go, of course. It won't be long, you know. Grandfather's looking desperately frail. Afterwards . . . afterwards, I'll see things straight with Con, somehow, and then I'll go. If he knows I'm leaving, there'll be no danger for me. We needn't meet, Adam."

"Neither we need."

I turned away abruptly. "I'll go now."

"Take your bridle."

"What? Oh, thanks. I'm sorry I spoiled your ride, Adam."

"It doesn't matter. Rowan would much prefer it with you. I've a heavy hand."

He picked his own bridle from the post, and heaved the saddle up over one arm. Then he smiled at me. "Don't worry, my dear. I won't get under your feet. But don't go away again, without saying good-bye."

"Adam," I said rather desperately, "I can't help it. I can't *help* the way I feel. Life does just go on, and you change, and you can't go back. You have to live it the way it comes. You know that."

He said, not tragically, but as if finishing a quite ordinary conversation, "Yes, of course. But it would be very much easier to be dead. Good-bye."

He let himself through the wicket, and went away across the field without looking back.

CHAPTER FIFTEEN

I lean'd my back unto an aik,
I thocht it was a trustie tree;
But first it bow'd and syne it brak—
Sae my true love did lichtlie me.

Ballad: *Jamie Douglas.*

LIFE GOES ON, I had told Adam. When I got back to the farm the men were arriving for the day, and the cattle were filing into the byres. I managed to slip into the stables and hang the bridle up again without being seen, then went into the kitchen.

Mrs. Bates was there, waiting for the kettle to boil. She cast me a look of surprise.

"Why, Miss Annabel! You're up early. Have you been out riding?"

"No. I just couldn't sleep."

Her bright black eyes lingered on my face. "What's to do now? You look proper poorly."

"I'm all right. I had a bad night, that's all. I'd love a cup of tea."

"Hm." The piercing, kind little eyes surveyed me. "Piece o' nonsense, getting up at all hours when you don't have to. You want to take care o' yersel'."

"Nonsense, Betsy, there's nothing the matter with me."

"Never seen anything like you the day you came back." Here the kettle boiled, and she tipped it, dexterously jetting the boiling water into the teapot. "If you hadn't 'a' told me you was Miss Annabel, I'd hardly 'a' knowd you, and *that's* a fact. Aye, you can smile if you like, but that's the truth and no lie. Depend on it, I says to Bates that night, depend on it, Miss Annabel's had a bad time of it over in America, I says, and I'm not surprised, I says, judging by what you see on the pictures."

"It was Canada," I said mildly.

"Well, they're all the same, aren't they?" She slapped the teapot down on the table, which was laid ready for breakfast, whipped off the lid, and stirred the tea vigorously. "Not but what you look a lot better than what you did, and you've begun to put a bit of weight on, aye, *and* get some of your looks back, and I'm not the only one that's noticed it. Have you noticed, says Bates to me the other day, that Miss Annabel's almost her pretty self again when she smiles. Which isn't often enough by a long chalk, I says. Well, he says, if she'd but get herself a husband and get herself settled, he says. Go on with you, I says, and her hardly home yet, give her time, I says, not but what men always thinks that's all a woman needs in 'er life to make her happy, so no offence meant, but all the same, he says to me—"

I managed a laugh that was, I hope, convincing. "Oh, Betsy dear! Let me get home first, before I start looking round!"

"Here's your tea." She pushed a steaming cup towards me. "And you did ought to take sugar in it, not a foreign black mess like that. And let me tell you that if you didn't sleep last night you'll only have yersel' to blame, with soup, and coffee, not to mention whisky and such, *as* I know by the glasses left in the kitchen bold as brass for me to find. Not that I'm one as concerns meself in things that are none of my business, but—oh, here's Mr. Con."

Con, I noticed sourly, looked attractive and wide awake even with last night's stubble on his chin, and in the clothes, carelessly hustled into, for his before-breakfast jobs. He threw me a look of surprise as he took a cup of tea from Mrs. Bates. "Good God. What are you doing up at this hour?"

"Taking a walk, she says," said Mrs. Bates, spooning sugar into his cup. "I thought she'd been riding, meself, but she says no."

His eyes flickered over my trousers and yellow shirt. "Weren't you? I should have thought Forrest's colt would have tempted you long ago."

I sipped my tea without replying. Already the scene in the meadow was growing dim, dulled, fading. . . . The hot tea was a benison, a spell against dreams. The day had started. Life goes on.

"Those things suit you," said Con. His glance held undisguised admiration, and I saw Mrs. Bates eyeing him with a sort of sour speculation. She pushed a plateful of buttered rolls towards him. "Try one o' these."

He took one, still watching me. "Are you coming out to lend a hand today?"

"That she is not," said Mrs. Bates promptly.

"I might," I said, "I'm not sure. I—I slept badly."

"You're not worrying about anything, are you?" asked Con. The blue eyes held nothing but mildly solicitous curiosity.

Mrs. Bates took his cup from him and refilled it. "She's worrying herself about her Granda, I shouldn't wonder, which is more than *you* seem to be doing, Mr. Con, *which* I may say you can think shame on yourself, for asking her to work in this heat, when you've as much help as you want up in the field, and that's the truth and no lie!"

"Well," said Con, with a glint of a smile, "I doubt it we'll get Bill Fenwick over today, so if you could relieve someone on one of the tractors some time, it would help. The weather'll break soon, you see if it doesn't. We'll have thunder before dark."

"I'll see," I said. "Will you be up there all day yourself?"

"As soon as I've had breakfast. Why?"

"I told you last night. I want to talk to you."

"So you did. Well, tonight, maybe."

"I'd rather see you before. I may come up to the field, at any rate when you stop to eat."

"Oh, sure," said Con unconcernedly, setting down his cup. "Be seeing you."

I went up to my room to change. If he hadn't been in his working clothes, I thought, he'd have smelled the horse on me. There were chestnut hairs on the grey trousers, and one or two on the shirt where Rowan had rubbed his head against me. I went along and bathed, got into a skirt and fresh blouse, and felt better.

I couldn't eat breakfast when the time came, but there was no one there to remark on the fact. Con wasn't yet in, Grandfather wasn't up, Mrs. Bates was busy elsewhere, and Lisa was invariably silent at breakfast time. Julie was taking hers in bed—this at my insistence, and more to keep her out of Con's way than for any other reason. She seemed to have completely recovered from last night's experience, and only accepted my ruling about breakfast because, she said, she had no desire to see Con again so soon, and certainly not before she had seen Donald.

Donald rang up shortly before half past eight, to ask for news of last night's truants. I told him only enough to reassure him—that Bill Fenwick's car had been involved in a mishap, and that Julie was unhurt, and wanting to see him some time that day. If, I added with a memory of the colleague from London, he was free. . . .

"Mphm," said Donald. "I'll be along in half an hour."

"Donald! Wait a minute! She's not up yet!"

"Half an hour," said Donald, and rang off.

I warned Julie, who hurled herself out of bed with a shriek and a "What shall I *wear?*" that reassured me completely as to her well-being and her feelings. I didn't see Donald arrive, but when, some half-hour later, I saw his car in the yard, I went to tell him that Julie wouldn't be long. He wasn't in the car, or indeed, anywhere to be seen; on an inspiration I slipped through the half-door of Blondie's stable, and there, sure enough, he was, stooping to prod a gentle finger into the pile of fur deep in the manger, while Tommy, sitting unconcernedly on top of the partition (which was at least half an inch wide), watched composedly, in the intervals of washing a back leg.

Donald straightened when he heard me come in. "She really is all right?" It was an unceremonious greeting, and I hoped it was symptomatic of his state of mind. He certainly betrayed no other outward signs of deep emotion.

"Perfectly. She'll be along in a minute or two."

I told him then rather more fully about the accident, but without mentioning Con, or, of course, what had happened later last night. If Julie chose to tell him, that was her affair, but I hoped she wouldn't. I wanted no more trouble until I had managed that overdue interview with Con, and after that, I hoped, all would be clear.

It was six minutes, in sober fact, before Julie came. She certainly looked none the worse for the stresses of last night. She wore her blue skirt and white blouse, and looked composed and immaculate, not in the least as if she had rushed shrieking for the bathroom only thirty-six minutes before.

She greeted Donald with a composure that amounted almost to reserve, and, when I made a move to go, held me there with a quick, imploring look that filled me with forebodings. These weren't diminished by Donald's attitude; he appeared to have retreated into silence, and, I noticed with exasperation, was even groping in his pocket for his pipe.

I said quickly, "You can't smoke in a stable, Donald. If you two are going off now—"

"Oh," said Julie, "are these Tommy's kittens? Aren't they *adorable!*"

She stooped over the bundle in the manger, exclaiming delightedly over the kittens, with every appearance of intending to remain there for some time. "And *look* at their tiny *paws!* Two black," she cried rapturously, "and three black-and-white, and *two ginger* . . . isn't it a *miracle?*"

"As a matter of fact," I said, rather sharply, "it's the ginger tom from West Lodge."

Julie had detached a ginger kitten from the tangle of fur, and was cuddling it under her chin, crooning to it. "How old are they? Oh, I'd *adore* to keep one! But they're far too tiny to take, aren't they? Six weeks, isn't it, till they can lap? Oh, isn't it a *darling?* Annabel, d'you suppose either of the ginger ones is a he?"

"They both are," said Donald.

"How do you—I mean, they're too small to *tell*, surely?"

"I should have said," amended Donald, carefully, "that the probability of both ginger kittens' being male is about ninety-nine-and-nine-tenths per cent. Possibly more. The ginger colour is a sex-linked characteristic."

The nearest we were going to get to romance today, I thought bitterly, was a discussion on genetics. And while there could, admittedly, be said to be some connection, it was getting us no further with the matter in hand. I sent Donald a quelling look, which he didn't see. He was watching Julie, who, with the kitten still cuddled close to her, was regarding him with respectful wonder.

"You mean you just *can't have* a ginger she?"

"No. I mean, yes." Donald's uncertainty was only momentary, and of the wrong kind. He stood there like a rock, pipe in hand, calm, slow-spoken, and undeniably attractive. I could have shaken him.

"Isn't that marvellous?" said Julie, awed. "Annabel, did you know that? Then I *shall* keep this one. Oh, lord, it's got claws like *pins*, and it *will* try and climb up my neck! Donald, look at it, isn't it utterly *adorable?*"

"Adorable." He still sounded infuriatingly detached and academic. "I'd be inclined to go further. I'd say beautiful, quite beautiful."

"Would you?" Julie was as surprised as I was at this sudden plunge into hyperbole. She held the kitten away from her, looking at it a shade doubtfully. "Well, it *is* the sweetest little love, of course, but do you think the pink nose is quite the *thing?* Cute, of course, with that spot on the end, but—"

"Pink?" said Donald. "I wouldn't have said it was pink."

He hadn't, I realized suddenly, even glanced at the kitten. Unnoticed at last, I began to edge away.

"But Donald, it's *glowing* pink, practically *shocking* pink, and quite hideous, actually, only so terribly sweet!"

"I was not," said Donald, "talking about the kitten."

There was a second's open-mouthed pause, then Julie, her poise in flinders, blushed a vivid scarlet and began to stammer. Donald put his pipe back into his pocket.

I said, unheeded, "We'll see you both this evening some time," and went out of the stable.

As I went, Donald was gently unhooking the kitten from the shoulder of Julie's blouse, and putting it back into the manger.

"We don't want to squash the poor little thing, do we?"

"N–no," said Julie.

Later that morning, after I had done the chores which I had taken on as my contribution to the housekeeping, I went to hunt up my gardening tools from the corner of the barn where they had always been kept. I had, of course, taken the precaution of asking Lisa where they were. The tools looked almost as if they hadn't been used since I'd last had them out more than eight years ago. It was queer to feel my hand slipping in such an assured way round the smoothed wood of the trowel, and to feel the familiar knot hole in the handle of the spade. I carried the tools along to the tractor shed and put in a little first aid on the shears, and the blades of spade and hoe, then threw the lot into a barrow, and went to see what I could do with the neglected garden.

I worked there all morning, and, since I started on the basic jobs of grass and path, it wasn't long before the place looked as if some care had been spent on it. But work, for once, didn't help. As I sheared the grass, and spaded the edges straight, and then tackled the dry, weedy beds with fork and hoe, memory, far from being dulled by the rough work, cut back at me ever more painfully, as if I had sharpened that, too, along with the garden tools.

That spring and summer, eight years back . . . the March days when the soil smelled strong and damp and full of growing; May when the lilac was thick on the tree by the gate, and rain lay in each cup, scented with honey; June, with the robin scolding shrilly from the waxy blossoms of the syringa bush, as I dug and planted with my back to the house, dreaming of Adam, and our next meeting. . . .

Today, it was June again, and the soil was dry and the air heavy. The lilac was done, and the syringa bush wasn't there, dead these many years.

And Adam and I were free, but that was over.

My fork turned up a clump of bulbs, autumn crocus, flat globes covered with onion-coloured crêpe paper. I went on my knees and lifted them out carefully with my hands.

Then suddenly I remembered them, too. This clump had been in flower the last day I'd been at Whitescar. They had burned, pale lilac flames in the dusk, as I slipped out to meet Adam that last, that terrible evening. They had lain, drenched ribbons of silk, under the morning's rain when, with the first light next day, I had tiptoed down the path and away, across the bridge towards the highroad.

I found I was sitting back on my heels with the tears pouring down my face, and dripping on the dry corms held tightly in my hands.

It was still an hour short of lunch time when Betsy's voice called me from the house. I thought there was some urgency in her voice, and when I stood up and turned, I could see her, in what looked like considerable agitation, waving for me to hurry.

"Oh, Miss Annabel! Oh, Miss Annabel! Come quickly, do!"

The urgency and distress could only mean one thing. I dropped my weeding fork, and ran.

"Betsy! Is it Grandfather?"

"Aye, it is that . . ." Her hands were twisted now into her apron, and, with her face paler than usual, and the red of the cheeks standing out like paint, and the black eyes at once alarmed and important, she looked more than ever, as she stood bobbing in the doorway, like a little wooden figure from a Noah's Ark. She was talking even more rapidly than usual, almost as if she thought she might be blamed for what had happened, and had to get her excuses in first.

". . . and he was as right as rain when I took his breakfast up, as right as a trivet he was, and *that's* the truth and no lie. 'And how many times have I tell't you,' he says, 'if you burns the toast, to give it to the birds. I'll not have this scraped stuff,' he says, 'so you can throw it out now and do some more,' *which* I did, Miss Annabel, and there he was, as right as rain . . ."

I took her breathlessly by the shoulders, with my earthy hands. "Betsy, Betsy! What's *happened?* Is he dead?"

"Mercy, no! But it's the stroke like before, and that's how it'll end this time, Miss Annabel, my dear. . . ."

She followed me up the passage, still talking volubly. She and Lisa, I heard, had been together in the kitchen, preparing lunch, when Grandfather's bell had rung. This was an old-fashioned pulley bell, one of a row which hung on their circular springs in the kitchen. The bell had jangled violently, as if jerked in anger, or some sudden emergency. Mrs. Bates had hurried upstairs, to find the old man collapsed in the wing chair near the fireplace. He had dressed himself, all but his jacket, and must have suddenly begun to feel ill, and just managed to reach the bell pull by the hearth as he fell. Mrs. Bates and Lisa, between them, had got him to bed, and then the former had come for me.

Most of this she managed to pour out in the few moments while I ran to the kitchen and plunged my filthy hands under the tap. I had seized a towel, and was roughly drying them, when a soft step sounded in the lobby, and Lisa appeared in the doorway. She showed none of Betsy's agitation, but her impassive face was perhaps a bit sallower, and I thought I saw a kind of surreptitious excitement in her eyes.

She said abruptly, "There you are. I've got him to bed and got him covered up. He collapsed while he was dressing. I'm afraid it looks serious. Annabel, will you telephone the doctor? The number's on the pad. Mrs. Bates, that kettle's almost hot enough; fill two hot-water bottles as soon as you can. I must go back to him. When you've got Dr. Wilson, Annabel, go and fetch Con."

"Lisa, I must see him. You do the telephoning. I can—"

"You don't know what to do," she said curtly. "I do. It's happened before. Now hurry."

She turned quickly away, as if there was no more to be said. I flung the towel down, and ran to the office.

The doctor's number was written there, largely, on the pad. Luck was in, and he was at home. Yes, he would be there as quickly as possible. What was being done? Ah, Miss Dermott was with him, was she, and Mrs. Bates was there? Good, good. I was to try not to worry. He wouldn't be long. Smooth with professional reassurances, he rang off.

As I went back into the hall, Lisa appeared at the head of the stairs. "Did you get him?"

"Yes, he's coming."

"Good. Now, will you go—?"

"I want to see him first." I was already starting up the stairs.

"There's nothing you can do." She did nothing to bar my way, but her very stolidity, as she waited for me in the middle of the way, had that effect.

I said sharply, "Is he conscious?"

"No."

It wasn't the monosyllable that halted me, three steps below her, it was the tone of it. I looked up at her. Even through my agitation I caught the surprise in her look. Heaven knows what she could read in my face and eyes. I had forgotten what lay between me and Lisa; now it whipped back at me, stinging me into intelligence, and caution.

She was saying, "There's no point in your seeing him. Go and get Con. He's in High Riggs."

"I know."

"Well, he must know straight away."

"Yes, of course," I said, and went on, past her, straight into Grandfather's room.

The curtains had been half drawn, and hung motionless, shading the sunny windows. The old man lay in bed, his only movement that of his laboured, stertorous breathing. I went across and stood beside him. If it hadn't been for the difficult breathing, I might have thought him dead already. It was as if he, the man I knew, had already gone from behind the mask that lay on the pillow. It, and we, were only waiting.

Lisa had followed me in, but I took no notice of her. I stood watching

Grandfather, and trying to calm my agitated thoughts into some sort of order.

Lisa had been in the kitchen when it happened, with Betsy. It had been Betsy who had answered the bell. All that Lisa had done had been correct, and obviously genuine. And Con was far enough away, in High Riggs; had been there since early morning. . . .

I turned to meet Lisa's eyes. If I had had any doubts about the naturalness of this crisis, coming, as it had done, so pat upon the signing of the will, they were dispelled by the look on Lisa's face. It was still, as before, obscurely excited, and she made no attempt to hide the excitement from me. And it was now, also, thoroughly surprised and puzzled as she stared back at me.

I could hear Betsy chugging upstairs now, with the hot-water bottles. Lisa had moved up to my elbow. Her voice muttered in my ear, "It's a mercy, isn't it?"

"A mercy?" I glanced at her in surprise. "But he was perfectly all right—"

"Ssh, here's Mrs. B. I meant, a mercy it didn't happen yesterday, before Mr. Isaacs came. God's providence, you might say."

"You might," I said drily. Yes, I thought, it was there, clear enough to see: Lisa, single-minded, uncomplicated, initiating nothing. The stars in their courses fought for Con; Lisa need only wait. Efficient, innocent Lisa. No doubt at all, when Doctor Wilson came, she would help him in every possible way.

I said abruptly, "I'll go and get Con."

The sun beat heavy and hot on High Riggs. A third of the field was shorn, close and green-gold and sweet-smelling. Over the rest of the wide acreage the hay stood thick and still in the heat. The clover, and the plumy tops of the grasses made shadows of lilac and madder and bronze across the gilt of the hay. There were purple vetches along the ditch, and the splashing yellow of ladies' slipper.

One tractor was at the far end of the field, with Con driving. It was moving away from me, the blades of the cutter flashing in the sun.

I began to run towards him along the edge of the cut hay. The men with rakes paused to look up at me. The cutter was turning, out from the standing hay, round, and in once more in a close circle, neatly feathering its corner and re-entering the standing hay at an exact right angle.

Con hadn't seen me. He was watching the track of the blades, but as the machine came into the straight, he glanced up ahead of him, and then lifted a hand. I stopped where I was, gasping in the heavy heat.

The tractor was coming fairly fast. Con, not apparently seeing in my visit anything out of the way, was watching the blades again. The sun glinted on the dark hair, the handsome, half-averted profile, the sinewy brown arms. He looked remote, absorbed, grave. I remember that I thought with a kind of irrelevant surprise, he looks happy.

Then I had stepped out of his path, and, as the tractor came level with me, I shouted above the noise of the motor, "Con! You'd better come to the house! It's Grandfather!"

The tractor stopped with a jerk that shook and rattled the cutter blades. The boy on the reaper hauled on the lever and they lifted, the hot light quivering on the steel. Con switched off the motor, and the silence came at us with a rush.

"What is it?"

I said, shouting, then lowering my voice as it hit the silence, "It's Grandfather. He's taken ill. You have to come."

I saw something come and go in his face, then it was still again, but no longer remote. It had gone blank, but it was as if something in him was holding its breath, in a sort of wary eagerness; there was a tautness along the upper lip, and the nostrils were slightly flared. A hunter's face.

He drew a little breath, and turned his head to the boy. "Uncouple her, Jim. I'm going down to the house. Ted!" The farm foreman came across, not hurrying, but with a curious look at me. "Ted, Mr. Winslow's ill. I'm going down now, and I may not get back today. Carry on, will you?" A few more hurried instructions, and his hand went to the starter. "Oh, and send one of the boys across to open that gate for the doctor's car. Jim, get up on the tractor here, then you can drive it back. I'll send news up with Jim, Ted, as soon as I see how he is."

As the boy obeyed, swinging up behind him, Con started the motor. He gestured with a jerk of the head to me, and I ran round and stepped up onto the back of the tractor. It went forward with a lurch, and then turned sharply away from the ridge of cut hay, and bucketed down across the uneven ground towards the gate. The men paused in their raking to watch curiously, but Con took no notice. He sent the tractor over the grid with hardly any diminution of speed. I was close beside him, standing on the bars and holding on to the high mudguard. He began to whistle between his teeth, a hissing little noise that sounded exactly what it was, a valve blowing down a head of steam. I think I hated Con then, more than I ever had before; more than when he had tried to bully me into marrying him; more than when I had wrenched away from him and run, bruised and terrified, to Grandfather; more than when he had tried to claim Adam's place as my lover; more than when he had brought me back, an interloper, to damage Julie.

He said nothing until we were getting down from the tractor in the yard. "By the way, wasn't there something you wanted to talk to me about? What was it?"

"It'll keep," I said.

Grandfather was still unconscious. The doctor had come, stayed, and then, towards evening, had gone again to a telephone summons. This was the number . . . we were to call him back if there was any change . . . but he was afraid, Miss Winslow, Miss Dermott, he was very much afraid. . . .

He lay on his back, propped on pillows, breathing heavily, and with apparent difficulty, and sometimes the breath came in a long, heaving sigh. Now and again there seemed a pause in the breathing, and then my heart would jerk and stop as if in sympathy, to resume its erratic beating when the difficult breaths began again. . . .

I hadn't left him. I had pulled a chair up to one side of his bed. Con was on the other. He had spent the afternoon alternately in sitting still as a stone, with his eyes on the old man's face, or else in fits of restless prowling, silent, like a cat, which I had stood till I could stand it no longer, then had curtly told him to go out of the room unless he could keep still. He had shot me a quick look of surprise, which had turned to a lingering one of appraisement, then he had gone, but only to return after an hour or so, to sit on the other side of the old man's bed, waiting. And that look came again, and yet again, as the blue eyes kept coming back to my face. I didn't care. I felt so tired that emotion of any kind would have been an exercise as impossible as running to a wounded man. Heaven knows what was showing in my face. I had ceased to try and hide it from Con, and I could not, today, find it in me to care. . . .

And so the day wore on. Lisa, quiet and efficient as ever, came in and out, and helped me to do what was needed. Mrs. Bates finished her work, but offered to stay for a time, and the offer was gladly accepted. Julie hadn't come home. After the doctor's visit, Con went out and sent one of the men up in the car to West Woodburn, but on his return he reported that neither Julie nor Donald had been seen at the site since that morning. They had gone up there some time before luncheon, had walked around for a bit, then had gone off in Donald's car. Nobody had any idea where they had gone. If it was into Newcastle . . .

"Forrest Hall!" I said. "That's where they'll be! I'm sorry, Con, I'd quite forgotten." I explained quickly about the alleged Roman carving that Adam had described. "Ask him to go to Forrest Hall—he'd better go by the river path, it's quicker than taking a car up past the gates."

But the man, when he returned, had found nobody. Yes, he had found the cellars; they were accessible enough, and he thought someone had been there recently, probably today, but no one was there now. Yes, he had been right down. And there was no car parked there; he couldn't have failed to see that. Should he try West Lodge? Or Nether Shields?

"The telephone's easier," said Con.

But the telephone was no help, either. West Lodge was sorry, but Mr. Forrest was out, and had not said when he would be back. Nether Shields—with a shade of reserve—was sorry, too; no, Julie had not been there that day; yes, thank you, Bill was quite all right; they were sorry to hear about Mr. Winslow; sorry, sorry, sorry. . . .

"We'll have to leave it," I said wearily. "It's no use. They may have found something at Forrest, and all gone into Newcastle to look it up, or something; or Julie and Donald may have gone off on their own after they left Forrest Hall. But it's only an hour to supper time now, and surely they'll come then? After last night—was it really only last night?—Julie *surely* won't stay away again without letting us know?"

"Do you know, you sound really worried," said Con.

I said, "My God, what do you think—?" then looked up and met the blue eyes across the bed where Grandfather lay. They were bright and very intent. I said shortly, "Oddly enough, I am. I'm thinking of Julie. She would want to be here."

His teeth showed briefly. "I always did say you were a nice girl."

I didn't answer.

The doctor came back just before seven, stayed a while, then went again. The day drew down, the sky dark as slate, heavy with thunder, and threatening rain.

Still Julie didn't come, and still Grandfather lay there, with no change apparent in the mask-like face, except that I thought the nostrils looked pinched, and narrower, and his breathing seemed more shallow.

Con went over to the buildings shortly after the doctor had gone, and only then, leaving Mrs. Bates in Grandfather's room, did I go downstairs for a short time, while Lisa gave me soup, and something to eat.

Then I went back, to sit there, waiting, and watching the old man's face, and trying not to think.

And, well within the hour, Con was back there, too, on the other side of the bed, watching me.

Mrs. Bates went at eight, and soon afterwards, the rain began; big, single, heavy drops at first, splashing down on the stones, then all at once in sheets, real thunder-rain, flung down wholesale from celestial buckets, streaming down the windows as thickly as gelatine. Then suddenly, the room was lit by a flash, another, and the thunderstorm was with us; long flickering flashes of lightning, and drum rolls of thunder getting nearer; a summer storm, savage and heavy and soon to pass.

I went over to shut the windows, and remained there for a few moments, staring out through the shining plastic curtain of the rain. I could barely see as far as the buildings. In the frequent flashes the rain shimmered in vertical steel rods, and the ground streamed and bubbled with the water that fell too fast for the gutters to take it.

Still no Julie. They wouldn't come now. They would stay and shelter till it was past. And meanwhile Grandfather . . .

I drew the thick chintz curtains and came back to the bed. I switched on the bedside lamp and turned it away, so that no light fell on the old man's face. Con, I saw, was watching him abstractedly, with a deep frown between his brows. He said under his breath, "Listen to that, damn it to hell. It's enough to wake the dead."

I was just going to say, "Don't worry, it won't disturb him," when Con added, "It'll have the rest of High Riggs as flat as coconut matting. We'll never get the cutter into it after this."

I said drily, "No, I suppose not," and then, sharply, all else forgotten, "Con! It *has* woken him!"

Grandfather stirred, sighed, gave an odd little snore, and then opened his eyes. After a long time they seemed to focus, and he spoke without moving his head. The sounds he made were blurred, but clear enough.

"Annabel?"

"I'm here, Grandfather."

A pause. "Annabel?"

I leaned forward into the pool of light, and slid a hand under the edge of the bedclothes till it found his.

"Yes, Grandfather. I'm here. It's Annabel."

There was no movement in the fingers under mine, no perceptible expression in Grandfather's face, but I thought, somehow, that he had relaxed. I felt his fingers, thin and frail, as smooth and dry as jointed bamboo, and no more living, lying in my palm, and remembered him as he had been in my girlhood, a tall, powerful man, lean and whippy and tyrannical, and as proud as fire. And suddenly it was too much, this slow, painful ending to the day. A day that had begun with Rowan, and the brilliant morning, and a secret that was still my own; then Adam, and the knowledge of our betrayal of each other; and now this. . . .

The storm was coming nearer. Lightning played for seconds at a time, flashing like some dramatically wheeling spotlight against the shut curtains. I saw Grandfather's eyes recognize it for what it was, and said, "It's just a summer thunderstorm. I don't suppose it'll last."

"That noise. Rain?"

The thunder had paused. In the interval the rain came down with the noise of a waterfall. "Yes."

I saw his brows twitch, very faintly. "It'll flatten—High Riggs."

Something touched me that was partly wonder, and partly a sort of shame. Con was a Winslow after all, and perhaps his reaction had been truer than mine—my dumb fury of grief that was a grief for the passing of, not this old man, but my world, the world I hadn't wanted, and deserved to lose. I said, "That's just what Con was saying."

"Con?"

I nodded towards him. "He's there."

The eyes moved. "Con."

"Sir?"

"I'm—ill."

"Yes," said Con.

"Dying?"

"Yes," said Con.

I felt my lips part in a sort of gasp of protest and shock, but what I might have said was stopped by Grandfather's smile. It wasn't even the ghost of his old grin, it was nothing but the slight tightening and slackening of a muscle at the corner of his mouth; but I knew then that Con was right. Whatever had been Matthew Winslow's faults, he had never lacked dignity, and he was not the man to slide out of life on a soothing flood of women's lies. He and Con had ground where they could meet, and which was forbidden to me.

My moment of protest must have communicated itself to him through our linked hands, for his eyes moved back to me, and I thought he said, "No lies."

I didn't look at Con. "All right, Grandfather, no lies."

"Julie?"

"She'll be here soon. The storm's kept her. She's been out with Donald all day. She doesn't know you're ill."

I thought he looked a query.

"You remember Donald, darling. The Scot, Donald Seton. He's the archaeologist digging up at West Woodburn. He was here last night at—" my voice wavered, but I managed it—"your party."

I could see him concentrating, but it seemed to elude him. I had to control myself sharply, not to take a tighter hold on the frail hand in mine. I leaned nearer to him, speaking slowly, and as distinctly as I could. "You met Donald, and you liked him. He's going to marry Julie, and they'll live in London. Julie'll be very happy with him. She loves him. You needn't worry about—"

An appalling crash interrupted me. The flash, the long, growing rumble and crack of chaos, then, after it, the crash. Through all the other preoccupations in that dim room it hacked like the noise of a battleaxe.

Matthew Winslow said, "What's that?" in a voice that was startled almost back to normal.

Con was at the window, pulling back the curtains. His movements were full of a suppressed nervous excitement, which gave them more than their usual grace, like the sinewy, controlled actions of ballet. He came back to the bedside, and bent over his great-uncle. "It was a long way off. A tree, I'm pretty sure, but not here. One of the Forrest Hall trees, I'd say."

He put a hand on the bed, where Grandfather's arm lay under the blankets, and added carefully and distinctly, "You don't need to worry. I'll go out presently and find out where it was. But it's not near the buildings. And the lights are still on, you can see that. It's done no damage here."

Grandfather said, clearly, "You're a good boy, Con. It's a pity Annabel never came home. You'd have suited well together."

I said, "Grandfather—" and then stopped.

As I put my face down against the bedclothes, to hide it from him, I saw that Con had lifted his head once more and was watching me, his eyes narrow and appraising.

There was only myself and Con in the room.

CHAPTER SIXTEEN

Nor man nor horse can go ower Tyne,
Except it were a horse of tree . . .

Ballad: *Jock o' the Side.*

IT SEEMED a very long time before Con cleared his throat to speak. I didn't raise my head. I could feel his scrutiny, and even through the first rush of grief, the instinct that I had been rash enough to disregard bade me hide my tears from him. I don't think I had any room, then, for conscious thought about the present danger of my position: the way my stupid, difficult safeguard against him had now become, ironically, a peril. I had known since yesterday that I would have to tell him the truth. To have discussed it today, across Grandfather's unconscious body, would have been unthinkable, like counting him already dead. And now, even if I had been ready to frame what I had to say, it was even less possible to do so.

I never knew what he was going to say. Somewhere, downstairs, a door slammed, and there were running footsteps. He checked himself, listening. I remember thinking, vaguely, that perhaps Lisa had somehow guessed what had happened. But would she have run like that? I had never seen Lisa hurry . . . somehow it seemed unlike her, even if she had cared enough . . . Julie; of course, it must be Julie. I pressed my fists hard against my temples, and tried to blot the tears off against the counterpane, steadying my thoughts as best I could. Julie was coming running, just too late, and in a moment I would have to lift my face. . . .

The steps clattered across the hall, seemed to trip at the bottom stair, then came on up, fast. Even through the thick panels of the door I could hear the hurry of sobbing breathing. She grabbed the knob with fumbling hands. It shook even as it turned.

I lifted my head sharply. There were still tears on my face, but I couldn't help that now. Here was something more. And Con had taken his eyes off me at last, and was watching the door.

It was thrust open—no sick-room entry, this—and Julie ran into the room. She must have come in so quickly from the dark and streaming night that her eyes had barely adjusted themselves to the light. I thought for a moment that she was going to blunder straight into the bed, and came to my feet in a startled movement of protest; but she stopped just short of the bed's foot, gasping for breath.

I had been right in my swift guess: this panic-stricken haste had had nothing to do with Grandfather. She hadn't even glanced at the bed. Her look was wild, dazed almost, and she groped for a chair back, to which she clung as if that alone prevented her from falling.

Her hair, and the coat she wore, were soaked, so dark with rain that it took me a moment or two to realize, in that dim light, that the coat was streaked and filthy. The gay summer sandals were filthy, too, and there was dirt splashed over her hands and wrists, and smudged across her jawbone. The flush of haste stood out on her cheeks like paint.

She was looking wildly from me to Con while she fought for breath to speak. Her eyes, her whole head, jerked from one to the other and back again, in a kind of distraction that was painful to watch.

"Annabel . . . Con . . . Con . . ."

The appeal was whispered—the sickroom atmosphere, and whatever news Lisa had given her had overborne her own distress—but if that distress, whatever it was, had driven her to appeal to Con, then something was seriously the matter.

"Julie!" This time my movement towards her was protective. I came between her and the bed. "Darling! Whatever's the matter?"

But something in the way I moved had got through to her. For the first time, she looked past me, fully, at the bed. I saw the shock hit her, as a stone hits a man who has been knocked half silly already. She wavered, bit her lip, and said, like a child who expects to be punished for behaving badly, "I didn't know. Annabel, I didn't know."

I had an arm round her. "Yes, darling, I'm sorry. It happened just a few minutes ago. It was very sudden, and he seemed quite content. I'll tell you about it later; it's all right . . . If there's something else wrong, you can tell us now. What is it? Something else has happened? Something's wrong."

She shook in my arms. She was trying to speak, but could only manage a whispered, "Could you—please—please—you and Con—"

It was apparent that there would be no sense out of her yet. I spoke across her, deliberately raising my voice to a normal pitch, and making it sound as matter-of-fact as I could, "Con, you'd better go down and tell Lisa, then would you telephone Dr. Wilson? And you might get the brandy; Julie looks as if she needs it. Julie, don't stay in here; come along to your own room—"

"The phone's off," said Julie.

"Off?"

"Lisa says so. It went off just now, she says. She's been trying. It'll be the ivy tree. When it came down—"

"The ivy tree?" This was Con.

I said, "The old tree by the gate-house. That was what we heard come down. Never mind that. Julie—"

"It sounded nearer. Are you sure it's that one?"

"It was split. It just split in two." Julie's voice sounded thin and empty, but unsurprised, as if the questions were relevant enough. "Half came down right across the gate-house, you see. It brought the rest of the roof down, and a wall, and—"

"That's nowhere near the telephone wires," said Con. "If that was all it was, there's no real damage done."

I said, "Shut up. This is something that matters. Go on, Julie." I gave her a little shake. "*Julie!* Con, for God's sake go and get that brandy, the girl's going to faint."

"There's brandy here." He was at the bedside table. There was the splash and tinkle of liquid being poured, and he put a tumbler into my hand.

"Here, drink this." I held the rim of Grandfather's tumbler against her chattering teeth. Behind me I caught the movement as Con drew up the sheet to cover the old man's face. The moment passed, almost without significance. I said sharply, "Julie, pull yourself together. What's happened? Is it something to do with the ivy tree? Were you near the gate-house when it—oh, my God, Con, she'd have been just about passing it when we heard it come down . . . Julie, is it *Donald?*"

She nodded, and then went on nodding, like a doll. "He's down there. Underneath. Donald. The tree came down. It just split in two—"

"Is he dead?" asked Con.

Again, it seemed, his tactics worked better than mine. I felt the shock run through her, and her eyes jerked up to meet his. She said, sensibly enough, "No. I don't think so, but he's hurt, he can't get out. We have to go. . . . We were in the gate-house, you see, and the wall came down when he went down the steps, and he's hurt, there underneath. He can't get out." Abruptly she thrust the back of one grimy hand against her mouth, as if to stifle a cry. "We—we'll have to go." She looked in a kind of childish helplessness at the bed.

I said quickly, "He doesn't need us, Julie. It's all right. We'll come now. Con, where's the car?"

"I—I brought Donald's," began Julie, "only—"

Con said crisply, "You're not fit to drive. Mine's at the door. You're certain the phone's off?"

"Yes. Lisa was trying again."

"Come on, then," I said, "quickly."

It was odd—I spared a fleeting thought for it as we hurried to the door—how deeply conventions are ingrained in us. Scratch the conventional man and you find the savage; look closely at the primitive, and you see the grain of the wood from which our conventions are carved. It was incredibly hard to go out of that room in a hurry, with the mind bent on violent action. It seemed like desecration, yet only a few minutes ago this had merely been the bedroom of an arrogant, difficult, temperamental old man. By some inverted process the departure of his spirit from him had hallowed the room till, shrinelike, it had become a place where normally pitched voices and decisive actions seemed shocking.

As we reached the door, I glanced back. The sheeted shape, the single dimmed light, made of the bed a catafalque, and of the room something alien and remote. Outside was a wet night, and a fallen tree, and something urgent to do. There was no time, yet, to sit quietly, and think; either of the past, or how to meet the future. Everything has its mercies.

Lisa was in the hall, having apparently just come out of the office where the telephone was.

She stopped when she saw us. "I've been trying to get through, Julie. It's definitely gone."

Julie said: "Oh *God,*" on a little sob, and stumbled, so that for a moment I thought she would pitch straight down the stairs. I gripped and held her.

"Steady up. We'll be there ourselves in a minute."

Con, behind me, said, surprisingly, "Don't worry, we'll get him out." He ran down past us, and across the hall, pausing with a hand on the baize door. "Go and get into the car. Torches and brandy, Annabel, you know where they are. I'll not be a minute. There's some pieces of timber in the barn, we may need them if there's any shoring-up to be done."

The door swung shut behind him. We ran downstairs. I paused to ask Lisa, "Are any of the men still around?"

"No. It's Bates' day off, and Jimmy left as soon as the milking was done. The others went when the rain started. There's only Con here. You'd better go too, hadn't you? I'll go upstairs."

"Lisa—" She guessed, as soon as I spoke; I saw it in her eyes. I nodded. "Yes, I'm afraid so; just a few moments ago . . . But would you go up? It seems terrible just to—to run out like this."

She said nothing. Her eyes took in my face with one of her queer, dispassionate glances, then Julie's. Then she merely nodded, and crossed the hall towards the stairs. I think, in that moment, in spite of everything, I was sincerely and deeply glad I had come home. My own isolation was one thing; Grandfather's had been another. That he had made it himself didn't matter; he had cared, and Con had given him enough . . . but without me here, now, no one at Whitescar would have mourned him.

And, ironically enough, I was at the same time glad of Lisa, calm and impassive as ever, mounting the stairs to his room.

I pushed open the green baize door, and hustled Julie through it. "Hurry. I'll bring the things. And don't worry, Julie, pet, Con'll look after him."

It didn't even strike me at the time that the tally of irony was complete.

The big Ford was there in the yard. We had hardly scrambled into it, both close together in the front seat, when Con appeared, a shadowy, purposeful figure laden with some short, solid chunks of timber that could have been thick fencing posts, together with an axe and a ditcher's spade. He heaved these into the back of the car, slid in behind the wheel, started the motor with a roar, and swung the car round in a lurching half-circle and through the yard gate all in a moment. The lights leaped out along the rising track. Rain, small now but still thick enough and wetting, sparkled and lanced in the light. I realized that the storm had withdrawn already;

the lightning was only a faint flicker away to the east, and the thunder was silent.

The track was muddy, and Con drove fast. The car took a rising bend at forty, lurched hair-raisingly across a deep rut, swung into a skid that took her sideways a full yard on to turf, hit a stone with a bouncing tire, and was wrenched straight to pass between the posts of the first cattle grid, with scarcely an inch to spare on the off side.

Con said abruptly, "What happened, Julie? Try to put us right in the picture. Just where is he, how is he hurt, can we get to him?"

"It's the cellar," she said. "You know the place is a ruin; well, it had all fallen in where the old cellar stairs used to be, so they spent most of the day shifting that, and then—"

"They?" I said.

"Yes. Mr. Forrest had told Donald—"

"Mr. Forrest's there?"

I thought my voice sounded quite ordinary, even flat, but I saw Con turn to look at me, and then away again. The car roared round a curve, slid a little on the clay bankside, and then straightened up for the next grid. High Riggs now. At the edge of our lights the uncut fringe of hay along the track stood up like a horse's crest, stiff and glittering under the light rain.

"Yes," said Julie. "They'd been to the Hall cellars first—oh, well, never mind, but it turned out it was actually the cellars at the gate-house—"

"The Roman stones," I said. "Oh, dear heaven, yes, of course, they were still looking?"

"Yes, oh yes! When the ivy tree came down it brought down the chimney and most of that end wall, and the bit of the floor that those beams were holding. I—I was waiting outside, and—"

"Is he hurt?"

"I told you. He's down in the—"

"*Adam Forrest.* Is he hurt?"

"I don't know. But when the place came down they were both inside, and when I could get through the dust I tried to pull some of the stuff away from the cellar door, but Mr. Forrest—he was inside—shouted for me to hurry and get help, because Donald was hurt, and not answering him, and he didn't know how much because he hadn't found the torch yet, and couldn't get at him, and the stuff was settling. *Con, the gate's shut!*"

The car had been mounting the hill with a rush like a lift. She reached the crest, topped it, and even as Julie cried out, the lights, shooting out level now, caught the gate full on. The bars seemed to leap up out of the dark, solid as a cliff wall. Beyond, the headlamps lit a field of staring cattle.

Con jammed everything on, and the car seemed to dig in its hind wheels the way a jibbing horse digs in its hoofs, to come up all standing with her bonnet touching the bars.

Before we had stopped I was out of the car and wrenching at the stiff metal fastening. The gate went wide with a swing. As the car moved slowly forward Con, leaning out of his window, shouted, "Leave it! Get in quickly."

I obeyed him, and even before my door was shut, we had gathered speed once more.

I said, "Con. The cattle. They'll get through."

"The hell with that." I glanced at him in surprise. In the light from the dash I could see his face; it was preoccupied, and I thought it was only with the car, he was lost in the moment, in the driving, in holding the lurching, bouncing vehicle as fast as possible on an impossible road. Fast, violent action, a summons coming out of the dark like a fire alarm, that suited Con. Just as (I had had time to see it now) it suited him to save Donald; Donald would take Julie away.

"I'm sorry about that," he was saying. "I thought sure you'd have left the gate open, Julie."

"I—I came over the grid."

"But it's broken."

"I know." She gave a little gulp that might either have been a laugh or a sob. "I—I broke something off the car. There was an awful bang. Donald'll be livid with me . . . if he . . . if he—"

"Hold up," I said sharply. "We're nearly there."

"Is the top gate open?" This from Con.

"Yes."

"Okay," he said, and a moment later the Ford shot between the posts where the white gate swung wide, and skidded to a splashing halt in front of the looming, terrifying mass of debris that had been the ivy tree.

The lightning had split the great tree endways, so that it had literally fallen apart, one vast trunk coming down clear across the lane that led to the road, the other smashing straight down on to what had remained of the ruined gate-house. It was the branches, not the trunk itself, that had actually hit the building, so that the masonry was not cleanly hacked through by the one gigantic blow, but smashed and scattered by a dozen heavy limbs, and then almost buried from sight under the mass of tangled boughs and leaves, and the heavy, sour-smelling black mats of the ivy.

Con had swung the car slightly left-handed as it stopped, and he left the headlights on. They lit the scene with hard clarity; the huge clouded mass of the tree, its leaves glittering and dripping with the rain, among which the scattered masonry showed white; the raw new gash of the split trunk, where the black trail of the lightning could be clearly seen; and, sticking up through the boughs with a sickening kind of irrelevance, those fragments of the building that still stood. The surviving end wall and its chimney were intact, and half the front of the house, as far as the door with the heavy carved lintel, and the date, 1758 . . .

We thrust ourselves out of the car, and ran to the black gap of the doorway. In my haste I had only found one torch to bring, but there had been another in the car, and with this Con led the way through the doorway, where the car's headlamps served only to throw deeper shadows. Inside the wrecked walls was a black chaos of smashed masonry and tangled wet boughs and splintered beams.

Con hesitated, but Julie pushed past him, one hand up to keep the whipping boughs from her eyes as she thrust through the debris that blocked the hallway.

She called, "Donald! Donald! Are you all right?"

It was Adam who answered her, his voice sounding muffled and strained. It came from somewhere to the left of the hallway and below it. "He's all right. Have you brought help?"

"Con and Annabel. Here, Con, they're down here."

Con had shoved after her, stooping under the barrier of one biggish branch, and was kneeling by what seemed in the torchlight to be a gap in the left-hand wall of the passage. I followed him. This was, I suppose, where the door to the cellars had stood. Now there was merely a hole through the shambles of broken masonry, not quite big enough to admit a man. It gave on darkness.

Con flashed the torch into the gap, lighting the flight of cellar steps. Twelve steps led steeply downwards, looking undisturbed, and solid enough; at the bottom was a short length of stone-flagged passage which must have led to the cellar door. Now, the doorway had disappeared. Where it had been was a pile of stones and rubble where the ceiling and one wall had collapsed, taking with them the splintered wreckage of the doorposts. But the crossbeam still held. It had fallen when the uprights collapsed, and was wedged now at an angle, within a foot or so of the floor, roofing a narrow, triangular gap of darkness which was the only way through to the cellar beyond. Above the beam pressed the weight of the broken wall, and the broken building above, all thrust down in their turn by the pressure of the fallen boughs. Stones were still falling here and there, I heard the patter of loose stuff somewhere; the other passage wall showed a frightening bulge; and there was fresh dust dancing in the torchlight.

Adam was lying right underneath the beam, face downwards. His feet were towards us, and the top half of his body was out of sight. I recognized the faded brown corduroys, his working garb, now thick with dust. For one sickening moment I thought that the great beam had fallen clean across his back, then I saw there was a gap of perhaps four inches between it and his body. He must have been somewhere on the cellar steps when the crash occurred, and he had been trying to creep under the fallen stuff to reach the place where Donald lay.

And, for the moment, the crossbeam held.

"Forrest?" Con's voice was subdued. A shout, it seemed, might bring the whole thing down, irrevocably in ruins. Even as he spoke, there was the slithering sound of something settling, and the whisper of dust chuting on to the steps below us. Somewhere, some timber creaked. I think it was only a broken bough of the ivy tree, but it lifted the hair along my arms. "Forrest?" called Con softly. "Are you all right?"

"I'm all right." Adam spoke breathlessly; it was as if he was making some violent effort, like holding up the beam with his own body; but he didn't move. "Seton's inside here; there's another pile of the—stuff—just in here, past the beam, and I can't—get any purchase—to move it. He'll be safe enough . . . it's a groined ceiling, it won't come down in there, and he's lying clear of this . . . I can just reach him if I lie flat, but I can't get—any further—and we'll not get him out till this stuff's moved. How long will the doctor be?"

"We couldn't get him. The lines are down."

"Dear God. Didn't Julie say—?"

"Look, if Seton's not badly hurt, you'll simply have to leave him, and come out, for the time being." Con had propped his torch where it could light the gap, and was already, gingerly, beginning to widen this. "You say the roof's safe over him; if you come back, we could probably shift enough stuff between us to get clear through to him. In any case, first things first, if this place isn't shored up pretty damn quick, I wouldn't give twopence for your own chances. That stuff's settling while you wait."

I heard Julie take in her breath. Adam said painfully, "My dear man, you'll have to prop it round me as best you can, and take the chance. Otherwise it's a certainty. I can't leave him. He's torn an artery."

Beside me, Julie gave a little gasp like a moan. I said, "Julie! Get a way cleared back to the car, and fetch the props. Pass them to me under that bough."

"Yes," she said, "yes," and began, with savage but barely effectual hands, to push and break a way back through the tangle to the doorway.

"I've got a tourniquet on, of a sort." Adam's voice was still muffled, so that I hoped Julie, working a yard or two away, couldn't hear it. "And it's doing the trick. I don't think he's losing much, now. But it's tricky in the dark, and I can't hold it indefinitely. You'll have to get the doctor straight away. Annabel?"

"Yes?"

"The car's there?"

"Yes."

"Will you go? If you can't find Wilson straight away—"

Julie had heard, after all. She turned among the wet branches. "The tree's down across the road, too. We can't take the car, and it's four miles."

I said, "The telephone at West Lodge, Adam? It's the same line as Whitescar, isn't it?"

"I'm afraid so."

I was on my feet. "I'll go on foot. It's all right, Julie, once I get to the road I'll get a lift."

"There's never anything along the road at this time of night," said Julie desperately, "you know there isn't! If you drove the car into the field, couldn't you get it round the tree, and—?"

"No use. We've nothing to cut the wires with, and anyway she'd bog down in a yard. We're wasting time. I'm going. I'll run all the way if I have to."

Con said: "It's more than four miles, it's nearer six. And you might get a lift or you might not. Your best chance is Nether Shields."

"But there's no bridge!" cried Julie.

"No," I said, "but I can drive right up to the footbridge at West Lodge, and then it's barely two miles up to the farm. Yes, that's it, Con." I turned quickly back. "Adam?"

"Yes?"

"Did you hear? I'm going to Nether Shields. Their telephone may be working, and I can get Dr. Wilson from there. If it's not, one of the boys will go for him. I'll send the others straight over here."

Julie said, on a sob, "Oh, God, it'll take an hour. Two miles up from West Lodge, and all uphill. You'll kill yourself, and it'll be too late!"

"Nonsense!" I said. "Run and open the gate."

"It's open. Con left it open."

"Not that one. It's quicker if I go by the top track through the Park. If I go down by Whitescar, I've to use the little track up behind the house, and there's three gates on that. Hurry, let's go!"

But she didn't move. "A horse! That's it!"

I was propping my torch where it would help Con. I turned. "What?"

"A horse! If you took the mare you could go straight across the ford and across the fields, and it's hardly any further than from West Lodge, and you'd be there much quicker!"

Con said, "That's an idea," then I saw it hit him. He paused fractionally, with his fingers curled round a lump of sandstone, and I caught his bright sidelong look up at me. He said, "The mare's not shod."

Julie cried, "That doesn't matter! What does the mare matter?"

I said impatiently, "She'd be lame in half a mile, and I'd get nowhere."

Con said, "Take Forrest's colt. He'll let you." Even then, it took me two heartbeats to realize what he was doing. Then I understood. I had been right, none of this touched him. The agonizing emergency was nothing more to him than an exciting job. In this moment of terror and imminent death, he was unscathed. By everything that had happened, he was untouched. And I had liked him for it; been grateful for it.

Well, he still had to get Adam out.

I said shortly, "It would save no time. I'd have to catch him."

Adam's voice again from beyond the beam. It sounded, now, like the voice of a man at the limits of his control. "Annabel, listen, wait, my dear . . . it's an idea. The colt's in the stable at West Lodge; I brought him in today. Take the car across there . . . if he'll face the water . . . only a few minutes to Nether Shields. He'll go, for you, I think. . . ."

The gap in the wall was open now. Con laid a stone down, and sat back on his heels. The twin torchbeams held us, Con and myself, in a round pool of limelight, one on either side of the gap. We stared at one another. He was no longer smiling.

I said to Adam, without taking my eyes off Con, "All right. I'll manage."

"The second door in the stableyard. You know where the bridles are."

"Yes. I know."

Adam said, "Take care, my dear. He doesn't like thunder."

"I'll be all right." I said it straight to that stare of Con's. "I can manage him. Don't worry about me."

"You'll take the horse?" cried Julie.

"Yes. Open the top gate for me. Hold on, Adam, darling."

As I went, I saw Con sitting there, back on his heels, staring after me.

CHAPTER SEVENTEEN

"The water is rough and wonderful steepe,
Follow, my love, come over the strand–
And in my saddle I shall not keepe,
And I the fair flower of Northumberland."

Ballad: *The Fair Flower of Northumberland.*

IT WAS IMPORTANT not to think about the scene I was leaving behind me in the dark gate-house; to blot out Donald, his life ebbing slowly behind the wall of debris; Julie, helpless, holding panic on a thin thread; Adam, prone in the dust under that settling mass. . . .

And Con there to help. I mustn't even remember that. I didn't know how that quick brain would work; what he would seize for himself out of this new situation. Con, if it suited Con, would work like a galley slave, and do miracles; but if it didn't, God alone knew what he would do.

But I put it out of my mind, and ran to the waiting car.

It seemed to take an hour to turn her, reversing out between the pillars of the gateway, over mosses made slimy with rain, and liberally strewn with fallen twigs, and fragments of rotten timber, and stray stones scattered from the smashed lodge. I made myself take it slowly, but even so, the wheels spun and slithered crazily among the fallen rubbish, and my hands and arms, shaking now as if with fever, seemed powerless to control the car. I heard the ominous sound of metal scraping stone, then we were free of the driveway, and swinging to face west again, and Julie had run across to open the gate to the upper track.

As I passed her, I called out, "Keep your eye open for the doctor's car! He may already be on his way to see Grandfather."

I saw her nod, looking pale as a ghost in the momentary glare of light, and her mouth shaped the one word, "*Hurry!*"

I drove my foot down as far as I dared, and tried to remember what I could of the road.

It was eight years since I had driven along the upper track to West

Lodge. Two fields first, I remembered, then trees bordering the track, young firs, waist-high, that the forestry people had put in; for even then Adam had been trying all means to make the estate pay its way. It was a shock to run suddenly between black walls of spruce that shut out the lighter night, and towered well above the roof of the car. Time was, and they had grown a foot a year. The headlamps lit a narrow black canyon through which we ran at a fair speed, as the track was paved with pine needles which had acted as drainage, and the walls of trees had kept off the worst of the storm.

Then a gate, standing open; a long hill curling down between high banks; an avenue, planted in more leisurely days, of great beeches that soared up silver in the lights, then a twisting, up-and-down quarter-mile along the gully cut by some small stream, where all I could do was hang on grimly to the controls and hope that the track was reasonably well-drained.

It wasn't, and I soon throttled down to a safe and cowardly fifteen miles an hour, which felt slower than walking, and brought the sweat out on my body till my hands slipped on the wheel.

Then a gate, shut, hanging a little crookedly across the way.

It was almost a relief to be out of the car, and running to open it. The lever was stiff, jammed by the sagging of the hinges, but I fought it out of its socket at last, and shoved at the heavy gate. This shifted a couple of inches, and stuck. It had sagged into a muddy rut, but that was not what prevented it from opening. As I bent to heave it forcibly wider, I heard the rattle of a chain. A loop of chain, dark with rust, and with a rusty padlock tightly locked, was fastened round gate and gate post, holding them together.

A locked gate; no place to turn the car; the choice facing me of either reversing down that dreadful piece of track till I could turn for the long trail back, and round by Whitescar; or of abandoning the car and running the half-mile between here and West Lodge. Either alternative, unthinkable . . .

There are times when your body and nerves think for you. Adrenalin, they tell you nowadays. They used to say, "Needs must, when the devil drives," or even, "God helps those who help themselves."

I seized the chain and yanked at it, with the fury of desperate need, and it came off in my hands. It had only been a loop, flung loosely over the posts, to hold the gate from sagging further open. I think I stood for four precious seconds, staring at it in my hands, as if by some miracle I really had snapped its massive links like horsehair. I should have known that Adam wouldn't have let me come this way, if it had been barred.

Adam. I dropped the chain into the soaking grass by the gate post, shoved the heavy gate wide as if it had weighed an ounce, scrambled back into the car, and was through the gate and away before the grasses had stopped shaking.

A sharp rise, then, away from the trees, and here was the straight, good half-mile across a high heathy pasture where the dry gravel of the track showed white in the lights, and as clear as if it had been marked with cats' eyes.

The crest of the moor. A single birch tree, its stem flashing white and then lost again in the darkness behind. Then the sudden, sharp dip of the descent towards the river, the swift, curling drop into the sheltered saucer of land where West Lodge lay.

I had forgotten just how steep the hill was, and how sharp the turn.

As my lights met the crest of the hill, we must have been doing forty-five. I stood on the brake, but as we switch-backed over the top and dived for the river, we were still traveling like a bomb. The car went down the drop like an aircraft making for the touch-down. I saw the bend coming, drove my foot hard down on the brake, and put everything I had of strength and timing into getting her round the corner.

I felt the front wheel mounting the edge, swinging, thrown wide by the force of our turn. I had the steering wheel jammed hard over to the left. I felt the rear swing, too, mount, pause . . .

We could do it. We were round . . .

On a dry night, we might have done it, even despite my bad judgment. But the track was damp, and the grass; and the wheels, at the very verge, had met mud. . . .

The front of the car drifted, slid, swam uncontrollably wide. The wheel topped the bank, was over. The car lurched crazily as she hit the rough turf of the slope to the river. The lights struck the water ten yards away, and the mirror-flash startled my eyes.

I must have straightened the wheel instinctively as we left the track, or we would have turned over. As it was, the car plunged down the last four feet of the bank dead straight, in a dive for the river, lurched over a nine-inch drop to the shingle, hit the edge of the drop with her undercarriage, and stopped dead, with the front wheels on the gravel, and the water sliding by not a yard from the bonnet.

In the silence after the engine stalled, the river sounded as loud as thunder.

I sat there, still gripping the wheel, listening to the tick of cooling metal, and stupidly watching the wipers still wagging to and fro, to and fro, squealing across the dry glass. It had stopped raining some time back, and I hadn't noticed. . . .

I don't know how long I sat there. Not more than seconds, I think, though it seemed an age. I was unhurt, and, though I must have been shaken, I had no time to feel it. This was a pause in the movement; no more.

I clambered out of the car. The stableyard lay no more than fifty yards away, at the foot of the hill. I retained enough wit to switch the ignition off, and the headlights, and then I abandoned the car, and ran.

I had forgotten the route, and crashed Con's car in consequence, but when I got to the stable door my hand went automatically to the light switch, and, as the light snapped on, I reached for the bridle without even looking for it. Leather met my hand, and the cool jingle of metal. I lifted it from its peg, and then stood still for a moment or two, controlling my breathing, letting my eyes get used to the light, and the horse used to the sight of me.

It was no use approaching him like this. A few more seconds now, to let my heart slow down to something near its normal rate, and to control my hands . . . I hadn't realized, till I lifted down that ringing bridle, that my hands were shaking still.

I leaned back against the wall of the stable, and regarded the Forrest colt.

He was in a loose-box opposite the door. He stood across the far corner of it, facing away from me, but with his head round towards me, and ears pricked, inquiring, slightly startled.

I began to talk, and the effort to steady my voice steadied me. When I saw the ears move gently, I opened the loose-box and went in.

He didn't move, except to cock his head higher, and a little sideways, so that the great dark eyes watched me askance, showing a rim of white. I slid a gentle hand on to his neck and ran it up the crest towards his ears. He lowered his head then, and snuffled at the breast of my blouse.

I said, "Help me now, Rowan, beauty," and cupped the bit towards him. He didn't even pause to mouth it; he took it like a hungry fish taking a fly. In seven seconds after that, as smoothly as a dream, I had him bridled. In ten more, I was leading him outside into the night. I didn't take time for a saddle. I mounted from the edge of the water trough, and he stood as quietly as a donkey at the seaside.

Then I turned him towards the river. The way led to his pasture, so he went willingly and straight, with that lovely long walk of his that ate up the yards. I made myself sit quietly. Momentarily blinded by the darkness as I was, I could neither guide nor hurry him. I talked to him, of course; it seemed that this was more for my own comfort than the horse's, but it took us both as far as the faint glimmer of the river, where a path turned off towards the pastures, from the foot of the narrow wooden footbridge.

Now, I had no idea if I could get Rowan to cross the water which, swelled a bit by the recent thunder-rain, was coming down at a fair speed, and with some sound and fury over its treacherous boulders. It would be a bad enough crossing by daylight, and in the dark it was doubly hazardous. But there is no horse living, except a circus horse, that will cross the unsafe echoing of a wooden footbridge—even if I had dared put him at the triple step at either end. It was the water or nothing.

At least here we had come out from under the trees, and I could see.

The bank shelved fairly steeply near the bridge. The river was a wide, broken glimmer, with shadows where the boulders thrust up, and luminous streams of bubbling foam where the freshets broke. The sound was lovely. Everything smelt fresh and vivid after the rain. As I put Rowan at the bank I could smell thyme and water mint, and the trodden turf as his hoofs cut it.

He hesitated on the edge, checked, and began to swerve away. I insisted.

Good-manneredly he turned, hesitated again, then faced the drop of the bank. Then, as his fore hoofs went down the first foot of the drop, he stopped, and I saw his ears go back.

Now, when one rides without a saddle, there are certain obvious disadvantages, but there is one great advantage—one is with the horse; his muscles are joined to, melted in with, the rider's; the rider is part of the beast's power, moves with him, and can think into his body a vital split second faster than when the impulse has to be conveyed through rein and heels alone.

I felt the colt's hesitation, doubt, and momentary fear, even before the impulses had taken root in his mind, and my own impulse forward was supplied instantaneously. He snorted, then lunged forward suddenly and slithered down into the water.

I held him together as he picked his way across between the streaming boulders. I was saying love words that I thought I had forgotten. His hoofs slipped and rang on the stones, and the water swirled, shining, round his legs. It splashed against his fetlocks, then it was to his knees; he stumbled once, and in recovering sent one hoof splodging down into a pool that drenched me to the thigh. But he went steadily on, and in no time, it seemed, the small shingle was crunching under his feet, and we were across. He went up the far bank with a scramble and a heave that almost unseated me, shook his crest, then plunged forward at a rough canter to meet the track.

This ran steeply up, here, from the footbridge, and, though rutted and uneven, lay clearly enough marked in the moonlight between its verges of dark sedge. I twisted my right hand in Rowan's mane, set him at the slope, and gave him his head.

He took it fast, in that eager, plunging canter that, normally, I would have steadied and controlled. But he couldn't, tonight, go fast enough for me . . . and besides, there was this magnificent dreamlike feeling, the flying night, the surging power that was part of me, the drug of speed that felt like speed, the desperate mission soon to be accomplished. . . .

The canter lengthened, became a gallop; we were up the slope and on the level ground. There was a gate, I knew. We would have to stop and open it. Even if I hadn't been riding bare-back, I couldn't have set him to jump it in the dark. I peered ahead uncertainly, trusting the horse to see it before I did, hoping he knew just where it was. . . .

He did. I felt his stride shorten, and next moment saw—or thought I saw—the dim posts of a fence, joined with invisible wire, with the shapes of cattle beyond. Across the road, nothing. The way was clear. The gate seemed to be open . . . yes, I could see it now, set to one side of the track, as if it were lying back, wide open, against the wire fence.

Rowan flicked his ears forward, then back, and hurtled down the track at full gallop.

I had hardly time to wonder, briefly, why the cattle hadn't crowded through the gap, when we were on it, and I saw. The gate for the beasts stood to the side, and was shut, as I should have known it would be. And, clear across the way, where I had thought there was a gap, lay the cattle grid, eight feet of treacherous, clanging iron grid that, even if it didn't break his legs, would throw us both. . . .

No time to stop him now, or swerve him to face the gate. Two tremendous strides, and he was on it.

This time, he thought for me. As the grid gaped in front of his feet, looking, in the dark, like a wide pit across his path, he steadied, lifted, and was over, as smoothly as a swallow in an eddy of air.

And then all at once, ahead of us, were the massed trees, and the lights of Nether Shields.

I learned afterwards that there had been some storm damage at Nether Shields, and that after the rain was off the men—Mr. Fenwick and his two sons—had come out to take a look round. They were in the yard when I got there, and they must have heard the horse's hoofs coming up the moor at the gallop, for all three were at the gate.

The main track went by some fifty yards from Nether Shields. We cut across the corner, and I sent Rowan headlong for the gate.

It is possible that they thought the horse was bolting with me, for nobody opened the gate. Rowan came to a slithering halt with his breast almost up against the bars, and then, seeing the men, shied violently sideways and began to circle.

Someone swung the gate wide, then, and the three men stood aside. It was all I could do to get Rowan in past them, through the gate, but he went in the end, fighting every inch of the way. One of the men shut the gate behind us, and would have reached for the bridle, but I thought the horse would rear, and said, breathlessly, "Leave him. It's all right. Keep back . . ."

Someone said, "It's Forrest's," and another: "It's the Winslow girl," and then Mr. Fenwick's voice came quickly, "What is it, lass? Trouble?"

I found I could hardly speak. I was breathless from effort, but it wasn't that. My teeth were chattering as if I was chilled. I suppose it was shock catching up on me; my whole body was shaking, now, and the muscles of my thighs felt loose against the restless movements of the colt. I think that if I hadn't had a hand in his mane, I would, shamefully, have fallen off him.

I managed to say, somehow, "There's been an accident at the gate-house. Forrest Hall. A tree's down on the gate-house, and someone's hurt, and Mr. Forrest's there too. They're both trapped inside, and if they don't get help soon the whole place looks like coming down on them. The phone's off at Whitescar. Is yours working?"

Mr. Fenwick was a man of swift action and few words. He said merely, "Don't know. Sandy, go and see. Is it for the doctor?"

"Yes. Yes. Tell him a cut artery, we think, and to come quickly. And could you come yourself—all of you, straight away? There's a wall collapsing, and the men underneath, and only Con and Julie there—"

"Aye. Bill, get the Land Rover out. Ropes, torches, crowbars. Sandy, tell your mother."

Sandy went in at a run. Bill had already vanished into a shed whose doors, dragged wide, showed the gleam of the Land Rover's bonnet.

I slipped off the horse's back, and held him. "Props," I said. "Have you anything to shore the stones up?"

"What sort of length?"

"Short. Just to hold them off a man. He's lying underneath. A foot, eighteen inches, anything just to hold them clear."

"Good Christ," said the farmer.

"We had fencing posts, and Con can push them in sideways," I said, "but there weren't enough. And some for the passage, too, if you've any longer ones—"

"There's plenty stuff in the shed, all lengths." He raised his voice above the sudden roar of the Land Rover's motor. "Put your lights on, Bill!"

The lights shot out. Rowan went back in a clattering rear, almost lifting me from the ground. I saw the farmer turn, and cried, "Never mind! Get on! I can manage him!"

The Land Rover came out of the shed, and stopped just short of the yard gate, with its engine ticking over and its lights full on. Bill jumped out of the front and ran back to where his father was dragging solid lumps of sawn timber from a wood stack. I saw the gleam of a metal bar, and the shape of a heavy pick, as they were hurled into the back of the vehicle. A couple of what looked like old railway sleepers went in after them.

"The rope from the tractor shed?" asked Bill.

"Aye." The farmer threw a shovel in after the rest.

Sandy must have told his mother something as he ran to the telephone, for she appeared now in the lighted doorway of the farmhouse. "Miss Winslow? Sandy's told me of the trouble. He's on the telephone now."

"*It's working?*"

"Oh, yes."

"Dear God," I said, meaning it, and put my forehead against Rowan's hot neck.

"My dear," she said, "don't worry. It won't be long. Doctor Wilson's not at home, he's up at Haxby, but Sandy's getting through now. He'll be down at Forrest in something under twenty minutes, and the men will be there in ten. Would you like me to go with them, in case I can help?"

There came to me, the first flash of warmth in an Arctic night, a vague memory that before her marriage to Jem Fenwick of Nether Shields, she had been a nurse. He had broken a leg and spent a month in the Royal Victoria, and taken her back with him when he was discharged. A long time ago now, but if the doctor were delayed. . . .

I cried, "Oh, Mrs. Fenwick, could you go with them? *Could* you? There's Julie's young man with a cut artery, and Adam Forrest trying to hold it, and the cellar roof going to come down on them, and only Con and Julie there to try and fix it up."

She was as decisive as her husband. "Of course. I'll get some stuff and be with you. Don't you fret, child. Can you leave that horse, and come in?"

"No."

She wasted no time arguing or persuading. She must have known that I was almost grateful for the job of holding Rowan quiet amid the bustle and shouting in the yard. She turned back into the house, and I heard her calling, "Betty! Pour some of that tea into the big flask, quickly! And get the brandy. Sandy, go up and fetch blankets—what? Oh, half a dozen. Hurry, now!"

The Land Rover was loaded; Bill had pulled the gate open, and was in the driving seat. Mr. Fenwick heaved a great coil of rope into the back, and then came over to me.

"I take it you came by West Lodge?"

"Yes. The tree that's down has blocked the lane to the main road. I drove over to West Lodge, and then took the horse."

"Is the river deep?"

"In places, but it's coming down fastish, and near the bridge it's all boulders. There's no decent crossing, even for that thing."

"I doubt you're right. We can drive her down and pile the stuff across into your car. It's at the Lodge?"

"No. You can't. I—I crashed it. I'm sorry, but—"

"Good Christ," he said again. "Are you all right?"

"Yes, quite."

"Well, we'll have to go the other way. It'll not take much longer; it's a good road. Ah, here we are." This as Sandy ran past us with a load of blankets, which went on top of the tools and props. Then a girl, with what must have been the hot tea and brandy. And finally, Mrs. Fenwick, diminutive but bustlingly efficient, with a box in her hands, and about her, clad though she was in an old tweed coat, the impression of a comforting rustle of starch.

Everyone piled into the Land Rover. The farmer turned to me. "Coming? Shove the colt in the barn, he'll come to no harm. We'll make room somehow."

I hesitated, but only for a moment. "No. I'll take the horse back. Someone ought to go to Whitescar and tell Lisa. We'll have beds ready there. Don't bother about me. And—thank you."

His reply was lost in the roar of the motor. The Land Rover leaped forward, cut across the field corner, her four-wheel drive sending her through the mud churned by the cattle, as easily as if it were an arterial road. I heard Mrs. Fenwick call something shrill and reassuring, then the vehicle was nothing but a receding roar and a red light in the darkness, making for the highroad.

I only remembered then, with a curious little jolt, that I had forgotten to tell them about Grandfather.

The girl said, shyly, beside me, "Will you come in, Miss Winslow? Just for a minute? There's tea made."

"No, my dear. Thanks all the same. I must get back. Will you shut the gate behind me?"

"Surely."

It wasn't so easy to mount Rowan this time, but I managed it with the aid of the gate itself, and presently, having said good night to the girl, I turned him out of the yard to face the darkness once again.

It was now, with the job done, that nature went back on me. My muscles felt as weak as a child's, and I sat the horse so loosely that, if he had treated me to a single moment's display of temperament, I'd have slid straight down his shoulders under his hoofs.

But, the two of us alone again, he went as softly as a cat across the grass, let me open the second gate from his back, and after that he walked, with that smooth, distance-devouring stride of his, till we came to the river bank.

Sooner than have to fight or cajole him, I'd have dismounted and led him across, myself thigh-deep. But he took to the water as smoothly as a mallard slipping off her nest, and in a few minutes more, it seemed, we were striding out at a collected, easy canter for Whitescar.

He swerved only once, as we passed the crashed Ford squatting down on the river gravel, but a word reassured him, and he went smoothly on.

It was now, when I had no more effort to make, when Rowan was, so to speak, nursing me home to Whitescar, with the sound of his hoofs steady and soft on the turf of the avenue, that the spectres of imagination had time to crowd up out of the dark.

Do what's nearest . . . I had done just that, and I was right. Someone had to go to Whitescar, and warn Lisa what to prepare for. There was nothing I could have done at the gate-house. And if I could do nothing for Adam, I could at least care for his horse, who was worth, in hard cash, at least as much as the garden and West Lodge put together. . . .

But this way, I should be the last to know what had happened. And in the darkness, as Rowan (whom I would never be able to see as "hard cash" in my life) strode steadily and softly on, I was forced at last, with nerves sufficiently stripped by shock, to admit openly to myself what I had known at some other level for long enough.

It might have already happened. This night, dark and damp and sweet-smelling, might at this very moment be empty of all I cared about. All. If Adam were dead (I acknowledged it now), there was nothing else, nowhere else, nothing. They are fools indeed who are twice foolish. I had had my folly, eight years back, and again this morning in the early dewfall, and now, tonight, it might be that the chance to be a fool again was gone.

The colt stopped, lowered his head, and blew. I leaned over his neck, and pushed open the last gate. The lights of Whitescar were just below us.

A few moments later Rowan clattered into the yard, and stood still.

As I slid from his back, Lisa came hurrying out. "I thought I heard a horse! Annabel! What's happened?"

I told her everything, as succinctly as I could. I must have been incoherent from sheer fatigue, but at least she knew that a bed, or beds, would be needed, and I must have made it clear that the doctor would soon be on his way. "I'll be with you in a minute," I finished wearily, "when I've put the horse in."

Only then did I notice how she looked from me to Rowan, and back again. "Yes," I said, gently, "I did manage to ride him, after all. I always did have a way with horses."

I left her standing there. As I led the lathered horse round the end of the Dutch barn, I saw her turn, and hurry back into the house.

The mare's box stood empty. I put the light on, and led Rowan in. He went without even a nervous glance round at the strange stable. Even when Tommy lifted her head from the nest in the manger, blinking at the light, Rowan only snorted, blew, and then lowered his nose to forage for hay. I fastened the bars behind him, slipped the bridle off and hung it up, then tipped a measure of feed down in front of him. He blew again, sighed, and began to munch, rolling an eye back at me as I brought the brush and set to work on him. Tired as I was, I dared not leave him steaming, and lathered, as he was, with ripples of sweat like the wave marks on a beach.

I had my left hand flat against his neck, and was currying his back and ribs vigorously, when, suddenly, I felt the muscles under my hands go tense, and the comfortable munching stopped. Rowan put his head up, and his tail switched nervously. From the corner of my eye I saw a shadow leap from the manger to the top of the partition, and vanish without a sound. Tommy, taking cover.

I glanced over my shoulder.

In the doorway, framed by the black night, stood Con. He was alone. He came quietly into the stable, and shut the half-door behind him.

CHAPTER EIGHTEEN

"I lo'e Brown Adam well," she says,
"I wot sae he lo'es me;
I wadna gie Brown Adam's love
For nae fause knight I see."

Ballad: *Brown Adam.*

He stopped just inside the door, and I saw him reach back to pull the upper half shut, too.

I hardly noticed what he was doing. There was room for only one thought in my mind just then. I straightened up, saying sharply, "What's happened?"

"They got him out. The doctor got there just before I left." He was struggling with the bolt, to thrust it home, but it was rusted, and stuck. He added, over his shoulder: "I see you did get the colt over to Nether Shields. Congratulations."

"*Con!*" I couldn't believe that even Con could so casually dismiss what must even now be happening up at the gate-house. "*What's happened?* Are they all right? For heaven's *sake!*"

He abandoned the bolt, and turned. He came no nearer, but stood there, eyeing me. Beside me, Rowan stood stiffly, not eating, motionless except for that nervously switching tail. I laid an automatic hand on his neck; it was beginning to sweat again.

Con's voice was subdued, even colourless. "I told you. They got Seton out safely enough in the end. The cut in the artery wasn't too bad; he'd lost a fair amount of blood, and he got a bump on the head, but the tourniquet saved him, and the doctor says it won't be long till he's as right as rain. They'll be bringing him down soon."

So fierce was the preoccupation in my mind, that only now did Con's manner—and his begging of my question—force itself on my attention. I noticed then that he seemed totally unlike himself; quiet, oddly restrained, not tired—that I could have understood—but damped-down in some way, almost as if his mind were not on what he was saying . . . or as if he was holding back what was in the forefront of it.

It came to me, quite clearly, what he was trying not to say. My hand must have moved on Rowan's neck, for the colt shifted his quarters, and his ears flattened.

I said hoarsely, "Why did you come down like this, ahead of the rest? What are you trying to tell me?"

He looked aside, for the first time since I had known him, refusing to meet my eyes—Con, who could lie his way through anything, and smile in your face while he did it. There was a horseshoe on a nail by the door; hung there for luck, perhaps, the way one sees them in stables. He fingered it idly for a moment, then lifted it down, turning it over and over in his hands, his head bent to examine it as if it were some rare treasure. He said, without looking up, "The beam came down. I'm sorry."

I must have been leaning back against the horse, because I remember how cold my own body seemed suddenly, and how gratefully the heat from the damp hide met it through my thin blouse. I began to repeat it after him, stupidly, my voice unrecognizable, "The beam . . ." Then, sharply, "*Adam?* Con, you're lying! It isn't possible! You're lying!"

He looked at me quickly, then down again at the metal in his hands. "He wouldn't come out. The beam was shifting, you saw it, but he wouldn't leave Seton, he said, he'd have to take the chance. We did what we could, but with just me and Julie there . . ." He paused, and added, "it happened just before the others got there."

While I had been riding home. It had happened then. *Then*. . . .

My hand had slid up the colt's neck, and was twisted in his mane. I think it was all that was holding me up. I said, so violently that the horse started, "So you let it happen, did you?" Con was looking at me again now. "'Before the others got there . . .' *Of course it was!* Because you let it happen! You did it, Connor Winslow, you wanted him dead!"

He said slowly, "Are you crazy? Why should I want that?"

"God knows why! Do you have to have a reason? I've stopped wondering how your mind works. I suppose it suited you to let him die, just as it suited you to get Donald out alive! You think nobody exists but yourself, you think you're God . . . every rotten murderer thinks the same! So Donald's alive, and Adam—" I stopped, as abruptly as if he had struck me across the face; then I added, quite flatly, without the faintest vestige of drama or even emotion, "You let him die, and me not there." And this time I wasn't talking to Con.

It must have been fully twenty seconds later that I noticed the silence. The quality of the silence. Then Rowan shifted his feet on the concrete, and I looked at Con again.

He was standing quite still, the horseshoe motionless in his hands. His eyes were wide open now, and very blue. He said softly, and the Irish was there, "Well, well, well . . . so it's true, is it? I thought as much, up there in your grandfather's bedroom, but I couldn't quite believe it . . . not quite; not till the clever little girl took the horse." His knuckles whitened round the horseshoe. "So that's it, is it? That's everything clear at last." He smiled. "Annabel, me darlin', what a fool you've made of me, haven't you, now?"

I didn't answer. The other thing was there in front of me still, a black questioning between myself and God. Con's voice seemed to come from a long way away, like a voice on the wireless, heard from next door through a wall. Irrelevant. A nuisance only, meaning nothing.

The horse threw up his head as Con took a step nearer. "So it was Adam Forrest, was it? Adam Forrest? Christ, who'd have thought it? What fools we all were, weren't we, and a damned adultery going on under our very noses?" All at once his face wasn't handsome at all, but convulsed, thinned, ugly. "And when you heard the wife was dead, you came back, you little bitch. You saw your chance to get me out, by God, and carry on your dirty little affair again into the bargain!"

That got through. "That's not true!" I cried.

"So, you wouldn't look at me . . . I thought there was someone, I thought there was. Your grandfather thought it was me you were meeting, but you wouldn't look at me, would you, Annabel? Oh no, it had to be Forrest of Forrest Hall, no less, not your cousin, who was only good enough to work for you . . ."

Suddenly, stupid and half-fainting (as I suppose I was) with fatigue and shock, I saw what all this time I had never even guessed: a cold rage of jealousy. Not, I am sure, because Con had ever really wanted me, but simply because I had never wanted him. It had been bad enough that I had pushed him aside without a glance, but to prefer another man . . . And the discovery of that man's identity had scored his vanity to the bone.

He took another step forward. "I suppose you thought he'd marry you?" His voice was cruel. "Was that why you came back? Was it? He's married money before, and you're well worth it now, aren't you? What was the game, Annabel? What have you been playing at? Come on, let's have it. You've been playing some game with me, and I want the truth."

He had come right up to the loose-box bar. Rowan was standing quite quietly now, head low, and tail still. But his ears moved with each inflection of our voices, and where I leaned against his shoulder I could feel the tiny tremors running up under his skin, like little flickers of flame.

"But Con . . . Con . . ." It was like groping through fog; there had been something I had to tell Con today, something about the money, that I didn't want it, and never had—that he could have it, just as he had planned, and I would take Mother's money, and go. . . . Something else, too, that I had torn up his "confession" to me, and that he was free to destroy mine, with its useless signature, "Mary Grey." . . . But above all, that he could have the money; that I was glad to let him have it for Whitescar, because Adam and I . . .

I turned my head into the horse's neck. "No, Con . . . not now. Not any more now. Just go away. *Go away*."

For answer, he came closer. He was right up at the loose-box bar. He had one hand on it; in the other he still held the horseshoe.

"You've made a fool of me all this time, so you have." The low voice was venomous. "Do you think I'd trust you now, with what you know about me? All that crap you talked about leaving the place, making over the money—what the hell were you playing at? Stringing me along, so you could hand me over? Or contest the will?"

I said wearily, "It was true. I wanted you to have it. And you did get Whitescar."

"How do I know even that was true?" he asked savagely. "You told me, yes, but why should I believe a word you say?"

"Oh God, Con, not now. Later, if you must . . . if I ever speak to you again. Go away. Can't you see . . . ?"

"Can't *you* see?" asked Con, and something in his intonation got through to me at last. I lifted my head and looked hazily at him. "Yes," he said. "I've taken enough risks over this, and I'm taking no more. I take my chances where they come, and I'm not missing this one. Lisa'll give me all the alibi I'll need, and there'll be nothing to prove. Even clever little Annabel isn't infallible with a young, wild brute like this . . . the Fenwicks said he was all over the yard with you at Nether Shields, and they won't stop to think he's so flat out he wouldn't hurt a fly." As he spoke, he was lifting the loose-box bar. "Now do you understand?"

Instinct had understood for me, where my failing sense did not. I shrank away from Rowan's shoulder, and came back against the cold iron of the manger. Behind me I heard tiny stirring sounds in the straw, as the sleepy kittens searched for their mother. I believe that the only coherent thought in my mind was that Con mustn't be allowed to find them. . . .

He was in the box with us. I couldn't have moved if I had tried; and if I had tried, I couldn't have got away. The scene seemed to have very little to do with me. The stable was curiously dark, swimming away into an expanding, airy blackness; it was empty, except for something that moved a little, near my shoulder, and Con, coming slowly towards me with some object held in his hand, and a queer look in his eyes. I thought, but not with any sense of its meaning anything to me, he can't kill me in cold blood. Funny! he's finding it difficult. I wouldn't have thought Con would even have hesitated. . . .

His hand moved out, in slow motion, it seemed, and took me by the wrist. At that same half-conscious level I knew that he wanted to frighten me into moving, screaming, running, fighting—anything that could spark off in him the dangerous current of violence. But all I could hear was my brain, repeating the words which, since that morning, it had repeated over and over again, like a damaged record, "It would be easier to be dead. . . ."

I must have said it aloud. I saw the blue eyes widen and flicker, close to mine, then the hand tightened on my wrist. "You little fool," said Con, "he's not dead. I only said that to make you give yourself away."

The light caught the edge of the horseshoe as he lifted it. The horseshoe—this was why he had picked it up. He had intended this. This was why he came down, alone. He had lied about Adam. He was not yet a murderer. This was the truth.

Then I screamed. I wrenched violently away from him, to get my wrist free. The movement brought me hard up against the colt's side, and jerked an oath from Con as he dropped my arm, and tried to throw himself clear.

But he wasn't quite quick enough.

As I went down into the whirling blackness under the colt's belly, I heard the high scream of the horse like a grotesque mimicry of my own, saw the hoofs flash and strike as he reared straight up over me . . . and then the red gloss of blood where, a moment before, Con's blue eyes had stared murder.

They told me later that they heard the scream of the colt above the engine when they were still halfway across High Riggs.

Adam wasn't with them. He, like Con, had not waited. When the horse screamed, he was already at the yard gate, and twelve seconds later he burst into the stable to find Con, thrown clean from the box by that first tremendous slash of the forehoofs, lying in his own blood with, oddly, a loose horseshoe three yards away; and in the box Rowan standing, sweating, but quiet, with me sprawled anyhow right under his feet, and his nose down, nuzzling at my hair.

He must have let Adam into the box to pick me up.

I remember, as in a darkened dream, swimming back through the mist to see Adam's face not a foot from my own. And it was only then that I accepted Con's last statement as the truth.

"Adam. . . ."

He had carried me out of the loose-box into an adjacent stall, and he knelt there, in the straw, with my head against his shoulder. "Don't talk now. It's all right. Everything's all right. . . ."

"Adam, you're not dead."

"No, dear. Now lie quiet. Listen, there's the Land Rover coming down the hill. It's all over. You're quite safe. Donald's all right, did you know? Just lie still; the doctor's coming with them, there's nothing we can do."

"Con's dead, isn't he?"

"Yes."

"He–he was going to kill me."

"It seems he nearly succeeded," said Adam grimly. "If it hadn't been for Rowan, I'd have been too late."

"You knew?"

"I guessed."

"How?"

"God knows. The old radar still working, I suppose. When the Fenwicks turned up, they all set to work and got the cellar walls made as safe as possible, and that beam shored up, then I came out from under, and Mrs. Fenwick–she's tiny, isn't she?–managed to creep through into the cellar to fix Donald up temporarily, till the doctor came. Your cousin was still around, then. Someone had said you were making straight back for Whitescar, to warn Lisa Dermott about beds and so forth. Then the doctor arrived. He couldn't get under the beam, of course, so everyone's attention was concentrated on getting Donald out; and in the general confusion of coming and going in the dark, it was some time before I noticed that Winslow wasn't there any longer. It was only then that I realized that I'd given you away to him, and I'm afraid I didn't even stop to wonder if this might have put you in danger. I just had a strong feeling that it was high time I came down here. As it was."

I shivered, and a muscle in his arm tightened. "I thought, when I heard you scream, that I'd come just too late."

He bent his head, and kissed me. The things he said to me then, in the straw of the dusty stable, with the smells of meal, and the sweating horse, all round us, and the damp of the gate-house cellars still on his coat, and Con's body lying there in its own bright blood under the raw electric light, were the sort of thing that one only says when one's controls have been violently lifted. They are not for retelling, or even for remembering in daylight. But they belonged to that night of terror and discovery, when both of us had had to be driven to the very edge of loss, before we could accept the mercy that had saved us and allowed us to begin again. . . .

Then the Land Rover roared into the yard, and Adam lifted his head and shouted, and the world–in the persons of the doctor, the Fenwicks, and a couple of strangers who had come down with the doctor when they heard of the accident at the gate-house—bustled in on our tragic little Eden.

Adam neither moved, nor let me go. It was as if those early months of lies and subterfuge were suddenly, now, to be purged and forgotten. He knelt without moving, holding me to him, and, as they exclaimed with horror, and the doctor got down beside Con, told them precisely and in a few words what had occurred. Not the attempt at murder, never that. Simply that Con (who had come down ahead of the rest to give Lisa and me the good news) had, not realizing the danger, walked into the loose-box, tripped, and startled the colt, which had reared back and accidentally caught him with its forehoofs. And I—explained Adam—had fainted with the shock.

"And this shoe?" Mr. Fenwick had picked it up and was examining it. "He cast this?"

I had been slow to grasp the significance of Con's choice of weapon. Adam, I saw, got there straight away. If he had noticed the thing earlier, he would no doubt have removed it. He said steadily, "It doesn't look to me like one of Rowan's. It must have fallen from a nail. Was it in the box? Maybe that was what Winslow tripped over."

The farmer turned the shoe over in his hand. It was clean. He glanced at Rowan's forefeet, which were (mercifully) out of my sight. "Aye," he said, "likely enough," and put the thing up on a window sill.

It was late next afternoon when Julie and I walked up through the fields towards the old gate-house.

The air was fresh and sparkling after the storm, the light so clear that each blade of grass seemed to stand separately above its shadow, and there were wild flowers out along the roadside where yesterday there had been only dusty and yellowed turf. We let ourselves out of the gate marked WHITESCAR, and stopped there, looking at the wreckage of the lodge and the ivy tree.

Even this, the day transformed. The great cloud of oak boughs with their golden leaves as yet unfaded, the dark trails of ivy, the pink roses still rioting over what remained of the stone-work—these, in this lovely light, clothed the scene in an air of pastoral, even idyllic melancholy. Last night's near-tragedy might never have been.

But there were the marks of the tires where I had turned the car, there, a few of the timber props still lying; here, most telling of all, the clearing that the Fenwick boys had cut through the part of the tree that blocked the roadway, to let the ambulance through.

Julie and I stood looking at this in silence.

"Poor Lisa," I said at length.

"What will she do?" Her voice was subdued.

"I asked her to stay, but she's going home, she says. I suppose it's best. What's done is done, and we can only try to forget it."

"Yes." But she hesitated. I had told her, now, the story of my conspiracy with Con and Lisa, and also the truth of what had happened last night. "I still don't really understand, you know."

"Who ever does understand what drives a man to murder? You know what he thought last night, of course? He only had my word for it that Grandfather had left Whitescar to him, and when he discovered that I really was Annabel, he couldn't imagine that I'd have stood by and let Grandfather will it away from me. Then he realized that Adam had been—was still—my lover. I believe he had an immediate vision of my marrying Adam and settling here. I doubt if he took time to think anything out clearly; he just knew that I was in a position to contest the will if it *was* in his favour, and even to arraign him for trying to get money by false pretences."

"I see." She gave a little shiver. "What I can't make out is why he *didn't* just let the beam down, last night? He could have done, so easily. It would have killed them both, but I don't believe he would have cared."

"No. But he wanted Donald alive . . . and besides, you were there, watching. It wouldn't have been so easy. And Adam's death would only have solved one problem; mine solved them all. Whether I'd told the truth about the will or not, Con stood to gain by killing me. There was the money, too, remember. He wasn't sure of anything, but he wasn't risking failure at that stage, and the chance was too good to miss. I said Con was never afraid to chance his arm."

"With me, for instance, that night by the river?"

"I think so."

We were silent for a while. Then she touched my arm. "Why do you look like that?"

"I find it very hard not to blame myself."

"Blame yourself?" cried Julie. "Annabel, *darling*, what *for?*"

"I can't help feeling that what happened last night was partly my fault. If I hadn't been so tired and stupid—and if Con hadn't shaken me to pieces with that lie about Adam—I'd have managed to make him see I wasn't hatching plots to do him out of Whitescar. Or if I'd seen him earlier—or even if I hadn't tried to be so clever in the first place, and come back here to outplay him at his own game—"

"Stop this!" She gave my arm a little shake. "Be sensible, for pity's sake! All the trouble and violence there's been has come solely from Con! He's to blame from first to last for what happened last night, you know he is! He went down to the stable with the intention of murdering you, just *on the chance* that you might do him some harm! Yes, it's true, *and* you know it. Even if you'd been fit to talk to him, do you suppose he'd have listened. Not he! And as for deceiving him over the Mary Grey business, whose fault was that? If he hadn't frightened you to death eight years ago you'd never had *dreamed* of trying it! And if you hadn't thought he was a danger to Grandfather and me—which he was—you wouldn't have come at all. Oh, no, honey, let's have no nonsense about blaming yourself. Come off it!"

"All right." I smiled at her.

"Advice from Aunt Julie." She squeezed my arm lightly, then let it go. "Tit for tat. I took yours, so you take mine. Forget all about it just as soon as you can; it's the only thing to do. We've an awful lot to be thankful for, if you ask me!"

"Yes, indeed." I tilted my head back and looked up where the oak leaves glowed golden against the deep blue sky. "Do you know what I'd like to do, Julie?"

"What?"

"Rescue that blessed oak crossbeam from under this mess when they clear it up, and have something made of it, for Whitescar. Something we'll both of us use, a small table, or a headboard, or even just a shelf for Adam to keep the stud trophies on, and the cups I got for riding."

"Why not? It seems a pity to let it rot underground. It saved them both. Keep a bit for me, too." She smiled a little. "I dare say there'll be room for an ash tray or two in our London rooms. What about the tree that caused all the trouble?"

"The ivy tree?" I walked across to where it lay in its massive wreckage. "The poor old tree." I smiled, perhaps a little sadly. "Symbolic, do you think? Here lies the past—all the lies and secrecy, and what you would have called 'romance' . . . And now it'll be cleared up and carted away, and forgotten. Very neat." I put out a gentle hand to touch a leaf. "Poor old tree."

"I wish—" Julie stopped and gave a little sigh. "I was just going to say that I wished Grandfather could have known that you and Adam would be at Whitescar, but then he'd have had to know the rest, too."

We were silent, thinking of the possessive, charming old man who had delighted in domination, and who had left the strings of trouble trailing behind him, out of his grave.

Then Julie gave a sudden exclamation, and started forward past me. I said, "What is it?"

She didn't answer. She climbed onto what remained of the parapet of the old wall, and balanced there, groping into the fissure that gaped wide in the split trunk of the ivy tree. Somewhere, lost now among the crumbling, rotten wood, was the hole which the foolish lovers of so long ago had used as a letter box.

It was with a queer feeling of *déjà vue* that I watched Julie, slight and fair, and dressed in a cotton frock that I might have worn at nineteen, reach forward, scrape and pull a little at the rotten wood fragments, then draw from among them what looked like a piece of paper.

She stood there on the wall top, staring down at it. It was dirty, and stained, and a little ragged at the edges, but dry.

I said curiously, "What is it?"

"It's a—a letter."

"Julie! It can't be! Nobody else—" My voice trailed away.

She came down from the wall, and held it out to me.

I took it, glanced down unbelievingly at it, then stood staring, while the writing on it swam and danced in front of me. It was young, hurried-looking writing, and even through the blurred, barely legible ink, and the dirt and mould on the paper, I could see the urgency that had driven the pen. And I knew what the illegible letters said.

"Adam Forrest, Esq.,
Forrest Hall,
Nr. Bellingham,
Northumberland.

And the blur across the top said: *"Private."*

I became conscious that Julie was speaking.

". . . and I met the postwoman at the top of the road. You remember her, old Annie? She retired that year. She gave me the Whitescar letters, and I brought them down for her. She shouldn't have done it, but that day there was just one letter for Forrest Hall, and you know how she used to, to save herself the long trail. . . . Well, I'd seen you and Adam putting notes in the ivy tree, and I suppose, being a kid, I thought it was quite the natural thing to do. . . ." Her voice wavered; I realized that I turned and was staring at her. "So I put that one in the ivy tree. I remember now. I never thought another thing about it. I—I climbed up on the wall and shoved it in as far as it would go."

I said, "And of course, once he knew I'd gone, he'd never have looked in there again."

"Of course not. Annabel—"

"Yes?"

"Was it—do you suppose it was a particularly important letter?"

I looked down at the letter in my hand, then up at the ivy tree, where it had lain for eight years. If it had reached him, all that time ago, what would have happened? His wife ill, and heading towards complete break-down, himself wretched, and an unhappy young girl throwing herself on his mercy and his conscience? Who was to say that it had not been better like this? The time we had lost had, most of it, not been our time. The ivy tree, that "symbol," as I had called it, of deceit, had held us apart until our time was our own, and clear. . . .

Julie was watching me anxiously. "I suppose it *might* have been important?"

"I doubt it."

"I—I'd better give it to him, and tell him, I suppose."

I smiled at her then. "I'm meeting him this evening. I'll give it to him myself."

"Oh, would you?" said Julie, thankfully. "Tell him I'm *terribly* sorry, and I hope it wasn't anything that *mattered!*"

"Even if it was," I said, "it can hardly matter now."

I might have been alone in a painted landscape.

The sky was still, and had that lovely deepening blue of early evening.

The high, piled clouds over to the south seemed to hang without movement. Against their curded bases the fells curved and folded, smooth slopes of pasture, fresh from last night's rain, and golden-green in the late sunlight.

The blocks of the Roman-cut stone were warm against my back. Below me the lough dreamed and ruffled, unchanged since the day I had first sat here. Two black-faced lambs slept in the sun; the same two, it seemed, that had lain there eight years ago, when it had all begun—

Time was. Time is. . . .

I sat there, eyes shut, and remembered, in the warm green-and-blue silence. Not a lamb called; the curlews were silent; there was no breeze to stir the grasses, and the bees had gone home from the thyme. It might have been the world before life began, and I might have been the first and only woman in it, sitting there dreaming of Adam. . . .

"Annabel."

Though I had been waiting, I hadn't heard him approach. He had come quietly along the turf to the south of the Wall. He was standing close behind me. The lambs, sleepy-eyed, had not even raised their heads.

I didn't turn. I put up a hand, and when his closed over it, I drew the scarred back of it down against my cheek, and held it there.

Time is to come. . . .